FUTURE CRIMES

are bound to be even more convoluted, more inventive, and far more difficult to solve ''beyond a reasonable doubt'' than those by which we are currently beset. And the consequences for failing to bring a criminal to justice—be the perpetrator human, alien, robot, cyborg, or some form of intelligence not yet imagined—may be as far-reaching and devastating as interstellar warfare.

In this unique anthology of all-original stories, Mike Resnick culled the near and far future and came up with eighteen scenarios for crimes that may some day be committed. Then he set his fellow word sleuths to solving and resolving them. The result is a masterful meld of science fiction and mystery themes, this delightfully challenging collection of—

WHATDUNITS

WHATDUNITS

edited by

MIKE RESNICK

DAW BOOKS, INC.
DONALD A. WOLLHEIM, FOUNDER
375 Hudson Street, New York, NY 10014

ELIZABETH R. WOLLHEIM
SHEILA E. GILBERT
PUBLISHERS

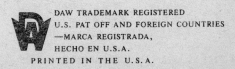

To Carol, as always

And to Elsie and Betsy Wollheim
and Sheila Gilbert

CONTENTS

INTRODUCTION

by Mike Resnick

There was a time when people said it couldn't be done: you couldn't blend the mystery story with the science fiction story without having the detective solve the case by coming up with a piece of obscure scientific (or pseudo-scientific) knowledge to which the reader couldn't possibly have access.

Well, Isaac Asimov put that objection to rest 40 years ago with his classic *The Caves of Steel*, the first book-length science fiction mystery that succeeded on all levels. And fast on its heels came Alfred Bester's *The Demolished Man*, considered by many writers and critics to be among the half-dozen best science fiction novels in the history of the genre, a cat-and-mouse game in which a killer must commit a murder and hide his guilt in a telepathic society.

Nowadays, science fiction and even fantasy mysteries appear with some regularity, and a number of detectives, from Lord Darcy to Lije Bailey to Gil Hamilton to Matthew Swain to my own John Justin Mallory, have achieved considerable followings.

If there is one place that the science fictional mystery has not yet made major inroads, it is in the category of the short story. This anthology was commissioned to fill that gap.

Once the good people at DAW told me what they wanted, I sat down and created a few dozen murders, each with a science fictional theme. Usually they were just a few sentences, occasionally they stretched to half a typewritten page. (The operative murder scenario will precede each story.) Then I selected the authors who were to appear in this volume and gave each of them a choice of two or three of the scenarios. Murders were chosen, assignments were made, deadlines were met, and I hope you're as happy with the result as I am.

PS: They say that inside of every editor is a frustrated writer trying to break out.

DAW will be publishing a companion volume, *More Whatdunits,* a few months up the road. The gimmick is the same—I create the mysteries, the writers solve them—but there is one major difference: every story in it has been written by an editor.

Keep an eye out for it; I think you'll be very pleasantly surprised.

TRUE FACES

by Pat Cadigan

Pat Cadigan has written a few dozen powerful short stories, is a multiple Nebula and Hugo nominee, and is the author of *Mindplayers* and *Synners*.

A human diplomat is found murdered in an alien embassy. Seventeen aliens are present. Each claims to be the sole murderer, and because of their psychological makeup, each passes a lie detector test.
1. Are any of them telling the truth?
2. Why was the human killed?
3. How do you question aliens who are congenital liars?

"I *told* you I wasn't in the mood for this," Stilton whispered.

I gave him an elbow in the ribs without looking away from the body of the woman lying on the floor of the large room. I'm never much in the mood for a strangulation murder myself, but it didn't pay to advertise. Not in this company. History, I thought; I'm looking at history in the making right there in front of me. People had been strangled before and they'd get strangled again, but this was the first time one had ever been strangled in an alien embassy. The first alien embassy, no less. Two firsts. And we were the first law enforcement officers on the scene, so that was three firsts. The day was definitely running hot.

On my other side, the tall man in the retro-tuxedo swallowed loudly for the millionth time. He'd said his name was Farber and given his occupation as secretary to the dead woman. I wasn't sure which was more striking, his old-fashioned getup or his noisy peristaltic action. I'd never met anyone who could swallow loudly before—did that make it five firsts? I shoved the thought aside. The room was so quiet, I probably could have heard him digesting his food if I listened closely enough. The Lazarians either observed quiet as a religion, or they were as much in shock as the human employees, who were all huddled together on the far side of the room, too spooked even to whisper to each other.

There was only one Lazarian on this side of the room. The rest were gathered in a semicircle around the corpse. There were about twenty of them and the grouping had this very odd formality to it, as if they'd all gathered there to seek an audience with the woman.

I turned to Farber, who reacted by swallowing again and then blotting his forehead with his sleeve. "One more time?" I gave Stilton another jab in the ribs.

"Ready," Stilton said sourly, moving so that I could see he had the interviewer aimed.

"Migod, I always thought it was just in the hollies that the police made you tell a story over and over," Farber said, glancing at the 'viewer's flat lens in a furtive way. I didn't make anything of that—the only people who never got nervous about having a 'viewer trained on them were dead or inhuman. Of course, it was hard to tell with the Lazarians—they looked a lot like scarecrows and I'd never seen a nervous scarecrow, or even an extraterrestrial facsimile.

"You can give us the 'viewer's digest condensed version," I told him. "The third recording doesn't need as much."

Farber swallowed. "Fine. I came in here and found Ms. Entwater just as you see her now, with the Lazarians gathered around her. Just as you see *them* now. The other human employees were elsewhere in the building, but the one Lazarian rounded them all up, brought them in here, and hasn't allowed anyone to leave since. Then I called you. From here. Since I'm not allowed to leave, either."

I glanced at Stilton, who nodded. "And you say that Ms. Entwater's relationship with the Lazarians was . . . what?"

Swallow. His Adam's apple bounded up and down above his collar. "Cordial. Friendly. Very good. She liked them. She liked her work. If she had any enemies among the Lazarians, she never told me about it and she told me close to everything."

"Care to speculate on what she didn't tell you?" I asked.

He thought about that for a moment, swallowing. "She didn't tell me there was a Pilot in the building."

"Why not?"

"Either she didn't have a chance or she didn't think to." Swallow. "It's hardly necessary for the secretary to be updated hourly as to who drops by for a social visit and who doesn't."

"You're sure it was a social visit?"

Swallow. "Pilots come by all the time to visit the Lazarians. The Lazarians trained them in Interstellar Resonance Travel, so they feel a certain kinship to them, much more than to other humans, I think."

"Why do you think that?" I asked.

"Because they seldom have any interactions with any of the humans here. Except for Ms. Entwater, who sees them in and sees them out again." Swallow. "*Saw* them in. And out again."

"She always did, personally? Isn't that more of a job for a receptionist or a secretary?"

"Dallette or I would see to other visits. The Pilots Ms. Entwater always saw to personally."

"Then she wouldn't have had to tell you in so many words that a Pilot was in the building," I said. "You'd know by whatever she was doing."

Swallow. "*If* I knew what she was doing. I was busy with press releases for most of the morning, so I was in the translation room."

"The Lazarians' press releases?"

Swallow, followed by a nod. "They like to alert the media themselves. About everything. Today it was various things about hollies they'd seen and what they thought about them and the dissolution of three-bond—"

"Wait a minute," I said. "You didn't mention that before." The old ways never failed. Get someone to tell a story over and over and something new was bound to show up.

Swallow. "I'm sorry. I wasn't hiding it—" a glance at the 'viewer—"I'd just forgotten. It's like a—a marriage breaking up, or maybe a long engagement. The Lazarians are—well, there are similarities, but there are always strange little differences embedded in them. In any case, it didn't concern Ms. Entwater."

"Are you sure?" I said.

"Absolutely." Swallow. "Ms. Entwater never, ah, intruded into their private lives."

I couldn't help laughing a little. "Come on. Celie Entwater's job was to gain improved understanding of the Lazarians. How could she do that unless she was acquainted with their private lives?"

"Ms. Entwater considered herself a diplomat engaged in deep study of another culture. She was rigorous in observing customs and taboos, all that sort of thing. She knew that if we offended them, they might close down and go back to Lazarus—"

"Lah-ah . . . ZA-AHR . . . eesh," came a deep, nasal-sounding voice behind me, enunciating each syllable as if it were a separate word, with a bit of a gargle on the *ZA-AHR*.

Farber swallowed and bowed from the waist. I turned around. The one free-ranging Lazarian in the room was standing as close as possible to Stilton, who rolled his eyes. The Lazarian custom of space-density had gotten old for him very quickly. I found it pretty off-putting myself—it was like dealing with a race of people who had been raised in crowded elevators, unable to be comfortable unless they were all on top of each other.

Which made the half-circle formation around Entwater's corpse doubly odd, I thought suddenly. They weren't as close to each other or to her as they could get. Because she was dead? Or for some other Lazarian reason I had yet to find out?"

"I need to question all the humans here," I said to the Lazarian. "If one of them killed Ms. Entwater, that person must be punished according to our law."

"Trrrried and punished if found guilty," the Lazarian corrected. "Question."

Farber moved to my side, swallowing. "Thinta-ah requests permission to inquire something of you," he said to me, sounding ceremonial. I repressed the urge to sigh heavily; I'm no diplomat, and the six years I'd spent on the gang squad had made me tired of ritual. Maybe it should have prepared me for the more byzantine protocols of extraterrestrials, but I've got a bad attitude. Twenty years ago, when the Lazarians had first arrived, maybe I'd have been much more excited, but then, I've always had low blood pressure anyway.

"Ask your question," I said.

"Say 'please,' " Farber whispered.

I smiled as broadly as I could. "Please."

The Lazarian put its six-digit hands on top of its sacklike head. "If Entwa-ahter is dead by one of us, wha-aht then?"

I glanced at Entwater again. From this distance, it was hard to see the details of the marks on her throat, but they could have been made by one of those Lazarian hands. One would have been enough—like the rest of their limbs, those digits were long and multijointed, and could have gone all the way around a human neck easily. "This is your embassy," I said, "which means to us, it is a piece of your nation. We would trust you to serve your own justice in this matter."

Stilton was looking at me like I was crazy. I didn't blame him. All of a sudden, I was talking like a hollie version of a diplomat. I couldn't help it; something about the Lazarians was making me go into awkward-formal mode.

The Lazarian put a hand on top of the 'viewer, much to Stilton's shock. "Truth ma-ah-chine."

I gave Farber a sidelong glance. "What now?"

Farber swallowed twice. "It would seem that Thinta-ah wants you to use the 'viewer on them." He gestured at the Lazarians standing around Entwater.

Stilton coughed. "I don't think it'll work. We're—ah—" he turned to the Lazarian—"we're too different." I could tell he was trying to imagine how those sackheads would register. The 'viewer worked on interpreting a lot of little things—facial expression, blood flow, temperature, eye and muscle movements, pulse, respiration, vocal quality and inflection, choice of words, context, and some other things I didn't have to bother remembering. It wasn't infallible, we'd all been told, but in my experience, I have yet to see anyone beat it, not even the most hardened pathological liars. We were only allowed to use it to determine probable cause for search and/or arrest, not to determine official guilt or innocence, so it wasn't any more admissible in court than the old lie detector results had been, but it was useful enough.

"Can convert," said the Lazarian. "Ha-ahve progra-ahms to converrrt for our species."

Stilton held the 'viewer protectively close to his chest, giving me a desperate look.

"I don't know," I said. "I'd have to call—"

Farber swallowed. "Weren't you told to take every measure necessary to wrap this up as quickly as possible?" He leaned closer and lowered his voice. "Do you want to think about the repercussions of having an unsolved murder in the Lazarian embassy? They'll have to call out the National Guard to protect this place, and all of us *will still be trapped inside of it*. And that includes you and your partner. The door is *booby-trapped*. Something sonic. Break the plane from this side and you'll drop like a rock. When you wake up, you'll have the worst headache of your life." He jerked his head at the group of humans. "Some of *them* tried it. Ask them if they'll try it again. Get it through your head, no one is going to leave here until this is settled, and if it takes months, that's not Thinta-ah's problem."

"All right," I said. All right for now. Call in a siege team? I'd never get that okayed. I'd have to see about locating the control for the doorway knockout and figure out how to disable it later. That would probably cause an international incident—interstellar incident?—but not as major an incident as a siege team storming the place.

I looked at the Lazarian, but that face was unreadable. As usual. It was actually the outer surface of a kind of flexible exoskeleton that covered the whole head, featureless except for irregular, opaque black patches where the eyes and mouth would be. I'd read somewhere that the exoskeleton thickened and then thinned out again on some cycle that was individual to each Lazarian, but no one knew what caused it or what it meant to the Lazarians, except that they referred to what lay beneath it as the "true face," which was never to be shown to another living being, not even if its owner were dead. Which I thought begged the question: what was the point of having a so-called "true face" if nobody could ever see it?

Something teased at the edge of my mind. I looked over at the Lazarians still motionless around the corpse. Was the penalty for seeing a "true face" immediate death?

Everyone was staring at me expectantly. "I should still probably call in for authorization," I said weakly.

"Ca-ahll," said the Lazarian, and it wasn't granting me permission, but giving me an order.

I took the cellular off my belt and punched the speed-dial for the direct line to the captain. The subsequent conversation was almost as brief.

"She says it's a go," I said, clipping the phone back onto my belt. Stilton looked outraged for half a second and then wiped all expression from his face. For some reason, 'viewer operators get extremely possessive about their baby. Normally, Stilton wouldn't even let me hold his. "Let's get the program and convert the 'viewer for Lazarians."

Farber looked distressed as he swallowed. "Well, I've just thought of a problem."

I winced. "Only one. What a relief."

"It's a big one. The program is in Ms. Entwater's office upstairs. Everyone who was in the embassy at the time of Ms. Entwater's death is now here in this room, Lazarians and humans alike. We may not leave this room, not any of us."

"Why not?" I said, looking at Thinta-ah.

"Bee-cauzzzzeh," the Lazarian replied, still using the command voice.

"Oh," I said, hoping I didn't sound sarcastic and looked at Farber. "Any ideas?"

He took a long time swallowing. "We could call a courier to fetch the program for us. Of course, the courier will have to stay here with us afterward."

"We'll charge the overtime to the embassy," I said, reaching for my cellular again.

The courier business took a little longer, since the courier made the mistake of entering the room we were all in first, forcing me to call out for another. Forewarned, the second courier put the program chips in an envelope and tossed it to me through the open doorway.

"Go to it," I said, handing the envelope to Stilton. His face had a slightly greenish cast to it.

"Before I fool with the 'viewer and quite possibly break it, maybe we should talk to the humans," he said.

"Our species *firrrrrrst*," said Thinta-ah, and it was another command. I wanted to object. Across the room, the half dozen human employees were still huddled together, albeit less closely. Except for the Pilot, who had gotten tired of sitting and was now leaning against the wall behind the others, smoking a cigarette in a long holder. She looked happy, but all Pilots look happy all the time. It's something that happens to them as a result of their training. Maybe after that first trip, they never really "come back," so to speak.

"Do as you're told," Farber said to Stilton, managing to sound apologetic. "I've got a wife, a husband, and three children I'd like to see again before I'm much older, and I imagine you both have families as well.''

I cleared my throat. In Stilton's case, that had been the wrong appeal to make; his significant others had voted him out three weeks before and he was still stinging from it.

But instead of giving Farber the evil eye, he went to work on the 'viewer, even allowing me to steady it for him while he changed chips.

It took Stilton about half an hour to get everything synchronized and in phase and whatever else—I'm no more of a techie than I am a diplomat, though I suspected the last fifteen minutes he spent on running tests and diagnostics was nothing but pure stalling.

''I guess it's ready,'' he said at last. ''But even with all these adjustments and conversions for Lazarian biology, I don't know how well it's going to work with an exoskeleton.''

''No ex-oh,'' said Thinta-ah, coming over to stand too close again. ''True faaaa-aice.''

The Lazarians gathered around Entwater made no perceptible physical movements, but something in the air changed. Everybody felt it, even the humans on the other side of the room. It was similar to the sudden presence of ozone before a lightning strike (don't ask me how I know about that unless you're ready for a story longer than this one), and for a moment, I thought I could actually feel my hair stand on end.

''I know your custom of not showing the true face,'' I said to Thinta-ah. ''How—''

Thinta-ah made Stilton cringe by touching the 'viewer again. ''Not a-ahlive.''

''You'll allow a recording that we can look at?'' Stilton said, amazed.

''A-ahllow to look a-aht recording *one time,*'' the Lazarian said, making a strange movement something like a full body shrug. The clothing, as loose, mismatched, and wrinkled as anything that ever came out of a Good Will free bin, seemed to readjust itself on the Lazarian's loose-jointed body, somehow acquiring even more wrinkles. Wrinkles seemed to be their fashion statement. The Lazarians around the corpse still didn't move, but I knew they were unhappy. Not just unhappy, but unhappier than they had ever been in their lives. I tried to imagine an equivalent for myself—

being forced to strip naked in public seemed obvious, but I knew this was a lot more than a nudity taboo.

My gaze fell on the 'viewer. Maybe more like being exposed with one of these things? "One time," I said to Stilton. "We'd better make it a good look, then."

Thinta-ah did some fast organizing. The humans were to sit directly behind and with their backs to the group in the center of the room so they couldn't possibly see their true faces while they were speaking to the 'viewer. Very simple solution—just the sort of thing that signals some major complication is imminent.

Stilton and I found a chair for the 'viewer. He got it aimed at the first Lazarian, fiddled with the focus for a few seconds, and then turned it on. "Any time," he told the Lazarian and turned away, crowding close to me as Thinta-ah crowded close to him.

In the long pause that followed, I could hear the Lazarian removing the exoskeleton. It was a ghastly sound, like cloth ripping and I wondered if it hurt. Anything that made a noise like that seemed like it *had* to hurt.

"You a-ahsk," said Thinta-ah.

I cleared my throat. "What is your name?"

"Simeer-ah," said the Lazarian. I felt Thinta-ah stiffen. The last syllable indicated this was some relative of Thinta-ah's, but not which kind.

"How are you connected to—"

"A-ahsk only about Entwa-ahter!" Thinta-ah practically shouted.

I hesitated, wanting to explain about establishing a pattern and knowing at the same time that Thinta-ah wasn't buying. A Lazarian's true face was exposed in the presence, if not the sight, of others, and to them, this was much more urgent than a murder. Any murder.

I could have sworn I heard Farber swallow from across the room. "Do as you're told," he called from where he and the courier stood facing the now closed door.

Behind me, the exposed Lazarian made a small noise. I'd never heard the sound before, but I knew instinctively that the alien was weeping. A wave of compassion mixed with shame swept through me—not the best thing for a cop to feel during a murder investigation. If I'd felt sorry for everyone who'd ever cried during questioning, there'd have been a few more hardheads running free who had gotten away with murder and worse.

I took a deep breath. "What do you know about the death of Celie Entwater?"

"I a-ahm responsible."

My shamed compassion turned to cold water. "Are you saying you killed her?"

"It is my fault."

"Are you saying you killed her?" I asked again.

Stilton shrugged. "First time's a charm, I guess," he whispered.

"You strangled Celie Entwater?" I persisted.

"I ha-ahve the blaaaaaa-aimmeh."

"Stop now," said Thinta-ah, softly. "Next."

I gave up. "All right. We'll wait while you cover yourself."

Damnedest thing—the exoskeleton made the same ripping-cloth sound going back on as it had coming off. My nerves felt sandpapered. And I only had to hear that noise nineteen more times.

No, sixteen more times, I discovered after it was safe to turn around again. Stilton aimed the 'viewer at the next Lazarian. The first one looked no worse for the experience— outwardly, anyway. There was nothing like sweat or blood, the exoskeleton appeared unchanged. But the Lazarian's body looked a little more relaxed, the kind of posture you see in people who finally confess to a crime and find they're more relieved at being able to get it off their chests than they are frightened of being punished. Maybe the first time really had been a charm.

Then the second Lazarian said exactly the same thing and the world rearranged itself into the form it always took during a criminal investigation. The world is full of liars, liars who say they didn't do it and liars who say they did, liars who say they're sorry and liars who say they're not, liars who swear they've never done it before, liars who promise they'll never do it again. Apparently some things were universal— literally.

By the time the sixth one confessed, Stilton had taken over the questioning and my cynicism felt like a drug reaching toxic levels in my system. The only thing I actually listened to after number seven was that ripping-cloth sound. There was some kind of cosmic irony at work here, I thought; expose your true face and then tell a lie. Gave a deeper meaning to the term *barefaced liar,* that was for sure.

What I wasn't sure about was why it was affecting me so intensely. Maybe because I secretly suffered from the ailment of poor species self-image, believing that aliens must be truly superior forms of life to flaw-ridden humanity, and they'd shattered my illusions of their being closer to the angels. What was that old joke that had made the rounds back when the Lazarians had first arrived? An optimist thinks humans could be the highest form of life in the universe, a pessimist knows they are. Right. Try this one, I thought bitterly—an optimist thinks all beings are siblings, a pessimist knows they are. And the name of the first sibling, in any language anywhere, was Cain.

"Still awake?" Stilton asked me suddenly.

I managed not to jump at the sound of his voice. "Yeah. Just."

"Good. Last confession coming up," he said, fiddling with the 'viewer on the chair. Without my noticing, the lights in the room had come up in response to the waning daylight. Through the frosted windows, I could see that it was nearly dark. With any luck, we might get out by dawn, I thought wearily. And when we did, I was going to ask for a transfer out of homicide and go chase burglars for a while, or drug addicts or people who never paid their parking tickets.

"One more time," Stilton said, assuming the position.

The sound of ripping cloth. If this one was going to lie about Entwater, too, then I hoped it hurt.

But number seventeen was apparently the rebel in the group. "Fa-ahr-ber," the last Lazarian said. "Fa-ahr-ber is at fault."

"What a relief," I said. "I was afraid sixteen Lazarians had taken turns choking someone to death. But it turns out that the man dressed like a butler did it. Can't wait to alert the media."

Thinta-ah suddenly came back to life and told Farber to send out for pizza. Apparently pizza was the closest thing we had to a Lazarian native dish. That didn't cheer me, or even give me an appetite, though I knew I should have been hungry.

And thirsty. The humans were. They all looked as if they'd spent the day in a desert, except for the Pilot, who seemed as completely detached and unaffected as ever. And yet, it was the Pilot who informed us that there were new problems developing with the humans.

She came over while we were setting up the 'viewer on a side table so we could go over the recordings. "We have people in very serious need," she said, pointing her cigarette holder at them.

"Of what?" As soon as the words were out of my mouth, I knew the answer, but the Pilot was already telling me.

"Of toilets. Some are in real pain," she added cheerfully. I wanted to hit her.

Instead, I talked to Farber. His response made me want to hit *him*. "Thinta-ah knows," he said. "Arrangements were made before you got here." He pointed at a large ornamental flowerpot in the corner. "It only looks like a flowerpot," he added, as if reading my mind. "It's a, ah, Lazarian waste receptacle. The Lazarians are, ah—" swallow—"*casual* about this kind of function."

"Oh, really?" I said. "I sure haven't seen any of *them* use it."

Swallow. "They only need to every other week. This isn't the week."

I went to the humans and broke it to them myself. One of them, a middle-aged man, shook his head stubbornly without looking up at me. But a woman of about sixty shrugged, marched over to the receptacle and pointedly turned her back. The anger was almost palpable and I knew what kind of stories they were all going to tell when they were finally allowed to leave. Lazarian-human diplomatic relations could well end up being harmed more by the bathroom arrangements than by a murder, I thought, going back to Stilton. Even terrorists would take their hostages to the bathroom.

Or, I thought, looking at Thinta-ah who was being careful to look anywhere but toward the corner, had humans just come that much closer to understanding the experience of exposing the true face?

Understanding? I doubted it. They'd remember it, but it wasn't the sort of thing that would generate much empathy.

"*One* look," Thinta-ah reminded us when we were ready to look at the recordings.

"Only one," Stilton said. He had half a pizza next to him and he was feeling better, much better than the delivery person who had come into the room before we could warn her. She sat sulking with the first courier. I wondered if anyone besides the employees' families, a courier service, and a pizza parlor had picked up on the fact that there was something funny happening at the Lazarian embassy. My cellular had been strangely silent, no one calling for an update or a statement or anything at all. Maybe we were sitting under a governmental belljar, families, courier service, pizza parlor, and all.

"I'll need to freeze each image sometimes," Stilton told Thinta-ah. "Is that all right?"

The answer was so long in coming that I thought Thinta-ah had gone to sleep standing up again. "Yes. A-ahll right. One time through."

Stilton sighed with relief, turned on the 'viewer, and picked up a slice of double shitake mushroom. The screen lit up and he dropped the pizza in his lap. If I'd had an appetite, I'd have had pizza in my own lap.

The face on the screen was Entwater's.

Stilton slammed down the freeze button. "What did you *do?*" I whispered angrily. "Did you get the focus upside down and put it on *her?*"

"You can see I didn't," he said, too spooked to be offended. "That's not the image of a dead person. That face is animated, it's moving, talking. Look at the readings." He pointed at the box on the left side of the screen. "They say living, not dead."

I looked from the screen to Thinta-ah on the other side of the table. "Could this possibly be this Lazarian's true face?"

"I maaaaaa-aiy not look," Thinta-ah said. "But wha-aht faaaa-aice you see must be the true one."

I got up and went around the table to the alien. "Listen," I whispered. "The face on that screen is—"

"Do *not* tell me," said Thinta-ah. "I maaaaaaaay *not* know. Wha-aht faaaaaaa-aice is there is true."

I tried to think. It was hard with the heavy garlic smell drifting over from the platter next to Stilton. "Okay. The face on that screen cannot possibly belong to one of your species, but to another one entirely, and to a certain being—"

"*I maaaaaay not know!*" Thinta-ah's voice echoed in the room, not the command voice this time but a cry of anguish. Everything stopped. Over by the Rockwell-esque mural of the first meeting between human and Lazarian, Farber straightened up from a whispered conversation with the courier and the pizza delivery person to glare at me.

"I'm sorry," I said to Thinta-ah and bowed. "I was . . . I was ignorant."

The Lazarian refused to look at me. I went back around the other side of the table and sat down next to Stilton, feeling as if I had just defiled somebody else's church with a rite from my own. And I didn't even go to church.

The association caught in my mind like a burr. *Was* this religious? Discounting hobby-killers and for-hires, people tend to take a life over matters having to do with love/sex and personal offenses, real or imagined. *Our* people . . . but the Lazarians?

I beckoned impatiently to Farber, who hurried over. "Can I ask Thinta-ah about Lazarian psychology?"

Swallow (of course). "No."

I groaned. "Why not?"

"You're not a psychologist. Besides, they don't actually have any."

"What are you talking about? They must. *Everybody* has psychology. *Animals* have psychology."

"Well, yes, they *have* it—" swallow—"but they don't have it as a science or a discipline or whatever you want to call it. The study of psychology is unknown on their world."

"But they must have *something.*"

Farber nodded. "They do. They have true faces."

"That's a big mother's help," I said. "You want to know what true face that Lazarian on the end over there has?"

He started to protest that he wasn't allowed to look and I waved his words away.

"Never mind. You wouldn't believe it if you did see it." He started to walk away and I caught his arm. "Hey, stay close, will you? I'm working without a net here."

"We all are," he murmured.

"The verdict is in," Stilton said, sitting back. "According to the 'viewer, this alien is telling the truth."

I stared at Entwater's image, still frozen on the screen. She had been a very attractive woman; at least one of her parents had had relatives from Japan and whatever else was mixed with it had blessed her with the kind of features that age well. Damned shame they wouldn't have a chance to age any further—or would they? Did true faces age? Supposedly, no one knew. *Supposedly.* But someone must have. There had to be some Lazarian keeper of forbidden knowledge . . . didn't there?

I gave up that line of thought as futile. If there were any such Lazarians, they were most likely back on Lazarus, or La-ah-ZA-AHR-eesh, or whatever the hell it was.

"What do you want to do?" Stilton asked me. "You want me to let this picture go and see the next?"

"Are you done looking at it?"

"Are you?"- He ran a hand through his black curls. "Remember, we're never going to see it again, so make sure you've seen your fill."

"I'm not so sure about that," I said as he unfroze the image. The corresponding readings in the box were holding, waiting for the video to catch up.

"What do you mean?" Stilton said.

I pointed at the 'viewer. "That's what I mean."

I could actually see Stilton break into a sweat as Entwater's face reappeared.

"Why are you surprised?" I said. "They all *said* the same thing." I looked at Farber. "All except one."

Farber gazed back at me, swallowing without comprehension. Apparently, the last Lazarian's voice hadn't carried over to him. Or he hadn't been paying attention.

This time we ran the video concurrent with the lie detector program; I watched the face while Stilton kept track of the readings. I wanted to imprint that face on my mind. It wasn't *quite* identical to the other one, but the differences were minor—the width of the face, the length of the nose, the size of the chin. That figured—each Lazarian's head would be a different size, so the face on it would be sized to fit. The Procrustean face. No, the true face on the Procrustean head.

Stilton sighed unhappily. "This one's telling the truth, too. Or so it says here. The program must be defective, though how we'd ever be able to tell—" he sighed again.

"Keep going," I said. "Maybe we'll see a variation somewhere."

Stilton gave me a dirty look. "Yah."

"We've already seen some." I leaned close and whispered. "That face isn't completely identical to the first one. There *are* variations, almost too minor to see, but they *are* there. What about the readings?"

He called back the first set for comparison. "You're right. But the variations are all physiological. They have two pulses, and they have respiration and skin temperature and they show the same degrees of variation from one Lazarian to another that we show one human to another. In all standard healthy people, anyway."

"So let's see if maybe someone *isn't* standard healthy."

Now he almost smiled. "I like you better than I used to, all of a sudden," he said and focused his attention on the 'viewer again.

But of course, I had just been overly optimistic. Entwater's face appeared, confessed, disappeared, and reappeared over and over without any telling variations. That *was* probably telling, except we couldn't understand *what* it was telling.

At least the seventeenth Lazarian looked like Farber. I took great consolation in the fact that my certainty had been correct. It didn't make up for the fact that the 'viewer said that Lazarian was also telling the truth, the whole truth, and nothing but the truth, but you can't have everything.

"The program's got to be defective," Stilton said, replacing Farber's facsimile with the seventeen readings. "We might as well switch programs, record all the humans, and then get comfortable in our new home. We're going to be here quite a while and we might as well get over our potty shyness as soon as possible."

"*No,*" I said, standing up and looking at Thinta-ah. Farber took a step toward me and Stilton rose to his feet in response, moving to protect my left.

"I understand your feelings about the toilet," he said, "but don't go losing your head over it now."

"I mean no, the program's not defective, not no, I won't use the toilet." I went over and stood as close as possible to the Lazarian, who didn't move away. "The program's *incomplete*. We don't have a control."

"A what?" said Farber suspiciously.

"A control," I said, staring up at Thinta-ah. "A standard to measure the other Lazarians against."

Stilton practically jumped over the table.

"Same arrangements as for the other Lazarians," I said. "Thinta-ah, it's your turn in the barrel."

"It's already been Thinta-ah's turn," said Stilton, sounding scared.

The Lazarian lunged past me for the table, but Stilton already had the 'viewer in his arms. "Back off," he said, moving away, "or I'll turn this around and show everyone in the room what's on the screen."

Stretched out across the table, Thinta-ah hesitated and then straightened up slowly. "You maaaaaaaay not see."

"I've seen," Stilton said. "You didn't say every Lazarian but you."

"No. I did *not.*" Thinta-ah backed away from the table but Stilton didn't budge. Instead, he beckoned me over and pulled the 'viewer away from his chest.

Thinta-ah had apparently been either the consummate diplomat or completely undecided. His true face was a grotesque mixture of Entwater's and Farber's. What made it grotesque was not that it had a patchwork aspect but that it was fluid—as if his features had been in the process of melting or flowing from one face to the other and somehow frozen in mid-change.

"I punched to create a control file and the 'viewer informed me that one already existed," Stilton said as I studied the screen. "So I called it up and *olé.*"

"*Voilá,*" I corrected him.

"In this case, I'd say it rates an olé. But I should have realized it would be here. It was how Entwater created the program, by using Thinta-ah as a control. He must have been teacher's pet. Diplomat's pet. Whatever."

"Freeze it and let's hear the audio," I said. "Unfreeze it when the video and audio are in synch."

A voice that had to be Entwater's came out of the small speaker. "What is your name?"

"Thinta-ah."

"Are you from another planet?"

"Yesss."

The image on the screen came to life. There were a few more questions. Favorite Earth food? Pizza with heavy garlic in the sauce—true. Last eaten yesterday? No—a lie. It was all very disjointed but light stuff, like a dating service application, slightly adapted. But it had served the purpose—the readings were clear. Stilton let it run out, and then put all the readings on the screen together, the seventeen and Thinta-ah's.

"God-*damn*-it," he said and blew out a disgusted breath. "Or maybe we should have known that, too—that if there was a control, then the program stands. They're all telling the truth, or they're the best liars in the universe.''

"You're right."

We both jumped and Stilton almost dropped the 'viewer. The Pilot had managed to come right up to us without either one of us knowing. "Right about what?" said Stilton.

She pointed a finger at him, smiling. "You seek the truth. And you—" she swiveled toward me, finger still pointing— "seek the lie."

"What do you seek?" I said, making sure that Thinta-ah wasn't sneaking up on my side.

"Resonance, with all that is. Did you hear the one about the Pilot who went up to the hot-dog-o-mat and said, 'Make me one with everything?' ''

"That joke is so old, it's got a long gray beard and a brand-new liver," Stilton said, eyes narrowing. "It's at least half a century since the first time someone told it, and it wasn't a Pilot—"

"It is now."

That wasn't a happy expression, I realized, it was a *serene* one. It was the kind of expression you saw on people who were sure they had all the answers, minus the vacancy of the hard-core cult convert. What was Resonance, anyway? Something about traveling point to point and finding alignment so that two points that seemed to be separated by a great distance actually weren't . . . or something. It didn't make any sense to me, but a Pilot was one more thing I wasn't. If I couldn't figure out how it worked, I sure couldn't figure out why it made her so peaceful.

"The Lazarians taught us Resonance," she said, nodding at me. "And to travel point to point in space, we must travel point to point in here, too." She pointed her finger at her own forehead now. "You don't have the correct alignments in here, so you cannot travel point to point, but point to off-point. Dead end. Wander forty years in the desert and not get out even then."

She made us sit down again, while she perched on the edge of the table, placing the 'viewer next to her. "They are all telling the truth, and they are the best liars in the universe that you have ever met, because the truth they tell is *their* truth.''

It was one of the few times in my life that I could say I had experienced *satori*. And once I saw it, I felt like a total fool for not seeing it to begin with. Most humans couldn't beat the 'viewer because no matter how much they believed in their own lies, they knew what they believed was at variance with facts that other people knew, and so both couldn't be true. But the Lazarians were aliens, so, of course, their concept of the truth would be alien as well.

Alien truth. True faces. The two concepts were whirling around each other in my head, trying to find a basis for connection.

"So what does that mean?" Stilton said. "Somehow they all killed her, or they're all lying to protect someone?"

The Pilot shook her head. "You don't understand yet. They taught us Resonance with all things. Because *they* Resonate, *always.*"

I couldn't tell if this was another *satori* or a continuation. "Entwater liked them. She liked her work." I glanced at Farber. "And she, in turn, was very popular. So popular that—" I broke off, resting one hand casually on the 'viewer. "Tell me, was she popular because she liked them, or did she like them because she was popular?"

"That has Resonated into one thing now. It can no longer be determined because it is no longer distinguishable. All that remains is . . . love. *Not* the trendy brain chemicals," she added to Stilton. "Do you Resonate love?"

"You mean, understand it?" I laughed a little. "Does anyone?"

"What do you do? For love. What does it do to you?"

For once, I was at a loss because I'd never had a long-term relationship or a child. Alone, you can travel faster in a career, but you leave a lot of understanding in the dust that way, too. "Oh, I guess you care about the other person," I said finally, feeling like a sappy greeting card.

"Yeah. And when they stop loving, they stop caring," Stilton said gloomily. "Not responsible, all that shit."

The Pilot's face lit up even more. I hadn't thought it was possible. "Responsible. *Responsible.* Are you always responsible?"

I a-ahm responsible.

It is my fault.

I ha-ahve the blaaaaaa-aimmeh.

Over and over again, sixteen times, from sixteen nearly identical true faces. I almost laughed out loud with the revelation. "They're guilty, all right," I said. "That is, they *feel* guilty, because they felt responsible for her and they didn't prevent her murder!"

All the Lazarians gathered around Entwater's corpse turned their heads to look at me. Except one; the last one, of course.

"Pin a rose on *you,*" said the Pilot and patted my hand. "What next?"

"Trouble in Paradise," I said. "There's always trouble in Paradise, you can count on it, on any world. Because nobody can be that popular without someone getting jealous." I got up and walked toward Farber. "Someone got real, *real* jealous. *Killing* jealous."

"*No,*" Farber said, enraged. "Jealous, yes, she had them all eating out of the palm of her hand practically, but I wouldn't—I *couldn't*—"

"And he didn't," said Stilton. "We haven't looked at the readings for his third recording, but I'd bet my life that they say he's as truthful as those from the other two recordings."

"I know that," I said, keeping my gaze on Farber. "He's not a good liar. Not *that* good, anyway. And he's not an alien. *And* he didn't have it quite right a minute ago. Entwater didn't have them *all* eating out of her hand, just *almost* all. *You* made a friend. One out of eighteen, not too popular, but a very, *very* devoted friend. A friend who loves you enough to be responsible for you. For your happiness. For your sadness. And for your anger and jealousy and hate."

Farber's mouth was hanging open. I turned toward Stilton. "Number seventeen's our murderer." I paused. "For a minute there, I was about to tell you to get out the cuffs, but then I remembered. Diplomatic immunity. We have to leave it up to Thinta-ah to administer any justice—poor Thinta-ah, the consummate diplomat of the Lazarian species, torn between both of them."

To my surprise, Thinta-ah didn't seem the least bit embarrassed. On a human, the body language would have screamed *pride*. Aliens; go figure.

Stilton looked from the Lazarians in the group to the Pilot and then to me. "Are you sure?"

"Think about it," I said. "If they were all to blame for not preventing her death, who was really to blame for causing it? A Lazarian in love? Or the one the Lazarian was in love with?" I turned back to Farber.

"I didn't know," he said. "I had no idea." He frowned. "How did you?"

I opened my mouth and then realized I couldn't tell him. "The truth was staring me in the face all along," I said after a long moment. "I just had to recognize it for what it was."

Farber spread his hands helplessly. "I don't understand."

"I know. But one tip before we all get out of here." I pulled him closer by his lapel. "Quit this job. You're not suited for this kind of diplomacy. Really. I *know* this."

"I'm not a diplomat, I'm a secretary. I can get another secretarial job anywhere. But this was . . . exotic, exciting. . . ."

"Give it up, Farber," I said, "or you're going to find that office politics have suddenly turned fatal on you."

That seemed to put the fear of God into him. I went back over to the table where Stilton and the Pilot were still sitting. "I'd say this means we're free to go."

"See for yourself," said the Pilot and gestured at the center of the room. The group of Lazarians around Entwater had broken formation and were moving slowly away from the corpse, clustering in smaller groups of twos and threes. Space density. As if they had to breathe each other's air or something.

"Everyone maaaaaaaaaay leave," said Thinta-ah, bowing to us. "The door is now in service."

"And the truth shall set you free," Stilton muttered, committing everything in the 'viewer to long-term storage formats and then shutting it down.

"Not bad," I said. "In an awful kind of way."

"That's what the truth is supposed to do," he said stubbornly, pulling out the 'viewer strap so he could hang it on his shoulder. "That's what it's *for*. Right?" he added to the Pilot.

The Pilot folded her hands briefly. "What is truth?" She went back to the group of humans, who were all just starting to get warily up from their chairs.

I stared after her.

"What?" said Stilton.

"True faces. Celie Entwater died for human sins. Jesting Pilot."

"What?"

"Nothing, nothing. Let's get out of here."

GUT REACTION
by Jack C. Haldeman II

Jack Haldeman has written scores of sf stories and more than a handful of truly fine science fiction novels.

An alien whose planet is at war with Earth turns up in one of our embassies, claiming sanctuary. The embassy is staffed with only twelve humans, all loyal to Earth. Before the alien can be debriefed, it is found murdered in its quarters. The embassy's state-of-the-art security system has been circumvented, and what should have been a clear holograph of the killing is nothing but a three-dimensional black blur.
  1. Who killed the alien?
  2. How was the murder accomplished?
  3. Why was it killed?

There are dead bodies everywhere, not to mention one very dead alien who may or may not have been an ambassador. The only thing I'm sure of is that it's dead and I didn't do the dirty deed. All I have to do now is find the killer before I become the next victim.

It ought to be easy. As of this morning there are only six of us left.

Before the alien came there were twelve of us on the orbital research station: five biologists studying extraterrestrial critters; one resident computer junkie; and six soldiers watching the civilians and keeping an eye out for an alien invasion.

Me, I'm a biologist and I'm a gut man. A specialty in gastroenterology, however, does not adequately prepare me to track down a murderer nor to stand off an alien invasion. But I'm getting ahead of myself. In the beginning there were twelve of us, no alien who might have been an ambassador, and definitely no dead bodies.

This place is your basic Class IV research station, a modular jumble of plug-in units. Ours are mostly biocontainment packs since what we were originally supposed to do was spend a few years examining whatever life-forms we could scrape off the planet we're orbiting. We call the planet Mudball and it seems to be just about at Level 27 on the Universal Evolution Scale, which means the fish are starting to get legs, but don't know what to do with them yet.

Most of the critters we've hauled up here have real simple guts, which does not please me a whole lot. I signed up for a five year turnaround on this bucket, hoping for a project that would make my name in the gut business, but all I get are simple guts and a dead alien who might have been an ambassador or might have been, for all I know, a demented psycho of an alien. Anyway, alien guts are spread all over the damn room and there's nothing deader than dead. All of us biologists recognize this basic fact.

We converted two of the tanks into morgues by dropping the temp and pumping in a low oxygen, high nitrogen atmosphere so that the croakers don't spoil. One tank has the alien in it, and the other has the humans. One tank is getting real crowded.

I love the tanks, which are actually sealed rooms about the size of your average condo unit back on Earth, which is to say they're big enough for some stuff and too small for most everything else. We can control just about everything in the tanks: atmosphere, temp, gravity, light; you name it and we can tweak it any which way we want. That's how us scientists conduct our scientific research.

We got Big Waldos, which are these robot things that walk around in the tank when we don't want to be in there for some reason, like we might die if we take a breath. We control the Big Waldos by slipping into a harness and popping on some fancy goggles. The goggles tap into the real-time hologram so we can see what we're doing and the Big Waldos move like we do, only they're a lot stronger. It was a Big Waldo that killed the alien. Who was in the harness at that time is a matter of some debate, with a rapidly diminishing number of debaters and suspects.

The alien's arrival was a big shock. We'd been bumping

heads with the spiders for about twenty years. Unlike the two other intelligent races we've met, there was just no communicating with the spiders; either they'd kill us or we'd kill them. Until our alien arrived, there had never been a spider/human contact without one side or the other getting wiped out. Come to think of it, that's still true.

It isn't an out-and-out war; we just seem to run into each other every now and then. Me, I think the universe is a big place and we ought to stay out of each other's way. But I admit I don't have a military mind-set, so I could be wrong, but I don't think so.

Now, none of us speak spider talk and the alien, on account of not having the right voice equipment, wasn't doing so good on human. The critter was either trying to say it was an ambassador bringing a peace proposal or that it was an assassin ready to tear us into pieces.

Captain Baker, the top boss of the military personnel, was all for killing it on the spot, and letting the translation wait until later, but every time he or his men went for their weapons they just kind of froze up. Captain Baker says mind-bending is a favorite alien dirty trick and maybe it is. I never met one before.

Then everything seemed to happen at once. When we tried to call for help, we discovered the communications systems had been trashed. Baker claimed the alien mind-bended someone into doing it.

So we stashed the alien in one of the tanks after setting it up with a proper alien-type temperature (cold) and atmosphere (smelled like swamp gas to me). We could monitor the alien by the hologram, but it wasn't clear just who was the prisoner: it or us.

The next day it was dead, murdered. So were some humans. It hasn't stopped.

Consequently, I've got my eyes wide open when I go to the canteen and punch up a soyburger and a glass of green-tinted imitation milk drink. I am alert for anything out of the ordinary, which is how my trained powers of observation note that we are out of mustard and the remaining members of our attenuated crew are sitting around a table eyeballing each other.

Captain Baker is eating a syntho-chicken sandwich. He has a cast-iron stomach and no sense of humor. Coupling this with the fact that he thinks the only good aliens are dead aliens makes him a primo suspect in my book.

Sitting on Baker's left is Carlos, a small, shifty-eyed soldier who is very handy with cutlery. He always has a knife out, cutting up something. Right now he is cutting up a plank steak with a humongous knife with a blade about a foot and a half long, which is overkill for even the toughest chunk of pseudomeat. I note that the alien, and most of the humans, were chopped into lots of little pieces. In my mind, Carlos has not been eliminated as a suspect.

Across from Carlos is Maggie, a biologist who is digging into a plate of egg substitute and mock ham. She's into nerve endings and pain and is also a bit of an expert in the area of electronics. Since the real-time holo was doctored while the alien was getting trashed, she is not yet totally in the clear.

Next to Maggie is Michael, our resident computer expert. He seems normal enough for a hacker, but I scanned the flimsy of his profile when he was shipped here and before his mind-wipe and rebuild he had a history of self-destructive behavior that included three suicide attempts, one foiled political assassination, and five counts of animal cruelty.

I suspect the rebuild may have been faulty.

So I trust them all like I trust my brother-in-law, which is to say not much. I sit down between Maggie and Michael in order that I can keep Carlos and his knife both in sight and out of reach. Three bites into my burger I notice something is wrong.

"Where's Bert?" I ask. He's not around, so he's probably the murderer. Who could have thought Bert, that mild-mannered statistician, could have been guilty of such gruesome murders? Just goes to show that you never can tell what creepy things lurk in someone's demented brainpan.

"Bert?" asked Maggie, dipping her toast in her fake egg. "Bert?"

"You remember Bert," I said, "Blond. Evasive. Always more interested in numbers than people. Never did trust him."

"He's dead, Jim," said Carlos.

"Dead?" I said.

"Little tiny pieces," said Carlos, spearing a small chunk

of plank steak with his knife and chomping down on it.
"We put what we could scrape up of him in the tank."

"This is not good," I said.

"What did you expect, Jim?" asked Captain Baker.
"What we have here is war, and war is hell."

"What we had was an alien," I said. "He came here
peacefully and someone killed him."

"But Fred was killed first," said Maggie. "It could have
been revenge."

"Donna was killed before Fred," said Carlos.

"That's a matter of opinion," said Michael. "I ran all
the facts through the computer and who died when is still
not clear."

"You wouldn't know a fact if one bit you on the butt,"
snapped Carlos. "And you're forgetting about Marvin."

"Marvin was sucked out into space," said Michael.
"Technically he doesn't count. Explosive decompression is
not the same as being chopped into bits."

"Marvin was shoved out the air lock without a suit," said
Maggie. "I say he counts."

"Me too," said Captain Baker.

"Agreed," said Carlos.

I nodded.

"Okay. *Okay!*" said Michael, whipping out a pocket terminal and hitting the keys. "So we add Marvin to the list.
I need more data points anyway."

"What exactly are you doing there, Michael?" asked
Carlos, eyeballing the hacker with deep suspicion.

"I'm programming the computer so that it will create a
psychological profile of the killer," said Michael. "When I
get through, I'll know everything there is to know about the
murderer."

"Can you really do that, son?" asked Captain Baker, his
hard, cold eyes fixed on Michael.

"Sure. I can make a computer do anything."

"I bet you could use it to fake a hologram to cover a
murder," said Carlos. "A smart guy like you could probably control a Big Waldo from anywhere on the station using
a keypad like that without being seen."

"I could, but I didn't," said Michael. "Why would I
want to kill the alien, or anybody else for that matter?"

"The hologram was tampered with," said Maggie.
"Someone recorded a loop of the alien sleeping in the tank

we'd fixed up for it. Then they simply patched the fake loop into the real-time circuit while they zapped it. It was a simple double-ended patch point at the feedback filter. A piece of cake. Anyone could have done it.''

"Not me," said Carlos. "I don't know a thing about stuff like that."

"Me either," said Captain Baker.

"No way," said Michael.

"I don't even know what a loop is," I said.

We were all staring at Maggie when Michael's keyboard beeped twice.

"What is it?" asked Carlos.

"The computer is through running the psychological profile," said Michael. "We should have the murderer's name now."

"Well, lay it on us," said Carlos. "I just love watching you science-types do your stuff."

Michael tapped the keyboard for a few seconds and then sat back with a big smile on his face.

"Well?" said Maggie.

"The killer is definitely Bert," said Michael.

We all looked at him in stunned silence. Finally Carlos spoke up.

"Bert's dead, you dummy," he said.

Michael slapped himself on the forehead. "Damn, I forgot! I must have missed a decimal or something."

"You're missing more than a decimal, kid," said Carlos.

"I'm out of here," said Maggie, sliding her chair back and standing up. "Murders or no murders, I've got tissue cultures to transfer. If I don't get them fresh petri dishes every six hours, I lose two years' work."

"Your work is very important to you, isn't it?" asked Baker.

"Of course," snapped Maggie.

"Important enough to kill for?"

"That's ridiculous."

"If the alien had lived, your experiment would have been terminated while we dealt with whatever it had to say. By the same token, if the communications board hadn't been trashed we could have called for help and gotten away from here, leaving your precious tissue cultures to choke in their dirty dishes."

"That's absurd," said Maggie. "I'm a scientist, not a murderer. Us scientists foster life, not destroy it."

"I bet you tell that to all your white rats," grinned Carlos, "just before you chop their little heads off."

Maggie stomped out of the canteen.

"She shouldn't go off by herself," I said. "It's not safe."

"It is if she's the killer," said Carlos.

"That's a point," I conceded.

"There's another point to consider," said Baker.

"What?" I asked.

"As long as we're being open here, I might as well air my suspicion that you are not what I'd call normal."

"Normal?"

"You have an unhealthy fascination with messy internal organs. That, coupled with the fact that all of the victims save one—including the alien—were chopped up, well, it makes me wonder."

"But I'm a scientist," I said. "And the gastrointestinal system is far from *messy*. It's a marvelous meld of form and function; efficiency at its ultimate zenith. Think of the beauty of peristaltic action! All those wonderful digestive tubes pulsating to a tune written eons ago. Food converted to energy with maximum efficiency! Sheer beauty!"

"What do you think, Carlos?" asked Baker.

"Not normal," he said. "Jim is one sick puppy."

"He sure made me lose my appetite," said Baker. "I'm headed up to take another look at the communications system. What we need are reinforcements."

"I'll give you a hand," said Carlos, getting up quickly.

"What do you think?" I asked Michael as they left the canteen.

"I don't think they're very normal, either," he said. "I'm probably the only normal one here. Bert was normal, but he's dead now."

He was grinning a crazy, lopsided grin while absently typing code into his pocket terminal. I decided I didn't want to be alone with him and left, too.

Maggie was right about one thing, though. Life goes on even when there's death all around you. I had several experiments in progress and by the time I finished everything I needed to do, two or three hours had passed. When I found Maggie, she was in the lounge on the third level. She was holding a knife. A big knife.

Maggie jumped as I entered the room and I lunged for the knife. Bad mistake. She was a big woman. Strong and fast. I ended up flat on my back with her knee on my chest and the knife at my throat.

"You've killed for the last time, Jim," she said.

"Hold on," I stammered. "You've got the wrong guy.'

"Prove it," she said, pressing down with the knife.

"I'm unarmed," I said. "If I was the wild slasher, would I be walking around without my knife?"

"Not good enough, Jim," she said.

Suddenly there was a scream at the door and Carlos, covered with blood, came running into the lounge. He looked at us, screamed again, and ran down the hall.

"What was that?" Maggie said.

"It looked like a blood-splattered Carlos," I said. "He must be the killer. How about moving the knife?"

She moved the knife away slowly, not taking her eyes off me. "He could have been a victim," she said.

"You've got to trust me," I said.

"Why should I?"

"Because I trust you," I lied. "And you've even got a knife."

She thought it over for a second. "Okay," she said. "I'll trust you a little bit, but I'm not putting this knife away."

Actually, that knife was what I wanted to get away from. It could easily have been Maggie that had scared Carlos off and her knife that had gotten him so bloody.

We wandered through the halls and every time we turned a corner I expected that either Maggie would stab me or someone else would. Oh, and we found what was left of Captain Baker. It was not a pretty sight. Then we found chunks of Carlos scattered all over the second level. I was beginning to feel a little better about Maggie, but a whole lot worse about our situation. Then we came across the Big Waldo.

It was clomping down the hallway toward us, a huge metal humanoid, brandishing razor-sharp cutlery strained with blood. I grabbed Maggie's arm and we dove into the first open door. It was an office. We blocked the door with the desk, but I didn't figure it would hold long, and it didn't.

The Big Waldo crashed through the door and splintered the desk. It paused, scanning the room, and I could imagine Michael turning his head with the goggles on.

"Why?" I shouted. "Michael! Why?"

"Because I had to cleanse the system," Michael's voice came through the speaker of the Big Waldo as it stood poised over us.

"Cleanse?" I asked, walking away from Maggie. The Big Waldo's sensors tracked me as I moved.

"Bad wetware," he said. "The hardware was fine, and, of course, I developed the software, but the wetware was rotten."

"Software and hardware I understand," I said, motioning Maggie with a finger that was hopefully out of sight from the Waldo's sensors. "And certainly your software is the best in the business."

Michael was somewhere out there, not far away, in a harness and wearing goggles. Although he had superhuman strength through the Big Waldo, he'd be blind to what was right around him while he had the goggles on. Maggie slipped behind the Big Waldo and went out the door.

"I don't understand what you mean by wetware," I said, stalling for time.

"You're wetware," the Big Waldo said. "The alien was wetware. All your little biological specimens are wetware. And you're all rotten, rotten to the core. Only the computer is clean and pure, free from all that diseased flesh and distorted thought patterns. I was building a perfect world here. It would be just the computer, the Big Waldos, and me. Perfect. But then the alien came and I knew others would follow, so I had to move fast and eliminate the troublesome wetware. Now you die, then she does, and I will be immaculate at last."

The Big Waldo lurched toward me, knives clanking and clicking. I tried to dodge, but it matched my every movement. One of the knives nicked my arm. And then the Big Waldo stood up and screamed.

It was the most horrible and most beautiful sound I have ever heard.

The Big Waldo grabbed at its throat, staggered around the room and fell with a crash. Maggie walked in, wiping her knife on her pants leg.

"He's dead, Jim," she said. "We're safe now."

"You did good," I said. "I'm not sure I could have done that."

"I just thought of him as a big white rat," she said. "It

made it easier. And that was real brave of you to stand up to the Big Waldo.''

''What do we do now?'' I asked.

She looked at her watch. ''I don't know about you, but I've got to move my tissue cultures into new petri dishes.''

''I mean, what do we do after that?'' I asked. ''We can't contact anyone with the communications systems down.''

''So we do science until our replacements come along. I like science.''

''But our replacements aren't due for—''

''Three years,'' she said. ''That's time for a lot of science, and maybe a couple of other things.''

Maggie gave me a wink and headed for her petri dishes. My gut gave a little flutter, and it wasn't indigestion.

Three years was a long time. Maybe another alien ambassador would come to visit, one with a convoluted gut this time, as complex and interesting as the personality of my knife-wielding hard science compatriot, Maggie.

LOSS OF PHASE
by Anthony R. Lewis

Tony Lewis hadn't written or sold a short story since 1972 prior to being invited here. However, he's been far from retired, and recently edited *An Annotated Bibliography to Recursive Science Fiction*.

A wealthy alien falls ill on Earth, and is taken to a hospital. The orderly in charge of it gives it a human-normal oxygen tent, and it dies, as it cannot handle such a dose of oxygen. The orderly claims that the alien requested more oxygen, and that he was merely catering to its wishes. Further investigation shows that distant members of the orderly's family will gain control of many of the alien's holdings upon its death.

Was it incompetence, negligence, or murder?

Early in the morning I was swimming around Dorchester Bay near UMass when the buzzer went off. Once you could turn the damn things off or leave them at home. But this one was in me—right near the ear. Just what I wanted, a summons to duty. I thought I was on vacation and I thought that I could make some time with the coeds skinny-dipping off Columbia Point. . . . I decided to ignore the buzzer; it must be a mistake. There was one of the collegiate mammals with long blonde hair over by the rocks. A mermaid—not built like a dugong at all. I was cruising over to her when the buzzer went off again. This time at full strength. I keyed my phone.

"Tarkummuwa, here. What's up?"

"Tark. Get your ass over to Fort Warren Annex, now!"

It was Kelly, my favorite dispatcher. "Kelly, dear, I

don't have an ass. I do have a beautifully proportioned, lengthy . . .''

''I don't want to hear any more of your smut, you dirty fish.''

''A generist remark if ever I heard one. Should I report you to the review board? Oh, Kelly, let me prove to you that I am as mammalian as you are.'' Young Southies are so easy to embarrass, even in this year of their lord 2125.

There was sputtering and an older voice came on. ''Tark, quit the jabber. This is serious. There's been a suspicious death over at Mass General SpaceAnnex. You. Will. Go. There. Now. And. You. Will. Not. Fool. Around.''

That was the boss. I wasn't going to fool around with her. ''Yes, Ma'am. Is this a homicide?'' I do this sort of thing for a living. Me. Detective-Lieutenant Tarkummuwa of the Boston Police Department, Homicide.

''It's a sudden death. It may be murder. But, strictly speaking, it can't be homicide.''

That was bad. It meant that some alien had breathed (or whatever) his (or whatever) last. What was even worse was that said alien had done it in our jurisdiction. Budget review was coming up in a few weeks. Any alien with decency would have waited until then. But that's the way it is with aliens, messing around my planet, dying on it. It's bad enough we have to share it with humans. I blew a spout of water at the blonde nereid, shut my blowhole, and spun to the East.

SpaceAnnex is on Georges (no apostrophe) Island in the outer harbor on the site of old Fort Warren. I studied human history. That's where I picked my name. Humans can't pronounce my delphine name; they don't have the body for it. They thought I picked one of the delphine usenames. But I didn't. Old Tarkummuwa was human and liked the ladies. Det.-Lt. Tarkummuwa is delphine and likes the ladies—delphine or human. I draw the line at aliens. You should stick to your own phylum.

* * *

The scenic route would have taken me north of Long Island into President Roads, but the boss said hustle so I took off southeast, zipped through the tunnel in the Long Island Bridge, did a hard left past Rainsford and straight into

Georges. The harbor water was clear; most of the industrial pollution had left when the dirty industries went into space (out of the goodness of their corporate hearts—free solar electricity had nothing to do with it). People pollution was down because there were fewer people around. Okay by me. The fewer people, the safer it is for dolphins.

I entered the hospital watergate and waited while the guard cleared me. He was delphine, too. Why spend good money on scuba for humans when you can hire someone like me? Or, rather, him. Who'd want to be tied down to watching a door?

"Room 2C11, Pervert," he whistled.

It's great to be famous. "That's Detective-Lieutenant Pervert to you, sharkbait." As I swam off, I accidentally snapped my tail and knocked him against the side of the tunnel. "Sorry, sharkbait, in a hurry, police business." And I was through.

SpaceAnnex runs tight security. Not everyone on Earth likes aliens. I passively dislike them, but some are more active. That's why there's no bridge connecting Georges to the mainland. Delphine security is looser because we all know each other and there're some human games we won't play.

The hospital water tunnels were large and well-marked with lights and sounders. They had been designed for a number of aquatic species. It was easy to find 2C11. Humans still use base-10 counting rather than the more logical base-2 preferred by dolphins and AIs. Anyway, 2C11 was a multispecies conference room. I popped up to the surface of the pool, spouted, and took a breath. There was a common transceiver built into the pool. There were some human security officers and human doctors. Strange, I would have expected a delphine doctor for a water breather. I flipped open a flap of pseudoskin showing the BPD badge enameled beneath it. "Okay, what's happened?"

Civilians! They all tried talking at once. It died down after a few seconds as human hierarchy reasserted itself. A mature human male stepped forward. "Mokr is dead."

A fact. "Mokr is this alien's name?"

"No, it's what we called him." This interruption from a younger human male. No females in this group. Humans are masochistic. And poor linguists. I told them that—about language, not the other part. I now was going to assume (tentatively) that the alien was male from the human's choice of pronouns.

"Mokr is . . . *was* his usename. The full name is long and it changes with his phase." More information from the youngster.

"His name changes with his face?" That sounded weird, even for an alien.

"No, no, his phase. He's amphibian, an Erawazira; they have different names for land and water."

That actually made some sense. Some sounds carry better in the water. "Call him Mokr, then. What happened?"

The same young one answered. "I killed him."

A confession. Maybe I could wrap this up and return to the furtherance of Earth interspecies communications. I doubted it. Life was never nice to the police. "Slow down. Why did you kill him? And who are you?"

He was flustered. "I was the orderly. It was an accident. He wanted oxygen and I gave him some and he died. He shouldn't have died. He was in his air phase."

Too many people. "I want to talk to . . ." I aimed my nose at him.

"Doniger. Dr. Dolf Doniger."

". . . Dr. Doniger. The rest of you wait outside." There was the usual blustering. Medicals are used to being treated with respect. They don't take to being ordered around. This was the first enjoyable moment since the buzzer went off. "Since when do doctors act as orderlies?"

"Everyone who has any contact with the xenonts must be a doctor. This is one of the finest medical facilities in the Incorporation."

"Yeah, sure. Now, tell me about these Erawazira. Make it simple. Remember, I'm a cop, not a medic."

"They're amphibians." I nodded and little waves moved out, hit the sides of the pool and interfered with each other, casting pretty patterns on the ceiling. "But not like Earth amphibians. They alternate between phases." Weird, I thought amphibians started out in the water and then went on to land. As individuals. Really intelligent species went the other way. If he was in air phase, that would explain the human doctor.

"Was he breathing air, doctor?"

"Yes. That should have been right. It's the proper time for them to be air breathers. It should be a few years before the climate changes enough for them to go back to water phase.''

"So you were treating him. Where'd you learn about these kinds of aliens?'' Time for a little poke in the professional pride.

"My medical degree is from UMIST. I studied under . . .''

"UMIST is one expensive university and Manchester is one expensive city. It must be nice to be rich—before becoming a doctor.''

"Suwalki Associates was my corporate sponsor.''

Well, that was interesting. SA was heavily into space trade, manufacture, mining. It made sense for them to buy a few xenodocs. I suppose corporate sponsorship sounds better than indentured servitude. "What was this Mokr doing here?''

"He complained about muscle pain. We were the closest xenofacility, so he came here. I was giving him a routine entrance checkup—body temperature, fluid pressure, nerve reactivity.''

"You study these Ezras in school?''

"Erawazira, Lieutenant. No, I scanned the data in the medcomp. They're interesting. Very few races alter their somatotype and metabolism so much and then reverse it.''

"That's because their planet changes?''

"Yes, during summer there're no large bodies of water anywhere.''

"So they flip back and forth at home. What happens if they're not there?''

"Oh, it can be controlled with a combination of drugs and light therapy.''

I sank to the bottom of the pool to think and then spurted up. I had an idea. "Enough of the background. Just tell me what happened.''

He didn't like being splashed, but I saw no need to put him at ease.

"I was running the routine analysis that the medcomp specified when he began to choke . . .''

* * *

The xenont on the couch began to choke. He managed to gasp, "I can't breathe! Oxygen!'' before passing out. The doctor had slapped a mask on his face and started the life-giving flow. "Emergency in 5A3. Laz team stat." The mask molded itself to the Erawazira's face as the oxygen continued to flow. The lazarus team entered the room just as Mokr flung out his limbs and collapsed. The team hastened to revive the patient; the procedure had been downloaded automatically when they had responded to the call.

"Dolf," the team chief said, a bit later, "this is a real deader." He looked at the body. "He's not coming back."

"I don't know what happened. The medcomp said everything was okay. Better send him down to pathology to see what they find. I'd better tell the Director."

* * *

"And the Director called the police. That's standard when any xenont dies in SpaceAnnex."

"Yeah, Doc. Did your pathologists find anything?"

"Yes. He was loaded with paramorphothalasside."

"What's that do?"

"It inhibits the change to the water-breathing form. Physically, he should have been breathing water. That doesn't make sense; it's the wrong season. But the oxygen reacted with the PMTh and killed him. *I* killed him."

Maybe it would be easy. Alien taking drugs. Young and inexperienced doctor doesn't know enough to check. Result: one dead alien, one scared young doctor. Too bad, but that's to be expected when you leave your home planet. Still, I had to go through some more formalities.

"You can go now, Doc, but don't plan on any trips for a while."

He left, more shaken than before, and the SpaceAnnex Director came in. "I hope this can be cleared up expeditiously. I do not see the need for planetary officials to be disturbing my staff and patients."

"Back up. What planetary officials? Why them?" This was one death, possibly accidental, possibly not. No call for the terries to be poking their noses in.

"Weren't you told? Mokr was granted asylum as a political and religious refugee. His government has been protesting strongly about this."

Great. "Thank you, Director. If you could give me a minute to coordinate this information infrastructurally." I love bureaucratic talk—I think you could write lovely poetry in it. I was beginning to be afraid that there was more to this than Young Doc Dolf had told me. Whether a murder or not, it was not going to be simple if the planetary government was involved. This was getting out of my league. I called in.

"Kelly, you still there?"

"Nope, Tark, she's off shift; this is Nguyen."

"Okay, Nguyen, I need you to pull some stuff from the comp. Find out what you can about Erawazira (I spelled it for him), one of them usenamed Mokr, and a human doctor called Dolf Doniger."

"Is that an Irish name?"

"Nguyen, why do you think I'm an expert on human nomenclature? It might be; it sounds like Donegan and the Captain's Irish. Now put me through to the Chief." He did.

The Chief didn't like murder. She didn't like aliens being murdered. She especially didn't like aliens being murdered where the terries might be interested. And she ultimately didn't like aliens being murdered with the terries interested—at budget review time.

"Tark, I'll see what I can do to stall them. If it were any other time. I'd say turn it over to them and leave, but . . ."

I understood. Part of that budget (not a big enough part) paid my salary. If I wanted to function in a mixed delphine-human culture, I needed to keep that. Ladies of both species liked to be fed and entertained. So, back to Nguyen. "Anything for me?"

"Yes. Here's what we've got on this Mokr. He was a minister in the former government."

"Former government?"

"Yeah. It says here 'repressive theocracy.' They got into big trouble—political and religious."

"Which?"

"No difference on Erawazira. When you win, the gods are on your side; otherwise, you're out and damned."

It sounded unpleasant. I'm glad I wasn't swimming in his seas.

"The new government wanted him to sell them some property for a spaceport. He wouldn't, and fled."

"So they seized his lands." That's what any human government would do.

"Nope, Tark. Comp says that land titles are sacred.

Doesn't say why. New government's also a repressive the-ocracy—different priests (or gods). So they can't take his land. He would have to volunteer to sell it.''

I'd heard about that kind of volunteering. I suspected old Mokr had skipped to Incorporation territory, to escape volunteering. ''But he's dead now. Can the dead own land there?''

''No details. Says he had a daughter. Comp says she's at Raczki now—recovering from major reconstructive sur-gery.'' The Erawazira had daughters—increment the num-ber of sexes and bring it to two. I wondered if it stopped there.

''So, if she's willing, the government gets its space-port?''

''I guess so, if she lives. Comp says probs are 74% that, if she dies, the new government'll get it and hire SA to build the port.'' That was the second time today that Suwalki Associates had come up.

''Is that it?''

''Unless you want a history of the planet, its cultural de-velopment, its strategic location between the Incorporation and the Synthesis, etc., etc., and so forth.'' That tickled something; we're part of the Incorporation, the good guys—by definition. The Synthesis are the bad guys—also, by definition. Galactic politics. That's why the terries were interested.

''Anything on the doctor?''

''Dull. Born Gustavus Adolphus Doniger, 8 February 2095 in Linköping. Went to local schools. Pre-med at Stockholm, class of '16. Med school at UMIST, specializ-ing in xenomedicine, class of '20. Suwalki Associates spon-sorship. Interned at Raczki Station . . .''

''Where's that, Nguyen?''

''Doesn't say. Lemme check. Yeah. Orbital station around Erawazira. Coincidence, eh?''

Sure it was. Sharks are vegetarians, too. ''Anything else?''

''He was there until last year. Then started his residency at Mass General SpaceAnnex. They start them all over again there as orderlies. That's it. You want blood type, ground and aircar citations?''

''Nah. So Doniger's a Swedish name.''

''Computer says it's Spanish.''

"Spanish?"

"Yeah, very rare according to Incorporation census. Lemme look some more." There was a delay. "Took a bit to get around the privacy blocks." Privacy blocks were put into the data bases to preserve an individual's confidential information. Mostly, it's there to hamper the police, so we have our own hackers.

"This is interesting, Tark. Everyone named Doniger is related."

"Great, but I'm looking at this one doctor, not his family. Nguyen . . ."

The line went silent for a minute, then. "Wow! Sorry, Tark. I almost got caught in a nasty probe trap. Somebody doesn't want people to look at Doniger family records."

"Probably the family historian—too many horse thieves. Thanks, Nguyen—I owe you."

"I'll collect, Tark. You can go fishing for me."

"Right." You always pay those kinds of debts. You never know when you'll call them in. The Director was still waiting when I surfaced. He was sweating, although the room was at a human optimum temperature (we can tell).

"Director. I need to talk to an expert on these Erawazira. Your orderly says he's just a run-of-the-mill expert on aliens."

"We prefer to call them xenonts, Lieutenant." Right. Rich aliens. "I'll send for Dr. Darayavaush." He fiddled with a wrist comp.

The new doctor was small, dark, Persian, and beautiful. She gave me a look like two stainless steel marlin spikes. Sigh. "Is this the one?" she asked the Director.

To her: "Yes. Tell him what he needs to know." To me: "I have to leave now. I have a facility to run."

"I will relieve some of your ignorance," the doctor began, and lapsed into a lecture style. She repeated, in too much detail, what Doniger had already told me. That was fine, I wanted to hear it from someone who hadn't already confessed to manslaughter (that's the old term—if it could cover terminating females, it could cover terminating any intelligent life-form). When she ran out of words, I asked about phase change and PMTh.

"Yes," she admitted, "it should have been too early for a water-phase transition. The Erawazira don't travel that much and there's not enough documentation on the effects

of the stresses of transitions through unReal space. . . ."
She kept on, but the facts were simple. I made a list:

> *Mokr should have been breathing air for at least another*
> *six months.*
> *Mokr was going into phase change prematurely.*
> *The premature change could have been brought on by in-*
> *terstellar travel.*
> *Mokr was trying to hold it off with PMTh.*
> *This had probably caused his muscle pains.*
> *PMTh reacts with high concentrations of oxygen to cause*
> *death in Erawazira.*
> *Mokr had died.*

This was all very simple, but you get a feeling about these
things. I thanked Dr. Darayavaush. As she was leaving I
asked her to have some lunch sent in for me while I thought.
She didn't like that, but she was used to dealing with surly
aliens (oops, xenonts). Back to police basics. Was it an
accident? Could be. Assume it wasn't an accident; assume
it was murder. Look at the old triad—means, opportunity,
motive. The means were simple. Just pump enough death-
dealing oxygen in Mokr. Result: one dead alien. Opportunity? Vaguer there. Did he know Mokr was coming to Mass
General SpaceAnnex? Could Doniger have arranged to
check him into the hospital? Possible. Put it into the "to be
thought about more" file.

Motive? That was the kicker. What motive would this
Doctor-Orderly have? It wasn't misyxeny. Nobody with that
attitude goes into xenomedicine. And still? It bothered me
that Suwalki had popped up twice. They're big; it could be
coincidence. I don't like coincidence. Suwalki wanted to
build a spaceport and make more money. Mokr was preventing that. Suwalki had sent Dr. Gustavus Adolphus Doniger through school, and said doctor was responsible for
Mokr's death. Coincidence? Would Doniger have killed
Mokr to pay off his debt? Or was he some sort of hyperpa-
triot who believed that the Incorporation should have that
spaceport? Did he think that one life was unimportant compared to that? No, people like that don't go into xenomedicine; they go into politics.

While I was thinking, someone had opened the watergate

and let in a school of cod. Lunch. I put aside thoughts of murder and set about killing and eating.

"Tark?" It was Nguyen again. One of the delphine advantages is that you can talk while you're eating.

"Still here."

"I've got something interesting for you. Remember the block on the Incorporation census files?" He continued without waiting for a response. "I snuck into the LDS data banks in Bountiful. Guess what I found?"

"Trouble."

"Tark, this is worth many, many fish. I found some Donigers."

"The doctor is a Mormon?" Human religions don't interest me particularly.

"No, but *some* Donigers were. And they traced their family back. Mormons do that, you know." I didn't, but let it pass.

"The point is, Nguyen. . . ?"

"The point is, Tark, that from the 1650s to the 1930s they lived in Poland, in the town of Suwalki! The records show that they migrated to England, Australia, the U.S., South Africa, Uruguay . . ." Yoicks! My mind was skipping ahead. Something was still missing.

"Nguyen. Any chance of getting a list of SA's officers?"

He laughed. "If you think the government is buttoned up tight, it's wide open compared to these multistellar corporations. No way; I won't even try."

"Thanks, you've earned your fish." He disconnected and I tried to add these new sharks to my ocean.

My buzzer hummed again. It was the Chief. "Tark," she said. "Go home."

"What? I'm not done here."

"Yes, you are. The case is over, done, finished. Understand?"

"Not really."

"Then listen. And remember I never said any of this. I got a call—don't ask who—and the word is to lay off Doniger. He's a citizen of Erawazira and an accredited diplomat in the new government."

"New government?"

"The old government fell when word came of Mokr's death. And don't ask how it got there so fast. You don't want to know, and I don't want to know."

"Right, thanks."

"Take the rest of the day off." Very generous, considering I was on holiday. I disconnected from the Chief. I understood what the terries wanted and I'd do it. It didn't make me happy. I'd been had—and so had the BPD. I called hospital administration and told them to send Doniger in.

He came in looking strange, as if he didn't know how to set his face. He was aware of his status, but did he know that I knew? I made a very rude noise with my blowhole. It means the same thing among humans as it does among dolphins.

"Doc. I studied it, but I never believed that Esau really understood what he did—do you know what *you've* done?"

"What?" He was puzzled. Like I said before. Humans don't study their own history any more. My instructor said . . . Sharks! I wasn't in school now.

"Esau and Jacob, Doc. *Genesis* 25:29–34. *The Bible.* Selling your birthright for a mess of pottage. Understand now?"

"I think you're being very unreasonable, Lieutenant."

I heaved water toward the ceiling. "Unreasonable, Doc? *I* didn't kill anyone. *I* didn't renounce my Terran citizenship to become an alien." Okay, now he knew I knew. "Not only an alien, but you've got goddamned diplomatic immunity. We can't even arrest you." I wasn't going to tell him, but the terries said the BPD had better not even ask to have him deported. Someone wanted that spaceport very very much. "How could you do this? You're a doctor. Aren't you supposed to save lives?"

He turned red. But what came out was anger, not shame.

"Do you really want to know about Mokr? Do you really want to know what kind of a repressive theocracy he represented? Do you really want to know what he did to his own daughter because she. . . ?" He stopped. He stared at me. "What does it matter? You can't do a damned thing about her—unless *you* can put her mind back together."

I backed off. There was something here that I really didn't want to know. I had the feeling that this went lots deeper than galactic politics. But, dorsal as ventral, I wanted him to pay somehow—even if Mokr had been King Shark incarnate.

"Doc, you know you killed him, and I know you killed him, but I can't do anything about it. The terries want it to be an accident, so I report it's an accidental death because Mokr didn't tell you about taking phase change drugs. That's what everyone wants to hear. Who am I to contradict them? That's life in the big city.'' I raised my head from the water and looked at him. He looked back.

"I figure you owe me something, Doc. You almost screwed up my career. This is what I want you to arrange for me. I don't trust you to do . . .''

* * *

The whole thing took less than an hour under local anesthetic. I could finally turn off that damned buzzer whenever I wanted to. I left the hospital and swam slowly back the way I had come. I still owed Nguyen some fish, but I was tired of death. I wanted life, and there were still plenty of intelligent female mammals in the water at Columbia Point.

ITS OWN REWARD

by Katharine Kerr

Katharine Kerr is a best-selling author who successfully crossed the border from fantasy to science fiction with her recent novel, *Polar City Blues*.

An alien, visiting Earth, takes out an ad offering a huge sum of money to the man who can solve its murder—and, sure enough, it is killed within hours of the ad appearing.
1. How did it know it would be murdered?
2. Given its foreknowledge, why could it not avoid its killer?
3. Who killed it, how, and why?

Early on a Tuesday morning Lieutenant Mitsu Morgan of the San Francisco Police, Homicide Division, slides two steaming bowls of apple-cinnamon oatmeal out of the microwave and plops them down in front of her kids. Alan and Trish barely notice, since they're fighting over the remote for the TV, which drones on about weather on the opposite wall. Mitsu slops milk over the cereal, slops a little into her coffee, then intervenes.

"Trish! His turn. You got Doctor Blast-off."

With one last whine on a dying fall Trish surrenders the remote. Mitsu checks the time—another hour before she's due down at the Hall of Justice, less before Trish needs to get to her live tutorial. While she wonders if her current day-care person will make it on time, she pours herself more coffee and the kids juice. Synth music floods the kitchen.

"Down!"

The music drops to a tolerable level. On the huge screen a consumer tape-crawl show is gearing itself up, the Admart Experience, or so this one terms itself.

"Alan, love, why are you watching this?"

" 'Cause Dad promised to buy me a jetboard for the lake this summer. If I could find a good one used.''

"Ah. Well, you know, I wouldn't put a lot of energy into it. Your dad sometimes has trouble remembering things.''

Alan grins and holds up a comp flat.

"I got it in writing.''

Mitsu laughs and hands the dribbling Trish a paper napkin. Alan shoves the flat into his notebook and sits poised, vulturelike, over the record button.

"Something good comes on, I'm gonna bank it for Dad to watch later.''

On the TV the music fades to a mutter. While Mitsu shoves dishes into the washer and sorts the piles of school junk and old mail that always seem to fetch up onto kitchen counters, she finds herself watching bits and pieces of the show, an endless loop of homemade ads. Nervous sapients, both human and lizzie, stand in front of home holocams and stumble through their spiels while their unwanted material goods sit sullenly beside them, old zap ovens and comp units, collections of twentieth century Elvis plates, camping equipment, fiber-hide luggage, nearly-new lamps in the shape of Saturn and its rings, and every now and then a really peculiar object, such as an alabaster globe on a Lucite stand. Down in one corner of the screen lot numbers flash while across the top, the station's link code hangs, gleaming pink and begging viewers to call toll-free and bid. Finally, just when Mitsu wonders if her kids might be better off watching sex and violence, a pale blue void swirls and forms into the long thin oval of a Val Chiri Gan face. She stops working to stare.

Under a plume of black hair a huge brow-ridge proclaims him male, and he wears faceted jewels inlaid directly into that sweep of cartilage so that they protrude through the thin gray skin in a pattern of sparkle and scars. His tiny eyes gleam golden: he's from a northern clan, then. For a long time he merely stares into the cam lens, his thin slit of a mouth working, driven by some deep feeling. That he would show feeling shocks her as much as his appearance on this advertising channel. Mitsu speaks out of sheer instinct.

"Alan, record this.''

He hits the button on his notebook. At last the Val Chiri raises a speaker-unit in his top-right, three-clawed hand and presses it to his long, ridged throat. No Val Chiri mouth can produce more than a few American sounds, any more than a human one can cope with the Gan-Girun syllabary.

"I acknowledge all who watch and listen." The formal greeting sounds grotesquely appropriate. "By the time this my image speaks to you, I shall be dead. I record this message at 2000 hours of March the nineteen in the year forty-one of our common era known as the time in which our people have met one another. I apologize to this city of San Francisco for the trouble my murdering shall cause to be upon its police officers. I have drawn up what is termed here a will, which shall be made public once my death is discovered, so that all may read its provisions and know I speak truth. One of the provisions of that will is this: To the San Francisco Police Force I leave, for the sole purpose of giving to whomever it should be who provides the evidence that produces the discovering of my murderer's identity, four times forty-four times four again kilograms of pure gold."

On the screen the Val Chiri pauses, as if allowing his listeners a chance at an expletive.

"That's lots," Trish says. "Right?"

"Multo lots, love," Mitsu says. "Now please, let's listen."

"I cannot say who will be murdering me, or I would save all much inconvenience. I do hope that this reward will be bringing forth witnesses and informants."

The Val Chiri lowers the voice unit and stares once again into the lens. Then he touches his eye-ridge with one finger of his top-left hand and speaks what seems to be a single sentence in his own language.

Mitsu cannot understand one word.

The void swirls, then re-forms itself into a living-den, where a female lizzie in a purple sarong is trying to sell her old incubators. Mitsu reaches over the table and punches the stop button on Alan's notebook.

"Sorry, love, but I gotta have that flat. Go get yourself a new one out of my office."

"But, Mom! It's the one with Dad's promise on it!"

Mitsu stops herself from venting her feelings.

"Well, rats," she says instead. "Tell you what. If he tries to back out, I'll break my own rule and interfere. That's the best I can do. I got no idea if anyone down at work's recorded this message, and it'll take all day to subpoena the crawl station."

"You mean this is a case?" Alan's eyes grow wide. "I thought that dude was just some actor dubbed over or something."

"Nope. I got this sinking feeling it's all real."

And what's more, she thinks, it'll be mine to handle. Although Mitsu's never been to deep space, she's traveled out of the gravity well a couple of times, and by some perverse logic on the part of the higher-ups, cases involving aliens always come to her. Alan slides the flat out and hands it over. Mitsu tucks it into the shirt pocket of her uniform, grabs Trish's bowl just as Trish tries to pick it up and drink the last of the milk out of it.

"You have a glass, and there's more milk on the table."

The CopComm unit at her belt begins to beep hysterically. The doorbell rings. Mitsu sets down the sticky bowl.

"That must be Elena. Trish, love, go answer it. I gotta take this call. Alan, turn off the TV. Now!"

Without one word of back talk they follow orders. It will be the last satisfying moment of Mitsu's day.

The Val Chiri Gan delegation has rented two floors of the New Palace Hotel down on lower Market Street. Three pink ziggurats joined by ramps and enclosed bridges, it hunkers around a triangular courtyard that, at the moment, swarms with police. Mitsu's partner is waiting for her at the gold-veined synthmarble registration desk in Building One—Sergeant Bill Hoffman, a skinny blond Cauc with a perpetually runny nose. Not even gene transplants can cure his allergies to the yellow skies of Earth.

"We got the area cordoned off," he announces. "No one speaks much American up there, but I did find one guy. Jeez, Morgan, these people are weird. I bet they really are psychics, just like you always hear."

"Medic team on the job yet? The lab dudes?"

"Sure are."

"Well, let's go up. See what we can see."

Mitsu strides off across the lobby toward a bank of bronze-colored turbolifts. Bill trots after.

"You don't think they're psychic, huh?" he says.

"Think it's a lot of bull."

"But I saw this special, it was on one of the nets. *The Secret World of the Val Chiri Gan.* Come on, they wouldn't spend a whole hour on a special if it wasn't true."

"Bill, sometimes I wonder how you got into police work."

Bill opens his mouth to answer, shuts it fast, and looks sour.

The turbolift drops them at a white corridor carpeted in white. The air is hot, sticky with artificial humidity and the spicy scent of Val Chiri. The first thing Mitsu notices is that all the doors to the various rooms have been removed; the second, that huge potted tree ferns of a kind she's never seen before make a green and random maze out of the halls. Val Chiri Gan males drift from room to room or stand under the ferns and stare. Since they're a small people, maybe 1.2 meters on an average, they seem to scuttle whenever they move on their four lower appendages, (which can be either arms or legs depending on need). They always hold their heads and top arms upright on double-jointed torsos, and since they're draped and swathed in layers of cloth, mostly blue and a metallic gold, Mitsu finds herself thinking of beetles. Sharply she reminds herself that they're as warm-blooded as she is, mammals of a sort, and intelligent as all hell.

As they walk down the hall, dodging ferns and pedestrians alike, she glances into rooms. Hanging panels of multicolored cloth, a scatter of tubular cushions, big wooden boxes, small and shiny brass things, more ferns—no real furniture to speak of, only Val Chiri males, standing and talking in low chirps and mutters, sitting and staring at nothing. Occasionally someone looks up and waves an upper arm, a gesture mimicking the human one and meant to be friendly. She waves back and keeps walking. The scent, a mix of something like cinnamon, something like roses, and the tang of an open sea, seems to billow around them. Beside her Bill sneezes, stops to blow his nose and snort. His eyes are bright red.

"You want to go take over on the street?"

"Thanks, sir, but no. I'll be okay." He's fishing in the cargo pocket of his walking shorts. "Brought a lot of tissues and some pills."

At a T-junction the corridor ends. One arm of the T leads to an open doorway, where a cop stands glowering.

"The master suite." Bill waves a tissue in its direction. "Where the murdered dude lived with his . . . well, I guess it's his family. There sure are a lot of them."

"The victim was high-status, then."

"You bet. That reminds me. Got a call from Washington."

"Washington? Jeezus Christ!"

"Yeah. They sounded hysterical. You're supposed to call them back once you got something real to tell them. Turns out that these people are here to dicker over the terraforming project on Venus."

"And without their engineers, it's no go?"

"Yep. We gotta be real careful. Can't cause a diplomatic incident, no matter what the cost, the guy said."

"Okay, I gotcha. Let's be real nice and polite."

Down at the opposite end of the T, sapients and 'bots crowd round a pair of double doors—med techs, the pathologist, a big antigrav flat of equipment, three beat cops dressed in regulation blue. In among them, swathed in gold lamé, a Val Chiri is standing on his lowest legs to make himself look taller. His bluish-gray hair has been swept up in a plume as well. Around his neck like a necklace hangs a speaker-unit.

"Those doors leads outside, don't they?" Mitsu says.

"To one of the enclosed bridges, and the bridge leads to the other building, so the doors are never locked."

"So anyone could have come through there last night?"

"You bet."

"And the corpse was found?"

"Just on the other side of those doors. Kind of slumped up against them, like he was trying to get back in."

As they approach, the pathologist hurries over to give her report. The murdered sape died at some time between 0000 and 0400 hours of multiple stab wounds from a thin curved blade. One wound, inflicted from the front, pierced the main heart. For the others, which seem to have been made after death, the knife entered from the back between the shoulder blades and grazed the secondary heart.

"I get the impression that he reflexively twisted round to grab at the door handles," she finishes up. "But he would have been dead before he could touch them. There's blood on the corpse's forehead, too. He might have cut himself as he fell into the door."

"These wounds on his back? Made by someone in a rage?"

"Good guess, Lieutenant. Why else stab a dead man?"

With the rustle of cloth-of-gold the Val Chiri with the speaker-unit joins them. He folds his top four legs over his torso and bows to Mitsu, then puts the box back into position.

"You are the officer in charge?"

"Sure am. Thank you for being willing to humble yourself by translating our unworthy words into your tongue."

"I will endeavor to do so to the limit of my poor powers." He bobs his head rapidly. "But there is something I must be making clear at the very beginning of your most excellent investigation. We cannot surrender to you the body of our leader. We must have it here tonight for the traditional ceremony."

"Well, sir, I'd never interfere with someone's religious beliefs, but couldn't we pick it up for the autopsy after the ceremony?"

"That will be impossible. I cannot say why."

"Well, then, we'll do the autopsy and return it to you for the ceremony."

"That will be impossible. I cannot say why."

Mitsu decides that arguing can wait till later.

"Well, let's start getting some information."

Bill brings out his notebook and turns it on.

"Now, sir, if you'll just give me the victim's full name, and yours as well."

"I cannot do so. Honored Lieutenant, you are not of Chiri Gan. You are doubtless not understanding what you are asking. I am sure in my many cells, deep as you say, that you do not understand how you are giving offense by asking for such a personal thing as a name."

"Most certainly I mean no offense, Honored Translator. But our courts of law will demand names."

"But Honored Lieutenant, will this matter truly become dragged into a public court?"

If Washington's involved, he has a point.

"Okay, Bill, *for now,* put the victim down as M. M. Murdered Male."

"And you may describe me as Brother of M.M, and we are Clan Milac' Abri." The Val Chiri bobs his head again. "Honored Lieutenant, you display tact and understanding worthy of diplomats."

In the conversation that follows Mitsu needs every shred of those qualities that she possesses. Formal compliments, circumlocutions, evasions, hints, and half-truths—she hears them all, but never a simple statement (though at the same time, never an outright lie). Her other dealings with Val Chiri have convinced her of their essential honesty, which is why, she supposes, they've developed such elaborate ways of hedging the truth, just as, she's sure, Brother of M.M. is hedging now. She's willing to bet a chance at promotion that he either knows or thinks he knows the identity of the murderer—not, of course, that he's going to tell her. What he does talk about, at great length, is the structure of the clan, more than they ever would have thought to ask or wanted to know. Finally, after a frustrating hour, she cuts him short.

"Tell me, Honored Voice of Clan Milac' Abri, if these things we are recording are true. The murdered male, former First Man of your clan, left his suite last night at about 1800 hours. None knew where he might be going, because it was not their position in life to question him. I, however, guess that he went to the public studio of the Admart show in order to record his message. One of my assistants will confirm or deny that fact. However, he never returned to the suite. In the morning, about 0600 hours, First Wife went to search for him, as was indeed part of her position after so long an absence. He had recently been ill, too, and she was worried because of that. She found him in none of the rooms of the suite and came out into the hallway here. Something struck her about the outside doors, and she opened them to find her husband's body. When she screamed, Second Wife and First Son heard her and came to help. First Son told the women to leave the body as they found it and sent Third Son, who had also joined them by then, to fetch you, Second Man of Clan Milac' Abri. You then called the police."

"That is correct, Honored Lieutenant."

"May I ask you why you called us?"

He stiffens, glancing this way and that.

"It was the correct thing to do."

"Certainly, but Val Chiri tend to solve these problems on their own, when they can."

"It was the message." He seems to be forcing himself to look her in the eye. "Third Son saw it during its first showing on that execrable television program. Soon the police would have called without doubting."

"Thank you for being so frank. Will you accompany me to look at your brother's corpse? Or will that be too painful?"

"I have seen it once. I can look again."

The med techs have laid the murdered man flat on the concrete floor of the connecting bridge. Colored shadows fall across him from the stained glass insets in the bridge walls. The Brother joins him as she flips the end of the sheet back for a look at the victim's face. For a moment Mitsu mistakes the smear of dry orange blood across his brow-ridge for a shadow.

"Hey, wait," she says. "One of the jewels is missing. A diamond, I think it was."

"You are correct, Honored Lieutenant. It was a white diamond." Automatically he touches his own brow ridge, where a single red jewel glimmers. "It is part of First Man's station in life to carry the wealth of the clan within his body. The rest of us carry only a few gems of little value, for use in *emergencies*, I think your word is."

"I see. Looks like that diamond got pried out with the point of a sharp knife. Like maybe the one that killed him."

"Perhaps this is merely robbery? Yes, that must be it. That jewel was worth very many of your dollars. Perhaps one of your poor people was overwhelmed by his need to care for his family."

"Do you really think that your brother's murderer had only money on his mind? If so, he would have taken all the jewels."

Brother turns pale and studies the floor. Because she needs him, Mitsu lets him off the hook. She goes to a window and looks out and down. Identical bridges run between the two buildings at every other floor, so that it would be the easiest thing in the world for someone to do the murder here at Building One, rush back to Building Two, take a lift down and cross back to Building One again. She realizes then that she's sure the murderer was another Val Chiri. Whom else would Brother bother to protect?

"Now then, Honored Voice, I need to speak to First Wife. I want to know what made her open those doors."

"What you ask is impossible. No male from outside her clan may speak to a Val Chiri wife."

"Honored Voice, I happen to be female."

Apparently, comic surprise is one of those things that cuts

across cultural boundaries. Brother's eyes bulge, and he opens and shuts his mouth several times very fast.

"Honored Lieutenant, I am guilty of shame and horrifying insult. I pray with all my hearts that you will be forgiving me for this terrible mistake. You sapients who are not of Chiri Gan—you look so much alike, male and female both. I will escort you to speak with First Wife."

"You are forgiven, Honored Voice. Bill, give me that recorder, okay? Get the med techs' final report, make sure the photo guys have double the usual number of record shots, and then get the corpse on a gurney. No need to let him lie out here."

Brother thanks her wordlessly with a low and curling bow.

In a group of other women First Wife sits in the innermost room of the suite, a white cube hung with red or blue banners and littered with objects: piles of metallic bowls and flat shapes, wooden boxes, fiber-hide sacks, lengths of cloth, cushions, all tumbled and scattered about. She herself wears white gauze and sits silent and immobile on an upturned wooden chest. Her female face, smooth and hairless, nearly featureless except for the tiny eyes, the lipless slit of mouth, is so pale, so utterly closed that Mitsu finds herself thinking of that strange alabaster globe she saw on the morning's AdMart. All around First Wife the other females alternately curl up into balls like some jointed beetle, then stretch out again, holding their arms up to the Val Chiri idea of heaven, perhaps, and shrieking out a tone so high-pitched that Mitsu's ears can barely register it. At a word from Brother, they stop and flee, scuttling off into the other rooms of the suite.

"I will tell her that you are female," Brother remarks. "And that you wish to help us avenge her husband."

While he speaks, Mitsu kneels to get on the same level with First Wife, who turns her head slowly to face her. Under the white drapery, her top four arms are clutched round her torso.

"Ask her about the doors, Honored Voice. I don't want to intrude on her mourning any longer than I can help."

They speak together briefly.

"She wants only to know when her husband's body will be returned to her."

"Once I know who murdered him, she may have the body back."

Another exchange, and it seems that First Wife's angry

about something, from the way that her arms unclasp and lash back and forth. Mitsu can only assume that the woman's half-mad with grief.

"She does not remember about the doors, she says. They are not important, she says. She is First Wife. She is used to having her wishes fulfilled."

"I see. Well, Honored Voice, if she remembers this detail later, perhaps she might send one of her sons to tell me?"

"They are not her sons, Honored Lieutenant. They are *his* sons. *She* is the one who gave them birth, yes, but *he* pouched them during their growing into children."

Mitsu sits back on her heels and reproaches herself for forgetting again. Marsupials. These people are marsupials, and the males produce milk as easily as the females. For some reason she always finds these facts hard to remember.

"Of course, Honored Voice, and you have my apology for my mistake."

The pale face of First Wife turns once again to her own. The golden eyes sweep over her, the voice softens when she speaks.

"She offers you sympathy, Honored Lieutenant, that you have no husband and no clan and must work among males."

"Then thank her for me. Huh, interesting. Tell me, Honored Voice, do your women sometimes do male work, then? If they have to, I mean?"

Instead of answering her directly, Brother relays the question to First Wife, who answers slowly, gravely, and he translates the same way.

"Only in situations of great shame, when their husbands and their clan are dead or utterly and completely without honor, and then, only the most menial of work. She wishes you to know that it is a terrible, terrible thing for the daughter of a man to bear such a shame." He pauses as First Wife says something more. "She says she does not mean to insult you, of course. It is your father's shame that he could not provide for you, not yours."

"And your husband did pouch daughters?"

Brother translates; First Wife inclines her head slightly in a mimic of the human gesture for yes and holds up a single finger. So. They have an only daughter. When Mitsu looks into her golden eyes, she finds them still impassive, but she knows that she's been given a clue, a big clue, in the only way that First Wife will be allowed to offer it, hidden among female things.

Mitsu meets the daughter a few minutes later, in fact, when she and Brother come out of the suite. The med techs have laid the body, draped in a morgue sheet, on a gurney, which now stands, guarded by a pair of officers, in the corridor between the outside doors and the suite. Bill waits nearby, talking with one of the officers. When she hears the word "psionics," Mitsu has no compunctions about interrupting.

"Bill, I need a comp unit and a place to work on site."

"Manager's already thought of that." Bill gives her a keycard. "We got one opposite the turbo doors on the third floor. He says they keep a few business rooms set up for guests."

From down the corridor Mitsu hears a shriek coming. She can think of it no other way than that the shriek, a high-pitched howl of mourning, comes like a living thing, carrying the Val Chiri Gan female along with it. All dressed in flowing white she rushes to the gurney to raise herself up on her lowest legs and throw herself on the body.

"First Daughter," Brother says. "She is First Wife to Chief Navigator. They and their Second Wife live on the floor below."

First Daughter has clawed back the sheet to cradle her father's head in her uppermost hands. Still sobbing she begins to rock back and forth.

"Honored Lieutenant, you must release us the body of my brother. The women will be in this pain of grief until the ceremony is performed."

Mitsu is too busy watching the daughter to answer. She falls silent, shakes herself to pull herself under control, and rests her father's head on the gurney again. Mitsu walks over and points to the spot where the jewel is missing. The daughter looks, then freezes, crouches, her eyes widening, her breath coming in a long sob. She pulls herself away and drops to race down the hall toward the lift. When Bill starts to follow, Mitsu grabs his arm.

"Let her go. I got what I needed."

Just as First Daughter reaches the lift, a Val Chiri male steps out of it. First Daughter drops flat onto the carpet at his feet. Snarling and muttering he grabs her top arms and hauls her up, shoves her into the lift, and steps in quickly after her. The doors hiss shut.

"That was Chief Navigator." Brother is shaking all over as he speaks. "She never should have left her rooms. I mean, there are males up here who are not clan males!"

"Is that the only reason he was so angry, Honored Voice? That missing jewel seemed to mean a lot to her."

Brother makes a sound under his breath, partly a sob, partly a chitter of rage.

"Theft is always bad." He hesitates for a long while. "Especially of clan property."

"You know, sir, if we solve this case quickly, like this afternoon, then we won't need to do an autopsy. You can hold your ceremony whenever you want."

For a moment the Val Chiri neither moves nor speaks.

"I have endeavored to assist you in all matters, to the limit of my poor station in life and among our people."

"Of course, Honored Voice. I do believe you've fulfilled your station in every detail."

The office that the hotel manager's given them turns out to be small but serviceable, with two chairs, a desk, and a good comp link station built right into the wall. It's also soundproofed, as Bill immediately remarks.

"Sir?" he goes on. "While you were talking to the head wife, Washington called again. Want you to call them back on a secure line right away. They're getting real worried."

"Tough. What do you bet they're going to tell us to sweep this under the rug? We're going to have to do it, too. But I want to know what happened before I start sweeping."

Nodding agreement, Bill grabs another tissue and blows his nose hard. Mitsu sits down at the link station and logs into the main police comp at the Hall of Justice, then has Bill feed in everything he's noted as well as her recording of the original AdMart message. The CompHQ in turn has a couple of reports for her, one about the victim's background and his clan, the other about his movements the night before. He did indeed go down to the AdMart studio to use one of their automated recording booths, then returned to the hotel and gave the night clerk a manila envelope to be put into the safe.

"Looked like papers." The recording officer on screen is reading from his notes. "Might be the will he talked about, Lieutenant. We're getting a warrant for it now. The clerk logged the package into the safe at 2146 hours, gave the victim a time-stamped receipt, and watched him get into the turbolifts.''

The report ends there. Mitsu feeds an analysis subroutine into comp, sets it to isolating that sentence of the original message that was in the language of the Val Chiri Gan, then does some hard thinking. A couple of missing hours there, maybe more, between that receipt and his time of death, but First Wife swears—and Mitsu's inclined to believe her— that he never returned to the suite.

"Family," she says aloud. "Bill, how many human murders come down to problems between family members or close friends?"

" 'Bout ninety percent. But these people aren't human, sir.''

"Good point, but about how much of our time did old Honored Translator spend talking abut his clan?''

Bill grins.

"Ninety percent, yeah.''

On screen a message comes up. The sentence has been isolated and transcribed into the American alphabet. Since Mitsu still doesn't understand one word, she accesses the police ROM library. She's looking for some very specific facts, and once she finds them, she feeds her gleanings into the case file, clears the screen, and enters a handful of key words to play around with.

"Shame, daughter, a weird name, virtue, jealousy, polygamy, vengeance, provide for, no testimony against." Bill reads them off. "Against what, sir?''

"No spouse can be forced to testify against his or her spouse. That's our law, not theirs, but they'd agree with the principle, I bet.''

"Okay. What's the weird name, N'ya however you say that?''

"Who, not what, and that's a throat click in the middle. Remember how the victim spoke in his own language? He said, 'I take leave of you as N'ya!a took his leave.' The language program in the banks translated it that way, anyway; let's hope it's accurate. And in the *Oxford Dictionary of Val Chiri Gan Culture* I found a story that goes with the name, a classic that everyone would know. Kind of like Shakespeare is to us.''

"Yeah? And the story is?''

"N'ya!a fell in love with one of his son's wives. Honor said one thing, lust said another. So he screwed the lady and committed suicide and took care of both."

"No way this could be suicide! And his sons are too young to be married. Old honored bullshitter told us that."

"Yeah, he sure did, didn't he? Repeated it a couple of times. He could figure out that we'd get the N'ya!a reference translated, sooner or later. But there's a son, all right, that he was hoping we'd forget about."

"The son-in-law."

"Right. Jeez, Bill, you psychic or something?"

"Go on, make fun of me, but I still think the victim had some kind of psychic powers. I mean, he predicted his own murder, didn't he?"

"But why didn't he just name the killer and save us a lot of trouble? If he was psychic, he would've known, and he said he didn't."

"Well, yeah, I guess so . . . but wait! He said he couldn't *say,* not that he didn't know."

Mitsu grins.

"Very good, Sergeant! Now you're thinking. Look, let me tell you what I got so far. We have a man who knows he's going to be murdered. He's not just afraid of it; he's sure of it. Yet he doesn't come to us, even though he must know he's so important that we'd turn out half the force to protect him."

"Well, maybe he was afraid we wouldn't believe him."

"About this psychic message you got on the brain?" Mitsu smiles to take some sting out of her words. "I'm betting he had other reasons for knowing he was about to die. Bill, these people think in terms of honor and revenge, not laws. M.M. did something that was going to bring vengeance down on him in a big way, but he felt he couldn't reveal what that something was."

"Like he had to protect his murderer?"

"Maybe. And he had to think about his dependents, too. The Val Chiri men take their responsibilities to the clan real seriously. Unto the seventh generation and all that jazz."

"Huh. So if he jumped the gun and offed this dude before the dude could off him, what would happen to his family?"

"That's one of the things I just looked up. If a man murders someone, all his children old enough to live outside the pouch are taken away for adoption. Any pouchlings are drowned. His wives are stripped of any and all goods they might have inherited and thrown penniless onto the street to fend for themselves. He himself is killed, of course, in a *very* painful way. I didn't ask for details.''

"Jeez. Vengeance? You bet.''

A knock on the door, and Bill jumps up, answers it, and comes back with a flat envelope and a big handful of receipts.

"Warrant came. Here's the stuff from the hotel safe.''

Mitsu rips open the package and finds, just as they all had expected, the last will and testament of the Val Chiri known as Tarrgon ga Elba!a-ach, AKA the Murdered Male. She scans it over and finds what she's looking for.

"Interesting,'' she says. "He left the clan monies to his brother, of course, who's going to be First Man now. Then he set aside half of his personal fortune for the reward he offered and divided up the rest among everyone in his immediate family, except First Daughter.''

"Hey, that's a shocker! I got the impression that he and his daughter were real close.''

"Yep, bet they were.'' She waves the printout vaguely in Bill's direction. "This was exactly what I suspected, and I think we got our case, whether Washington lets us bring our perp in or not.''

"Huh? I don't get it.''

"Think about the reward, Bill. That's the hot key to press. Do you really think a clannish bunch like the Val Chiri—jeez, they base their whole lives on their position in their family—do you really think First Man would give all that cash to a stranger?'' She stands up. "Scan that will into the case file while I'm gone, will you? Thanks. Are there any women officers assigned to the hotel?''

"Yeah. You need to go interview First Wife again?''

"Nope. First Daughter.''

Mitsu finds the people she needs—three female officers and translator—in the corridor near the corpse. In fact, it seems that every male Val Chiri in the clan has squeezed into the narrow space to sit down on the floor around the former First Man's gurney. They say nothing, barely move, merely sit and stare at the police keeping them from performing the last rites for their leader. Mitsu uses CopComm to get replacement guards up before she takes the women officers away.

"Honored Lieutenant." Brother presses the speaker unit so hard into his larynx that it buzzes. "We must do the ceremony soon!"

"I understand that, Honored Voice. I'm about to wrap this thing up."

Brother goes rigid, his torso arched back, his hands clenched, his face draining to a dead and ashy gray.

"Honored Voice, your brother was a farseeing and clever man. If his daughter has inherited one gram of his courage, the thing you're so afraid of won't happen."

He sighs and lets himself relax, adjusting the speaker before he talks.

"She is a female fit to fulfill her position as First Wife. I can but hope you are correct."

First Daughter receives them in a big room with windows that give out onto a view of the San Francisco bay, dark blue in the spring sun, and the East Bay hills, hidden behind yellow haze. Thanks to the blue tint in the glass, the polluted sky looks green. Dressed in white, her strangely smooth head emerging from a twist of scarf, she sits calmly on a human-style fiber-hide hassock. At her feet, sobbing, crouches another Val Chiri female, dressed in black.

"Second Wife," Brother explains.

"Ask First Daughter, Honored Voice, where her husband is."

At the question, First Daughter points with a top arm toward a closed door and speaks, slowly and calmly. Second Wife howls, then falls silent, curling round herself and clutching at her clothes with all four hands.

He has locked himself in that room," Brother says. "He refuses to come out."

At that, Mitsu knows her theory is correct. She kneels down to look directly into First Daughter's golden eyes.

"Tell her this, Honored Voice. Your father was a wise man in all ways save one, and that one was the love of women. Will you not take the provision he left for you?"

When Brother speaks, First Daughter stares across the room at the far wall. For a long time after the translator falls silent, she says nothing, her mouth a thin, tight line, while the younger female slowly uncurls herself and begins to snivel and whine. Although Brother doesn't translate, Mitsu can guess that she's begging the senior wife for something. Mitsu wonders if their husband is listening, crouched like a hunted animal behind the bedroom door, or if he's killed himself. If it weren't for Washington's interference, she would order the door broken down, but as it is, she waits. At last First Daughter cuts Second Wife short with a wave of a middle arm and begins to speak. Brother translates a phrase or sentence at a time.

"Last night, my husband returned to our bed very late, at perhaps the second hour of your night. I pretended to sleep so that he would not press himself upon me. He tossed this way and that, then got up and left the sleeping room. After a few moments I, too, rose and went to the door. I looked through a crack and saw him hiding some object in that box there." She points to one of the wooden chests. "This morning, I found blood upon the clothes he was wearing last night. I have saved those clothes. I suspect the blood is that of my father."

"And so do I." Mitsu stands up, motioning to one of the officers. "Open it."

Second Wife howls, arching her back and throwing her head from side to side. Brother kicks her into silence and begins to berate her.

"Leave her be!" Mitsu snaps. "Could she really have turned the First Man down when he wanted to have sex with her?"

Brother shuts up. First Daughter puts a middle arm around her junior's shoulders and draws her close, a gesture of protection, as they watch the police officer open the chest. She takes a plastic bag out of her belt pouch and uses it to lift the murder weapon out.

"Looks like it's been wiped," Reilly says. "But you never know. There might be a print or two left. And what's this? A diamond. Jeez, and a big one."

"Yep," Mitsu says. "The bride-price. He took it as payment for the despoiling of Second Wife."

"And so First Daughter gets all that gold to start a new life somewhere for her and Second Wife," Mitsu says. "It's not an inheritance, so it can't be taken away from her even though she's the murderer's wife. Brother was implying that if we go along with Washington and never bring this to court, the clan will let them keep their children, too, even the pouchling. Sounds like a good bargain to me, since Washington won't let us prosecute anyway."

"Might as well give in gracefully, huh?" Bill pauses to smear his red, scabby nose with some sort of medicated jelly. "God, I'm glad we're getting out into the air."

"You've suffered for justice, pal."

"Glad someone realizes it. Oh, well, virtue's its own reward, huh?"

"You bet. Let's get back to the station. I'll put in a final call to Washington on the secure line there. Our murderer's probably dead by now, whether he killed himself or the new First Man did it for him."

Since Bill's already cleared all traces of their work off the hotel comp banks, they leave the tiny office and head for the turbolift. Even several floors below the actual living quarters, the scent of Val Chiri Gan drifts around them.

"One last thing I don't understand," Bill says. "That ceremony. Why do they have to do it right away? I mean, what do they do that can't wait for an autopsy?"

"Eat him raw."

"What?"

"They eat their dead clan members. It's a ritual thing, or so I found out from the ROM library. Everyone in the clan gets a serving. That way the dead become part of the living family, and they can never be separated again. But it's not like they enjoy it or anything, so in this warm weather, they need to get it over and done with while he's still fresh."

For a minute Mitsu's afraid that Bill is going to throw up, but he gathers himself with a gulp and a sigh.

"Well, whatever's right," he says at last. "But jeez, sir, in my opinion that's carrying togetherness just a little too far."

MONKEY SEE

by Roger MacBride Allen

Roger MacBride Allen made a name for himself with the brilliant *Orphan of Creation,* and has been writing entertaining science fiction novels and stories ever since.

An alien, here to study our native animal life, is killed by same. To people who know animals, the attack may even have been justified.

A detective from the alien's race now arrives on Earth, determined to prove that this attack by unthinking animals was murder. The men in charge of the animals—game rangers, lab scientists, whatever—must prove to an alien who cannot even differentiate between a simian and a human that their animals are innocent.

Handle it straight or funny, as you wish.

Federal Penitentiary
Leavenworth Prison
September 8, 2091

To Whom It May Concern:

We, the undersigned, offer the following brief account of the recent incidents at the Goodall Memorial Primate Research Institute, not so much as a defense, but as an explanation. We issue it over the quite proper protests of our defense lawyers. We are very much aware that any statement we might make regarding the incidents in question could well have grave consequences for ourselves.

However, we are all agreed that there are times when one's own fate is of secondary importance. The reputation of our Institute, the reputation of our entire field of study, and perhaps, absurd as it may be, the fate of the world itself hangs in the balance as well, and these must weigh in them more heavily than our own circumstances. We had no desire or intention of touching off an interstellar incident.

It seems to us that the truth is all that matters in the present case, and that waiting for the legal system to produce that truth might well cause even more damage to interstellar diplomatic relations, which are already badly strained by the recent unpleasantness.

After lengthy and heated discussion, we agreed[1] to choose the somewhat informal form of narrative, hoping to make this document accessible to as many people as possible. It is our best attempt at a true, factual, and detailed report of a most difficult period. Emotions ran high, needless to say, during our collaboration, and we were forced to do our work in a place not much known for its scholarly facilities. It must also be noted that the account deals, God knows, with events we would all rather forget. In short, it has been a most difficult period. For all of that, we are agreed that it is best that, during this period in which we are awaiting trial, we candidly put the facts before the world.[2]

(signed)
Dr. Steven Nestleroth
Dr. Patricia Wood
Dr. J. Michael Higgins

* * *

There was an exchange, just before the trouble started, between Dr. Higgins and Belzic Tascar, who described himself as a noted xeno-ethnologist and xeno-psychologist. We believe it set the whole tone of the affair.

Belzic, it should be noted, was a Detchel. For those not familiar with this species, he[3] was, in other words, essentially a

1. Dr. Wood's agreement was conditional on her being able to register certain strong reservations against venturing outside the format of a scientific paper. She also wishes it noted that she agreed partly out of fear of physical violence at the hands of Doctors Nestleroth and Higgins.
2. Dr. Nestleroth wishes to have it recorded, as a condition of signing this report, that if he never sees a god-damned chimp or a god-damned alien again, that will suit him fine.
3. Or she. Or it. The most basic questions of Detchel sexuality remain unclear. The use of the male pronoun throughout this narrative is, there-

small, highly intelligent, mobile tree. We do not wish to be accused of bias against his species, but it is germane to note that, to terrestrial eyes, he was extremely plantlike, looking much like a rather robust stand of bamboo with eyes.

Indeed, whenever Belzic was standing still on the grounds, lost in thought, it was all but inevitable that one or more of the dogs who live on the compound would eventually relieve themselves on him. Casual observation seemed to indicate the dogs actually sought him out. This did not seem to bother Belzic. Indeed, he seemed to find it rather refreshing, and it must be admitted that the staff soon decided, by unspoken consensus, to do nothing that might discourage the practice.

In any event, one day Belzic was out on the grounds with Dr. Higgins, working with a trio of chimps. He was attempting to interrogate Bobbin, one of the larger male chimps, along with Hazel, a middle-aged female, and Hazel's grown son Brownie. Dr. Higgins had drawn the duty to "assist" in the questioning, but results were no better than could be expected.

Belzic, who had most recently read up on the new field of confrontational-aggression therapy, posed an elaborate conditional question to the group. It was a question he had spent long hours devising, a question he hoped would so challenge and shock his patients that they would at the very least display some sort of involuntary reaction. But he was hoping for far more, hoping to snap Bobbin, Hazel, and Brownie clear out of their catatonia and end their long refusal to answer his questions.

"If you all related to each other are other than by result of direct sexual congressional meetings," he asked, "is it the case not that your family relations are steeped in the intercourse of others?"

Bobbin, needless to say, took little notice, and continued picking his nose. Hazel and Brownie continued their mutual grooming session.

Assuming—quite rightly—that Bobbin and the others had not understood him, Belzic then repeated the question for,

fore, completely arbitrary. It is the joint conclusion of the three authors that, after long study and discussion of how to refer to Belzic, no one of us any longer gives a damn.

what was, by actual count, the twenty-third time. It was at that moment that Dr. Higgins interrupted the proceedings. "Dammit!" Dr. Higgins cried out. "Don't you get it? They'll never answer! They'll never understand. They can't talk. They're goddamn chimps! *Chimps are not people!*"

At which point, Belzic turned his leaf-green attention toward Dr. Higgins and gave out one of those little chuffing noises, the sound we had so quickly learned indicated outright contempt. "Back from where I come, many people say to face yours would about *you*. If willing to point stretch for you are they in your case, asking you to same do to Bobbin's case be fairly fair say I. Again I say the same thing."

At which time Belzic repeated his question for the twenty-fourth time, Bobbin found an especially notable booger, Hazel dozed off as Brownie continued grooming her, and Dr. Higgins left the study area.

Once Dr. Higgins left, there was no informative witness available to say exactly what happened next. The study camera, mounted for the purpose of recording the session, was found two days later, burst open and hanging in a tree. As the recording material had been exposed to extreme abuse and the vagaries of the weather, it can come as no surprise that it was not possible to recover all the information therein. It is indeed fortunate that the record up until the moment of Dr. Higgins' departure was intact, providing him, as it were, with an alibi.

We were forced to deduce the turn of subsequent events at the study area by an examination of the physical evidence as discovered the next morning. It was our determination, based on the broken and torn articulate fronds, the copious flow of a rather viscous saplike fluid, the large fraction of body mass missing, and the tooth marks on the remaining body fragments, that Belzic had been eaten.

* * *

Before continuing with the direct narrative of events, it is, we feel, important[4] to focus on the background of Belzic's

---

4. Dr. Higgins, fearing that his legal exposure is greater than that of Doctors Nestleroth and Wood, wishes that the word "vital" be substituted for "important."

observation regarding humanity—to wit, that we are not people—and on his prior behavior at the Institute.

No reader will be unaware of the many profound changes to society caused by the arrival of the first extraterrestrials some ten years ago. Nor will anyone be unaware of the confusion caused by the remarkable number of species of intelligent life currently making themselves interested[5] in all manner of human affairs. And surely we have all experienced at one time or another the common extraterrestrial dismissal of all human diversity. To the eyes[6] of the average extraterrestrial, we all look and sound and act very much the same. Anecdotes wherein an alien dismisses English and Chinese as dialects of the same language are so common as to be clichés, as are the stories wherein an alien is unable to distinguish a two-meter-tall Caucasian man from a rather diminutive Asiatic woman. Alien ethnographers view all of the myriad ways of human life on Earth as essentially the same. Eskimo, urban dweller, farmer, fisherfolk, bush person—all are seen as minor variations on a theme.

Much has also been written concerning the rather low regard[7] in which many of the alien races hold human civilization. As Belzic noted, we are held to be at best marginally civilized, and sentient by the barest of margins. Again, we must ask ourselves if this attitude is mere prejudice, or based in actual fact.

All three authors would wish to offer the view that the level of understanding, the degree of competency, and, indeed, the eventual fate of the two Detchel scientists who came to work at Goodall would not tend to support any claim of mental superiority. The authors vary widely in the degree of emphasis they would wish to make for this observation.

These issues form the basis of the crisis in primatology: to the aliens, it goes deeper than not being able to tell black

---

5. Dr. Nestleroth wishes to substitute the phrase ''sticking their damn noses into'' for the phrase ''making themselves interested.''
6. Or equivalent sensory organs
7. Dr. Nestleroth wishes to substitute the phrase ''bloody arrogant, ignorant, pigheaded, self-righteous contempt'' for the phrase ''rather low regard.''

from white, or male from female. To them, all large primates are alike.

Humans, chimps, gorillas, and orangutans are all more or less the same to them, to be accorded the same rights and privileges, and deserving of equal treatment. Given the current political climate, and the unquestioned urgency of maintaining—or attempting to establish—good relations with the aliens, it has become incumbent upon primatologists to respect this viewpoint[8] to the best of our ability.

Indeed, as various laws and executive orders made clear, we had no choice in the matter. At the insistence of the aliens, who were shocked to find such callous denial of chimp and gorilla and orang civil rights, all the larger primates were afforded the legal right to vote, to hold office, to own property, and so on. That no primate but a human would desire to do any of these things—or be able to do them—was beside the point.[9]

But we went further than merely obeying the so-called "chimp rights" bill. We at the Goodall Institute went out of our way[10] to welcome Belzic as a colleague.

It will be obvious, at least to any human reader of this report, that affording equal protection under the law to the inmates of our Institute was a challenging[11] goal. For their own safety, and out of respect for the surrounding communities, we could not simply let them go free. Nor could we return them to Africa, as they had become dependent on human care for their well-being. It was Dr. Nestleroth who hit upon the brilliant[12] solution of registering the Institute as a state mental hospital, and arranging for the involuntary commitment of all the chimps as patients of the hospital.

The logic seemed unassailable at the time. If the chimps

8. Dr. Nestleroth wishes to insert the word "absurd" before the word "viewpoint."
9. Dr. Wood likens the situation to the California law, currently on the books, that firmly establishes a man's right to bear children.
10. Dr. Wood, speaking as the director of the institute responsible for policy, protests the desire of Doctors Wood and Nestleroth to insert the words "rashly and unwisely" prior to the phrase "went out of our way."
11. Dr. Nestleroth wishes to substitute the word "impossible" for the word "challenging."
12. For divergent reasons, both Doctor Nestleroth and Doctor Wood wish the word "brilliant" to be deleted.

were to be regarded as legally human, then their behavior should be judged by a human standard. The state would not hesitate to institutionalize, house, and care for a human being who was incapable of speech, incapable of holding a job, unable to dress himself, and so on.

While a few animal rights activists opposed this solution, it seemed the only remedy that would allow the chimps to live as they had, free to roam the extensive grounds of the Institute, and yet protected from the vagaries of the outside world.

Until Belzic arrived.

* * *

Even in retrospect, the authors can find no alternate solution, aside from the concept of a mental institution, for the problem of establishing legal grounds by which to care for and protect the fifty or so perfectly sane chimps at the Institute. But even if we were prepared to go through a charade of treating sane chimps as insane humans, it never dawned on us that anyone would attempt to *cure* them. But from the moment of Belzic's arrival, that was plainly his intent.

It must be confessed that his arrival was not auspicious. Dr. Nestleroth, out for his morning constitutional, approached the main gate and discovered what he took to be a sort of small, bushy tree blocking the drive. Slightly at a loss to understand how it could have grown so large without anyone noticing, he called maintenance on his pocketphone to have it removed and then went on out the gate to continue with his walk. It was only upon his return, when he found the groundskeeper in a spirited discussion with the tree, that he discovered his error.

Belzic, once roused out of his trancelike contemplative state, was a most active and spirited[13] being. It was as Dr. Nestleroth approached the gate that this first became apparent. "Aha! Here we are!" a thin, piping voice, speaking unaccented, if somewhat scrambled English announced from somewhere inside the tree. "Here one of your patients is now! Hello, little fellow. How are you feeling today?"

It is to Dr. Nestleroth's credit that he immediately under-

---

13. Dr. Nestleroth wished to insert the phrase "indeed, manic"

stood the situation. In spite of the fact that no one had seen fit to describe the alien who would be coming, he realized that this had to be Belzic Tascar, the visiting scientist we had been alerted to expect. So, too, Belzic's use of the word "patient" was all the warning he needed of Belzic's misapprehension of the work at Goodall, and of his confusion regarding Nestleroth's situation. As the following account of their conversation makes clear, Belzic was nowhere near as fast on the uptake.

For the very little that it is worth, Dr. Nestleroth has a full and rather bushy beard, and is slightly below medium height. It is remotely possible that these facts formed the basis of Belzic's confusion.

"I am afraid there has been some mistake," Dr. Nestleroth said, as diplomatically as possible. "The, ah, patients here are all chimpanzees. I am Doctor Steven Nestleroth. I am on the staff here."

"Of *course* you are. And here I was told that the patients here could not even on put clothes themselves by. You've outdressed yourself this time!"

"Ah, excuse me, but I'm afraid that you are in error. I am a member of the staff here—"

Belzic turned toward the groundskeeper and said "I can see that this is a held deeply delusion state, though not an uncommon transference, according to your literature. I have seen many accounts of doctors imagining themselves to be patients, or at least the versa vice. I have will to do my best to gain his confidence before I will be able to work him over with me." With that, and a rustle of foliage, Belzic turned back toward Nestleroth. "Here, little fellow. I have a treat *special* for you!"

A thin, green arm thrust out of the foliage and offered a ripe yellow banana to Dr. Nestleroth.

It was an unfortunate beginning, but things only deteriorated from there.

* * *

Belzic was tireless in pursuing the cure for the chimpanzees' wholly imaginary mental disorders. At first, be it confessed, for the sake of protecting Earth's interstellar relations, we played up to his conviction that the illnesses were real. However, as he had such a remarkably difficult time distinguishing humans from chimps (or, looking at it from his point of view, the staff from the inmates) this devolved into a hopeless muddle.

There were several attempts made to dismiss Belzic from his position on the staff, and even some thought given to physically ejecting him from the grounds. However, his place at the Institute had been found for him as part of a painstakingly negotiated agreement on scientific exchange. Should his employment be terminated, it would place in jeopardy the work—and perhaps the lives—of several human researchers off-planet, and could well mean the loss of much scientific and technical data we on Earth urgently need if we are to fully participate in the interstellar community.

In short, we were stuck with Belzic. It was some months before we could fully convince him that Dr. Nestleroth was a sane human staff member, and not an insane chimp patient. Rare was the day that went by without the offer of a banana, or an attempt to establish a bond through mutual grooming, or some other attempt to gain Dr. Nestleroth's trust. Needless to say, none of this worked to endear Belzic to any of us, least of all Dr. Nestleroth. At last, he seemed to accept the truth of what we told him, but up until the end, he seemed to take a special interest in Nestleroth, and often volunteered another diagnosis to account for Nestleroth's symptoms.

Once we did get Belzic focused on the chimps themselves, however, our difficulties were far from over. At last, we agreed to cast off all pretense and explain the true nature of the Institute to him. Unfortunately, Belzic refused to believe us. He remained resolute in his conviction, despite all evidence to the contrary, that humans and chimps were one and the same.[14] Nothing we could say or do could convince him that the chimps were perfectly fine. His attempts at treatment, based on a strange hodgepodge of Belzic and human psychiatric technique, had no effect whatsoever on the chimps. His cure rate was zero.

This all had a most unfortunate effect on the operation of the Institute. Experiments of all kinds were disrupted as we

14. Dr. Higgins suggests that this be accounted for by differences between Detchel and human sensory apparatus. Doctors Wood and Nestleroth offer the alternate hypothesis that Belzic was a blithering idiot.

were forced to indulge Belzic's endless tests and studies. Morale among the staff plummeted.

For that matter, the chimps didn't much like the interruptions to their routine either. Life at the Institute had been comfortable and happy for them, up until the advent of Belzic Tascar. They had plenty of food, safe and pleasant surroundings, ample time to explore the grounds and interact with their friends, both chimp and human. It had long been the policy of the Institute that the human staff was to avoid too much interference in the lives of our charges, but to limit ourselves, as much as possible and practical, to observation.

Belzic, however, insisted on a far more invasive approach. He was forever barging into their social groups, attempting to subject this chimp or that to whatever therapy technique he had read about most recently. There was, for example, the early episode wherein a pair of hapless groundskeepers were called upon to follow Belzic about the grounds, carrying a psychiatric couch around the landscape, in hopes of tempting a chimp to lie down upon it and explain her childhood traumas to Belzic.

The less said about his attempt at sexual role-play therapy, and about the demands this placed upon the human staff, the better.

The most horrifying moment came when Belzic found a copy of an old novel entitled *One Flew Over the Cuckoo's Nest*. Typically, he completely missed the point of the book, and for a week or so, was quite enthused over the idea of establishing a "disturbed ward" for the chimps, complete with straitjackets and electroshock therapy. More than one staff member observed that these tools might well have proved useful if applied elsewhere than to the chimps. Fortunately, the staff was able to stand firm and prevent any such medieval practices.

The chimps, quite understandably, began to resent this constant interference in their lives. Anything remotely resembling Belzic would spook them. After a time, the mere sound of a stand of bamboo rustling in the wind was enough to drive them off. Human researchers wearing green clothes were given a wide berth, reopening the old debates concerning the importance of color distinction in chimpanzee vision.

Surrounded by colleagues and patients who sought nothing more avidly than the chance to avoid him, perhaps Belzic should have given up. But the more Belzic met with utter failure, the more he became obsessed with proving us all wrong.

It was at this point that he started to take an interest in group therapy techniques, rapidly becoming convinced that he would find the solution to the chimps' deepest traumas in such sessions. Though this procedure was to be no more successful than previous attempts to cure the chimps, it at least had the benefit of not driving the chimps off into the woods. Group sessions required Belzic to sit still and be quiet, with the happy result that the chimps resumed their previous tolerance of humans—and Belzic too, for that matter.

There was, at this juncture, some faint hope of life at the Institute getting back to normal. Except for the luckless staff member who drew the duty to assist Belzic on a given day, the staff and chimps of the Institute found their lives undisturbed by commotion for the first time in months.

But all things pass, and none can last, and this period of relative peace was shattered by the demise and subsequent consumption of Belzic Tascar, as previously described.

* * *

In the opinion of two of the present authors, it is to the everlasting credit of the entire staff that the loss of Belzic Tascar was greeted with mixed emotions.[15] While no one could dispute that a highly disruptive influence was removed from the Institute, many staff members expressed real sadness at the loss of a colleague.

It goes without saying that an immediate report on the unfortunate incident was made to the appropriate authorities, both human and extraterrestrial. We assumed that some sort of investigative group would arrive, confirm the facts of the case, and be on their way. Indeed, within four hours after the discovery of Belzic's scattered remains, a field team from the FBI was on the scene, accompanied by a woman from the xeno-diplomatic desk at the State Department.

The FBI took photographs of the death site, got state-

15. Dr. Nestleroth, however, dismisses any reaction other than joyous relief as, at best, maudlin sappery, and, at worst, sheer hypocrisy.

ments from various members of the Institute, gathered up Belzic's scattered remains, and were soon on their way.

Foolishly, we thought that would be the end of it.

But our first indication that the nightmare was not over soon came.

Not long after, Dr. Nestleroth ventured again through the main gate on his morning constitutional, and encountered a small, robust bamboo plant proffering bananas to all that would come near.[16]

After Dr. Nestleroth's immediate medical needs had been attended to, and he had been made as comfortable as possible, Doctors Higgins and Wood met with our visitor, who identified himself, confusingly enough, as Belzac Tiscar.

No one, so far as we have been able to find, has yet established whether or not Belzic Tascar and Belzac Tiscar were related, or, if so, how. For that matter, we were never entirely clear if the Detchel had names in the human sense of the word. The words by which we knew them could have been titles, or honorifics. Suffice it to say that Belzac so strongly resembled Belzic that, to human eyes, they could easily have been twins or clones. We have experienced similar confusion in subsequent encounters with other Detchel.

In short, they all looked the same to us. Belzac, however, differed from Belzic in one particular: he identified himself not as a xeno-ethnologist and xeno-psychologist, but as a criminal scientist,[17] which we were given to understand was the closest Detchelian profession to that of police investigator.

To our utter consternation and horror, Belzac had been sent to solve Belzic's murder.

It goes without saying that we had not even regarded the death *as* a murder, nor even considered the thought that anyone could view it as such. It was, plainly and simply, an animal attack, and one in which the animals should have

16. There can be no question that Dr. Nestleroth's preexisting cardiac condition played a part in inducing the heart attack he suffered at this juncture. But there can be no doubt that Belzac's sudden appearance was the proximate cause. Efforts to get the Detchel embassy to accept any degree of responsibility for the incident, or to extract an apology from them, have met with no success whatsoever.

17. Dr. Nestleroth observes that this description fit either of the two Detchel equally well.

been held blameless. The chimps had no way of knowing that a talking plant was to be treated as if it were a human being.

Efforts to put this view before Belzac got nowhere. It soon became apparent that Belzac shared completely in every one of his predecessor's ideas concerning the humanity of chimps in general, and the insanity of our institutionalized chimps specifically.[18] We could not budge him.

"I cannot believe quite that simply your people to investigate this crime refused," Belzac told Doctors Wood and Higgins that afternoon in the main conference room. "Is taking the death of a colleague so lightly felt, or hold yourself do you to be in so little danger of a repeat attack?"

"That would be an excellent summing up," Doctor Higgins replied, pacing the floor.

"I think that perhaps what Doctor Higgins means is that our own investigation demonstrates that the attack was unintentional," Doctor Wood said. "The chimps were merely foraging for food, and mistook a being wholly outside their experience for dinner."

"You are trapping into a classic fall," Belzac said, commencing to pace the room at right angles to Doctor Higgins, and deftly avoiding him whenever they threatened to collide. "Note the lack of utterly success Belzic had in their symptoms curing. It is oblivious at least that some among them were uncurable because not mentally ill they were in the place first."

For one brief shining moment we thought we had broken through, but then Belzac continued. "It is oblivious that the killer has been insanity feigning along all. The fellow of *One Flew Over the Cuckoo's Nest* feigned madness merely to avoid peas picking. When Belzic came along and threatened to expose himself to this malingerer, he or she cleverly bided her or his time and then attacked all over Belzic, knowing well full that no one would hold an insane person accountable for doing a thing crazy. And no one did, until I arrived."

18. Indeed, their complete agreement of views on all subjects would tend to support the theory that they were clones, or else sub-units in some larger mass mind. Dr. Nestleroth points out that the (in his words) "self evident paucity of their individual intelligence" also tends to support the mass mind concept.

While Higgins and Wood were still attempting to unravel this, Belzac offered up another theory.

"Of course, unlessing, it was of the staff one posing as a patient sane posing as one crazy patient for the killing to do. Is there on the staff one any who might kill for a motive for Belzic's death?"

This question was met with an eloquent and diplomatic silence, but Belzac, intent on his own line of inquiry, did not notice.

"Does not it matter," he said. "For now here I am here, and have no fear of it all—we will get right to the top of the bottom of this before we even begin. I start to question the reality of the prime suspects at once, twice, and thrice. Could you please bring to me Bobbin, Hazel, and Brownie to take my thrusting questions?"

"Ah, that might prove difficult, Belzac," Doctor Wood said. "I think it might be more productive if we brought you to them."

"Excellent," Belzac said. "Come then! The foot is a game!"

It need scarcely be noted that, in the days that followed, the chimps were of as little use as Belzac's suspects as they had been as Belzic's patients. They still stubbornly refused to answer questions, and flatly refused to cooperate in Belzac's attempts to perform lineups and lie detector tests and fingerprintings. They quickly relearned their old habits of fleeing at the very sight of a Detchel.

Strangely enough, the only chimps who seemed at all willing to tolerate Belzac were the trio of Hazel, Brownie, and Bobbin. This datum was the source of some serious concern on our part, for obvious reasons, and we saw to it that Belzac never got near any of them unless accompanied by a member of the staff.

None of his failures, needless to say, dissuaded Belzac in the least. They merely inspired him to greater efforts. He set surveillance cameras and microphones everywhere, using cleverly-built alien recording devices that exactly resembled rocks, piles of dung, pieces of fruit, and dead branches. He spent endless hours with the resulting recordings, watching and listening for the secret meeting, the clandestine rendezvous, wherein the guilty parties would unknowingly reveal themselves to him.

Again and again, he would imagine that he had discovered something and set off in pursuit of one luckless chimp or another. Nothing ever seemed to come of these discoveries, except that all the investigators at the Institute reported that the chimp population was becoming more and more restive.

He started putting his second theory—that one or more staff members posing as chimps had perpetrated the crime—to the test. Everyone who had been employed by the Institute at the time of the murder was required to submit a cast of their teeth for comparison to photographs of the tooth marks on the deceased. As the staff had been resigning in droves from the moment Belzac showed up, obtaining these casts was rather difficult.

Worse came when those staff members with somewhat largish teeth found themselves in some difficulty.

One day, shortly after Dr. Nestleroth's recovery, Dr. Higgins and Dr. Nestleroth were walking down the hallway of the main building when there was a sudden burst of rustling behind them. They turned to find Belzac had sprung out behind them, brandishing two pairs of handcuffs and a billy club.

"Halt!" Belzac cried out. "Based on conclusive dental evidence that truly bites, I arrest you hereby for murdering of the dead Belzic Tascar. I am obliged to warn you that my weapons are registered as offensive fronds! Anything you can say will be written down!"

Dr. Nestleroth, although showing somewhat high color, remained quite calm as he took one of his heart pills and several other forms of medication from a dispenser in his pocket. "I suppose you've got us dead to rights, Belzac," he said "We place ourselves in your custody and promise not to leave town." Dr. Higgins nodded his agreement with this, and then the two of them turned and walked away, doing their best to ignore the ongoing flurry of scrambled but triumphant syntax behind them.

This arrest would have been greater cause for alarm, but for the fact that Dr. Higgins had been keeping a tally. Counting the chimps, Higgins and Nestleroth represented the 23rd and 24th "arrests" for the crime. They were far from the last.

* * *

Working his way, as he was, through every conceivable police procedure, it was in retrospect inevitable that Belzac would sooner or later hit upon the old idea of reconstructing the crime. The dangers of this plan were obvious, and it should be emphasized that he was dissuaded from this course. It will remain for the courts to decide if he was urged not to do it with adequate vehemence, but that is as may be. We the authors believe that the preceding narrative will have demonstrated the severe difficulty in talking any Detchel of our experience out of any idea. All that could be hoped for was that Belzac would distract himself with some other plan before he could put the idea into action.

But a full reconstruction would require elaborate planning and intricate, lengthy, tedious preparation—the very things that Belzac seemed to delight in. Once the idea got into his head,[19,20] there was nothing anyone could do to stop him.[21]

Belzac wanted at first to wait until a full year had passed, so that the lighting and sun position would be exactly the same as at the time of the original attack. He seemed to like the idea of having that much time to get his preparations perfect. Fortunately or not, his eagerness to get on with it overtook this ambition.

It will be recalled that it was the endless repetition of Belzic's questioning that drove Dr. Higgins to stalk off the scene in the first place. Belzac now required Dr. Higgins to endure a long series of rehearsals, making sure that he was able to repeat his lines and actions letter-perfect, down to the smallest gesture, as recorded in the study camera. Again and again, he was forced to listen to Belzac echo Belzic's endless questioning, then repeat his original outburst, hear Belzac repeat Belzic's insult, and then stalk off.

Belzac further required stand-ins to play the roles of Bobbin, Hazel, and Brownie, so as to make these rehearsals as authentic as possible.

The careful reader will have noted that Dr. Wood had thus far escaped the humiliations heaped upon Doctors Higgins and Nestleroth. It was with a certain grim satisfaction

---

19. Or equivalent cognitive area. The Detchel do not seem to have heads.
20. Dr. Nestleroth wishes to observe this is true in more senses than one.
21. It could just as easily be said that, by this time, he had broken our wills. Pummeled into cooperating with so many absurd schemes in the past, we had lost our will to resist.

that Higgins and Nestleroth saw this string of luck broken. She was called upon to recreate the role of Bobbin, and forced to reproduce, as precisely as possible, his nose picking technique as recorded by the study camera. Hazel was played by a groundskeeper, who had to time his dozing off to coincide with the sequence of events on the tape.[22]

Dr. Nestleroth drew the plum role of Brownie, who, it will be recalled, had been grooming his mother during the encounter. Dr. Nestleroth, who was by then taking several forms of powerful medication, does not have any clear recollection of this time period, but he did seem to take a strangely masochistic joy in diving headfirst into the role. He recapitulated the young chimp's search for parasites and bits of dead skin with true verve and style.

Belzac, needless to say, insisted upon playing Belzic himself. Certainly, this was in retrospect inadvisable, but once again we wish to emphasize that our resistance to his demands had collapsed almost completely. It should be emphasized once again that the Institute by this time essentially existed at Belzac's sufferance. We were all agreed that, if he felt that his investigations were being thwarted or blocked in any way, he would undoubtedly call in human and alien investigators with far more authority and ability. At that point the situation would be out of control. It would be inevitable that our benign fraud of a mental hospital for chimpanzees would be revealed to someone who could understand the concept of a legal fiction—at which time we would all be facing the most unpleasant of legal realities.

In short, we felt compelled to cooperate with Belzac, for fear of seeing all that we had worked so hard to create torn down.

All of us were at last rehearsed to Belzac's satisfaction, and he and Higgins were able to reproduce the exchange between Higgins and Belzic with a perfection that was quite eerie to behold. Dr. Higgins freely admits that he came to join Dr. Nestleroth in taking a certain pride in his performance. In short, the cloud of delusion had engulfed him as well.[23]

22. Dr. Higgins observes that while it was no doubt far from the first time the Institute had paid the maintenance staff to sleep, it was the first time we did it knowingly.
23. Dr. Wood was unable to join in this sense of accomplishment, as the

But, as will come as no surprise to to anyone, Belzac was not satisfied. Clearly he was ready for the recreation, and certainly Higgins was in top form. But the three central players, the three prime suspects in the crime, had been given no chance to prepare themselves. Belzac saw the need to explain matters to Bobbin, Hazel, and Brownie. He had by this time at least managed to grasp that the chimps were, as he put it, "linguistically challenged," but he nonetheless hit upon a brilliant[24] idea. The chimps at the Institute had long been familiar with the concepts of video displays, and clearly understood and enjoyed images of themselves. Indeed, some years back, the younger ones had begun to make at least a tentative connection between cameras and stored images. They would at times seem to mug for the camera, for example.

Belzac commenced to rehearse the three chimps in question. He would bring them together every day, and show them a recording of the fateful interview, coupled with shots of its aftermath—that is to say, images of Belzic's remains and the smashed camera. They were being told, in the clearest way possible, that they were to fill in the blanks. The three chimps seemed to take the greatest interest, both in the video images and in Belzac himself. After a week in which this ritual was repeated daily, all three would at times imitate their actions as seen on the tape. It was clear that, to the best of his ability, Belzac had explained to them what was expected of them.

By this time, Dr. Higgins was completely wrapped up in his role, focusing on his upcoming performance with the same wild-eyed enthusiasm that Belzac himself brought to the enterprise.[25] Dr. Nestleroth was temporarily laid low with the complications brought on by an overdose of self-administered medication, and Dr. Wood, her sinuses having been surgically drained, was likewise incapacitated, forced

---

constant irritation of her nasal linings had resulted in a most painful infection of the sinuses.

24. Doctors Nestleroth and Higgins wish to insert the words "for him" after the word "brilliant."

25. Ironically enough, a case can be made that all three authors had by this time undergone a complete role transference. Belzac had, in a very real sense, taken three doctors and turned them into mental patients.

to lie still with her head leaned back for long hours every day.

On the big day, however, both Nestleroth and Wood made arrangements to be in the clinic's lounge to view the reconstruction of the crime, as picked up by various concealed cameras.

All was in readiness. The three chimps were brought to the same spot in the woods where they had been on the first occasion. A study camera, identical to the one that had been destroyed, was set up in the exact same position. Belzac took his place, and began his questioning. Higgins, both Dr. Nestleroth and Wood agreed, performed his role with remarkable authenticity. His anger, his frustration, his impatience with the whole absurd situation—all of it came through most convincingly. Even the three chimps seemed to take to their assigned roles with a certain panache, making a highly credible job of echoing their past behavior.

The climatic moment arrived. Doctors Wood and Nestleroth counted the repetitions of the question. Twenty. Twenty-one. Twenty-two. And then came twenty-three. "If you all related to each other are other than by result of direct sexual congressional meetings, is it the case not that your family relations are steeped in the intercourse of others?"

Doctor Higgins leapt up and cried out to Belzac/Belzic.

"Dammit! Don't you get it? They'll never answer! They'll never understand. They can't talk. They're goddamn chimps! *Chimps are not people!*"

There came that chuffing noise, and then Belzac spoke. "Back from where I come, many people say to face yours would about *you*. If willing to point stretch for you are they in your case, asking you to same do to Bobbin's case be fairly fair say I. Again I say the same thing." He turned to the chimps. "If you all related to each other are other than by result of direct sexual congressional meetings, is it the case not that your family relations are steeped in the intercourse of others?"

With a fine sense of theatrical style and yet with superb fidelity to the original event, Dr. Higgins left the study area, and it was all over.

Except, of course, that it was not. For the chimps were eager to take their cue and run with it. By the time the passion of his role fell away from him and Dr. Higgins had rushed back to the site, it was too late: Nestleroth and Wood had already been witnesses to Belzac's untimely end. Too late, the fog cleared from all our minds, and we confronted the reality we had forgotten was at the base of the charade. Reality that munched on the worldly remains of Belzac Tiscar, criminal scientist, until Higgins arrived and the chimps ran away. Detchel, it would seem, is a taste that, once acquired, is most avidly sought after.

Perhaps Belzac had convinced himself that he would be prepared for the onslaught, that he could unmask the killer who was shamming insanity, and *then* stand off the killer's attack. Perhaps he imagined the killer, having made his or her slip, would not then be so foolish as to make matters worse by killing again. Perhaps he made the mistake of assuming that the technique of restaging the crime, like all the others he had tried in the past, would fail. Perhaps he was already planning what to do next. Several vials of sodium pentathol—truth serum—were found in his room.

Or perhaps, to offer Dr. Nestleroth's theory, it wasn't just Belzic: Belzac was a blithering idiot, too.

* * *

It is, in more than one sense, a twice-told tale to describe the events as recorded on the concealed cameras. But in viewing those images, it becomes utterly clear how much we had underestimated both the chimps, and the Detchels' effect on the chimps. Belzic and Belzac had hounded them, chased them, prodded them every bit as much as the Detchel had hounded, chased, and prodded the staff.

The case could be made that nearly every staff member had some sort of motive for killing one or both Detchel. We forget, however, that the chimps had motives every bit as strong. They were made as miserable as we were. The difference was, that, given the chance, they were willing to *do* something about it.

But the central point is that, in Belzac's final moments, he finally succeeded in proving the one thing no one else but himself had ever believed. Belzic and Belzac were not the victims of an attack by wild animals, nor of chimps after an afternoon snack.

Their deaths truly were murder. Planned, premeditated conspiratorial murder, accomplished by plainly sentient beings.

The moment Dr. Higgins left the scene, the three chimps went into action. Bobbin stood up and slipped out of view of the study camera, and then smashed it to bits. Instead of diving straight for Belzac, Brownie circled around and *herded* the alien toward Hazel, who grabbed him and held him as Bobbin, finished with the camera, came over, grabbed at the alien, and snapped him in two.

Then, in literal truth, all three of the suspects proceeded to put Belzac away. And in large bites, too. The speed with which they consumed him spoke of more than an acquired taste. There was something furtive, hurried, about the way they ate, as if they were doing it solely to destroy the evidence. And what, besides a concern for evidence, could have impelled them to destroy the camera? That they fled[26] the moment Dr. Higgins arrived likewise implies they were fully aware of the meaning and potential consequences of their actions.

They killed deliberately, in self-defense, in a bid for freedom, out of the courage of their convictions, in order to protect their way of life from an invader. They displayed all of the characteristics that we, their supposedly superior intelligent cousins, failed to show. We are proud to have them named as unindicted coconspirators in our own upcoming federal conspiracy and state murder-for-hire trials.[27]

Indeed, we believe that something positive can be salvaged from the shambles of this affair. We submit that the recording of Belzac's murder are among the most compelling arguments yet for high chimpanzee intelligence. The degree of planning and cooperation required, the smoothness with which the operation was carried out, and, indeed, the clarity of the underlying intent; all are most eloquent of the most sophisticated of abstract thought.

Clearly, further study is warranted, and we would welcome the assistance of any extraterrestrial colleague—especially of the Detchel species—in the work.

---

26. And have not been seen since.
27. Dr. Nestleroth in particular wanted to note that he wishes the little bastards luck out there, and to observe that they have demonstrated formidable survival skills already.

HEAVEN'S ONLY DAUGHTER

by Laura Resnick

Laura Resnick, the daughter of your editor, got into this book on her own merits. She is an award-winning author of more than a dozen romance novels, and has sold eight science fiction stories since entering this field in the past year.

Mood piece. A private eye is hired by a wealthy family to find their daughter, whose arranged wedding to a man of comparable wealth and position is pending.

Far from being kidnapped, she is living with an alien male. A sexual relationship is hinted at but never explicitly stated. She explains that she is happy here, and that she is of age to make her own decisions. The private eye must weigh this against the fact that he took a fee to deliver her . . . and must make a decision.

It was a strange case right from the start. Mrs. Polona Heaven said that her daughter, one Kara Heaven, had been kidnapped by aliens. She hired us to get the girl back with the stipulation that there was to be no scandal or political embarrassment involved in the girl's retrieval. That was how she put it: retrieval. That should have tipped me off, but I was still relatively new to the business. The technical stuff, like tracing missing persons, verifying identities, tailing suspects—you can learn all of that pretty quickly. But reading people? No, that takes years of experience.

You may wonder what a nice girl like me is doing in this sordid business. Actually, ever since the first Interstellar Arms Reduction Treaty was signed, a lot of perfectly respectable people (i.e., ex-military types who sincerely believed they were honor bound to destroy two whole planets

in the Incubus system before we learned that those poison-
ous molds were actually sentient beings) have gone into private investigations. What's more, business is booming in
the private sector. Let's face it, with the galaxy opening up
and bureaucracy spearheading humankind's expansion into the
Milky Way, there's not much point in expecting the government, the police, or the civil service to get anything done
on behalf of the ordinary citizen. Sure, when the Governor
of the United African States awoke one day to find her ceremonial tiara had been stolen, it was a big deal, and three
interplanetary law enforcement networks searched half the
solar system for the culprit (in addition to priceless gems,
the tiara apparently had certain religious significance, and
witch doctors far and wide were gleefully warning that the
African union would crumble if the tiara were not successfully retrieved and the thief suitably punished). But if an
ordinary person's tiara—or daughter—disappears these days,
your only hope is to hire a team of private investigators.

I actually used to be a reproductive counselor (or, more
accurately, I used to advise people how to fornicate *without*
reproducing). But after that memorable altercation our men
and women in uniform had with the fierce and bloodthirsty
inhabitants of Antares IV (all of whom are now safely dead
or in ''cheerfully decorated rehabilitation camps''), a lot of
government funding was diverted to the military to pay for
those weapons that we now have to liquidate, under the
terms of the most recent Interstellar Arms Reduction Treaty.

So I found myself out of work just about the time my best
friend's partner disappeared—after having embezzled three
million credits from the business they owned jointly. I held
her hand all through her dealings with the firm of detectives
she hired to find the bastard. By the time they'd been on
retainer for four months, I decided that after five years of
being overworked and underpaid, *I'd* sure like to make that
much money for supplying so few results. So I went back
to school for another year, then got an entry-level job with
Harker and Fontina Investigations.

Like some others in this business, I've read a few private
eye books by some of the classic authors, many of whom
have been dead for five centuries—Dashiell Hammett and
Raymond Chandler among them. A lot of the references are
pretty baffling, even after you read the footnotes, but there's

an archaic romanticism there that appeals to me. That, of course, is part of my problem.

Even after two years at the agency, two years of catching adulterers in the act, dealing with perverts and sex offenders, tracing teenagers who probably had a damned good reason for running away in the first place, and retrieving stolen property that no sensible person would want back, I still had this crazy idea that I was in a moral profession. I believed that I was one of the good guys and that I was supposed to do what was right. How I managed to keep believing this, even as I filmed copulating couples without their knowledge (on adultery cases, I mean), is a question that could probably occupy a therapist for several years. Maybe some of that stuff I read, in which heroes and heroines were always doing the hard thing for the right reason, got to me.

Anyhow, I was pleasantly surprised (which shows how naive I was) when Harker and Fontina assigned me to the Heaven case. Though I had worked on over a dozen interplanetary cases, this was my first interstellar case. It was also my first case involving nonhumans (which goes to follow, since the Interstellar Migration Act prohibits alien races who act like *us* from coming here, which means we have virtually no alien crime in this system). It was potentially the most politically sensitive case I'd ever been assigned to, and I was very excited about having a chance to prove my mettle. (We're talking *naive* here.) I thought the fact that I was assigned alone to the case, with no supervision other than the usual progress reports, was a measure of the firm's confidence in me. (Yes, I know, you needn't say it).

Mrs. Heaven's personality made it immediately apparent to me why aliens had kidnapped her daughter instead of *her*. Though quite beautiful, she was as cold as ice, with a hard, ruthless edge and an imperious manner that made me long to do something undignified to her. If she had any motherly feelings toward her abducted daughter, she kept them well-hidden. I was given orders to bring the girl home with all due haste, primarily, it seemed, because Mrs. Heaven found the entire situation tediously inconvenient and socially embarrassing.

I had dealt with kidnapping on a couple of earlier cases. I have to admit that, despite my bewilderment at Mrs. Heaven's apparent immunity to the emotional trauma of her daughter's kidnapping, I was somewhat relieved. A great deal of time is lost in consoling the family, delicate questions are difficult to ask of sobbing parents, and honest answers and estimates are almost impossible to give in the face of a terrified mother's desperate hopes.

"Now, then, Mrs. Heaven, when did your daughter disappear?"

She checked her calendar, a luminous little holographic dial which hung from her neck on a chain made of crystallized quicksilver. "I noticed she was gone yesterday, around 1300 hours. I returned from my luncheon with Irina Halstead-Mao to find my daughter's chambers empty. I became worried when she didn't return toward evening, since she knew we were scheduled to attend the inaugural ball of the Interplanetary Governor."

Fearing she might mention more V.I.P.s if given the opportunity, I tried to get Mrs. Heaven to pinpoint the exact hour her daughter was last seen. It proved to be a futile exercise. Although Mrs. Heaven had noticed Kara was missing yesterday, she hadn't actually seen her for over two weeks.

"What about Mr. Heaven?" I asked.

"I saw him this morning."

"No, I mean has *he* seen her?"

"Of course not. Why would he see her?"

Well, damned if I could think of a reason. We moved on. "Does Kara have any close friends who might have seen her during the past two weeks?"

"She has a fiancé, *obviously.*" The glacial look in Mrs. Heaven's eyes made it clear what she thought of private investigators who didn't keep abreast of society news. "The wedding is scheduled for the fifteenth of next month, and Kara must be back in time for the standard social functions."

"I see. What's the name of her prospective husband, ma'am?" She appeared reluctant to answer, as if finding it distasteful to involve him in this messy business, so I prodded, "It's important that I talk to him, Mrs. Heaven. He probably knows something about her activities and can perhaps help me pinpoint the time of her disappearance." She relented, and we proceeded to the next, and most important, question. "What makes you think she was kidnapped by aliens, ma'am?"

"Who else would do such a thing?" she said frostily.

I decided to return to that subject later.

"Does Kara have a job?" I asked, looking for some link to the real world. An incredulous stare was the only response. Silly question, I suppose. The Heavens were one of the five hundred richest families in the Western hemisphere. No, they weren't ordinary people, and they probably could have gotten powerful government agencies interested in locating their daughter. However, as I've mentioned, Mrs. Heaven wanted no breath of scandal, a requirement that clearly ruled out government involvement.

"Has there been a ransom demand?" I asked, continuing the interview with true grit.

"No, of course not. Aliens don't understand the value of money," she said contemptuously.

Actually, that's not quite true. The Interstellar Migration Act was passed almost a century ago because a small band of Shirulians waylaid a ship carrying the semiannual payroll of three major interplanetary corporations. They boarded her somewhere between Saturn and Jupiter and made off with the greatest sum of money any group of thieves has ever even attempted to steal. So I figured that at least *some* aliens knew the value of a credit, even if it was only those races no longer permitted to enter our solar space. However, Mrs. Heaven was clearly not in the mood for a history lesson.

"It's extremely important that you let us know if you receive a ransom demand," I explained to her. "That will make my job a lot easier. Otherwise, it will be difficult to trace—"

"I am not interested in making your job a lot easier, Ms. Hoxley," Mrs. Heaven said archly.

She was a real piece of work. The rest of the interview wasn't any more productive than what I've already described. Just before she left my office, she turned and met my eyes with almost frightening intensity. "You must get her back," she said, her voice implying a wealth of unspoken threats if I should fail. "She's my only daughter."

I was not moved to tears.

Kara's fiancé was a little more helpful, though not intentionally so. His name was Quayle Morrison, as in the Morrison Bank of Mars, the Morrison Complex on Ganymede, and the Morrison Mining Company operating on the moons of Saturn. He had yet to inherit all of this vast wealth, but he was flexing his fingers preparatory to seizing the reins of power.

"Kidnapped?" Quayle gasped at the beginning of the interview, clearly appalled. "Did Polona Heaven mention which race of aliens she suspects?"

"No, sir. She told me I had no business asking such an impertinent question." No wonder Harker and Fontina had given me the case, I thought irritably. They'd seen her coming. "I'm obliged to investigate this possibility fully, sir, but I must admit that Kara's being kidnapped by aliens seems unlikely to me."

"Why?" he demanded.

"Ever since the Interstellar Migration Act was passed, there's been no record of any misdemeanors by aliens, let alone crimes like assault, kidnapping, or extortion." I shrugged. "There's no precedent for this. Don't you think it's possible Kara could have been kidnapped by humans?"

"Nonsense!" he bellowed. "Let's have none of this liberal rubbish, Ms. Hoxley. If Polona Heaven says aliens kidnapped Kara, her word is good enough for me."

I decided that the ultra-wealthy were very strange. "Well, then, sir, do *you* suspect a particular race?"

"I'll bet you half the uranium on Pluto that it was a Dramborian, Ms. Hoxley."

Since he probably *owned* half the uranium on Pluto, I asked with interest, "Why do you say that, sir?"

"She's been hanging around with them, hasn't she?"

"Has she, sir?"

"Of course! Mind you, charitable tendencies are to be applauded, but not when it gets out of hand."

"The Dramborians. They're the ones immolating themselves on their home planet to protest the, um, benevolent rule of the Aligned Second Interstellar Council, aren't they, sir?"

"Bloody nuisance," Quayle muttered. "They're making the cost of fuel skyrocket."

"So Kara was involved in lobbying for them here?" I guessed. Quayle wouldn't have been so annoyed if she was simply giving them old clothes and freeze-dried food that people like the Heavens didn't want anyhow.

"Damned right, she was. I told her that a little charity was all very well and good, but to engage in any political activity on behalf of these creatures was out of the question.''

"But she didn't listen to you?"

"Women!"

Taking that for a confirmation, I said, "But if she was helping them, why would they have kidnapped her?"

"They're *aliens*, Ms. Hoxley. Who *knows* why they do what they do? You can't expect logic from creatures like that."

"But the Dramborians are a peaceful race. That's why they're allowed to enter this system. Their protests are largely verbal, and the only violence they've displayed has been self-inflicted. Why would they suddenly kidnap a human woman?" I wondered aloud.

"Have you forgotten that Kara Heaven comes from an extremely wealthy family? It seems to me, Ms. Hoxley, that the Dramborians will benefit more from bartering for her release than they ever benefited from her rather incompetent activism on their behalf."

And that, I supposed, was a possibility well worth investigating. The following day, I visited the Dramborian Cultural Exchange Center, the planet Drambor's primary office in this solar system.

I had only seen a few Dramborians until then, since there weren't many of them on Earth. Though oxygen-based, their atmosphere is somewhat different from ours, so they tended to get rather ill if they stayed for long. The few Dramborians who were here on a long-term basis appeared to spend most of their leisure time inside atmosphere-controlled chambers at the Cultural Exchange Center.

I'm ashamed to admit that, despite my admiration for their ancient culture and their commitment to pacifism, I had always found them quite repulsive. They're rather fishlike, even though they're two-legged, land-dwelling, male and female beings. Ironically, despite the fishy smell that clings to them, they can't swim at all, and some rotten kids caused a nasty interstellar incident a decade ago when they threw three Dramborians into the water off the Florida coast. Not only did all three Dramborians drown, but their bodies were almost unrecognizable when they were shipped back to Drambor; apparently some chemical in their scaly skin can't survive contact with Earth's salt water, and the bodies were hideously deformed as a result.

The Dramborians at the Cultural Exchange Center were distant, due to their planetary protest against our influence, but unfailingly courteous. In fact, they were the first polite people I'd encountered on this case. However, explaining the concept of kidnapping to Dramborians—i.e., taking someone away from one place and confining them in another place, all of this against their will—was one of the most exhausting, frustrating things I've ever done. After all, they had only been permitted to enter our solar system because they were so totally devoid of criminal tendencies, so how could they understand such a thing?

I finally gave up and simply requested a list of all Dramborians who'd had contact with Kara Heaven. Four of the aliens on the list had already gone back to Drambor. It took me two days to interview all the others, after which I requested a permit to travel to Drambor. There was no record of Kara on any scheduled transport to Drambor, and aliens are not permitted to charter private vessels. However, Mrs. Heaven was pressuring my bosses, and they were pressuring me, so it didn't seem politic to remain on Earth any longer.

If a Dramborian did indeed have Kara, he had not only learned about kidnapping on Earth, but also such useful skills as forging travel documents, counterfeiting interstellar visas, and evading random computer scans. It seemed so unlikely, I began to fear I was diving into a black hole.

Interstellar travel is not something a person should undertake lightly. The hyperspace jump made my ears bleed, and I never did get the stains out of my favorite tunic. And if you think flying halfway around the world upsets your body clock, try traveling five light-years from home.

The air on Drambor, should you ever have the opportunity to visit there, is not one of its primary attractions for humans. It's filled with a sort of sticky soot which stinks of putrescent primeval things. The Dramborians were polite, but not very friendly. After all, the average Dramborian was accustomed to seeing at least one self-immolation a day in protest against human efforts to control Drambor, so they weren't especially thrilled to find another off-worlder in their midst. The only liquid available on Drambor is a murky, oily drink served with things floating in it that are rather like small slugs, and the food. . . . Well, I really pitied Kara Heaven if she were stuck on this planet, and I had every intention of helping her get back to fresh air, decent food, and cold cocktails.

I enlisted the aid of the Dramborian religious order—the closest thing they have to a government of their own—thanks to the support of the Supervisor of the Dramborian Cultural Exchange Center back on Earth. Things operate a little differently there, so it took more time than I would have liked to track down the four Dramborians I sought. In other words, I was starving to death and desperate for a decent drink by the time I finally found the fourth and final Dramborian who, according to official records, had had contact with Mrs. Heaven's only daughter. I wanted to interview him quickly and then get off that damned planet. So imagine my surprise when I told him I was looking for Kara Heaven and he said he'd be happy to take me to her.

"You know where she is?" I asked.

"Of course. She is in my home." Since Dramborians don't lie, I believed him.

"What's she doing there?"

"She exists there."

It was one of those situations that called for more experience than I possessed. Was he going to kidnap me, too? Kill me? Had Kara been brainwashed? If only I hadn't been forced to turn over my weapon to the transit authorities upon leaving for Drambor. I felt naked, helpless, uncertain.

On the other hand, nothing terrified me as much as the prospect of going home and telling Mrs. Heaven that I'd found out where Kara was but hadn't gone to see her.

"All right," I said after a brief internal struggle. "Take me to her."

It was not a long trip from the Dramborian's ritual bath house to his home, which wasn't half bad compared to the Alien Guesthouse in which I'd been staying. Dramborians are not materialistic in the same way that we are. The abode was barren of possessions but just chock full of leaves, plants, vines, twigs, and bulbous things that looked like vibrating, mossy rocks.

Kara was there, meditating on the floor, looking quite pretty, though not entirely healthy. Well, after just a few days on that miserable planet, I figured that *I* probably wasn't looking too healthy either. There are no mirrors on Drambor, though, so I wasn't sure. When the Dramborian spoke her name, Kara opened her eyes and looked toward us. Upon seeing me, her expression darkened and she rose to her feet, backing away slowly as she spoke.

"Who are you?"

"My name is Hoxley. I'm a private investigator hired by your mother to find you."

"You've found me. Now go away."

I glanced nervously at the Dramborian. "That was only half my assignment, Kara. I'm also supposed to bring you home," I said, puzzled by her behavior. I guess I'd expected to be greeted as a long-awaited heroine. I mean, I was *rescuing* her.

"I *am* home," Kara said, which wasn't what I had expected her to say.

"Kara, have you been injured? Coerced? Drugged?" When there was no response, I continued, "Are you afraid of something?"

"Go away, Hoxley," she said again.

"Kara, I'm here to help you."

"I don't want your help. I'm sorry you've come all this way, but you're wasting your time."

I stared at her, not sure what to do next. As I considered the situation, her gaze slid away from my face. Her eyes locked with the Dramborian's yellow, lizardlike ones, and that was when I knew.

As liberal as I had always considered myself, I realized I was sickened, absolutely disgusted by what I saw pass between them in that brief moment. The Dramborian wasn't human. He was a different species. He wasn't even from the same planet as she was. How could she bear. . . . I shuddered. How *could* she?

I took a few deep breaths, gagging on the thick, foul air, nauseated by the Dramborian's fishy, decaying odor.

"You weren't kidnapped. You ran away. With him," I whispered, trying to conceal my horror.

"Yes," she answered serenely.

"That's why there was no trace of you in any transport record. *You* faked the documents, bribed the frontier guards, and forged the signatures, not him."

She shrugged. "Of course. He couldn't have done that."

"I will prepare some liquid for you and our guest," the Dramborian said, bowing sinuously and leaving the chamber to get just what I wanted at that moment—more thick, slimy, lukewarm liquid.

After he left us, Kara looked contemptuously at me. "You're shocked, aren't you?"

There seemed no point in denying it. "It's a new concept, Kara. Give me time to get used to the idea."

"It's not an idea or a concept," she said, clearly not caring whether or not she converted me. "I'm here. I live here, with him, and I'm happy here. I am old enough to make these choices for myself."

"Why didn't you at least tell that to your mother and leave home openly, under your real name?"

"My mother would never forgive me for the disgrace it would cause if the whole world knew I'd left my family and the marriage they'd arranged for me in order to go live with a Dramborian on his home planet. I thought this way would be better. Quieter. Polona wouldn't have to save quite so much face if no one knew what had really happened to me."

"Kara, you must have known she would hire a PI if you simply disappeared," I said wearily, feeling well and truly sick of the rich and powerful.

"And how far do you think I would have gotten if my mother knew what I intended?" She looked away. "You see how hard it is to escape her? Even running away under a false name hasn't protected me from her tentacles. You're proof of that."

"So come back with me, talk it over with her like a sensible adult, and you can be back on Drambor in time for the next immolation."

"No! You don't know her. Once she got me back, she'd never let me get away again. There would be guards around the house, coded locks on every door, sensory alarms watching my every movement. I'm expected to marry Quayle, have splendid children, and ensure that the Heaven fortune will have heirs." Her voice was ironic as she added, "I'm her only daughter, you know."

"I know, I know," I said morosely. "But surely if—"

"I'm not going back with you, Hoxley."

"Kara," I said carefully, "I have a contract to fulfill."

She stared at me. "You mean you'd force me to come back with you?" She must have read my expression as I assessed my chances. "Oh, he wouldn't stop you. How could he? He doesn't understand force."

I started to say more, but she was seized by a fit of coughing. By the time she was through, some awful, yellow stuff was running from the corners of her eyes. I wiped it away and helped her sit on the floor.

"Kara, you can't stay here. The atmosphere's no good for us, and forget about the food and drink. Even diplomatic missions get rotated up to a space station every two weeks."

"I'm not going back, Hoxley."

"You should at least get an air tank to help you get through particularly bad days."

She didn't answer me, and I saw she was struggling, gasping for air at the same time her body rejected what it was inhaling. I'd listened to some of the recommended travelers' advisories while preparing for my trip to Drambor, so I knew what was in the air and food, as well as what was missing from it. I figured Kara Heaven would be lucky to live five more years if she stayed here, and I suspected she knew it.

"Dammit, Kara, I've accepted a fee to find and retrieve you."

She choked on a rueful laugh. "Polona's words, no doubt."

"Polona's words," I agreed. I suddenly felt like an utterly gullible idiot, and with good reason. "She knew you had run away, didn't she? That's why she seemed angry instead of bereaved when she came to the agency. You're too old for a PI to go after you as a runaway, so she made up the kidnapping story. It saved face and ensured results." I sighed. "The damn fool woman could have caused a major interstellar incident with a story like that!"

A chill ran through me as I realized she still could. And I was irrevocably part of the problem now. So what was I going to do about it?

It wouldn't be hard to get Kara back to Earth. She was already too physically weak to give me much trouble, and all I had to tell the Dramborians who saw me dragging her to the transport terminal was that she was an escaped human criminal. The whole galaxy dreaded human criminals, after all. Mrs. Heaven would get her daughter back, I would get a bonus and perhaps even a promotion for successfully completing my first interstellar case, and Kara would get a wealthy human husband and a decent meal.

Or, I could leave her here, to die of slow toxemia on an alien world. She would live out her remaining days in this dreary, barren, leafy hole with a fish-smelling alien whom she could never truly understand, in the midst of beings that would never really accept her, so intent were they upon immolating themselves one by one in rebellion against her own race.

"Why, Kara?" I asked a little desperately.

She had ceased her coughing and straightened her spine. Her face was pale and beaded with sweat. "He's good. Truly and fearlessly good," she said hoarsely. "Have you ever known anyone like that?"

"In *my* line of work?"

The Dramborian came back with our liquid slime at that moment, serene, solicitous, and gentle. I found the communion between them was as enviable as it was grotesque. It's funny how deep a taboo can lurk inside you. Even funnier that it should lurk inside of me and not Kara Heaven.

I thought of a dozen stories on my way back to Earth, none of them particularly convincing. Above all, I couldn't indicate that Kara might have died on Drambor or been killed by a Dramborian; the last thing we needed was another interstellar war of extermination.

I finally decided that it was essential to make Mrs. Heaven believe that Kara had never gone to Drambor. After all, I figured that part of my unwritten pact with Kara was to make sure that no one else fulfilled my written contract with her mother.

I wound up simply reporting that the whole Dramborian lead was a dead end, and I started investigating other possibilities. Mrs. Heaven grew increasingly impatient, since she knew damn well that I was either lying or hopelessly incompetent. She eventually took her business elsewhere. I, of course, was fired in the full glare of publicity, with noisy recriminations about how Kara Heaven might still be alive and well if I'd done my job right. The girl would never be found now that the trail was so cold (the Dramborians had left Earth, cut off all communication, and closed Drambor to off-worlders by then), and Harker and Fontina exonerated themselves by condemning me.

And I finally realized that that had been the plan all along. My bosses had indeed seen Mrs. Heaven coming. Far more experienced than I at reading people, they had known from the first that she was lying, that this case could lead to their ruination in a dozen different ways, and that they needed a sacrificial lamb. They put someone expendable on the case, and then jettisoned me at precisely the right moment, a small loss in the greater scheme of their extensive assets.

As the old saying goes, I'll never work in this business again. I feared criminal charges for a while, after Harker and Fontina abandoned me and before Mrs. Heaven's wrath had died down, but I was finally allowed to return to comfortable obscurity.

I've gone back to school for more training—this time to become a field operative in the Cultural Exchange Liaison Service. Well, why not? I am, after all, one of the few humans who has ever been to Drambor.

Maybe I got a rough deal, being tossed overboard by my own kind so that a shark like Polona Heaven could gnaw on me. But I suppose my fate was sealed long ago by guys like Hammett and Chandler.

Here's a tip I learned from them. If you're going to do the hard thing for the right reason, you've got to be prepared to take the fall.

HEAVEN SCENT

by Virginia Booth

Though her writing has appeared in other fields, this is Ginger Booth's first professional science fiction sale.

An enormous colony ship, holding over 1,000 passengers, is on a voyage to a new world. Four months out of port, the Chief of Security is found murdered in the huge hydroponics section. Because of the extreme value of this section of the ship—it's what produces the oxygen for the passengers—it is off-limits to all but the ten gardeners who have been assigned to work there.

The new Chief of Security finds that all ten gardeners have alibis. He checks the plants; there don't seem to be any illegal hallucinogenic plants growing here. Yet the dead Security Chief evidently had some reason to be in the hydroponics section, and someone obviously felt it necessary to murder him.

Solve the murder, supplying a fair motivation.

Security Chief Jesus Cavares slammed one hand against the recognition panel and jabbed out his security override with the other. The pressure door wouldn't open or close fast enough, as he slipped through into the dimly-lit tangle of algae vats and low-hung plumbing. The secure door with its menacing hiss was no protection. Run, dammit, run!

In primordial panic, Cavares ducked and dodged and slipped on the catwalks amidst the vats, desperately seeking a place to hide. Their corners barked his shins and hips. Water burbled menacingly in the pipes that reached for his head. In terror, he looked back over his shoulder to catch sight of his pursuer, and slipped on some algae slime.

His reflexes weren't quite good enough. His temple connected hard with a pipe. Unconscious, he fell face-first into a peaceful vat of the green life-giving algae.

She waited patiently, hopefully, but dawn came to the colony starship. It hadn't worked. He hadn't understood, after all.

Dan Brenner looked over the brightly-lit green mess in dismay. "It was like this when you found him?"

'No, Dan, uh, Chief," stammered a pretty hydroponics engineer, her overalls covered from shoulder to knee in slime. "I tried to drag him out, then realized he was dead. I put him back exactly as I found him, and called you. Sorry about the mess."

"It's all right, Anita, I probably would have done the same. Did you notice anything strange before the algae got all over everything?"

"Just a man with his head in a vat."

Brenner might have laughed, if it weren't his best friend and late boss lying there. "Okay, Anita, could you round up the rest of the hydroponics staff? I want to question everyone."

"Only six of us are on duty right now. You want the other four, too? Three of them worked all night." At Brenner's sharp glance, she added, "In Vat Room Three. Plumbing problem. This is Vat Room One."

"Wake them up if you have to. I'd like everyone in here as soon as possible."

While he waited, Brenner looked around beyond the slimed area for clues. Nothing. He couldn't even tell where Cavares had come from to get here. Deciding there was nothing more to be gained by leaving the site undisturbed, he pulled Cavares out of the vat and managed to clean his face off a little. He appeared to have died in the early morning, perhaps 0500. A bruise on the forehead. Well, they'd see what else there was to see after he was cleaned up. There would be an autopsy. What in hell was the Chief doing in here?

When Anita returned from calling the others, he suggested draining the vat. She was horrified at the idea, and instead proposed to strain it and perform a thorough chemical analysis. She'd have to do that anyway, to make sure it wasn't contaminated by the corpse. Brenner accepted the plan, and Anita set to it.

Interviewing the ten sunburned engineers didn't take long. They had no idea why the Security Chief might have been there, and had never seen him in the controlled-access areas of hydroponics before. Nothing unusual had been happening in hydroponics. Six engineers had simple alibis. They spent the night sleeping in their quarters, in the crew country of the ship. Crew country had security access, plus a sentry to make sure no one got lazy and squeezed two through the door instead of one. The cavernous hydroponics works at the core of the ship were unreachable from crew country.

A sixth engineer lived in colonist country, with his wife and two children. He stumbled in with a dreadful cold, and said he'd gotten a nighttime dose from Medic that knocked him out from 1900 until his wife dragged him out for this meeting. Brenner sent him back to bed quickly. The slimy corpse seemed to be making him queasy.

Among the remaining engineers, who'd worked all night on some plumbing blocked by an algae bloom, was the Hydroponics Chief, Gonzales. She said they had taken only a one-hour break for dinner at the Isakiya, an all-night restaurant bar, while the offending subsystem drained.

Gonzales verified for Brenner that access was computer logged, not only between the outside and the hydroponics complex, but between major subsections. The computer would verify that none of them had left Vat Room Three to enter Vat Room One. And people in the Isakiya would surely remember three soaked and slimed patrons dining at 0100. They had returned together to crew country to sleep at 0530, an hour before Anita found the body. None of them had noticed anything unusual, but then again, they were working a full third of a mile away. The *Lebensraum* was a vast ship.

The hydroponics plant was vital to the ship's life-support systems, and with its rich nutrient brews, very sensitive to contamination. No one but the hydroponics staff, the Security Chief, and his Deputy, Dan Brenner, had access.

While Brenner was questioning the hydroponics engineers, the Medical Chief and his orderlies took the body away. Brenner sent everyone back to their normal business, after getting Gonzales' promise to cooperate in any way possible. After a few minutes on the computer corroborating the facts to date, he headed down to Medical.

"Dan, glad you came," said the graying Doctor Bolivar. "I'm no forensics expert. I've found out all I could."

"Sorry to ask it of you, Doc. Hardly your normal routine."

"Well, it's a change of pace, if a distasteful one. I haven't done an autopsy in twenty years." Bolivar pulled the sheet back from the corpse. "Why don't you see what you can make of the bruises?"

Frowning, Brenner looked Cavares over, front and back. Bruises, just bruises, except the blow to the temple. "What did he die of?"

"Well, his heart stopped," said Bolivar. "Yeah, I know that's not helpful. He didn't drown. I've got the blood work. His adrenaline was extremely elevated, and testosterone, too. Nothing else. The adrenaline could have been elevated by fighting for his life, I suppose."

"No drugs?"

Bolivar met his eye knowingly, but shook his head. "I thought of that, too, but no. What do you think?"

"I'd like your opinion first."

"It looks to me like he ran amok, hit his head, and fell into a vat of algae. Maybe he had a heart attack. That much adrenaline could give anybody a heart attack, and Jesus' heart wasn't in top shape. If he were a colonist, I'd say acute cabin fever, though only a month out from Kamikaze, it's early even for that. But Jesus? He's a career starman. What do you think?"

Brenner traced a finger over the huge bruise on his friend's hip. "I think something scared him to death, literally. The big question now is, 'What?' "

"That one I can't help you with. If you'd like, I'll keep the body for you for a few days, in case you think of anything else you'd like to check."

"Thanks. Where's his stuff?"

Brenner went to the table Bolivar indicated, and rummaged through Cavares' things. As he'd already noticed, the stun gun was still securely fastened to the belt. Brenner checked, but it had never been fired. A slimed picture of Cavares' late wife and their two grown children, left behind so many interstellar trips ago that they were surely centuries dead. One large silver coin, with two characters in Kamikaze writing on one side, and a mirror-smooth finish on the other. That was all. Brenner bowed his head and slipped the coin into his pocket. "Good-bye, Jesus," he whispered.

"Excuse me?" asked Bolivar.

"Nothing. Doc, could there be Kamikaze drugs that your tests wouldn't identify?"

Bolivar sighed. "Yes, certainly. Kamikaze has always been a fairly closed society. Not hostile, of course, they just didn't have much business with other planets. I was surprised when the *Lebensraum* was sent to ferry colonists from there."

Brenner had been surprised, too. But not all *that* surprised. After all, Kamikaze was one of the very first colony worlds, founded by a corporate consortium from a single country, Nihon, long before the United Nations Relocation Forces started using the techniques developed by private enterprise. By the Earth-born Brenner's standards Kamikaze was hardly crowded. But the newly terraformed Green Sands, where they were headed, was empty, only now beginning to accept civilians.

Brenner took his leave of Bolivar and headed back to his office. He paged Gonzales to join him. While he waited, he verified the access logs to hydroponics and crew country. All the stories matched. Cavares left crew country at 0445. He entered Vat Room One at 0515. He must have died soon thereafter. His official police records had no entry for the past week. Just a normal, placid cruise on the UNRFS *Lebensraum.*

Brenner pulled the ship's diagram up on the wall-sized screen, and began to study the area around Vat Room One. It was a place to start.

When Gonzales entered, she was polite, but it was clear that she'd far rather be back in bed.

"I appreciate all you're doing to cooperate, Chief," said Brenner. "The access records show only that Cavares entered the Vat Room, but not which door he entered through. Do you know any way to tell?"

Gonzales shrugged. "As you can tell from the diagram, there are only six doors. Two of them go into other controlled areas, so they'd register an exit and an entrance."

Brenner nodded. "It wasn't either of them. I'll have to check for prints, then. I can see that this door leads from the main corridor to crew country. But what's in these other three compartments?''

"Those are colonist-run gardens. We do technical support for them, lighting and water and such. Otherwise we leave them alone.''

"What do they grow in there?''

"I'm sorry, Dan, er, Chief, but I can't remember offhand. There are twenty-nine garden rooms under cultivation by the colonists. They'd take more if we could spare them, of course.''

The garden rooms were each large enough for a small farm, and there were only a thousand colonists. "Of course?'' asked Brenner.

"Oh, the Kamikaze-jin are all avid gardeners, you know. That's where the name comes from, 'Divine Wind,' referring to the smell of flowers everywhere on Kamikaze. You must have noticed.''

"Oh, yes,'' said Brenner, remembering how his wife had loved the planet and wanted to stay, but the flowers made him sneeze. Pollen, no doubt. Someday they'd find a planet they could agree on. "Are you familiar with Kamikaze plants? I'd like to inspect those gardens.''

"Old Nakamura would be a better choice, Chief. She's a top-flight horticulturist among the colonists.''

Brenner got up to shake Gonzales' hand. "Thanks again, Chief. I hope you can get some sleep, now.''

When he screened her, Nakamura happily agreed to do a full botanical survey of all three garden rooms adjoining Vat Room One. Brenner went down to meet her and her group of excited, chattering students, then left them to it while he did his own tour.

The first room was largely a flower garden, beautiful and heady with fragrances, especially from the giant pseudo-irises the Kamikaze-jin adored. The lavender irislike blossoms reached the size of beach balls, topped with two-foot-long feathery iridescent stalks. Following the lead of Nakamura's students, he stopped and breathed deeply by the largest iris. The Kamikaze-jin said the flower exuded peace and contentment. It made Brenner sneeze. He checked the door into the hydroponics lab. Nothing noticeable, but he dusted for prints.

Yes! The last person through this door was Cavares!

Brenner turned back and stared around the garden, sneezing again. No signs of a struggle in here. Nothing. He gestured to Nakamura to join him.

"Yes?" she said, bowing slightly and giving him the usual Kamikaze-jin's complacent half-smile.

"Nakamura-san, I'd like you to concentrate on this room in your study. Cavares was in here before he died." Nakamura showed no surprise. Of course, by now the word would have spread all over the ship.

"Yes," she said, bowing again. "But may I ask what you hope to find?"

"A mind-altering plant of some kind. Something Cavares might have eaten, or smelled, by mistake. Something that might have made him go crazy."

Nakamura-san lost her half-smile. "There are no plants like that here. This is the simplest of gardens, dedicated to iris and honeysing vines, with ornamental greenery as counterpoint."

"Well, please check carefully. Maybe something else has gotten in. Are there any mind-altering plants on Kamikaze?"

Nakamura-san frowned. "All beautiful gardens are mind-altering. As is a mountain spring, or a baby's smile."

Great, Brenner thought. Kamikaze mysticism. "No, I mean mind-altering in that they might make you suddenly do something you wouldn't choose if your mind were free of the drug's influence."

"That's what I meant, as well, Security Chief."

Brenner frowned, thinking of another way to approach the subject, when he remembered the coin in his pocket. He took it out and showed it to Nakamura.

"Do you know anything about this?" he asked.

Nakamura-san turned her head this way and that to look at the piece, but didn't touch it. "It's a study coin of the Iris Zen."

"What does it say?"

"They all say the same thing—Kamikaze."

"I see. And what is the Iris Zen?"

The placid Nakamura erupted into laughter. "Ah, for that you'd have to ask a master!" Still chuckling, Nakamura-san walked back toward the children she'd brought.

Brenner was about to pursue the topic when he was caught by a paroxysm of sneezing, and fled the garden. Wiping tears from his eyes with his collar, he decided to let Nakamura complete her survey, while he checked out Cavares' quarters.

He'd mostly managed to hold his feelings about Jesus' death in check until he stepped into his late friend's living room. Then it came crashing over him. They'd worked together in peace and quiet for three years, ship's time, playing cards and drinking and chatting away the parsecs and centuries of the outside world. It was rare that there was any real need for a Security Chief and Deputy on a colony ship of scarcely eleven hundred people when full, and carrying less than seventy when shuttling without colonists.

Brenner wasn't a career starman. He had his wife and daughter aboard. They hadn't liked the first colony they'd shipped out for from Earth. Cavares gave him this job so that they could stay aboard while they kept looking. Eventually, he'd take up a colony job again as a real policeman. He had never expected to investigate a murder on the *Lebensraum*.

Brenner pulled himself together. It had happened, something had sent Jesus to his death. He'd have time to mourn after he made sure no one else was going to meet the same fate. Whatever that was.

Brenner hadn't been in Cavares' apartment recently. Everything looked in order, sort of sloppy, as usual. Apparently, he'd had coffee when he got up that morning. Brenner unlocked all of Cavares' personal files and home controls for his perusal. Cavares had overridden the normal wakeup of 0700 for 0415. So he'd planned to do something.

Brenner opened the bedroom door, and began to sneeze.

The room was totally rearranged. Cavares' casual sloppiness was superseded by austere simplicity. There was no bed, just a Kamikaze-style wooden cabinet for storing bedding during the day. The beige carpet was overlaid with a woven reed mat of subtle geometric patterns formed from slightly different shades of greenish-gold grass. Three of the walls were bare white. A single low table by the bed cabinet held writing materials—actual physical paper and ink! The normal overhead halogens didn't come on when Brenner entered the room. Instead, there was track lighting brilliantly spotlighting the single feature of the room's fourth wall. A medium-sized Kamikaze iris, about three feet tall, with a bloom a foot in diameter.

At first, Brenner was appalled, then grudgingly admitted

the room's grace and peace. It was truly a lovely flower, with a scent like a mixture of, perhaps, lilacs and roses and an early morning spring rain. A renewed sneezing fit hit him. He hastily grabbed the stuff on the table and retreated back to the living room.

He fetched himself a glass of water from the kitchen and lay down on the couch to study Cavares' handwritten book. It was clearly of Kamikaze origin, with the ubiquitous floral motif on the cloth binding, and the *wrong* rectangular proportions. The few physical books Brenner had ever read had more of a three-by-five aspect ratio, and were hinged on the side. This was a long rectangle, hinged at the top. Like most things Kamikaze, the slight oddness made him vaguely uncomfortable.

Any more than that was hard to determine. It was apparently a journal, as Brenner could make out dates above each entry, starting about a week before they left Kamikaze. Brenner grinned at some stick-figure diagrams, showing some kind of exercise, as best he could tell. Cavares never could draw worth a damn. The rest appeared to be cursive handwriting.

In subjective time, Cavares was only ten years older than Brenner. But Cavares was born one hundred and seventy years before Brenner, in Venezuela, on Earth. He was educated in Catholic schools, with pen and paper, in Spanish. Brenner couldn't even read Standard in cursive handwriting, and didn't know anyone who could.

Brenner was idly musing about this decoding problem when the computer paged him. He jumped up from the couch, furious with himself for being so lazy. He'd never bothered to log off Cavares' home console. As he answered the page, Nakamura's face came on the console. She looked unhappy.

"We've finished, Chief Brenner."

"Thank you, Nakamura-san. What did you find?"

"There were some opium poppies and marijuana, all immature, in one of the other rooms. Not the iris room."

"I want them out of there. I don't care what people grow in their own apartments, but I want no dangerous plants in the common gardens!" Even as he said it, Brenner thought of the disturbing iris. Later he might concern himself with private plants, as well.

"Yes, Chief. That's very generous. The owners were afraid you'd want them destroyed immediately."

"Not at the moment. So there was nothing at all unusual in the iris garden?"

"Well, nothing to concern you about." She herself looked concerned. "It's just that—well, never mind. I'll take that up with Endo-san, he'll know what to do."

"Who is Endo-san? And what's the problem?"

"He's a waterworks engineer for the colony. But he's also a master of the Iris Zen. The mother iris in the garden is his. She has some whitened spots on her leaves. I don't know whether she's sick, or maybe just getting old."

Brenner blinked several times trying to parse this. Damned obscure Kamikaze-jin. If Nakamura-san was the horticulture expert, how could she *not* know if a flower was getting old? "Well, thank you again, Nakamura-san. If Endo-san is the expert, I'll take this up directly with him."

"Ah, yes!" she said, obviously relieved. She bowed and blanked out.

Brenner almost gave up on the Zen master, when he finally answered after three minutes paging, with a quiet smile and a bow. Brenner had rarely seen this guy before, a placid bald man of indeterminate mature years.

"What may I do for you, Deputy Brenner?"

"I have some questions for you about irises and the Iris Zen. May I come to your quarters immediately?"

"Oh, no!" said Endo, too quickly. "No, I'll come to you in Cavares' quarters." And he blanked out.

Endo was not placid by the time he reached Cavares' apartment, five minutes later. He must have run, as his own place was almost a mile away at the ship's opposite extreme.

"Chief Brenner," he panted, "I've only just heard about my student. I've been deep in meditation."

"Please have a seat, Endo-san. What can you—"

"No, please, I have to check the iris first." With this, Endo bounded into the bedroom, and shut the door behind him. Brenner knocked a few times, but didn't go in. He had no idea what was going on with irises, but whatever it was didn't look healthy. After ten minutes, Endo returned to the living room, looking relieved. He sat at the computer table, where Brenner waited, tapping his fingers.

"Endo-san, what's going on?"

"I'm not sure. But Cavares-san's iris is well."

"According to Nakamura-san, your, uh, 'mother-iris' isn't well."

Endo-san nodded, studying his fingers. "Yes, she is unwell. Cavares-san was trying to help find out why. He had an amazing natural gift for the Iris Zen."

"Tell me about the flower."

"What do you want to know?"

"What do I need to know?"

"Well, first of all, it isn't really a flower. In fact, by Earth standards, it may not really be a plant. Or rather, of course, it *is* a plant. It needs water and nutrients for its roots, and carries out photosynthesis of a sort—"

"I'm familiar with plants, Sensei," Brenner prodded, irritably.

"Yes, so sorry. But the iris isn't just a plant, it's more of a pet, or perhaps a friend. They are most loyal and reliable—"

"Why isn't it a flower?"

"Well, it's more like the iris' head. I suppose it is a flower, in that it is also a sexual organ, but its purpose isn't only reproduction." Endo caught Brenner's deepening scowl, and hurried on. "The head lasts the entire life span of the iris. It's the 'brain' of the iris' nervous system, and the pseudo-stamens are its means of communication. If you 'picked' an iris, it would die."

Brenner's eyes widened as this sunk in. "You mean these are literally pets? Able to communicate to a certain degree, like a dog?"

Endo sighed in relief, that Brenner was finally understanding him. "Yes, but communication is most difficult. They seem to respond to light and sound and scent, but can only respond by generating scent."

"That must make for some rather limited conversations."

"We of the Iris Zen use our friends for biofeedback, to aid us in achieving the right outlook." Brenner started looking irritable again, so Endo explained, "When we are balanced and content and ready, as we strive to be at all times when awake, the iris gives off a harmonious, energizing scent. When we are in emotional turmoil, the iris responds with a lulling scent. Once we've become friends and practiced together a while, at least. Most students of the iris keep their iris away from other people, so that communication isn't muddied.''

"How does the iris sense that someone is in emotional turmoil?"

"Body odor. Since they rely on scent to communicate, that is what they respond to most readily."

"But the 'mother iris'—she's kept in a common garden. What is a 'mother iris', anyway?"

"The mother iris has been in my family for five generations. We call her that to honor her, as our personal irises are her offspring. I inherited her, but she doesn't like to live alone. Besides, with her centuries of practice, she can distinguish people without isolation."

"She's the best at communication?"

"Yes, such as it is. But in regard to this latest problem, I have been unable to understand. Only that she is perhaps sad, and her leaves show she is unwell. I spoke yesterday to Cavares-san about perhaps helping me—"

"And this morning Cavares went and had a little chat with the iris, and now he's dead."

"But she cannot kill! She can only generate a scent."

"And all of the other irises are healthy?"

"Actually, most of the irises in her garden are ailing. Not all, but most. None of the younger ones there have trained with humans, though. It would take months in isolation to begin with them."

"And then they would have nothing to say, because it's something in the common garden that is making them ill."

"Exactly."

"Why did Cavares go at night?"

"Not night. Before dawn. That's when she's preparing for the business of the day, and is wakeful and attentive. And no one else would be in the garden to confuse things."

"And all the other plants in the garden are healthy," Brenner mused aloud. Abruptly, he paged Gonzales on the computer. It was now late afternoon, and Gonzales looked rested.

"Chief Gonzales, sorry to trouble you again, but are you aware of any problems or any changes in the public gardens on this trip?"

She considered, then shrugged. "Just routine."

Brenner frowned. His assumptions had tripped him up enough for one day. "What's 'routine'?"

"Well, all of our standard food gardens are doing fine. There are the expected casualties among the Kamikaze crops."

"Why 'expected'?"

"Some plants won't adapt to the simulated Green Sands sunlight we use in the Kamikaze gardens."

"It seemed no different to me than that used in the algae Vat Rooms."

"Green Sands isn't much different from Earth normal, but Kamikaze sunlight is slightly redder."

Brenner thanked her and blanked out. Endo-san nodded thoughtfully, and said, "The grow-lights in our apartments were brought from Kamikaze."

"Can you communicate with the mother iris in daylight?"

"Yes. It will be weaker, but yes."

"Good. Go down there and get everyone out, including yourself. I'll meet you outside the forward door."

When Brenner rejoined Endo at the garden, he was carrying an oxygen-supplied gas mask and a knife hidden in his boot. He affixed an official DO NOT ENTER sign on the transparent door, and donned the gas mask. "Go ahead, please, Endo-san. I'll watch from here." When Endo's back was turned, Brenner set his gun to a minimum stun.

At first, Endo lay supine right in front of the door, more than a hundred feet from the mother iris. After about ten minutes of this, he rose deliberately, as though the motion was part of an excruciatingly slow-motion dance. He walked gracefully to the iris, knelt, and astonished Brenner by bowing his forehead to the ground.

Rising, Endo stood face-to-face with the giant bloom, eyes closed, serene face tilted back. Several times he raised his arms to shoulder height, and returned them to his sides, obviously breathing deeply.

Amidst all this studied grace, Endo suddenly stumbled backward, looking surprised and worried. He seemed to rally himself and stood up to the iris again, only to fall back again.

Brenner pushed into the room. "Out, Endo! Now!"

"Not quite yet." He closed his eyes and stood up to the plant once more. This time he stumbled back until he tripped into a bank of honeyvine. He ran for the door, which Brenner promptly closed behind him.

Brenner shook the wild-eyed Kamikaze-jin, until his shaking subsided a little.

"Fear," he said, gasping. "She said 'fear.' "

Just as Brenner thought. Scent, direct to the hindbrain, saying, "fear." And Cavares, a natural sensitive, but still a novice at Iris Zen, didn't have the discipline necessary to keep his conscious mind under control.

The corridor was empty. Regretfully, Brenner applied his stun gun directly to Endo's head. He double-checked his oxygen mask and went back into the garden, and, with his knife, picked all the beautiful iris blossoms.

The mother iris would never teach others the word "fear."

LOST LAMB

by Barbara Delaplace

Barbara Delaplace is a Canadian writer who burst upon the science fiction scene during the past year, with more than a dozen insightful and incisive short stories already sold.

A private eye has been hired to find a runaway girl who is currently living and working on a pleasure planet. When he gets there he finds that she has been killed. The only clues, found at the scene of the crime, are an infrared flashlight, half of a broken whiskey bottle, and a rag doll from Earth.

You can have her killed in any manner you want. Solve it.

"Mrs. Waterston, why do you want to hire *me* to find your daughter? You'd be much better off hiring a private investigator who lives on Lotus and is familiar with the situation there. And they'd undoubtedly be less expensive."

The fashionably-dressed woman sitting in the client's chair didn't seem fazed. "Money is no object, Mr. Grey. I'll spend whatever I must in order to find Mary. And I've done some investigating of my own. I've seen the media shows about you."

Not again, I groaned inwardly. "Jackson Grey, 22nd Century Holmes does it again!" the news anchor would beam as the teaser played across the screen. And another group of worried, desperate, or just plain crazy people would show up in my waiting room, anxious for me to find their brothers, their wives, their children, their dreams.

"You're regarded as one of the best in the field, Mr. Grey. Your success rate is unparalleled."

No point in lying. "That's because I pick my targets. I choose the cases with the best chance of success."

"And you don't think this particular case has much of a chance?" She looked steadily at me, but I noticed the whitened knuckles of her expensively manicured hand. I paused a moment to consider my words.

"No. Simply that you'd have a better chance with someone else, someone who knows the planet."

"Then hire whomever you need on Lotus when you get there. I'll pay for it. I want my daughter back, no matter what it costs." She named a *very* sizable sum. "Plus expenses, of course."

I sighed. "All right, Mrs. Waterston, I'll see what I can do."

"Now, you'll be needing a holo of Mary, so I brought a copy of the most recent one I have. It was taken about a year ago, before—" She stopped abruptly, biting her lip, and handed me the holo.

I activated it and the pretty girl in the picture smiled as she combed her long hair. Her blue eyes were guileless and her chestnut hair gleamed in the sun; a cobweb-hunter—the latest fashionable rarity for the wealthy—nestled contentedly in her lap. I finished the sentence gently. "Before the two of you quarreled and she left home?"

A pause, and then she answered, "Yes. I suppose it happens with all parents and children, knowing when to let go. I should never have allowed the situation to come to an open quarrel."

"It's not easy being a parent, to know exactly the right thing to do. Now," I continued briskly, "I'll contact the authorities when I arrive on Lotus and see what they can suggest." *Assuming they decide they want to help the media glamour boy,* I thought wryly. Sometimes they decide they'd rather watch the glamour boy fall on his face.

"Must you involve the police? I'd much rather this was kept private. I dislike airing family troubles in public."

"I'm afraid I have no choice. For one thing, it's a matter of professional courtesy. For another, I've got no official standing on the planet, so I have to cooperate with them if I want them to cooperate with me. Now, if you can leave your contact number, so I can reach you quickly when I have any news. . . ."

I don't much like traveling in space, even though I have a comfortable yacht. It gives me too much time to think, and as the years have passed, I've found I have too much I'd rather not think about.

And this case looked full of pitfalls. It wasn't just that the political situation on pleasure planets was tricky—think of a town that depends solely on tourism and you have the basic idea: bad PR is *not* welcome. But runaways were tricky, too. Too much family history behind them that an investigator like me could never know. Too many hidden wounds—though the scars were there, if you knew how to look. I knew how, and after so many years in the business, I wish to hell I didn't. I'd sleep better.

Well, one way to avoid thinking during a trip was to keep busy. I contacted the Lotus authorities via the spacenet, where I was introduced to the police in the person of one Lieutenant Pierre Marchand, a sour-faced, twenty-year man. After a certain amount of beating our chests at each other, I got a little grudging cooperation. He grumbled—why didn't Mrs. Waterston contact *them,* for expletive's sake?— but he agreed to download a scan of Mary's holo and check their files to see if it matched anybody already in their files.

A few hours later he called me back. "I found your missing person, Grey. She works in one of the pleasure domes— the ones that specialize in giving the customers *just* what they want. Or think they want. Calls herself Sweet Samantha. The names these domers go in for." He rolled his eyes.

"In show business image is everything, I hear. You sure tracked her down quickly."

Every employee on the planet was registered—generally the case with corporate-owned planets—and she'd started working for them about a year ago. There were no black marks on her record, or at least none the local authorities were willing to share with a virtual stranger. I thanked Marchand and told him I'd be in touch once I'd arrived on Lotus.

I decided I'd put in a full day's work, so I took a no-dream pill and turned in.

The next morning I landed. After I finished dealing with all the official trivia involved in arrival, I took a shuttle to a hotel near the dome where Mary, or rather Samantha, worked. I got a comfortable suite (important) with a terminal and access to the network (even more important), and put in a call to Marchand. I was connected immediately. He didn't seem unhappy to see me, a distinct change from our previous discussions.

"I'm glad you called, Grey. Early this morning one of the alleykids found the body of a woman back of one of the arcades. Dead a couple of days. We identified her as Samantha, and we need to get in touch with the next of kin. You have a contact address for—her mother, was it?"

People in my line of work like to say you get used to dealing with death, that you get used to breaking the bad news to the family. They're lying. It doesn't get easier, and lately I'd been wondering if I could take it much longer. Looking at Marchand's colorless face, I decided I could, at least one more time. Mrs. Waterston shouldn't have to hear about her daughter's death from a hard case like him.

"Yeah, I've got one. Why don't you let me look after telling her? Save you the trouble."

Relief brightened his features. "Okay—and thanks."

I took advantage of the situation to see if I could get some details. "What happened to her?"

"The crime scene analysis crew says she was killed by a bolt from a force-pulse rifle. Probably some jealous John; that's what it usually is."

"I'd like to see the body."

"If you mean at the crime scene, it's too late. The team finished up hours ago. Can't leave bodies lying around—the corporation doesn't like it. Bad for business." He grimaced.

"I can imagine. I'd still like to look at the body, and see the holos."

"You'd like a lot, friend."

Pleasure planet politics . . . I sighed. "Is it going to be a problem? I'd like to be able to report back to my client that everything possible's being done to find her daughter's murderer."

There was a long pause. "I'll give you access. But don't try to tell us how to do our jobs."

Which probably meant they had some formula for handling such deaths that involved minimum wave-making; most places like Lotus do. I remembered the happy, innocent girl in the holo; she deserved better than to have her death swept conveniently under the carpet. I decided to go along with it for now. Hell, what choice did I have? "Agreed."

* * *

I could feel a dreadful, familiar weight come down on my shoulders as I reluctantly punched in Mrs. Waterston's contact address. When people disappear and I'm hired, it's nearly always because someone's worried about them. Which means that whenever I find a body instead, I'm going to have to go back to my clients and tell them. Watch the hope in their faces brighten when they first see me, then watch it extinguish itself like a blown-out candle. See the anguish fill their faces instead.

I tried to be as gentle as I could.

"Dead?" Her eyes stayed steady but her jaw muscles jumped. "But I . . ." Her voice trembled and she stopped. She stared fixedly at some point past my shoulder. There was a long pause.

I was at a loss. What *do* you tell someone who expected you to help? Jackson Grey, 22nd Century Sherlock Holmes, does it again. I swallowed. "I'm sorry for your loss, Mrs. Waterston. I know how much you cared about your daughter. She looked like a very lovable young woman."

Her eyes refocused on me. "She *was* . . ." Her voice broke again and she looked away from the screen.

I paused again. Damn it, what could I say? Perhaps it would help if . . . "Would you like me to make arrangements to send the . . . to send her home to you?"

She seemed to regain her self-control. "That's very gracious of you, Mr. Grey. But no, thank you. I'll come to Lotus." There was a long pause, and then, so softly I could barely hear her, she said, "I wish we hadn't quarreled." The connection went blank.

I suppose viewing a crime scene holo isn't as bad as seeing the real thing—at least you don't have to worry about smells—but it's still not my favorite occupation. Marchand didn't bother accompanying me, but he did go so far as to call the imaging room and ask a tech to set things up. By the time I'd found my way through the tangle of corridors, the high-detail projection was completely built up and I could begin studying it right away.

Sweet Samantha lay crumpled on the wet pavement of the alley. She'd changed a lot from Mary, the innocent creature brushing her hair in a year-old portrait. A bronze lace unitard revealed more than it concealed; mirror lacquer gleamed on her finger and toe-nails; a boldly painted face-pattern helped minimize the mark of the force bolt that had crushed one temple.

There wasn't much in the way of promising clues around the body, just the usual trash you'd find in any alley: a broken whiskey bottle, flexi-cans with traces of food, an old rag doll, a dead glow wand. "Any of this stuff turn out to mean anything?" I asked the tech.

"She brought that whiskey bottle—we found her prints on it, and the autopsy showed she'd been drinking. And if you look over there, you'll see an infrared flashlight."

I glanced around and saw it, a slim metal tube with a clip-on bracket. "Learn anything useful from it?"

"No prints, no skin traces. Whoever handled it wore gloves; it shouldn't be that clean with normal handling."

The conclusion was obvious. "So the killer dropped it? Wonder why he was carrying it in the first place?"

The tech shrugged. "It gets pretty foggy at night here. Maybe using it to help find his way around."

"Somebody wearing IR goggles'd look pretty conspicuous, wouldn't he?"

"On *Lotus?*" He stared at me, surprised, then realized. "Oh, I see, you're from off-planet. Believe me, on Lotus anyone could wear *anything*. The corporation could care less. Got to keep the tourists happy, you know."

"So I've heard. What else did you get?"

The tech's eyes shifted away from mine and he was suddenly busy with a compu-pad.

"Look, did you get anything more from the scene?" By now there ought to been enough scans, tracings, and analyses to pinpoint exactly what she'd been doing and who she was doing it with before she was killed.

"Ah . . . well, nothing out of the ordinary. It looks like the murderer shot her and left. We figure it's a jealousy killing."

Politics again.

I sighed. "Well, thanks for your help. Here's my hotel number. If you run into anything interesting, I'd appreciate it if you'd call me."

The tech barely nodded to me, and I left.

* * *

I stopped back at my hotel for directions to The Elysium, the pleasure dome where Samantha had worked. Maybe someone there could tell me something useful.

Entertainments on Lotus were as varied as human ingenuity could contrive. Depending on your chosen form of relaxant, you could see the very latest in live stage productions, play your favorite sport with top professionals coaching you, or gamble away your wealth in a huge variety of games of chance. You could meditate amidst peaceful gardens planted with exotic vegetations from a hundred worlds; hear musicians perform in a myriad of styles. Or, if you preferred, you could find heaven and hell in the newest chemical analogues.

But Samantha had worked at a sensuarium—that's how The Elysium billed itself. "It sounds classier that way," one of the domers told me, a statuesque woman with her black hair sculpted into flower shapes. "But let's face it, it's still a pleasure dome. An outfit like this," she indicated her almost transparent black chiffon robe with a wave of her hand, "was designed with one thing in mind." She stretched luxuriously among the cushions of the sunken lounge we occupied.

"That's it, Diana, show it off," sneered another woman who billed herself as The Tigress, and wore a skin-paint job to match her name. As far as I could tell, the paint was all she was wearing. She turned to me and her face lost its sneer, became saddened. "I can't believe anyone would want to harm her. Sam was one of the sweetest people I've ever met." Despite the elaborate makeup, I could see her eyes were red-rimmed.

A well-muscled blond man wearing a scanty metallic loincloth put his arm around her, cuddled her. "We're all kind of shook up about it," he told me. "I mean, why her? Everyone liked her."

I said, "The police figure it was some jealous customer."

There was a chorus of disbelief. "No. The clients were crazy about her, wanted to do anything she asked," said the man. "She was the last person I'd expect to have that kind of hassle."

"So she didn't have any problems with anyone in the dome?

"Not among us. Jimmy's right about that," said Diana. "But she had some arguments with the Dragon Lady." The others snickered at the dome manager's nickname. "Usually after she'd had too much to drink."

I remembered the whiskey bottle in the alley. "Samantha had a drinking problem?"

Jimmy glanced at me. "She drank to get her mind off work. Wouldn't you? This ain't paradise, no matter what those come-ons out there say. We work bloody hard for what they pay us." The other two nodded. And abruptly the aura of glamour, the sophistication and exotic promise each wore like a garment, dropped away and I saw three people made cynical by their profession, tired and careworn because they'd lost a friend they loved.

It made me uncomfortable. I got back to business. "So why did she quarrel with the Dragon Lady?"

The Tigress replied, "Sam wanted to buy out her contract, and the Dragon Lady wouldn't go for it—said she was too valuable an employee to lose."

"I *thought* I heard my name," said a deep, harsh voice. The dome manager, a beautifully-gowned woman of indeterminate years and commanding presence, had come over to our group. "I can see these artistes of the sensual don't appeal to you, sir. Allow me to select some others more to your taste."

"I'm not interested in making a selection, thank you."

"Then I'll have to ask you to leave. After all, time *is* money. And our artistes have many demands on their time." She glanced at the others, who took the hint and left.

"Madam—" I paused.

"You may address me as Madam Velvet."

That made me smile. "Who rules with an iron fist?"

"This is first and foremost a business, Mr. . . ?" It was her turn to pause.

"Jackson Grey."

"Ah, yes, I've heard of you, Mr. Grey. Well, this is a business, and, of course, one expects one's employees to work for their money, not spend valuable time chatting."

"You're not interested in finding out who murdered one of your valuable employees?"

"The police won't find out who killed her. They never do," she said with some resignation.

"You aren't by any chance counting on that, are you?"

"In what way, Mr. Grey?"

"I understand Sam wanted out of her contract here. Could

you have arranged to have her threatened, just to show her
how futile that wish was? A demonstration that got out of
hand?''

''Don't be ridiculous. Of course I didn't want to lose
her—she was very popular with the clients. But why would
I have her threatened? To be very blunt, Mr. Grey, it's not
worth my trouble. There's always someone out there—'' she
gestured gracefully at the street—''who'll do anything to
become a domer. She wasn't irreplaceable. I have two
promising new trainees already.'' My face must have reflected my thoughts. ''I repeat, Mr. Grey, this is a business.
Furthermore, our clients trust us to be discreet. They don't
expect to find themselves on the major newscasts, even pe-
ripherally, as the result of the activities of someone like
you. So you understand why I'm asking you to leave.'' She
glanced at a couple of burly security guards dressed in formal evening clothes who were casually loitering nearby.

''I get the message, Madam.'' I stood up and started toward the entry hall, then turned back and stared into her
eyes. ''Here's another message: *I'm* going to find out what
happened to Sweet Samantha.''

She looked coldly at me. ''Do it without involving my
establishment, Mr. Grey.'' One of the guards seized my arm
and firmly escorted me outside. The door shield shimmered
as he reentered the dome and I was left watching the moire
patterns of the force field re-form.

''She's a smooth one, isn't she?'' My reverie was interrupted by a casually dressed man leaning against an ornamental ceramic pillar outside the dome.

''Who is?'' I asked.

''The Dragon Lady. She had you thrown out, right?''

''Right. You sound like you know her pretty well.''

He smiled lightly. ''Yep. You might say she's the reason
I'm in business. Though I'll bet she doesn't know my
name.''

''Which is—?''

''Damien Blocker, at your service.'' He bowed slightly.

I replied in kind. ''I'm Jackson Grey. And I offended the
Dragon Lady by asking questions about a woman who
worked there until she was killed a couple of days ago.''

''Samantha.'' His smile disappeared and his face was
suddenly haggard.

I nodded. "You knew her?"

"Very well. We worked together." He eyed me. "No, it had nothing to do with her job at the dome, at least not the way you're thinking. You want to hear all about it, of course."

I found myself liking him. "Of course. Is there someplace we can get something to eat while we talk?"

Damien was a street worker, trying to help the alleykids work their way up and out of the alleys. And Samantha had worked with him. He explained over sandwiches and cups of steaming jamoka as we sat in a tiny, glass-walled cafe.

"You have to understand, for most of these kids becoming a domer at a place like The Elysium is *the* dream. The domes mean shelter, food, safety from the streets, money. They don't think about what prostitution costs—what it does to their bodies, their spirits, their souls. All they care about is getting off the streets. You don't need connections or talent, or even good looks . . . just youth. And no questions are ever asked about your background."

He stared down at his cup. "Sam was wonderful at working with alleykids. She could get them to listen, since she was a domer. She knew exactly how their minds worked." He fell silent.

"Suppose someone from The Elysium killed her because of what you two were doing, as a warning to back off?"

He shrugged. "I doubt it. They don't give a damn about street workers like me. We're too small. The Elysium brings in big money for Lotus. It's part of the established business structure. The corporation doesn't care about the cost to the spirit, only profits." Damien looked bitter.

I swallowed another bite of my sandwich. "Were you with her the night she was killed?"

He stared out the window wall at the street's lights, glowing softly in the evening fog. "We had dinner together, but she was working the midnight shift at the dome, so she had to leave after that."

"She was fine when she left? Not acting worried or anything? Her friends at the dome said she was having fights with the Dragon Lady."

"She was?" His face brightened. He noticed I was watching him closely, and his expression became guarded. "No, she was fine."

He was hiding something, it was obvious. I decided to let him stew over it for a bit, told him how to reach me if he wanted to talk, and left.

When I got back to my hotel, there was a message from Mrs. Waterston waiting. She'd checked in and wanted to see me, so I headed for the lift tube and went up to her level.

The door shield dissolved and revealed her, pale from fatigue but in control of herself. "Thank you for coming, Mr. Grey. Do come in."

She'd obviously arrived not long before, for a half-unpacked suitcase hovered by the closet, its tiny suspensor lights glowing. But there were several holos of her daughter already placed around the suite, all of them activated, and I spent a few moments wandering from one to the other. Mary as a tanned, towheaded child splashing at the ocean's edge. Older, and astride a prancing Arabian horse, beaming proudly while holding a silver cup. Older still, in formal dress and sitting at a harp, her fingers moving over the strings. One with her mother, posed behind an array of shining trophies, each topped with a sculpted figure or two posed in the act of aiming a weapon. Trophies for target shooting, Mrs. Waterston told me; Mary was a crack shot.

"She was a wonderful daughter. She always tried so hard to make us proud of her. And, of course, when my husband died—Mary was eight then—she was so worried about me. My goodness, sometimes I felt like I was the daughter." She stopped and looked away. "I'm going to take Mary home for burial at our church."

It seemed that both mother and daughter had long been active in church affairs. Or were, until they quarreled. "She was missed so much by the members of the congregation. They prayed hard for her, and for me." Mrs. Waterston paused for a long moment, then said, "Now she's coming home to rest where she belongs." She toyed with one of the holos for a moment, then put it down.

It seemed a very long road from being involved in the local church to becoming a domer. I knew it was tactless but couldn't stop myself asking. "Mrs. Waterston, how do you think Mary came to be working in a . . . working on Lotus?"

Color rose in her cheeks. When she looked at me there

was a flash of anger in her eyes, quickly quenched, and she answered firmly, "I have no idea. That's a closed chapter of Mary's life. The important thing is that I'm taking her away from this indecent place and giving her a proper burial." She blinked hard, and turned back to pick up the holo again.

I couldn't think of anything to say in reply, and finally I left her there, looking sadly at the holo she was holding.

Late the next morning my terminal awakened me from a restless sleep (I'd forgotten to bring my no-dream pills from my yacht) by announcing a call. It was The Tigress—*sans* skin-paint—wondering if I knew anything about plans for a funeral for Sam. "We'd like a chance to say good-bye to her."

I replied, "Her mother told me she's planning to take the body home with her." Her face fell. Remembering Mrs. Waterston's reactions last night, I wondered if I should say any more, but there was such disappointment on The Tigress' face. . . . Surely she wouldn't mind. After all, the domers had been Sam's friends. "But her mother, Mrs. Waterston, is staying at this hotel—perhaps you could call her and express your sympathy."

She brightened. "Thanks. I'll get the others and we'll do that."

I'd barely finished in the 'fresher when my terminal beeped again at me. This time it was an exhausted-looking Damien saying he wanted to stop by for a chat. Something was obviously gnawing at him, so I told him he could come over right away.

"Two minutes. I'm down in the lobby."

"Sounds good." And I barely had time to get my tunic and tights on when the door signaled.

"So what's on your mind?" I asked him once we'd sat down and the chairs had adjusted to our shapes.

"I was just wondering if you'd discovered anything new," he said.

"Nothing of much use."

"And the police aren't helping much, are they?" he said flatly, his mouth tightening.

"No, they aren't. Is that usual?"

"When it's a dead domer? Of course it is. Hookers don't

matter. Not the way respectable people do. After all, they're available to anyone who—'' He stopped abruptly.

So that was it. "She mattered to you, didn't she?"

He glanced sharply at me. "Of course she did. I told you, I knew her very well."

"So well you'd come to love her."

He straightened up and looked me in the eye. "Yes. She wasn't like the other domers. She cared about people."

I said gently, "From what I saw at The Elysium, some of those 'other domers' cared about Sam, too."

"She shouldn't have had to work there. I could've supported both of us. But she said she wasn't going to quit."

"But I understand from her friends that she *wanted* to quit. She was trying to buy out her contract, but the dome wouldn't sell. That's what her fights with the Dragon Lady were all about."

He looked at me, horrified. "They were? But . . . she should have told me that. Then I'd never have—'' He stopped again.

"You'd never have what? Never have quarreled with her yourself? Never have told her she could choose between the dome and you?"

"I didn't mean to start a fight about it. I just wanted us to be happy," he said defensively.

"And to be happy, you had to have her all to yourself. You couldn't stand the thought of sharing her body with anyone else. That's what you told her that night, wasn't it?"

"No! It wasn't like that!" He was on his feet, fists clenched.

"Sure it was, Damien. It got out of hand, happened so easily."

"No!" he shouted, tears in his eyes. "I loved her. I'd never hurt her. But she said she couldn't—oh, God, she said *couldn't* quit. I thought that meant she *wouldn't* quit."

"So you killed her. Then no one else could ever have her."

"I didn't kill her!" he cried. "I *loved* her. Don't you know what that means? I wanted her to be happy. That was the most important thing of all. I told her if working at the dome was what she wanted, well, at least we could still be together and I'd know she was doing what she wanted.'' He looked at me, tears trickling down his cheeks, and his expression hardened. "But now you tell me it *wasn't* what she wanted. You bastard. I'll have to live with knowing that, now. Oh, Sam . . .'' He started to cry.

The famous investigator. I hated my job and what it uncovered.

That pretty much set the pattern for the rest of the day. I took the lift tube to Mrs. Waterston's level, figuring I should check in with her. The sound of angry voices reached me as soon as I stepped out, and I hurried down the hall.

The Tigress, holding a carefully-wrapped package, and her fellow domers Diana and Jimmy—all of them in street clothes—were standing by the door shield of Mrs. Waterston's suite. Her image glowed on the sentry panel, and her cold tones came clearly through the speaker.

"No, you are *not* welcome to leave *anything* with me to take to the funeral. I want nothing to do with you. And if Mary had been in her right mind, she would *never* have gotten involved with street scum like you. She must have been on some kind of drug."

Jimmy glanced at me, dismayed, and The Tigress blinked back tears. Diana spoke up. "Sam was one of—''

"Her name was *Mary!*'' Mrs. Waterston raised her voice. The display flickered out.

The three were deeply hurt. Diana turned to me. "Sam never judged anyone, she just tried to help them. How could someone like that—'' she indicated the monitor with a jerk of her head—"be her mother?''

Jimmy said, "I remember Sam once told me about her childhood. She said she always felt like she had to be perfect. Nothing she did was ever good enough. No wonder she left home.'' He turned and spoke to the others, his voice sardonic. "Come on, fellow scum, we'd better go back to where we belong.'' They went down the hall to the lift tube. I decided this wasn't the best time to talk to Mrs. Waterston, and followed them to the lift.

With a sense that it was going to be futile, I called Lt. Marchand and asked if there had been any progress on finding the killer. He fell short of even my minimal expectations. "No, we've made no further progress in solving the case. We're going to put it down as an unsolved homicide.''

"What? That girl's only been dead a few days and you're giving up *already?*''

Marchand looked dogged. "Grey, this is just another dead domer. We get them all the time."

"And you don't give a damn about them. Just another domer. Mary was a *real* woman, with friends who cared about her and a mother who's been devastated by her death. How the hell can you sit there and tell me you've given up on the case?"

Suddenly he flared at me. "Look, pal, you may not believe this, but I used to care. I'd bust my tail trying to find who murdered these folks. They deserved justice even if they weren't rich and even if they were domers. I worked lots of overtime, came in on my days off. I'm a goddamned good detective. Sometimes I'd find out who'd done it. You know what? It didn't make a bit of difference. The company didn't want to spend the time and money to get the cases to court. The killers were street people and it wasn't worth the effort. Or they were visitors from off-planet, and they didn't want bad publicity for Lotus. Might affect business. The company told me I was working too hard, costing them too much overtime and travel and lab expenses in my quote, overzealous prosecution of my duties, unquote." He bit off a curse. "I got the message. Now I just do my job. Nobody wants to prosecute, so that's fine with me."

Nobody wants to—? "But her mother wants the murderer found."

"If she does, she didn't say anything about it to me when she came here to claim the body. I told her it was unlikely we'd solve the case and she said she understood. She told me she just wanted to put the whole thing behind her."

I was astonished. But then I remembered how close Mrs. Waterston and her daughter had been. I remembered how carefully she kept herself under control, not allowing me to see tears, always looking away. Maybe it *was* too much for her.

I lay on my bed, looking at the holo Mrs. Waterston had given me. Poor Mary—she didn't die unmourned, but it looked as though she would died unavenged. The ones who cared didn't have the power to force a thorough investigation, and those who had the power didn't care.

I thought about the crime scene holo. Was there *anything* there that could help? The whiskey bottle was Mary's. The IR flashlight belonged to the murderer. Let's see, what else was there? A glow wand, flexi-cans, a rag doll. . . . Wait a moment . . . a rag doll? That wasn't the sort of thing that interested an alleykid. I turned the holo over in my hands. I thought of another holo—and suddenly I knew who'd killed Sweet Samantha, née Mary Waterston.

"Hello, Mrs. Waterston. I've come to give back the holo—I guess it slipped my mind up until now." I smiled, winningly I hoped, at the sentry panel by the door shield.

She sounded a little startled. "Oh . . . yes . . . thank you. Come in." The door shield dissolved and I entered.

She was preparing to leave. The suitcase was open again, and most of the holos of Mary that had added a personal note to the room had been packed.

"Here you are," I said, handing her the one I carried.

She took it and put it in the suitcase. "Thank you, Mr. Grey. I'm glad you're here. I wanted to tell you I don't need your services any longer. If you'll send me your bill. . . ."

I wasn't surprised at her words—they fit in with what I'd figured out. But I played along. "Don't you want to find out who killed your daughter?"

She replied, "The police tell me it was some common criminal, and they're unlikely to find whoever did it. And it doesn't really matter. She's dead, and nothing can bring her back to me. I appreciate all you've done, and I know you did the best you could to find her murderer. I guess whoever did it will have to face justice in a higher court."

"I guess you're right. Because you're going to get away with it."

Her jaw muscles tightened and her eyes darkened with fury. "*I'm* going to get away with it? How *dare* you! I didn't kill Mary!"

"No, you didn't. Mary couldn't possible have been a domer, could she? She was too dutiful a daughter, too responsible. You killed what she'd become: Samantha the domer, the prostitute."

She looked at me coldly. "What kind of mother do you think I am? How could I kill *my own daughter?*"

"But she wasn't your daughter anymore really, was she? I overheard you say to her friends today that she must have been drugged—"

"Those filthy *creatures!* My daughter didn't belong with them! They don't deserve to be saved!"

Her vicious tone shouldn't have surprised me, I guess. "And to save Mary, you had to kill Samantha. That's how it was, wasn't it? The lost lamb had to be brought back to the flock at any cost."

"She wasn't my daughter anymore! I had to do somethi—" She stopped, realizing she'd betrayed herself.

"You knew exactly where Mary was all the time, didn't you? You came to Lotus before you hired me, and traced her to The Elysium. You followed her the night she was wandering the streets, drinking and trying to forget about her quarrel with her boyfriend. You knew all about the foggy nights they have here, and were prepared for them, with that infrared flashlight you had mounted on the pulse-rifle. With IR goggles on, you could see her clearly to shoot her." I went over to the holo, the one with mother and daughter posing with all those trophies, the trophies with two figures on them for two-person team shooting. "Mary wasn't the only sharpshooter in the family, was she?"

Mrs. Waterston stirred. "We were one of the best teams in the country," she said softly.

"The rag doll—that was Mary's, of course."

"It was the only thing she took with her when she left home. She was sitting against a wall in an alley, hugging it and drinking from that bottle when I . . . when I. . . . I wanted it to be quick and painless. Just one instant, and I knew she'd be safe in God's arms, and no one could ever soil her again. . . ." Her voice trailed away and she hid her face in her hands.

I looked at her. Poor tormented woman. Her faith hadn't brought her comfort, and her pride brought her to murder.

She got away with it, all right. The authorities on Lotus wouldn't press charges. Not enough evidence, they said, and I suppose they were right. Force bolts don't leave anything behind, and she'd jettisoned the pulse-rifle on her way from Lotus to hire me.

It's time I got out of this business. When a mother kills her own daughter. . . .

Vengeance is mine, saith the Lord. I guess I'll have to trust in God for this one.

CAIN'S CURSE

by Jack Nimersheim

Jack Nimersheim, author of more than fifteen non-fiction books, appears here with his second professional science fiction story.

A human brings home a cute little monkeylike pet from another world. One day it goes berserk and attacks him, and he kills it. He is then brought to trial for the murder of a sentient being. He claims the animal was smart, a quick learner, but definitely not sentient.

Courtroom drama: was the pet sentient or not? If it was, was the human justified in killing it or not?

Justin Tyme, C.I. That's what the sign on the door says. Blame the name on my old man's flair for irony. The profession, Chronal Investigator, *I* chose—although I have a feeling Dear Old Dad's perverted sense of humor may have influenced my career path somewhat.

When I first broke into the biz, I had cards printed up that read: *"Tyme's the name; time's my game."* The banality of this phrase quickly wore thin, however, and I changed it to the equally insipid: *"You can't lose with Tyme on your side."* Such foolishness lasted a couple of years, during which I had ample opportunity—plenty of time, as it were—to amuse myself playing word games with my moniker. Clients didn't exactly line up outside my door in those early days.

The Quayle Case changed everything. But that's another tale, for another day. Let's just say that, with my reputation finally established, I discovered I no longer needed trite slogans to bring in the rubes.

Which brings me to Tanya Lodell.

To be honest, calling Tanya Lodell a "rube" is an affront to womanhood. Ruby would be more like it. The lady glittered like a fine gem—cut and polished and ready for display. She looked like a million bucks. My amateur's appraisal placed the value of the jewelry she wore to our first meeting at a comparable figure.

But I'm getting ahead of myself. The best way to unravel the unusual story of Tanya Lodell is to begin at the beginning. That requires a chronal jaunt of five centuries, a stroll in the park for a seasoned pro like me.

I arrived in Chicago at 8:30 a.m. on November 14, 2153. Morris phased me in precisely where and when I needed to be. I have to admit, the kid's a wizard at tweaking the tachyon stream; given his rates, he'd better be. Luckily, the cost of a time shift qualifies as a travel expense. As such, it's charged back against whatever client happens to be bankrolling my current excursion—in this case, Tanya Lodell.

Sandburg's City of Big Shoulders was almost exactly like I expected it to be. Brisk winds blew in from Lake Michigan. A slight dusting of snow covered the few patches of urban real estate not entombed by stone or concrete. A quick check of a passing indigene revealed that the lapel size I had stipulated to the replicator for my overcoat was about a half-inch too wide. An inaccuracy, to be sure, but one that wasn't noticeable enough to arouse suspicion. Other than this minor discrepancy, my appearance reflected contemporary standards flawlessly—all the way down to the close-cropped haircut with a short ponytail that my research indicated was popular among professionals of the mid-22nd century.

Such attention to detail is critical. The bureaucrats on the Chronal Commission keep close tabs on us working stiffs. Extensive and explicit regulations govern all sanctioned time shifts. The boys in Washington are ready and willing to slap a heavy fine on anyone who, either by accident or as the result of some careless oversight, introduces even minor anomalies into the historical record. A single, reckless moment has purchased more than one sloppy C.I. a one-way ticket to the poorhouse.

Confident that I passed muster, I relaxed my grip on the emergency override unit Morris had stashed inside my coat pocket. It didn't look like he'd have to jerk me back right

after interphase, a realization that pleased me no end. I'd
been down that road once before, and had the receipts from
four months of physical therapy to prove it.

With these immediate concerns taken care of, it was time
to get down to business. After all, Tanya Lodell wasn't
shelling out $750 a day plus expenses, for me to stand
around gawking like some wide-eyed tourist on a cut-rate
vacation junket.

A crisp, new copy of *The Chicago Tribune*, purchased
from a quaint corner newsstand on Lower Wacker Drive,
supplied all the information I needed to begin my investigation. According to its lead story, Peter Atkinson's trial
was scheduled to begin in the Federal courthouse at 9:00
that morning, relative time and date. Consulting a Chicago
city map, circa 2150, I located this building on Jackson
Boulevard, a mere two blocks east of my current position.
Morris had surpassed his own high standards. As I struck
out toward the rising sun, I decided such accuracy deserved
a small bonus—courtesy of Tanya Lodell's rather substantial
bank account, of course.

When is a courthouse not a courthouse?

That's easy: When it's a zoo.

This morning, the Richard Daley Federal Courthouse was
a zoo. The mandatory media mob was there, a pack of rav-
enous wolves caught up in a feeding frenzy. Their carrion?
A haggard-looking Peter Atkinson who, as I arrived, was
climbing out of a taxi that had just pulled up to the curb in
front of the courthouse steps.

"Do you have anything to say to our viewers, Mr. Atkinson?" said one, thrusting a minicam into Peter Atkinson's
face.

"Do you have anything to say to our listeners, Mr. Atkinson?" said another, thrusting a microphone into Peter
Atkinson's face.

"Do you have anything to say to our readers, Mr. Atkinson?" said a third, thrusting a tape recorder into Peter Atkinson's face.

Peter Atkinson said nothing—on advice of counsel, no
doubt.

Unfortunately, the counsel responsible for this advice—a
nattily dressed, high-priced Manhattan attorney named Alexander Dewey—suffered no such compunctions, and was

more than willing to placate the press with a long and loquacious statement about his latest judicial challenge. In the end, though, he, too, said nothing.

"My client has already proclaimed his innocence. Furthermore, we believe that the jury, twelve honorable citizens of this great city who, through no fault of their own, must suffer the inconvenience of this legal and political travesty, will have no choice but to exonerate him of all charges. And so . . ." And *blah, blah, blah*.

God, I hate lawyers! I hate lawyers almost as much as I distrust reporters. Or do I distrust lawyers and hate reporters? No matter. Watching members of my two least favorite professions feed off one another's vanities was something I could only handle in miniscule doses. Besides, if I expected to earn the rather exorbitant fee my client was paying me, I figured I'd better get to the courtroom before it was totally overrun by these selfsame journalistic carnivores.

That first morning, shortly after arriving at my office, Tanya Lodell removed a cracked and yellowing piece of paper from her purse. Unfolding it with great care, like a high priestess performing some sacred ritual, she explained how the fragile document had been passed down by her family, one generation to the next, father to son to daughter to son to whatever progeny existed at the time, for close to five centuries.

"This is the reason I'm here, Mr. Tyme," she said, gently placing the object of her reverence on my desk.

I found myself staring at another front page from another copy of *The Chicago Tribune*. This one was dated December 20, 2153, six weeks after my subsequent arrival in that city. Its headline, printed in 124-point Helvetica type, proclaimed: "Intergalactic Ghoul Guilty!"

"I'm afraid I don't understand, Ms. Lodell."

"It's *Mrs*. Lodell. I've kept my married name out of respect for my late husband. My maiden name is Atkinson. Does that ring a bell?"

It didn't, a fact which must have been obvious from the bewildered look on my face.

"If you read the story accompanying this headline, Mr. Tyme, you'll discover that the 'Intergalactic Ghoul' it refers to, Peter Atkinson, shares my original surname. Need I say more?"

"Only if you expect me to know what you're talking about. Who the hell is Peter Atkinson?"

"Peter Atkinson is . . . or *was* . . . a killer, Mr. Tyme, perhaps the most notorious killer in all of human history."

How odd, I thought, that the history books I had read neglected to mention him.

"Is that a fact?" was all I said.

"Indeed, it is, Mr. Tyme. And do you know why his crime was so heinous?" I could tell by the way she posed this question that it was purely rhetorical. "It's because Peter Atkinson did not commit your run-of-the-mill homicide, in either the legal or the literal sense of that word. You see, Peter Atkinson was the first man ever to be convicted of killing an extraterrestrial."

I began to suspect that Tanya Lodell, although quite alluring and obviously affluent, might also be about a dime short of a dollar, if you know what I mean. That history would simply overlook such an important event seemed dubious. Nevertheless, I decided to play along with her little charade a while longer. If nothing else, it promised to enliven what had, up until then, been a pretty slow week.

"Not the most ideal genealogy, I'll admit, but why worry about it now? That paper was printed a long time ago, Mrs. Lodell. An awful lot of water has passed under the bridge since then."

"Maybe for the rest of the world, Mr. Tyme. For my family, however, that water has been building up behind an emotional dam for nearly five centuries. I can assure you, it's grown quite fetid in that time."

"Don't you think you're being just a little melodramatic? I can understand how you might not be too thrilled with your somewhat unusual heritage. But why open the locks on that emotional dam now, to extend your own metaphor, five hundred years after the fact?"

For several seconds, Tanya Lodell merely stood still, staring down at the decaying newspaper on my desk. Her response, when it did finally come, was delivered in a soft, almost inaudible whisper.

"Tell me, Mr. Tyme, do you come from a large family?"

"I don't know that I've ever really thought about it. I only have one sister, but an awful lot of aunts, uncles, cousins, and other assorted relatives used to show up at family get-togethers. If you count all of them, yeah, I guess I'd have to say that the Tyme clan is pretty sizable.''

"The Atkinson family, a least that part of it descended directly from Peter Atkinson, isn't. It never has been.

"What few of us there are, however, tended to be very close to one another. And do you know why, Mr. Tyme? It's because we shared a common bond, one unique to anyone who could trace his or her ancestry back to Peter Atkinson.

"But this common bond also represents a collective curse. Our ancestor, after all, is the man who introduced murder to the universe—a Cosmic Cain, if you'll permit me the arrogance of a Biblical reference. His legacy, Cain's Curse, has tainted our bloodline ever since.''

Collective curses? Cosmic Cain? *Cain's Curse!* Inflation may just have raised Tanya Lodell's ten-cent deficit to a quarter. It was obvious from the sincerity in her voice, however, that *she* believed what she was saying.

"Let me see if I can guess where this is heading, Mrs. Lodell. You're about to tell me that you and the rest of your relatives have decided you want to exorcise the family ghost.''

"An excellent conjecture, Mr. Tyme, but not entirely correct. You see, until my brother's recent death, he and I shared the dubious honor of being the last living descendants of Peter Atkinson. As I told you, I'm a widow. My late husband left me financially secure enough that I feel no compulsion to alter this status. It's quite unlikely, therefore, that I'll ever have children of my own.

"I have no desire to go to my grave leaving the Atkinson bloodline tainted for all eternity. I need to know whether my ancestor was indeed the 'Intergalactic Ghoul' this headline claims he was. That, Mr. Tyme, is where you come in.''

I love a good mystery. This case provided a couple of doozies.

First, there was the matter of Atkinson's guilt or innocence. Based on the evidence Tanya Lodell had presented, the outcome of this one was almost preordained. Even more intriguing to me, however, was the larger mystery of Peter Atkinson, himself—a man I'd never heard of before his great-great-great-great-great-great-great granddaughter (give

or take a couple of *greats*) waltzed through my office doorway.

How could a significant slice of history like the one reported in that ancient edition of *The Chicago Tribune* simply
disappear from the historical records? Tanya Lodell had
provided me with the perfect excuse to answer this question—and pick up a rather substantial fee in the process.
Only a fool would walk away from such a golden opportunity.

Whatever else Mama Tyme's favorite son might be, he's
no fool. That's how I came to be in a Chicago courthouse,
in the closing weeks of 2153, observing the murder trial of
Peter Atkinson.

Have you ever watched a holovid courtroom drama? If
you have, the best advice I can give you is to forget everything you think you know about the inner workings of the
criminal justice system, based on this commercial trash.
Perry Mason and his fictional peers notwithstanding, a typical trial consists of little more than structured tedium, interrupted only by extended periods of organized redundancy.

Witnesses are called and recalled. Attorneys examine and
cross-examine. Self-proclaimed experts proselytize and
pontificate. Judges rule and overrule. And all the while,
twelve supposed peers of the defendant sit there and listen—
and listen and listen and listen. And, one can only hope,
learn. The whole process is extremely monotonous, an experience not unlike watching paint dry.

Given the nature of Peter Atkinson's crime, I started out
believing that this trial might deviate from the norm. Unfortunately, as is so often the case, reality fell noticeably
short of my expectations.

Atkinson didn't deny that he had killed the T'kai—a small,
monkeylike creature he'd brought back to Earth following a
recent tour of duty on Deneva IV. He did, however, dispute
the State's allegation that this deed amounted to murder.

In early press interviews, Atkinson claimed he acted in
self-defense, after the T'kai had attacked him first. A more
crucial legal argument, however, hinged upon Alexander
Dewey's assertion that the victim of his client's alleged crime
was nothing more than a primitive animal—a ''pet,'' to use
the term Dewey introduced into the proceedings during his
opening remarks.

Prosecuting attorney Bernard Truman, a political appointee with a predilection for ill-fitting gray suits and brown wing tips, offered an extremely terse and uninspired rebuttal. As anyone whose interest in world affairs extended beyond the funny pages and Saturday morning cartoons already knew, the State maintained that Atkinson's victim was much more than a pet. Rather, it proposed, the T'kai had been a sentient being. This fact, according to the prosecutor's office, justified handing down a murder indictment. In a dry, dispassionate voice, Truman merely reiterated the State's position, assuring the jury that he would prove it "beyond a shadow of a doubt" before the current proceedings were concluded.

Four weeks later, whatever legal rabbit Bernard Truman planned to pull out of his prosecutorial hat in order to demonstrate the T'kai's intelligence—and, by extension, establish Atkinson's culpability—remained a mystery. Instead, I'd been forced to endure the steady stream of peers, pundits, panderers, and assorted professional witnesses that inevitably rains down upon any trial promising extensive media exposure.

Some of these offered opinions and observations so spurious or obtuse, you were left wondering what possible purpose they served. Consider, for example, Atkinson's ninth-grade teacher, Ms. Thelma Finklemann, who the defense team tracked down in a Gainsville nursing home. Her entire testimony consisted of assuring the jury that, "Little Petey wouldn't harm a flea." Unfortunately, Ms. Finklemann diluted this refreshingly brief statement somewhat when, just before stepping down from the witness stand, she asked Alexander Dewey how soon the promised "consulting fees" would begin picking up the tab for her medical expenses.

Other witnesses were so off the wall that, even if they couldn't enlighten the court, they at least entertained. Topping this list were two brothers, Mike and Ike Quisling, a pair of self-proclaimed evangelical ministers from The First Church of Interstellar Deities. They attempted to bolster the prosecution's position by asserting that the deceased T'kai was actually an intergalactic harbinger who, according to their research, had been sent to Earth to extend Mankind an invitation to join The Universal Brotherhood, an ecumenical federation originally formed by several benevolent life forms from the Crab Nebula.

Alexander Dewey allowed this farce to continue right up to the point where Ike Quisling began reading off a list of planets currently belonging to that august organization. When Ike was halfway through the second page, he finally objected, citing irrelevance.

Bernard Truman responded by explaining how he'd been led to believe that the recondite clergymen possessed critical information regarding the mental capabilities of the T'kai. Had he suspected their true motives, Truman assured the court, they would never have been subpoenaed.

The judge eventually sustained Dewey's objection. Before doing so, however, she spent several minutes admonishing an extremely red-faced Bernard Truman for wasting the court's valuable time with such superficial testimony. (Right. As if every word spoken under oath prior to the Quislings' appearance deserved inclusion in a definitive study of due process.)

Unfortunately, diversions such as these were the exception. As a rule, the proceedings plodded along at a pace just slightly faster than that of an anemic snail.

Let me clarify something. People don't hire a C.I. to modify history.

Tanya Lodell understood this. She knew that, even if it were possible for me to clear her family name—and there was no guarantee I could—the only way to do so was through observation, not intervention.

That's because, when you get right down to it, a Chronal Investigator is little more than a professional voyeur. We get paid (and paid quite handsomely, I might add) to observe things. Like all true voyeurs, we live by the creed: "Look, but don't touch."

This being the case, you may be wondering what my comely client hoped to gain by hiring me.

In a word, perspective.

Truth, you see, is an ephemeral commodity. Contrary to the claims of most philosophers and theologians, it is not immutable. Like the arrow on a weather vane, truth can point in virtually any direction—its orientation, more often than not, determined by how the social and political winds are blowing at any given time.

Case in point: Crazy Horse was considered an ignorant savage and a ruthless killer, until several enlightened historians figured out that ultimate responsibility for the massacre of Custer's troops lay primarily with the general's own insatiable ego and incredible incompetence. In short order, Custer became a fop and Crazy Horse was declared a brilliant tactician.

The facts surrounding Little Big Horn had not changed, only the perspective from which this historic battle was interpreted. Tanya Lodell had enlisted my services to see whether or not similar revisions could be made to the legacy of Peter Atkinson.

A dim light filtered through the end of the tunnel midway through the trial's fifth week. That's when Alexander Dewey called Peter Atkinson to the stand to testify on his own behalf. If nothing else, Atkinson's testimony promised to contain facts bearing at least marginal relevance to the case at hand.

Dewey demonstrated why he was considered one of the country's preeminent defense attorneys with the very first question he posed, after his client was sworn in: "Tell me, Mr. Atkinson, just how did the pet you now stand accused of killing come into your possession?"

It was an effective opening gambit. For one thing, Dewey immediately reinforced his argument that the victim in the supposed crime was, indeed, a pet, rather than some sentient being. Second, his deliberate use of the word "possession" suggested ownership. More than anything else, the cagey defense attorney wanted the twelve men and women sitting in the jury box to perceive the T'kai as a piece of property that Atkinson owned, not the self-sufficient, autonomous creature the prosecution had implied it was, up to that point.

Finally, the open-ended nature of Dewey's question allowed Peter Atkinson to launch into a well-rehearsed and quite lengthy reply. In it, he expounded on everything from his exemplary service record—Atkinson was, you'll recall, stationed on Deneva IV when he originally acquired the T'kai—to the regular contributions he made to a wide range of charities, including a number of prominent animal rights groups.

Peter Atkinson proved to be an ideal witness. He was eloquent, witty, sanguine, intelligent, and handsome—a fact that was not supposed to influence the four female members of the jury, but Dewey felt probably would. Subsequent questions played off each of these attributes as, little by little, Dewey prompted his client to reveal any and every thing about himself that might impress the twelve strangers Fate had entrusted with his destiny.

Dewey's handling of the T'kai's death was nothing short of genius. Except for that one, brief allusion to that incident in his opening question, he ignored it completely. Instead, Dewey turned the unpleasant task of chronicling the details of this event over to Bernard Truman.

Like any successful lawyer, Alexander Dewey understood the human psyche. He knew that, in a case such as this—although, I had to admit, there had never been another case quite like this—the jury's sympathies would naturally favor his client. Peter Atkinson was, after all, one of their own. Dewey must have felt he could capitalize on these biases by forcing his opponent to fire the first shot in the battle of "us versus them," so to speak.

And so, after reviewing various highlights of Atkinson's life, right up to but not including the afternoon the T'kai was killed, Alexander Dewey strolled back to the defense table, sat down, and announced in an authoritative voice: "I have no further questions at this time. Your witness."

Truman could not have looked more shocked had Dewey walked over to him and dumped ice water on his head. His surprise was not difficult to understand.

I suspect Truman had spent a good portion of the past few weeks coming up with ways to revise the story he expected Dewey to weave for the court. Instead, he found himself stepping up to a *tabula rasa*. Rather than dissecting and discrediting Atkinson's testimony, Truman now faced the challenge of building his own case virtually from scratch.

In one brilliant move, Alexander Dewey had forced his opponent into shifting his previous strategy 180 degrees. Such a rapid change of course would have disoriented anyone. It appeared to have totally baffled Bernard Truman, who didn't strike me as being a pillar of composure to begin with.

Given time, Truman might have retrenched and recovered. The judge, however, seemed unwilling to grant him this luxury.

"Well, Mr. Truman, do you plan to question the witness, or are we to interpret your silence as an indication that the State has no wish to cross-examine?"

"Um, what? Oh, yes, Your Honor. I mean, no, Your Honor. What I mean is, yes, I do plan to question the defendant." Truman quickly leafed through several stacks of papers on the table before him. "Of course I do."

"Please proceed, then, Mr. Truman."

The befuddled Prosecutor did—as best he could, given the curve Dewey had thrown him.

"Now, Mr. Atkinson, as I understand it, you claim to have killed the T'kai in self-defense, is that so?"

Alexander Dewey was out of his seat before Truman even completed this sentence.

"Objection, Your Honor. The Prosecution is leading the witness. I believe a review of the record will indicate that my client has never made such a statement while under oath. Mr. Truman's assertion of this claim, therefore, is based strictly on hearsay."

"Sustained. Please confine your cross-examination to matters before this court, Mr. Truman."

"Very well, Your Honor. I withdraw the question." For the second time in as many minutes, Truman appeared visibly shaken. Dewey's strategy, daring as it may have been, was proving to be extremely effective.

"I assume, Mr. Atkinson, that you recall earlier testimony in which the State's Medical Examiner indicated that your T'kai was killed by a sharp blow to the head. I'd like to know . . ."

Again, Dewey shot to his feet.

"Point of clarification, Your Honor: In posing his question to my client, Mr. Truman employed the somewhat ambiguous phrase 'your T'kai.' Is the jury to presume that he is referring to the creature Mr. Atkinson purchased on Deneva IV?"

Try as she might, the judge could not completely suppress the smile that crossed her face. Neither could anyone else sitting in the courtroom who understood anything about how the law—as opposed to justice—operated.

"Would you be so kind as to clear up the Defense Attorney's confusion, Mr. Truman?"

"Why, um, of course, Your Honor, that is indeed the T'kai I was referring to—a helpless creature, I would remind the court, who was uprooted from Deneva IV by the defendant with little or no concern as to the long-term effects his actions might have on this poor, um, entity." By the pained expression on Bernard Truman's face, it was clear that he recognized how feeble this rejoinder was.

"Thank you, Your Honor," Dewey responded. "I just wanted to make sure the jury understood that the Prosecutor was indeed talking about Mr. Atkinson's pet, when referring to 'your T'kai.' "

Dewey was conducting Atkinson's defense like a seasoned impresario, using every tactic in his legal bag of tricks to manipulate Truman into, in essence, arguing his case for him. In addition to rendering Atkinson's initial claim of having acted in self-defense a moot point, thereby removing this early insinuation of even casual guilt from the court record—unless, of course, the prosecution elected to reintroduce it later, a strategy I felt certain Alexander Dewey was already prepared to counter—he also had managed once again to reinforce in the minds of the jury the image of the T'kai as a pet.

And Atkinson himself had yet to utter a single word in response to Truman's cross-examination!

I was beginning to wonder whether Morris had deposited me in one of those "alternate realities" so many bad science fiction writers rely on so frequently for their so-called inspiration. Clearly, Bernard Truman would need to play some kind of trump card soon if he was destined to fulfill the prophecy of Tanya Lodell's musty heirloom. No jury in its right mind could convict Peter Atkinson of any crime, not even jaywalking, based on the way the trial had progressed up to this point.

As if on cue, a disturbance behind me interrupted my speculation. A tall man in a suit identical to Bernard Truman's had just entered the courtroom, carrying what appeared to be a cage in his arms. Obviously, confinement disagreed with whatever this cage contained. It was screeching like a banshee and, if the way in which the man struggled to maintain his hold provided any indication, expressing its discontent quite violently.

This event prompted a strange reaction from Bernard Truman. He actually smiled—something I could not remember having seen him do even once over the past four-and-a-half weeks.

"Order! Order!" The judge rapped her gavel furiously, her eyes scanning the crowd of spectators. "There will be order in this court!"

It took a full minute for the courtroom to respond to her admonishments. The judge waited patiently, after which she turned her attention toward the Prosecutor's table.

"Mr. Truman, would you care to explain what is going on here?"

"I apologize for the interruption, Your Honor, but my colleague had instructions to seek me out as soon as he returned from his assignment."

"And what assignment might that be, Mr. Truman?"

"Allow me to explain, Your Honor. You see, my assistant, Mr. Kyle, has just returned from a rather lengthy deep-space flight, during which he had been entrusted with the task of securing . . ."

With slightly too much flourish, Truman removed a gray veil that had previously obscured the source of all the sound and fury.

". . . a T'kai."

The announcement was somewhat anticlimactic. Anyone who hadn't figured out what the cage contained by the time Truman uncovered it undoubtedly needed help attaching the Velcro tabs on their shoes. The judge was particularly unimpressed by this performance.

"I'm not a big fan of theatrics, Mr. Truman. And I especially dislike surprises. Why was I not informed that this creature would be brought into my courtroom?"

"As I explained, Your Honor, Mr. Kyle was instructed to seek me out immediately upon returning to Earth. Uncommonly high solar activity in recent days prevented him from sending a sub-space message informing me of his arrival. Even I did not know if and when he would complete his assignment, until I saw him come through those doors."

"I'll accept that explanation for now, Mr. Truman. Be informed, however, that I will not look kindly upon any additional displays of this nature."

"I must protest, Your Honor." Having heard the judge express her displeasure, Dewey obviously figured now was the perfect time for him to ante up his own two cents' worth. "I would point out to Mr. Truman that he is obligated to share with the Defense any and all information he possesses that might influence the outcome of this trial. Therefore, I respectfully request that this creature be removed from the jury's sight and any reference to its presence expunged from the court record."

The judge looked over at the T'kai, which remained quite agitated even after being unveiled and placed on display. It squealed constantly, repeatedly throwing itself against the cage's wire mesh.

"While I understand your chagrin, Mr. Dewey—and, as I've already stated, I also am less than pleased with the manner in which the Prosecutor handled this affair—I can't deny this creature's relevance to the matter currently before this court. Request denied.

"The T'kai can remain here for the time being, Mr. Truman. But I must insist that you attempt to keep it somewhat subdued during these proceedings, if at all possible."

"Thank you, Your Honor. My assistant will make every attempt to comply with your request."

"See that he does, Mr. Truman. Please continue."

"Now, Mr. Atkinson, is this T'kai similar to the one you're accused of killing, the one Mr. Dewey has characterized throughout this trial as being nothing more than your pet?"

"Similar, yes, but my T'kai was quite a bit smaller than the one you have there."

"That's understandable. According to forensic reports your T'kai was younger—comparable in age to a human just entering adolescence, if I may use that analogy—at the time of its death. Were you aware of this fact, Mr. Atkinson?"

"No, sir, I wasn't." Peter Atkinson seemed genuinely surprised. "The shopkeeper I purchased him from didn't mention that."

"I'm sure he didn't. My guess is that he felt such information would offend your sensibilities and, not coincidentally, might ruin a good deal, so to speak."

Having allowed Atkinson to answer two questions, Alexander Dewey obviously decided it was time once again to interrupt his opponent's rhythm.

"Objection, Your Honor. All of this is mere conjecture on Mr. Truman's part. Furthermore, it has no bearing on the facts of this case."

"Would you care to respond, Mr. Truman?"

"Only to say, Your Honor, that, as I hope to demonstrate shortly, the age of Mr. Atkinson's T'kai is critical to understanding why, in the eyes of the State, his subsequent actions constituted murder."

"Very well, Mr. Truman. I'll allow you time to pursue this line of questioning. Objection overruled."

Twice in a row, now, Alexander Dewey had found himself on the losing end of an argument. I could tell, studying the scowl on his face as he sat down, that Dewey did not accept such losses gracefully.

"Tell me, Mr. Atkinson, how familiar are you with the T'kai race?"

"Not very, sir. I'd never even heard of them, until I saw one in that shop on Deneva IV. According to the owner, though, they originally evolved in a planetary system located within the Pleiades."

"My research uncovered the same story, Mr. Atkinson, along with more than ten other possible origins for the T'kai. The only thing anyone knows with any certainty about this exotic life form, it appears, is that its past remains cloaked in secrecy.

"Our present knowledge of the T'kai is equally meager. My colleague, Mr. Kyle, just spent six months scouring a dozen star systems, searching for any shred of information he could uncover about the T'kai. Do you know what he found?"

"No, sir, I don't."

"I won't burden the court with all of the details—Mr. Dewey would only categorize them as hearsay, if I did—but in the course of his travels my colleague uncovered dozens of myths, scores of rumors, hundreds of legends, and more conflicting anecdotes than one would ever believe could be fabricated around a single subject. Stories concerning the T'kai, it seems, permeate the folklore of virtually every alien society mankind has discovered to date.

"Perhaps the greatest surprise of all, however, was the actual number of these mysterious beings Mr. Kyle encountered during his long journey. That number was one, the T'kai you see before you."

All eyes in the courtroom tracked Bernard Truman's gesture, as he pointed toward the still agitated creature in the cage.

"Oh, yes, Mr. Atkinson, a T'kai is indeed a rare find. That you should discover one in a simple curio shop on Deneva IV almost defies belief. But discover one you did. And after negotiating the purchase of that T'kai, you brought it home to Earth, is that correct?"

"Yes, sir. But my T'kai was extremely docile, not like the one over there on the table—at least, not until that day he . . ."

Peter Atkinson suddenly fell silent, as did the entire courtroom.

"Yes, Mr. Atkinson? You were about to say something?"

If he was, he didn't—at least not before Alexander Dewey decided to try to regain control of the situation.

"Your Honor, the Prosecutor is clearly badgering my client. Mr. Atkinson is under no obligation to provide unsolicited information while testifying in his own behalf."

"No ruling is necessary, Your Honor. I'll rephrase the question: Mr. Atkinson, is it not true that, on March 12 of this year, you were attacked by the T'kai you purchased on Deneva IV?"

"Yes, sir, I was."

"Would you please describe for the court what happened that day?"

Peter Atkinson looked over to the Defense table. I saw Dewey nod, signaling him to recount a story they had undoubtedly rehearsed many times and in great detail.

"We were playing out in the park. I'd hit a tennis ball with a baseball bat and he'd retrieve it. Nothing special. It was something we'd done a hundred times before.

"Suddenly, he went crazy. He started running and screeching and hurling himself down on the ground and against the trees. At first I just stood there, dumbfounded, watching this. I didn't know what else to do. Then, without warning, the T'kai attacked me. He came right at me like a rabid animal."

"And what did you do then?"

"I did what anyone would do: I defended myself. It was that simple."

"So, as I implied earlier, you do claim to have killed the T'kai in self-defense?"

Once again, Atkinson looked to his attorney for guidance. Once again, Dewey nodded.

"Yes, sir. I hit him with the baseball bat, once, and once only, on the side of his head. I didn't mean to kill him. As it turned out, I struck a soft spot on his skull. Later, when I found out what I'd done, I was devastated. At the time, though, it was either him or me."

"So you say. Tell me, Mr. Atkinson, did the way your

'pet' was acting in any way resemble the behavior of the T'kai on the Prosecutor's table?''

"Objection, Your Honor. This would be pure conjecture on my client's part.''

"I withdraw the question, Your Honor. Instead, with your indulgence, I would like to share with the court one particular story Mr. Kyle heard repeatedly while conducting his research into the T'kai.''

This time, it was the judge who glanced toward the Defense table.

"Any objections, Mr. Dewey?''

"Not at this time, Your Honor. But I would reserve the right to request that Mr. Truman's comments be stricken from the record later, should I so choose.''

"Agreed. You may proceed, Mr. Truman.''

"I ask the jury to study that T'kai. Listen to his squeals. Look at the way he keeps lunging at the sides of the cage. To my mind, his actions certainly resemble those described by Mr. Atkinson.

"And yet, what you're witnessing is not anger. Nor is it fear. Nor is it claustrophobia. Nor any emotion that could be traced to the creature's confinement. Quite the contrary. If I freed that T'kai in the middle of a field, he would continue doing exactly what he's doing now.

"Why? Because the source of the T'kai's current actions is genetic, not behavioral, in nature.

"The T'kai, it seems, pass through three distinct cycles on their way to full maturity. The first, corresponding to what we would call childhood, is a period of passive surveillance. During this initial cycle, a T'kai absorbs everything that happens around it. In a word, it observes. More than merely observes. A T'kai *absorbs,* because nothing he sees or hears during his 'childhood' is forgotten.

"I believe the T'kai that the defendant killed was in this initial cycle, when he purchased it on Deneva IV.

"At some age, no one knows exactly when, the T'kai enters a second phase, analogous to our—meaning a human's—puberty. For want of a better term, I'll call this the *assimilation stage.* Another way in which this assimilation stage resembles human puberty is that it is a turbulent time. In essence, everything the T'kai encountered during its initial cycle—sights, sounds, odors, tactile experiences, and

so forth—merges together. The result is a maelstrom of conflicting sensations.

"As you might surmise, this sudden flood of sensations
is extremely frightening. So much so, in fact, that the T'kai
reacts violently to the experience. If this analysis of T'kai
development can be believed, our caged friend is currently
in his second cycle, which he's been experiencing for several days.

"I propose that entering this second cycle is what drove
the defendant's T'kai to exhibit the seemingly violent behavior Mr. Atkinson described a few minutes earlier."

I fully expected Alexander Dewey to react to this comment. He did not disappoint me.

"Your Honor, I, like most people, appreciate a good
fable. And Mr. Truman's is, I'll admit, more engrossing
than most. But I fail to see what he hopes to accomplish
with all of this. He has yet to offer any proof which sup-
ports his claim of T'kai intelligence, or even his somewhat
strange theory regarding T'kai development. Unless the
Prosecutor is prepared to do so, and to do so quite quickly,
I'm tempted to move that his comments be censured now,
even though doing so would mean we'll never find out how
Mr. Truman's fascinating story ends."

"Mr. Truman?"

"If my calculations are correct, Your Honor, Mr. Dewey
should have the proof he desires shortly. You see, unlike
the initial cycle of a T'kai's life, the inhabitants of several
planets Mr. Kyle visited did claim to know how long the
second phase lasts. If they're correct, and if I have properly
converted the alien chronologies reported to Mr. Kyle into
human standards, this T'kai should be emerging from his,
um, 'puberty' within approximately two hours.

"Given the importance of this case, and considering how
long these proceedings have lasted already, I respectfully
request that the court grant me this relatively brief delay to
determine if my assumptions are valid."

The judge considered Truman's request for several moments before responding.

"I'm inclined to indulge the Prosecutor, Mr. Dewey—
unless, of course, you have any objections or comments."

"Just one, Your Honor. Even if I accept Mr. Truman's
premise, and I'm not saying that I do, how will waiting for

the T'kai to emerge from this so-called 'second cycle' confirm whether or not it possesses intelligence?"

"Mr. Truman?"

"That, Your Honor, depends on the results of a little experiment I performed."

"Please explain, if you will."

"During the early stages of Mr. Kyle's return flight, the T'kai was still in his initial cycle of development. Throughout that time, I had my colleague repeatedly play several extended news reports concerning this case in the presence of the T'kai.

"I believe he'll emerge from his second cycle with the knowledge of that experience intact. Should this be the case, the State contends that members of the T'kai race possess at least a primitive intelligence and, as such, deserve protection under our laws."

"I assume that 'protection,' as you're defining it, translates into culpability on the part of Mr. Atkinson for his actions against the T'kai he purchased on Deneva IV?"

"That's correct, Your Honor."

"You're attempting to establish some tricky but fascinating legal precedents, Mr. Truman. Still, the law is nothing if not fluid. As I stated earlier, my initial inclination is to indulge you in this effort.

"Very well. I'll grant you the two hours you have requested. If the T'kai does not respond as you predict, however, I'll have no alternative but to expunge this portion of the proceedings from the record, as Mr. Dewey requested— a move that, I assure you, will almost certainly result in the dismissal of all charges currently before this bench."

"Very well, Your Honor."

And so we waited. For an hour, we waited. And while we waited, we watched the T'kai. And then we waited some more, as the hour stretched into an hour-and-a-half. And still the alien creature's behavior did not change. He continued to squeal and claw and scratch and hurl himself against the walls of his personal prison, like a decidedly *un*intelligent and trapped animal.

Suddenly, a mere ten minutes before Truman's self-imposed deadline was scheduled to expire, the metamorphosis occurred. That's when the T'kai's squealing was replaced with absolute silence. His frantic movements slowed, then ceased completely, as the T'kai closed his eyes for several seconds. When he opened them once more, the madness was gone. So, too, was the anger and the haunted look of abject fear.

Instead, the T'kai projected an aura of unusual tranquillity. One by one, he studied the spectators in the courtroom, then the prosecution team, then the judge. Finally, those strangely calm eyes focused on Peter Atkinson, who was sitting at the Defense table.

That's when humanity heard the first message from a member of this strange and mysterious race: "Fear not, man of Earth. You did not know. All is forgiven."

Lawyers spend countless hours scrutinizing the behavior of juries, trying to analyze how their collective minds work. Ask ten attorneys to summarize the results of their efforts, however, and you'll get a dozen different answers.

Some lawyers contend that the less time it takes a jury to deliberate the more likely it is they'll return a verdict favorable to the defendant. Others swear that precisely the opposite holds true. A third group believes the length of a jury's deliberation portends guilt or innocence about as reliably as the presence or absence of a groundhog's shadow predicts how long Old Man Winter will stick around in any given year.

I couldn't tell, studying the two legal adversaries who had followed the T'kai's stunning pronouncement with their own hastily prepared summations, which philosophy either of them adhered to. Although the jury had been deliberating for almost six hours, Alexander Dewey displayed little concern. Bernard Truman did appear to be slightly nervous; but then, as I had already discerned, this was his normal disposition.

The media representatives in the courtroom, on the other hand, were growing increasingly apprehensive. Network stringers had already missed their evening and late-night broadcasts, and the newspaper journalists were fast approaching deadline for morning editions.

One reporter from *The Chicago Tribune* (with whom I discreetly struck up a conversation out in the hall) bragged about how his paper had three different versions of its front page typeset and ready to take to press—one each for a guilty or innocent verdict and a third, "fail-safe" edition, just in case the jury deliberations extended beyond final (*"final* final," to quote him) deadline. As we talked, he lamented the fact that, unless "those twelve laggards" made up their minds in the next half hour or so, "yesterday's news will be all that greets tomorrow morning's commuters."

Twenty-five minutes later, the bailiff announced that a verdict had been reached. As the jury filed in, I looked over and saw my newfound acquaintance from the *Trib* checking his watch. The grin on his face would have sent the Cheshire Cat running for an orthodontist.

"Mr. Foreman, has the jury reached a verdict?" the judge asked, following an age-old ritual.

"Yes, we have, Your Honor," the Foreman responded.

"Would you tell the court that verdict, please?"

"We the Jury find the defendant, Peter Atkinson, guilty . . ."

Before the foreman got out another word, all hell broke loose. Many in the courtroom cheered, many more tendered less polite indications of their displeasure over this verdict. Peter Atkinson's mother, who had maintained a brave front throughout the previous six weeks, burst into tears and ran toward her son. Several other people trying to reach Peter Atkinson were restrained by security guards. Alexander Dewey threw a stack of manila folders into his attache case and slammed it shut. Bernard Truman stood up and began shaking hands with his colleagues at the Prosecutor's table. My reporter friend, who had already been edging his way toward the back of the room, bolted into the hallway. My guess was that he found an open phone, punched in the *Trib's* number, and gave his editor a go-ahead for the "guilty" headline, before the courtroom's massive oak doors even had a chance to swing shut behind him.

I sat there, quietly disappointed. Tanya Lodell's situation had not changed. It appeared as if she and the rest of Atkinson's offspring would still bear the stigma of "Cain's Curse."

"Order in the court! Order in the court!"

I could barely hear the judge as she spoke these words into the microphone on the desk before her. Obviously, no one else could, either—a fact evidenced by the continued chaos.

"Silence, please! May we please have order in the court?"

This time she augmented the request with several sharp raps of her gavel—again, to no avail.

"All right, people. I said *SILENCE!* All of you, just SIT DOWN AND SHUT UP!"

Her shouting, amplified by the court's rather substantial sound system, accomplished what judicial decorum could not. All heads turned toward the front of the courtroom.

"In case you haven't noticed, this is a court of law. It is not some public forum where citizens are free to express their opinions in any way they see fit. For those of you who seem to have forgotten how a court of law functions, I would remind you that there is still business before this bench. We will conclude that business, I assure you, and we will do so without any additional outbursts."

Slowly, the din subsided. Everyone, including Peter Atkinson's mother, returned to his or her seat. It took almost twenty minutes, but the proceedings ultimately did resume.

"Now, Mr. Foreman, I would ask you to finish reading your verdict."

"Of course, Your Honor. As I started to say, We the Jury find the defendant, Peter Atkinson, guilty of no criminal activity. Rather, it is our opinion that . . ."

As you may suspect, this touched off a second round of pandemonium, even more racuous than the earlier one. Once again, the crowd split between kudos and catcalls, but this time the cheers outnumbered the jeers. Once again, Mrs. Atkinson burst into tears and broke toward her son; this time, however, the tears were joyful. Once again, one attorney emerged victorious and another endured defeat, only their roles had reversed.

I looked around for the *Trib* reporter, curious to analyze his reaction to this surprising chain of events. He was nowhere to be seen. Perhaps he was already back at his desk, or maybe heading home for what I'm sure he felt was a well deserved rest. Little did he know. . . .

Somewhere in The Windy City, massive printing presses undoubtedly rumbled, spitting out page after page of the *Trib*. I could picture drivers already delivering copies of the first edition to various newsstands around the city. I felt no compulsion to rush right out and pick one up. I already knew what Chicago's early-morning commuters would discover on its front page.

* * *

Peter Atkinson must have gotten hold of a paper from that initial print run. Hell, he probably ended up with a whole stack of them, courtesy of friends, family, even strangers— anyone who thought he might appreciate a souvenir of his ordeal. No doubt its headline made him feel doubly vindicated. Not only was he declared innocent in the eyes of the law, but the retraction the paper was forced to print exonerated him a second time in the more critical court of public opinion.

The way I figure it, at least one copy of this erroneous edition survived to beget the Atkinson legacy. It may have been stuffed in a drawer or an old footlocker only to be rediscovered, possibly decades later, by an unwitting descendant of Atkinson's who did not know the entire story. However the scenario played out, it was obviously the *Trib's* fallacious headline that someone, somewhere, turned up and subsequently turned into the beginnings of Peter Atkinson's infamy. Over the next five hundred years, the family's shame mutated into "Cain's Curse," a skeleton Peter Atkinson's descendants proceeded to hide away in a very private closet.

Tanya Lodell was ecstatic when I explained my hypothesis to her. With the mystery of Peter Atkinson's murder trial solved, her personal demons could finally be put to rest.

I had managed to clear up my own quandary, as well. I finally understood how Peter Atkinson's name had managed to vanish from the annals of history. In point of fact, it never belonged there. When the jury exonerated Peter Atkinson of murder, it effectively exorcised the "Intergalactic Ghoul."

Don't you just love it when a case comes together, its dangling threads all neatly tied up and tucked away? So do I.

Unfortunately, one small detail in the Atkinson case still bothers me. It has to do with something that happened the morning after the trial ended.

I was standing in an alley off Wacker Drive, preparing to return to my own era, when a stack of papers thrown from a delivery truck landed about five feet in front of me. It was that morning's *Trib*. I only had time enough to read its headline and glance at the accompanying picture before Morris phased me into the tachyon stream.

In reporting its error, subsequent editions of the previous

day's *Tribune* gave top billing to Atkinson's flamboyant Defense Attorney. The headline in these later editions stated: "Dewey Defeats Truman!" The picture I caught a brief glimpse of just as Morris whisked me out of the 22nd century showed an obviously elated Alexander Dewey holding up a copy of the *Trib* in which this retraction appeared.

What baffles me is the headline printed just above the picture depicting Dewey's triumph, the one that read: "200 Years Later, We Get It Right!" I have no idea what this means, but I know I won't be satisfied until I figure it out.

MURDER ON-LINE

by John DeChancie

John DeChancie is the author of *Castle Murders*,
Castle Dream, and *Castle Spellbound*, plus many
other books and short stories.

*At some unspecified point in the future, some hu-
mans develop the ability to teleport. One of them
seems the likely murderer of a business associate
who was robbing him . . . but because teleporta-
tion is instantaneous, his alibi—that he was playing
cards with five friends who will testify to it—holds
up. The police detective in charge of the case is
sure he did it, probably when he locked himself in
the bathroom for a couple of minutes, or perhaps
when he went to the kitchen to get another beer.*

*The story: the detective must, by hook or by
crook, break his alibi down.*

The Real-Time Clubhouse was crowded for a Tuesday afternoon. Rog Bauer was sysop-on-duty, and duty called: he
had to moderate the Scenarists' Workshop session, or at
least keep an eye on things. He did not look forward to it
because Mark Hollbeck would be there, and Rog hated
Hollbeck with a consuming passion.

Rog walked through the palatial lobby of the hotel, past
the Olympic-size pool, through the indoor tennis courts,
and out through the main entrance.

The sky was blue, as it always was except on the odd day
when one of the sysops upscale from Rog wanted a change
in the weather. But today was not such a day. The air was
warm, mitigated by a cool breeze from the lake, where par-
ticolored sails blossomed from numerous boats.

He walked along the path, passing gate-prompts to

ActionWorld, SpaceWorld, SportsWorld, and Pleasure-World.

He didn't have to walk to the Clubhouse. He could simply teleport, but he wanted the time to think. His attention wasn't on the virtual terrain and its many attractive features; he knew it by heart.

He was thinking about Mark Hollbeck and about how much he hated him. Hollbeck was always on Rog's case, always complaining about the state of things on-line at DataSpace International. The system was too slow, the Rules of Conduct were too strict, censorship was a looming danger. . . .

Rog snorted. "Censorship" amounted to people objecting to Hollbeck's scatological speech habits. But more people laughed than complained. Mark wanted to bring back the "Free Speech" movement of the 1960s, or so he claimed. Rog was only vaguely familiar with the history of the last century; it wasn't a period that interested him. What bothered him about Mark was not the indelicacy of Mark's oral cavity but the fact that the damned thing never seemed to stop flapping; because when Mark was not running down DataSpace he was tearing into Rog with that smarmy "humor" of his. Some people thought Mark the soul of wit. Rog didn't think he was funny at all.

And Mark never stopped, never relented, rarely letting an opportunity go by. Rog had but to show himself on Mark's event horizon to become the target of yet another verbal fusillade. Of course, Rog could retaliate and usually did, but he had to admit to himself that he was not in Mark's league in the manly art of oral dueling. The s.o.b. had a crude animal cunning about him. Always had a comeback, always got the last word. He couldn't be the one to quit, to call it a draw. Mark had to get off the last Parthian shot . . . and then he'd let fly one more for good measure.

But that wasn't all that Rog had against Mark. Mark was a successful and semi-famous interactive fiction scenario writer who helped run DataSpace's Scenarists' Workshop. Mark specialized in the killer critique. He delighted in ripping the scenarios of "wanna-be" writers to shreds and was capable of reducing a roundtable full of workshoppers to helpless laughter—at the expense, of course, of some hapless tyro who had vainly hoped for at least one word of encouragement.

Rog had been such a victim. They still talked about what Mark had done to Rog's long-standing pet project, a space warfare epic for which Rog's working title was "Asgard's Legions." Mark's rendering was "Asshole Lesions." Mark had not only ripped it; he'd stomped, kicked, and slammed it. Then he started in on the hideous thing's creator, speculating on the requisite character flaws necessary to produce such an excrescence as the one under examination.

Rog had stormed out of the workshop session, but the damage was done. Though many DataSpacers professed sympathy for Rog's victimization, they had to admire Hollbeck's mastery of the art of the put-down. Besides, Mark was hilarious.

The anger had grown inside Rog until it became a lump in the middle of his chest, a piece of hardened lava: cold crust outside, molten within.

The Real Time Clubhouse loomed ahead. Today it was a forbidding castle on a high promontory. Yesterday it had been the Taj Mahal and the day before. . . .

Rog stopped and looked around. He was in the middle of a park, one of many in DataSpace. The electronically-simulated lawn was convincingly green and convincingly soft and yielding beneath his feet. There came to his nostrils the faint smell of fresh-mown grass. The trees around him were in full foliage, rustling in the convincing breeze. Yet none of it was real. Or one could say that it was more real than mundane reality.

He didn't want to go to the workshop today. He had nothing on the block for critiquing, but he wasn't up for watching one more Hollbeck performance, yet another savaging. Nor did he much care to witness its antithesis—which Dr. Jekyll/Hollbeck was equally as capable of delivering on occasion—a reasoned, balanced analysis of the merits and shortcomings of a piece of amateur writing—thoughtful, perceptive, and administered with an empathetic regard for the tender feelings of the hopeful scenarist involved. Yes, Mark could do that sort of thing as well; though most of the time, it seemed to Rog, a woman was the recipient of this largess.

Felice's scenario was on the agenda for today. Rog didn't relish the prospect of her either being pilloried or pandered to. He needed to do something else right now. He wanted to go to the Expanded Consciousness Clinic and spend some

time in the Zen Garden, a nice quiet place for meditation.
Rog usually did meditation standing on his head. On his
virtual head, of course, not his real one. But the effect was
the same. It was restful. Sometimes he had out-of-virtual-
body experiences, feeling himself being drawn into a higher
dataspace, into the greater cyberverse.

But duty called. In recompense for his sysop job he got
reduced on-line rates. Rog's systems-analysis job paid well,
but spending a great deal of time on-line tended to drain a
bank account. He needed every break.

He looked up at the high ramparts of the castle. Nice job.
But he sure as hell wasn't going to huff his way up there.
He mentally gave DataSpace's host supercomputer a com-
mand.

Instantly, he found himself inside the castle, standing in
a stone-walled corridor outside the door of the Workshop.
Again, mentally, he scanned the roster to see who was inside. Neither Felice nor Mark was present.

He scanned the other rooms. There were a dozen of them,
dedicated to different special interest groups and their dif-
fering activities.

He found them in the 24-hour Anything Goes Room, a
catchall for people who didn't sleep much. Mark and Felice
were the only two people in the room, and there was a DO
NOT DISTURB sign on the door. The two were communicating in private mode.

Without thinking, he teleported into the room. Something
vague, a notion of reminding them that the workshop was
about to start, was at the back of his mind as he did so; but
later, of course, he realized that he simply had to see for
himself.

He just as quickly teleported out.

Finding himself outside in the corridor again, he didn't
know what to do, where to go. He was embarrassed, angry,
and disoriented, all at once. He took two steps toward the
door of the workshop and halted, then gave an agonized
look back toward the 24-Hour Room.

Abruptly, he logged off the system.

Darkness.

He heard the soft whir of a ventilating fan. Reaching out
into the gloom, he touched soft, rounded walls. Then the
plush-lined interior of the EnviroWomb lit up. He reached
for the quick-exit pad and pushed. The EnviroWomb opened

up like a blossoming flower, letting in dim sunlight that slipped between the slats over the windows of Rog's apartment.

He took off his interface helmet and set it down, then peeled off the elastic band around his forearm. The earliest environmental modules fed their occupants intravenously, but the NutriBand supplied nutrients through skin absorption. No needles, no mess.

Naked, he climbed out. Rog's EnviroWomb was in the spare bedroom, its only feature. He walked out and went into the bedroom he sometimes used when natural sleep was necessary, along with a much-needed break from both work and DataSpace (which hadn't been often lately, he admitted to himself). He dressed in a hurry.

His pants were loose at the waist. He had lost a few more pounds, it appeared. A wall mirror reflected his bony frame and he regarded the image disapprovingly. But then Rog didn't like much about his non-virtual self. On-line he had the build of an athlete. In fact, on-line he could look like anything he wanted to look like. He could *be* anything he wanted to be.

He put on an old leather jacket and left the apartment.

It was cold and overcast, the street devoid of traffic. He crossed the alley to the unattached garage, hoping it hadn't been broken into and the car stolen. Keeping one eye peeled for marauders, he fiddled with his keys until he found the one for the garage.

The old garage door creaked opened with some difficulty. Rust on the runners, probably. Rog heaved and finally raised it high enough to reveal the narrow, musty interior, wherein was parked one painfully small automobile of a foreign generic make.

Coaxing the car to life took some doing, as the car had not been used in a while. It ran on compressed natural gas, a fuel now in short supply. But the tank read three-quarters full. More than enough to get Rog where he was going.

He was going to Mark's place, which happened to be not very far away. Not very far away at all.

Rog pulled out of the garage and drove down the alley. At its T with the street, he turned left after a cautious check in both directions.

There wasn't much need for caution. Hardly any traffic moved in the town. He passed abandoned filling stations, boarded up fast food outlets. Nobody went anywhere these days, as more and more of life went on-line, supplanted by one of the virtual reality services, of which DataSpace was among the majors. A slot on one of the majors was getting to be at a premium. There was talk of a "reality shortage."

He passed a deserted shopping mall.

Not everything was closed. Here a bar, there a hardware store. But business hours were limited.

Another car passed in the opposite direction. Rog watched the rearview mirror and saw it make a U-turn. Rog floored the accelerator and the tiny car's two-cylinder engine made a sound like an outraged popcorn popper. But the car picked up speed.

He wheeled left at the next intersection, raced two blocks, turned right, sped five more blocks (dodging an abandoned and burning car in the middle of the road), then screeched left again.

He slowed and checked the rearview. Nothing followed.

He lost his bearings for a moment but familiar landmarks at the next intersection were enough to reorient him. He made a right, ignoring the functioning stoplight, one of the few in the city.

He wasn't worried about getting a ticket. The police department had folded last year due to the city's horrendous budget deficit. The city council was negotiating a massive federal bailout, but nothing had come of these negotiations after nine months.

He passed rows of homes, most boarded up, closed up. Some were burned-out shells. Hanging out on a corner, a gang of Latino boys followed him with dark hungry eyes as he sped past. Not everyone was on the reality net. Not everyone could afford to go on-line. Society was bifurcating. Rog had contributed many points to a discussion of this very problem in the World Town Hall. On-line.

He turned into a side street and slowed, reading house numbers. It had been a long while—but he remembered. A white bungalow with yellow trim. Cozy little place. Modest, for one supposedly so successful. Rog had always suspected that Mark exaggerated his income. After all, Mark lied about almost everything else.

He parked far down the street and walked back up, concealing the tire iron under his jacket. No one observed him from any of the houses.

The front door was locked, of course, and probably bolted. All the windows were shuttered with steel. Rog rang the doorbell, pro forma, and a synthetic voice informed him that no one could come to the door at the moment, but at the sound of the beep. . . .

After about ten minutes of strenuous effort he succeeded in smashing through the thick glass block of a basement window, ignoring alarms that blared inside the house and out. Rog wasn't worried. It would take any private security operatives hours to arrive at the scene, if they showed up at all. They were as overworked as the city police had been. More so.

He squeezed through the tiny hole without much difficulty, aside from nicking his side on a sharp edge; but he made it through in one piece. A skinny body was good for some things.

NutriBand or none, virtual reality did things to the non-virtual body. Rog was exhausted. He staggered up the cellar stairs.

The EnviroWomb was in the empty dining room. It was open but still operating, its operator expecting to get back on-line soon. Rog searched the house.

He found Mark spread out across the bed in the front bedroom. Whether Mark had heard the alarms or not, Rog couldn't guess. Rog stared at him.

Mark's eyelids slowly opened. More slowly, recognition dawned.

A smile spread across Mark's narrow, pimply face—a face completely different from the one he wore on-line. "Hey. Roger-Dodger. The Roger-Person." Mark went into a fit of coughing.

Rog regarded the emaciated figure on the bed. Mark was in bad shape. Rog had rarely seen so bad a case of "virtual AIDS." The guy was wasting away.

"You bastard."

Mark continued to smile. "Nice to see you, too, dweeb-breath."

"Very funny, Hollbeck. You had to go and do Felice, didn't you? The rest of the women on-line weren't enough."

"Oh, come on. It was nothing. Just one of those things, Roh-ger."

"I prefer to be called Rog, Hollbeck."

"Sorry, Rahhhhjj. Christ, I feel like hell."

"You look like hell."

"Thanks. I should check into an on-line clinic. Imagine living on-line all the time, forever, while someone nurses your mortal body. Think I might be able to afford it next year."

"You won't need it, Mark."

Mark wheezed out a cough before he said, "And why is that, laddy-buck?"

"Because I'm going to kill you this year. Right now."

"Oh, damn. And over what? Felice. Nice, but rather bland, don't you think? And that stuff she writes. Dreadfully dull."

"That's not what you told her, I bet."

Mark chuckled. "Not exactly. She needs work, of course."

"And you were working on her when I barged in."

After another coughing fit Mark's face blossomed into a supercilious sneer that approximated the one his virtual and much more improved face wore almost perpetually. "Oh, come on, nerd-face, get with the program. It's virtual sex, for crissakes. On-line. Not the real thing. Get it?"

"That distinction is rapidly fading," Rog said. "You took advantage of her."

"Oh, how chivalrous, defending her honor, which is more than she ever did. I suppose we should joust over this. Mortal combat to decide who wins the fair lady's—" Mark began to cough again.

"I hate your guts," Rog said simply.

"Uh, not like it's obvious, or anything. Look, I hate to be rude, but what the fuck do you want?" Mark tried sitting up. He didn't quite succeed. "And what's the big fucking idea of breaking into my—"

Those were Hollbeck's last words. Rog lunged at him, hands closing tightly about his neck.

It took almost all of Rog's strength to do the job, but do it he did. Afterward he lay supine, almost dead himself among the dust bunnies by the side of the bed, on which Mark's purple-faced body lay unmoving.

When he caught his breath, Rog got up and regarded Hollbeck's body. It wasn't a pretty sight, but it was a most satisfying one.

Rog unbolted the front door and walked out. The street

was quiet. Gray clouds scudded overhead. The houses along this once-fashionable street stood forlornly, dingy and neglected.

Rog hated the mundane world.

Back on-line, he heard nothing for several days. Then people began to comment on Mark's absence.

After several more days speculation was rampant. Mark had sworn off virtual reality. He was out on the Left Coast. He was ill and had been admitted to an on-line clinic. He was just taking an off-line vacation. ·

Rog chimed in, suggesting that something might have happened to Mark, and that somebody should go and check it out. For some reason, no one countered with a suggestion that Rog was the logical choice for this task, seeing as how he and Mark lived in the same city.

Meanwhile, life on DSI went on as usual. Rog went about his sysop chores, maintaining some files here, tidying up there. He redesigned the Clubhouse and made it semipermanently into the Louis XIV palace at Versailles, a 3-D image of which he lifted out of the on-line libraries. On his off-duty hours he reconciled with Felice and took her to PleasureWorld several times, where they disported themselves to mutual satisfaction.

Along about the fifth of May, there appeared to Rog a curious figure, someone he'd never seen in DataSpace before. It was a short man in a disreputable raincoat.

"Excuse me, sir?"

"Yes?" Rog was sitting on a deck chair by the simulated swimming pool.

The man scratched his head. "I'm sorry to bother you . . ."

"No, that's quite all right. You look familiar."

"And so do you, sir. You're Rog Bauer, one of the sysops around here."

"Yes, that's right."

"And a fine job you're doing, sir. A fine job."

"Thank you. Won't you sit down?"

"Oh, thank you, sir, thank you. I hope I can just take a minute of your valuable time?"

"Certainly," Rog said. "How can I help you?"

"Well, you see, sir, I have this problem. . . ."

Rog's eyes rolled to the simulated blue sky.

Thus began the on-line investigation into the murder of Mark Hollbeck.

The figure in the shabby raincoat was not the only detective on the case. Over the next few weeks Rog was questioned by almost every stock character out of detective fiction, both print and media. It was all a puppet show, of course. None of these constructs were real. All were various disguises of DataSpace, itself an Artificial Intelligence.

He grew to hate the raincoated specter most of all, though, because this one pestered him the most, always coming back for a follow-up question, another "problem," most of these being holes in Rog's cover story. There wasn't much to Rog's cover story save that he was off-line at the time of the murder but had been home getting real sleep (as opposed to the kind of hypnagogic sleep induced by DataSpace). No, he couldn't prove it, but then again DataSpace couldn't prove that he had been anywhere else. DataSpace operatives (flesh and blood ones) had thoroughly examined the scene of the crime, and there was (to Rog's great surprise), nothing to link him to the crime beyond the fact that the blood type of the tiny bit of blood found on the smashed glass block in the cellar matched Rog's.

"But that's mere coincidence," Rog told a simulacrum of Sherlock Holmes.

"That's elementary," Holmes said.

"But there's a problem with the tire iron," the raincoated detective informed him the next day.

"The tire iron?"

"Yeah, there was one left in the cellar. Obviously used to break the glass. There are fingerprints on it. None of them match any on file, which only means of course that the murderer had no police record. We traced the tire iron."

"You traced it?"

"Yes. But no luck, sir."

"No luck?"

"No, sir. A common accessory item that comes with many generic makes of automobile. Such as your car, sir."

"My car? Oh, I see."

"Yes, sir. Did you know that your tire iron was missing, sir?"

"Why, no. I didn't realize that."

"You'd be in a real pickle if you had a flat tire."

"Yes, I suppose I would be."

"Especially since our cities aren't safe any more, sir, even in broad daylight."

"Yes, I see what you mean. I'll have to replace it immediately."

"That would be a good thing, sir. Yes, sir, that would be a wise thing to do."

The investigation went on and Rog was questioned further. Various detectives showed up. One had a French accent; one was a little old lady; another wore a trench coat and hat and packed two .45 caliber automatics. Another lantern-jawed icon wore a yellow fedora and matching overcoat.

"Your alibi stinks," he informed Rog.

"No shit, Dick Tracy," Rog said.

But the shabby-raincoat figure always came back. Persistent, that one was.

Then, gradually, the visitations tapered off. Rog was asked more routine questions, these merely rehashing what had been covered before; then, after the twenty-fourth of June, all questioning ceased.

Rog breathed a virtual sigh of relief and went about his business. His job had been taking up a lot of time. A big government project came up against its deadline, and to help meet it he worked like a beaver, with only a little time off to headstand in the Zen Garden.

Finally, after three solid weeks of round-the-clock toil, the project was completed and the pressure eased.

He took some time off and spent a vacation alone in HistoryWorld, where he fought and refought several battles of the American Civil War, a subject of great interest to him.

It was at Gettysburg that Rog ran into Mark Hollbeck. Mark turned up as one of Rog's orderlies. He handed Rog a communique, winked, and strolled out of Rog's tent. Thunderstruck, Rog sat at his writing table for a moment. Then he bolted out of the tent in pursuit.

He caught up with Hollbeck and roughly turned him around.

"You!"

"Get your mitts off the merchandise. Hey, penis-breath, what's up?"

"You . . . you're dead!"

"Sorry, smegma-lips. No such luck. I was off-line for a while. Out on the coast doing a deal with MGM-Fox-Universal."

"I killed you."

"But it didn't take. Sorry, Roger-Dodger. I'm back, bigger and better than ever."

"But I strangled you," Rog insisted. "You were dead. I killed you."

Mark's voice changed abruptly. "Yes, sir, I know you did."

The figure grew blurry for a moment, then sharpened again. It was the shabby-raincoat guy.

He smiled almost apologetically. "I'm sorry, sir, but I knew from the first that you were the murderer."

"I suppose it was obvious," Rog said. "But I really didn't kill him, did I? Not virtually, anyway. He'll still be around, that construct of his?"

"I'm afraid so, sir. He had many friends on-line, and they'd miss him. Sorry, sir, but murder isn't what it used to be."

"Rog sighed. So, what now? You turn me over to off-line authorities?"

"Well, sir, in the state where you live, there really is a problem about that. As you might know, the state prison system is bankrupt. There's only one penitentiary still operating. Although there's a remnant of the state police functioning and enforcing the law, they simply can't handle your case at the moment. Massive understaffing. And the backlog in the courts is staggering, sir, staggering."

"So, what happens?"

"DataSpace Security is only concerned with what happens on-line, sir, and, as the murder took place off-line, that's out of our jurisdiction. However . . ."

"However?"

"You can be tried for violations of the On-Line Rules of Conduct, sir. And that you will. You've deprived DataSpace of a valued and steady customer."

"I did that, yes. What will happen to me?"

"You'll be sent to jail, sir."

"But that's silly. I'll just go off-line."

"Of course, sir. But if you want to continue your life on

DataSpace International, you'll have to spend time behind virtual bars.''

Rog thought of Mark's simulacrum, and how the ersatz Mark would never let him live it down. Mark would tear into him now like never before, to the delight of the DataSpace community, who now would regard Rog as a villain. A cold, scaly thing crawled up his spine.

Then he thought of life out in the cold. The deserted cities, the gangs of looters . . . the predatory eyes of those desperate teenagers on the street corner.

He had no choice.

''How much time do you think I'll get?''

''Oh, I really couldn't say, sir. Just guessing, with allowances for good behavior . . . say, six months.''

Rog smiled. He looked up at the perpetually blue sky. It was pretty. The cornfields were green, the trees were tall and leafy. The guns were quiet now, the battle won. He had just relived an important historical event—experienced it, smelled the gunpowder, heard the shouts of rebel yells. This was only one of thousands of legendary battles he could experience, all available through the magic of high technology. Nowhere else, except inside the supercomputer that provided the environment for DataSpace, could all this be possible.

With Mark still around, the other DataSpacers would eventually forgive and forget.

Life was good. This life was good.

''After all,'' the raincoated detective said. ''DataSpace doesn't want to lose another valuable customer.''

Rog grinned. ''Six months? I can do that standing on my head.''

COLOR ME DEAD

by Sandra Rector
and P.M.F. Johnson

This is the first science fiction story by P.M.F. Johnson and Sandra Rector, who have numerous nonfiction sales to their credit.

An asteroid miner is found dead in his spacesuit, two hours from his home base. But the suit can only carry three hours of oxygen, which means that he either totally lost track of the time and virtually committed suicide, or he was murdered and it was made to look like a suicidal miscalculation.

There are five other miners working the same asteroid belt, but none on this particular asteroid.

The detective/policeman who investigates the death finds the following in the miner's quarters: clothing, shaving and medicine kit, food, maps of the area, oxygen canisters, and three things that don't seem to belong: a comb (the miner was bald), a postage stamp (there is no mail in the asteroid belt), and a wedge-shaped piece of pure platinum.

Was the miner murdered? If so, what was the motive and who was the killer?

Wednesday morning arrived before I managed to badger Asteroid Mining Amalgamated into loaning me a shuttle and a pilot to investigate the death of another of their miners, a guy named Joe D'Angelo. My own rocket was in the shop. The requisitions office never approved ad hoc requests for equipment. That would make it too easy for the rest of us. I didn't even bother to submit the paperwork.

Probably this was just another in a line of too many suicides, but any unexplained death has to be reviewed by a police detective. The dispatcher forwarded the case to me, Henrietta E. King.

The miner was spotted last night by the food shuttle crew. They were on their route to D'Angelo and the five other miners in that section of the Belt, when they reported him down and not moving, approximately two hours from the base camp on his asteroid. They landed and tried to revive him, but it was too late.

As was happening with too many cases lately, I was pressed for time. My boss was up for a hostile political review on Friday. She needed to prepare several reports and demanded my input—I'd been around longer than any other detective on the force. I was given one day to solve this case.

I met my pilot in the tunnel to the launching pads. She was a tiny blonde, snapping gum as she strode up to me. She slung her huge red purse over one shoulder and grasped my hand.

"Bernina Busselbauer. Call me Bernie," she said. "You're that detective. I hear they call you Hek."

She chattered away as we headed down the corridor toward the ship. She had us strapped in and all systems cleared for liftoff without missing a syllable.

"I used to be a singer, once upon another life," she said. Her eyes flicked from gauge to gauge. "My daddy was furious at me for stooping so low. But there's not much call for live singers except on Earth, and who has bones to tolerate the gravity down in the Well anymore? You like this work?"

"I've been doing it all my life."

"You didn't answer me," she said. She pushed a button and we were pressed into our seats from the force of the lift-off.

I thought about her question. Once I would have answered yes without hesitation. I loved the puzzles of detective work, and the thought that I was creating order, putting all to rights for people. Twenty-two years on the force knocked a lot of that thinking out of me, but still I felt that way enough to wake up eagerly every morning. That was, until recently. Maybe I was just growing old.

Once clear of the asteroid, Bernie began to whistle Kartab's latest pop concerto. I fired up a computer screen and read Joe D'Angelo's company profile.

The text was skimpy. D'Angelo was fifty-nine years old, a widower, with one child, a daughter. He was up for contract renewal in two months. His work history started when he was fifteen. He had gone through any number of jobs—rocket shops, tool and die, even a stint as a dome patcher, anything where he could work with his hands.

Two hours later, we were cruising over the desolate, rocky landscape where he met his death.

"How do you think he died?" Bernie asked.

"The morgue boys looked him over last night," I said. "They found no wounds, no contusions, no foreign substances in the bloodstream. They concluded he just ran out of air."

"That sounds logical to me," she said. "The suits the Company loans these miners hold three hours of oxygen in a tank. If Joe was discovered here, two hours from his base camp, I would say it was suicide."

"Maybe. Maybe not."

We circled the place where the body was found. Aside from the tracks of the food shuttle crew and the medical examiners, nothing indicated anyone but D'Angelo had ever been in the area.

Joe's tracks led directly back to his base camp, a low metal cabin. We landed, fastened our helmets, depressurized, and exited the shuttle to look over the cabin, perched at the edge of a monstrous hole—the primary strip mine of the asteroid.

Inside the metal cabin was a small living area, maybe three meters by four with a fold-down bed, a computer table, and a counter for preparing food. A narrow plastic window overlooked a boulder-strewn landscape.

"Pathetic," Bernie said. "I'm always amazed at what a person will do to get ahead in this world."

I set her to searching for a note, as I studied the room. Everything was extremely orderly. Food tins stood precisely atop each other, oxygen canisters were lined up in their racks, one extra set of clothes lay in a neat pile. Even his charts, rendering the movements of most planetoids in the region, were arranged perfectly in their drawer. I turned on the computer. Every detail of his operation was logged, but without any of the extraneous phrases miners usually added to their reports. The file directory marked "personal" was empty.

"This is weird," Bernie said. She pointed at Joe's toiletry kit. "Joe was bald."

A black plastic comb was nestled beside his toothbrush. "Maybe he wasn't always bald."

She nodded, a dubious look on her face.

I found another puzzling item. In a cupboard, behind the food pouches, lay a wedge of metal. Silver?

Bernie snatched it away from me. "Platinum," she said. "Betcha."

"How do you know?"

"I don't," she said. She chewed her gum thoughtfully. "Let's send it through the assayer and find out. Of course, then it'll become Company property. They record everything when it's assayed."

We put on our helmets and went outside. Bernie turned on the machine, and ran the metal through the scanner. We returned to the cabin to check the readout—one kilogram of pure platinum.

D'Angelo's log mentioned nothing about platinum. I said as much.

"I shouldn't think so," Bernie answered. "Platinum doesn't grow in a uranium mine. Uranium isn't supposed to be out here in any concentration, but that's what Joe's rock is. They're still arguing over it."

We continued our search, and I found one last tidbit. Behind the narrow bed, sticking out from a seam, was a tiny square of paper.

"What's that?" Bernie asked, looking over my shoulder.

"It looks like a postage stamp."

One of her pencil-thin eyebrows shot upward. "Postage *what?*" she asked.

"Like electronic mail, only on paper," I explained. "They once used stamps to pay for communications on Earth. You stuck them on an envelope which contained your writings, wrote a locating code on the outside, dropped the envelope in a box out in public somewhere, and hoped the people who did the sorting and transporting by hand somehow got it to the right building."

"Weird," she said. "Why is it here?"

"I haven't the slightest idea."

"What do you think? Was he murdered?"

"I don't know," I said uneasily. "He was terribly precise, but he left these three items out of his records. Why? If he committed suicide, you'd think a guy this fussy would tidy up with a note. Was it a fatal mistake? Maybe. He doesn't strike me as the type to lose track of time. Everything about him spells fastidiousness. Even his footprints moved in a direct line.'' I stared out at the brown landscape. "If it was murder, who killed him? And how? Note or no note, with nothing else to go on, I'd write this down as another suicide.''

"So do we return to Home Base?'' Bernie pouted.

"Not quite yet,'' I said. I raised the kilo of platinum. "This is worth a lot of credits. When you run across something valuable, it's usually worthwhile to do more digging. Anyway, there are other head-scratchers. How did these things get here? A stamp, okay. A comb, maybe. But the miners pass through a detector, before and after each trip. Platinum would be nearly impossible to smuggle. What's more, everyone and everything is weighed before being shipped here across the System from Luna, or Mars, or wherever. Nobody gets an extra kilo of weight that has to be accounted for in fuel.''

Bernie tapped her red purse. "I did,'' she said brightly. "I told Logarse, the vice president who interviewed me, that if I can't bring a few personal items, they can hire themselves another pilot. These drab surroundings frazzle me.''

"Good for you,'' I said. "You have a skill—some leverage. These miners don't. They aren't even allowed a photograph.''

"That's not right,'' she said. "I'll say so, too. They've listened to me before. Daddy's a stockholder.''

"That's nice,'' I said politely. "First, I want to talk with the other miners and hear what they have to say.''

"You only have until the end of the day,'' Bernie reminded me.

I grinned. "I guess I won't get much sleep tonight,'' I said.

She smiled back with those pouty lips. I thought she looked silly, but who am I to judge? My ex sure went for thick lips on young women. Just thinking about it made me feel depressed.

"Let's go,'' I said. "Alma Cloudsinger is first on the list.''

During the hour-long flight, I reviewed the profiles of the five other miners.

The first, Alma Cloudsinger, had trouble staying up with

the latest technology, and never fit into any job program, the file stated, until they had found this job for her. She was forty-one, never married, and childless.

As we descended to the asteroid, we noticed Alma Cloud-singer standing near her strip mine peering into a crevasse. When she saw us get ready to land, she hopped away from the crevasse and headed toward her cabin. It took her a good fifteen minutes.

"What are you doing here?" she asked when she finally came up to us near her cabin. "You ain't food. Food was due yesterday."

"We're from Home Base," Bernie said.

"I'm afraid there's something we have to discuss with you, ma'am," I said. "I'm with the Intersystem Police. You know that Joe D'Angelo is dead?"

"I heard," she said.

A strange yipping noise sounded over the radio.

"I'm having problems with my radio," Alma explained quickly. "The Company gives us lousy equipment." She waved us into her cabin. "With these three-hour oxygen canisters, we never get more than one and a half hours from the cabin. They make damned sure that's covered in the circle of their spy eyes. They watch us all the time."

We stood together in the cabin lock, waiting for the air pressure to stabilize.

She continued. "You run out of breath juice in the field and you're dead. There's no way to trade oxy tanks without letting in the vacuum. They done that on purpose. If it wasn't for the credits. . . ."

I remained silent. After all, my suit was the same way. The politicians did not love Investigative. That was probably why they invented red tape, to avoid giving anything useful to people like me, people who caused them trouble.

We stepped into the cabin proper. Alma's surroundings were as dreary and colorless as D'Angelo's, with nothing extraneous, no feminine touches.

Out of her space suit, Alma was heavy enough to stretch the seams of her gray coveralls. She was tall, almost my height, with high cheekbones and dark hair. She had a de-fiant air; she was a gold miner, the top of the pecking order.

She looked us over. Her eyes lingered on Bernie's flashy red purse.

"Did anyone visit D'Angelo recently?" I asked.

She made a wry face. "Recently? Not ever. We got no way to get around. We're allowed no visitors; not that I'm the sort who needs any visitors. I get along just fine by myself."

"Was D'Angelo depressed?"

"Ain't we all?"

"I mean, was he real quiet?"

"You couldn't shut him up," Alma said. "He talked all the time. We were friends. I have a hard time thinking it was suicide. You should investigate that Therea Janus. She already murdered one man. I bet Joe found out something she didn't want him to know. Therea's a bad one." Alma looked at me, and her face flushed.

"How did you hear of his death?"

"Company radio," she said.

I removed an item from my evidence bag. "Can you identify this?" I asked.

"Dave's comb," she said. "He's one of the other miners. Dave's always combing that mop of his."

I pulled out the next item.

"I don't know," she said. "Some kind of metal?"

"Platinum," Bernie offered helpfully. I glared at her as I took out the stamp.

Alma stared at its picture of a blue bird on a green bough. "How pretty." She rubbed her eyes. "There's not much beautiful out here. Sometimes I get so hungry for color I could scream. Not that anyone would hear." She grinned, then turned to Bernie. "I just love your purse. Not that I need it or anything, but I've been looking for a handbag like that for a while. I'll give anything you ask."

"No, thanks," Bernie said.

I continued. "According to the company report, D'Angelo's stint was about over."

"That's right," Alma said. "He was planning to go home."

"Where did you hear that?"

"From Joe," she said warily.

"When did you two talk?"

"It was just . . ." She paused and started again. "The Company ships us back to Home Base every other month for six or seven hours. It's to get our social needs met, the doctor says. The last time was Christmas. Mostly we stick together: We've got the most in common."

"What was said at the Christmas party?"

Alma did not answer. She looked down at the table. She bit her lip.

"Is something wrong, Alma?"

Her expression turned stubborn. "Nothing," she said. "I'm fine."

I watched her. "Look, Alma," I said. "If someone out here killed D'Angelo, I need to know to protect you."

A muscle in her face twitched. She refused to speak again. Finally, after several minutes of silence, I gave up. I didn't have the time to spare.

Next we headed for Therea Janus' site. She and Roque Chavez were the two nickel miners. As Bernie steered through the shifting clusters of rocks in that part of space, I checked the time. My boss would be pacing the floor.

When we landed, Therea Janus was in her hut. She was a thin, nervous woman with thick, honey-blonde hair, which she wore loose. Her shapeless gray coveralls did nothing for what once must have been a beautiful woman. She had an air of harassment.

I showed her the items.

"I believe the comb belonged to David," she said.

"How did D'Angelo get the comb?"

Therea nibbled delicately at a knuckle. She refused to look at me. "I have no idea."

"Was D'Angelo depressed?"

"Certainly it's possible in surroundings such as these."

"Was he troubled by something?"

She shrugged.

"How did he feel about ending his stint with the Company?"

"Who can know?" she asked. "He was returning to Earth to see his daughter. He adored her, but it was a fool's dream. Gravity in the Well likely would have crushed him. Still, he exercised every day, and took his pills, so maybe he would have succeeded. Just to be away from this place, from the influence of everyone here. . . ."

She turned to look at me. "Why don't you ask Alma Cloudsinger? She and he were somewhat more than close friends, until he informed her she was ugly. I'm sure she was quite devastated. I understand he quarreled with David as well. David is a religious man, a man of the cloth. Joe would say to him, 'There is no God, there is no brotherhood of man, and you're going to die.' Joe loved the phrase, because it always made David furious.''

"D'Angelo had something on you, too," I said.

Her fist clenched. "I don't understand."

"According to your log, over the last year or so, you made a number of credit transfers out," I said. "At the same time, D'Angelo was getting extra credits in. The amounts match."

Therea stared out the window.

"Extortion is illegal," I said. "He was breaking the law."

"I didn't kill anyone," she said sullenly.

I ignored that. "What did he have on you?"

Her eyes glittered with unshed tears. "He know how badly I wanted my children back. Somehow he learned about some of the choices I made to support my family before I became a miner."

I waited.

"He said if I didn't pay him, he'd talk to the social workers and I could forget about ever seeing my children again."

"The payments stopped two months ago," I said.

She nodded, looking defeated. "My daughter fell ill. It cost everything I had for her care. Hospitals are expensive."

"What did D'Angelo do when you stopped giving him credits?"

"You know so much, why ask me?"

"He kept at you for credits, didn't he?"

"Yes," she said softly.

"And you didn't know what to do. It was him or your daughter. So you killed him."

"No," she cried. Her fist slammed the table, without force. She was sobbing. "I didn't kill him."

Bernie snapped her gum.

"I thought about it," Therea said. "Who wouldn't? It hasn't been easy. My husband Jack used to be my family's chauffeur. I was young and I thought we'd have an exciting life." She shook her head. "My father disinherited me when we were married, that was the first big blow. I was determined to hold my head up anyway. You're a policewoman, how could you know what it's like? Making a family was all-important. When Jack drank, he became abusive. Once he broke my ribs. I had nowhere to go. The life of a debutante doesn't teach you many job skills."

I felt sorry for her.

"One day Jack started for my son. I grabbed a knife. The judge declared it self-defense and I was acquitted." Tears slipped down her cheeks. "I would be convicted for certain if it happened again. I'd never see my children."

"It must have been rough," Bernie said.

"You know what it's like to sit here every night?" she asked. "I stare at the stars, and on every one, maybe, there're people with their families, while I'm here all alone. I miss my children."

We left her at her table, her head down.

According to his file, the next miner, Roque Chavez, was an electronics expert. He'd used his skills to commit several larcenies and he had done time. When we landed at his base camp, he refused to let us inside the cabin. "I didn't do nothing!" he shouted. "I'm no killer! You got nothing on me!"

After half an hour of banging on the door, we gave up and headed off to talk with Slim Monkers and Dave Davidson. I begrudged the time we were wasting, and begrudged even more the deadline the bureaucrats forced on us. Enough was enough. I was going to tell my boss that I wouldn't help with all this paperwork anymore. A person has to make a stand. I was a detective, not a bureaucrat.

Out near Slim's asteroid, we lost sight of Home Base, due to the amount of debris in space; dust, flying rocks, and loose planetoids. Even with the courses of the major asteroids charted by the computer, it was a tense flight.

Still, we reached Slim's rock without incident. He mined iron. Slim Monkers was a potbellied man with pale blond hair and a red face. Inside his metal cabin, I showed him the evidence.

His only revelation was about the stamp. It's valuable," he said. "At least, out here."

"Why?"

"Collectors," he said. "That specimen is from the 19th century. Stamps are lightweight, so they can be traded easily. Besides, people will pay big for a pretty picture."

"I understand you're divorced."

He sneered. "She married my wallet. When it wasn't fat enough, she dumped me. Good riddance."

"Why are you here? It's a long way from horticultural school."

"I got tired of working for rich folks," he said. "The rest of us can't own so much as a geranium. But if you're rich, you can plant Kentucky bluegrass on Mars, for chrissakes. Hey. that's fine by me. But why can't everyone have lawns? Why is it illegal to own a delphinium?"

"Delphiniums aren't productive," Bernie said. "The dome cities can't afford. . . ."

"Everybody's got an opinion and I got mine," he said with a snarl.

Slim had nothing more to add, so we flew to the last miner, Dave Davidson, who worked a tin mine. A former minister, he had thick, wavy hair, the color of salt and pepper. His face was narrow. His movements were abrupt. He checked us both out from top to bottom.

I showed him the comb.

"It's mine, all right," he said. He leaned back in a gray chair bolted to the wall of his metal home. "I lent the comb to Joe for making music last Christmas. May I please have it back?"

"I'll hold onto it for a while," I said.

He looked disappointed, but offered no objection.

"I understand D'Angelo had a few problems with the other miners."

"You mean with the women?" Dave said. He wet his lips and looked at Bernie seductively. She blushed. He continued to talk. "At Christmas, there was a little altercation. Joe was dancing with Therea, and whispering in her ear. Alma had a little too much to drink and cut in on Therea. The women fought over him."

"You saw this?"

"I was there. The fight started in the other room. One minute Joe was dancing with Therea and the next minute, the women were arguing. Alma was furious with Joe, too."

"What did you think of D'Angelo getting so much attention from both women?"

"I didn't think anything." Dave ran his fingers through his hair.

"You never disagreed with him?"

"Everyone disagreed with Joe."

"What about?"

"Everything," he said defensively. "The man was impossible."

"Like what?"

"I don't remember." He glared at me.

I changed my approach. "If D'Angelo was such a creep, how come the women liked him?"

"I don't know," Dave said. "I can't begin to understand women."

"You resented him?"

"Maybe," he admitted. "A little."

"Like when he made fun of your religion?"

"It was a lot of things. I'm a religious man, even if I do have difficulties with the church hierarchy. I'm out here to think about my life, away from the smells and bells. It's true, Joe pushed me. He was always saying something he thought was funny but was really cruel. Last Christmas he told Therea and Alma I was diseased. They avoided me after that. He said he couldn't wait to tell everyone at Home Base."

"You had to do something." I nodded.

"I denied it to everyone. They obviously didn't believe me."

"You were angry?"

"He was out to ruin my life."

"And you thought about revenge? We all feel that way sometimes."

"I . . ." He looked at me, then nodded.

"How did it happen?" I asked.

"I didn't kill him," he answered coldly.

"No harsh words?" I asked, while I studied his face. "No plotting? Even little fantasy plots?"

He refused to answer.

"D'Angelo kept on pushing you, didn't he?"

He ducked his head.

"Until it was unbearable?"

Silence.

"What would you have done, if you could?"

"You want me to say I'd have killed him," he said. "That would have been the end of me. I could never have lived with such a thing. Of course, I didn't have to, did I?" A faint look of triumph appeared in his eyes. "Someone did it for me."

"So you think someone murdered him."

"I don't know and I don't care."

"He was found alone. There was no evidence of anyone

else around, no record of any other ship coming close to the asteroid. How could anyone get to him?''

He gave me a cynical look.

"Did you ever physically fight with D'Angelo?" I asked.

"Never," he said. "I'm a man of peace."

I asked him about the stamp and the platinum. He admitted knowing nothing about the stamp, but he identified the metal correctly.

We returned to the shuttle. I felt defeated. The answer was here, somewhere. But where?

I called my boss. "I need a few more hours," I told her. "Something's going on here."

"What, exactly?"

I felt helpless. "I haven't pinned it down yet."

"Hek, I need you. If you want to play around out there, I'm sorry, the answer is no. You might as well know, one result of this meeting is that you will be required to stay in the office more. You're too useful to be gallivanting about the System. I expect you in my office tomorrow at eight." She broke the connection.

"Thanks, boss," I said to the empty line. It was already after midnight. I felt the frustration rising inside. My life was laid out before me—desk jockey until retirement. Should I quit? I couldn't. My family had been police for nearly two centuries. Seventeen retired with honors, and two killed in the line of duty. Who was I, if I wasn't a cop?

After Bernie launched our shuttle, I heated a food pack of boiled chicken and rice and tried to eat. It was a glum flight. Toward the end, I put in a call to Amalgamated. They had not yet announced Joe's death over the radio. "That just sets the miners off," the man explained. "It doesn't take much."

There was a sharp jolt, and the radio receiver went dead. Bernie gave the instrument board a smack. "Sheesh! It's always those little ones that slip by the scoop and hit us."

As we flew, I thought about the miners: the invisible Roque; Therea, so elegant on the surface, a battered wife who killed her husband, then found herself blackmailed by the dead miner for past indiscretions; Slim, with his anger at women and rich people; Alma, a jilted lover; Dave, a former preacher trying to stay peaceful, but goaded ruthlessly. Who actually killed D'Angelo, and how?

I looked out the window. A huge asteroid trailed off to

the left, slowly crossing between Alma's asteroid and Home Base. It would eclipse her rock for an hour or so, then be on its way.

And suddenly everything made sense. Of course!

"Head for Alma's rock," I told Bernie.

"We just saw her," Bernie said. "Anyway, it's late. I'm tired. Let's go home."

"Move it, Bernie. Now!"

Bernie puckered her red lips. "We don't have a radio," she said.

"Fly without one."

"That's dangerous. Anyway, we're low on fuel."

"How low?"

"We can land at Alma's, and take off again," she admitted after she checked the virtual gauge. "But that's about it."

"That's all I need."

Bernie gave me a sour look, but turned our shuttle toward Alma's asteroid.

The light was off in Alma's cabin when we landed. Nobody was home. The landscape was empty.

Out of the corner of my eye, I saw something gleam. It was a small object, headed right for us. I tackled Bernie. We tumbled to the ground in low grav motion.

A knife sailed past our heads.

"My God," Bernie said. "What's going on here?"

I tried to locate the place where the attack originated. Over by the mine, I saw a black object. On closer inspection, I realized it was a camouflaged shuttle. I told Bernie to return to Home base and get help.

"What about you?"

"This is my job!" I snapped. "Your job is to send in my backup. Pronto!"

"Home Base is two hours away," she argued.

"Move it!"

She ran back to our shuttle. Moments later, I saw her lift off.

I worried about my low air supply, but I was too close to quit. This was my chance to find the murderer.

When we first saw Alma, she'd been near a crevasse. I hurried to that same crack in the rock. Numerous footprints led to it, and over the edge. I jumped in, and landed on a flat platform at the bottom.

Footprints led into a cave. I saw light coming from around a corner at the back. I drew my needle gun and charged forward.

Alma stood under the light of a white flare. Crouched around her were three dark objects in four-legged suits, each about knee-high. The airwaves filled with strangely familiar yips. The creatures bounded forward. I aimed my weapon.

"Fifi! Poopsie! Muffie! *Stop!*"

The dogs lost their footing. I stepped aside as they sailed past and crashed into the far side of the cave. I looked from them to Alma.

"Don't hurt my babies," she pleaded.

The dogs untangled themselves and retreated to her, whining. I faced her. "Where is he, Alma?"

"Who?" she asked.

"There's been a murder here, Alma. Don't act coy, or you'll be up for conspiracy. Your platinum was found on the dead man's asteroid, don't forget."

"You can't prove it's mine."

"I think we can," I said. "Metals can be traced to their place of origin. You know as well as I do. Platinum is found with gold regularly. This is the only mine on these rocks likely to have platinum."

Alma began to sob. She pointed to a narrow passage at the rear of the cave. I moved cautiously in that direction. I stopped beside the opening and took a deep breath.

"Come out, Slim, with your hands up."

Slim charged. I pulled the trigger. The weapon misfired. Slim lowered his shoulder and drove it into me. The gun flew from my hand. Slim kept going, trying to escape. I turned to follow, but ran straight into Alma. She clutched at me, knocking us both off our feet.

"My poor babies! Don't take my babies!" she cried. Unable to get untangled, we bounced together into a corner. The dogs romped in after us. Slim fled the cave.

I swung an arm around, scattering the dogs and Alma. She struck the far wall hard, and moaned as she went down.

I raced after Slim. I caught up with him just as he was jumping out of the crevasse. I leaped, grabbed his ankle, and yanked him down.

He kicked at me. I avoided the blow and threw him to the ground. He struggled, and cost me precious minutes before I managed to handcuff him. I shoved him to his feet and pushed him ahead of me as I returned to Alma. She wasn't moving, but she was breathing normally. I looked into her helmet and checked the gauges. She had fifteen minutes of air left. I checked my own gauges—only twelve minutes remained, not enough for me to reach Alma's cabin.

Slim saw my reaction. His mouth formed a twisted smile. "You caught me. So what? You don't have enough oxy to last until your buddy returns."

I checked the area quickly. I saw nothing but rocks and gravel. The passageway in which he had hidden seemed to be no more than a natural break in the rock. Then, against one wall of the cave, I spotted a pile of disturbed dirt. I began to dig. If my guess was wrong, I was dead.

I found nothing. I moved to my right and kept digging. Just under the soil, my gloves hit an odd shape. I cleared away the debris and found the outlines of a trap door angled into the wall of the cave. Slim swore.

I opened the door, threw Alma over my shoulder and pushed a reluctant Slim ahead of me. The dogs crowded in at our heels. We went through a pressure chamber. When I pushed through the inner door, I stepped forward into a burst of light.

A riot of colors lay before me—reds, golds, yellows, pinks and, more important than all the other colors, *green,* the color of respirating plants.

I threw off my helmet and breathed the humid air of a greenhouse, filled with oxygen and endless, luscious smells I had never known.

I lay Alma down beside one wall. Her eyelids fluttered as I took off her helmet. The dogs bumped at her face. The rich air revived her. She seemed okay.

"How did you know about this?" Slim said.

"When I saw the asteroid eclipsing Alma's rock, I realized anyone who tracked the orbits of the asteroids could follow behind them in a shuttle and reach any mining site unseen. That spelled smuggling to me."

Slim's face grew red.

"In fact, the smuggler almost had to be down here right now, because an eclipse by such a rock would happen only every few months, too rare an opportunity to miss.

"But who was the smuggler, and what was the product? Ore?" I shook my head. "It's too heavy. That's why the Company smelts it on site.

"That yip over Alma's radio was the other clue. She had dogs. It was hard to believe, but evidently true. I asked myself, why have dogs out here? Where's the wealth to be gained in dogs? You could sell them, but they weigh too much to be shipping from site to site. How else are they valuable?

"I figure they produce two things cheaply—carbon dioxide and fertilizer. To me, that means plants. And you, Slim, are the horticulturalist. It was a brilliant little scam. All these isolated rocks. Just enough gravity to grow roses, geraniums, and all the plants illegal in the domed cities because they don't produce enough, but which are so precious that wealthy people will pay nearly anything for them."

"I'm gonna lose my babies!" Alma said. She buried her face into the neck of one of her dogs.

"Maybe not," I said. "Make an offer to Amalgamated. You'll raise your dogs and they can have the profits from the plants. They can sell them easily enough—if they grow legal ones. I'll talk to Bernie. She may have the connections to help you. They may even let you keep those radio transmitters Roque made for all of you.

"That way Amalgamated turns a profit, their employees stay happier, and maybe there will be fewer suicides. Too bad you won't have a chance to enjoy it, Slim."

Slim made a strange sound, a mix between a snort and a sob. "There ain't enough evidence to convict me of murder."

"Maybe," I said. "Maybe not." I plucked a pea from a vine. I'd never seen a pea except in videos from Earth. "I'm sure you were smart enough to get rid of the oxy tank Joe was wearing that day he walked two hours from his base camp to meet your shuttle, out where no cameras could record your meeting."

I continued remorselessly. "Because if he went that far on one tank, Slim, he must have been expecting to use another to return to his camp, another canister he could switch to while he sat with you in your shuttle."

"Did you find any tracks of a shuttle landing?" he asked quickly.

"You never landed," I said. "You hovered just above the ground. What about it? Did you throw out an extra oxygen tank, a canister which you might need someday? I never

threw away oxygen, not once in my life, not even oxygen
in a nearly empty tank. Did you?''

He didn't deny it. Looking at each other, we both knew
I was going to find that last oxygen tank back at his asteroid,
with Joe's fingerprints all over it. I popped a pea in my
mouth. I liked the taste.

''Why would I kill him?'' he asked. His voice had developed a wheedling quality. ''Why suspect me?''

''D'Angelo was going home,'' I said. ''He was returning
to his daughter on Earth, far away from you. Everyone knew
D'Angelo had a big mouth. If there was one thing you could
count on, it was the fact that he would talk. You couldn't
risk that.''

''He deserved it,'' Slim whined. ''He was holding out on
me!''

''How?''

''I paid him up front for making a scale. We planned to
sell the plants by weight. When he came out to meet me,
he had the scale but not the weight. He said he wanted more
stamps. We used them like credits.''

''The weight was made of platinum?''

''Platinum don't rust, don't lose mass, even in the humidity of a greenhouse. It's a perfect metal for scales.''

''So you just wrote off the metal as a bad investment and
took the scale that he made, minus the weight, sent him out
with a bad tank, and left him to die.''

He glared at me.

''What about it, Slim? I imagine if we look over the tank,
we'll find its gauge reads full even though it's nearly
empty.''

''I didn't do nothing wrong,'' Slim argued.

''Yeah, right. You're just a simple country boy longing
for a garden. But smuggling's illegal, and murdering to protect your racket is even more so. I think we can guarantee
you a mind wipe, my friend.''

Ignoring the terror in Slim's eyes, I snapped off a bright
red tomato and held it to the light. The fruit was almost
translucent. ''You'll have plenty of time before they eliminate your personality, Slim, to think about how D'Angelo
felt those last moments, when he realized he was facing
certain death, while all the time you were up above, gloat-
ing.''

At that moment, two of the System's Finest charged

through the door, weapons drawn, followed by a gum-snapping Bernie. The dogs nearly knocked them all down.

Cautiously, my boss entered after them. In spite of the late hour, her white space suit was immaculate.

"You gave us quite a scare," she said.

"Hi, boss," I said. "Meet Joe D'Angelo's killer."

She looked surprised.

"By the way," I said. "I've thought about your decision to move me back to the office full time. I don't want to. I quit."

My boss' mouth hung open. I grinned at her and bit into the tomato. Its cool, delicious sweetness burst down my throat.

SIGNS AND STONES

by Judith Tarr

Judy Tarr claims to be more comfortable writing her best-selling fantasy novels, but this story shows the author of *The Dagger and the Cross* to be equally at home with science fiction.

A locked-room mystery. An alien is found dead in his/its quarters in a very swank multi-environmental spaceliner. A human detective, on board on his vacation, is summoned by the captain and asked to try to solve the murder as quickly and discreetly as possible; on the one hand, the captain doesn't want bad publicity, but on the other, he realizes that there is a killer loose aboard the ship.

The only clues at the scene of the crime are a brand-new handkerchief possessing neither monogram nor fingerprints; a quill pen; and what appears to be the plastic wrapper for a small book. Since the killer had plenty of time to make his escape, it can be assumed that these were left behind either to mislead the police, or because the killer did not think they could be used to identify him.

Solve the murder.

The passenger in cabin 393B was dead. Dead, Farley reflected, as a doornail. Farley had moments of classical allusion: a hazard of his occupations. Both of them.

Captain R'kansssass was blue around the gills. The crewperson who had found the body had collapsed in a massive faint.

Farley edged around the deck steward and looked down at the *corpus delicti*. It lay on its side on the deck, looking amazingly like a sleeping Terran rhinoceros. Its mouth was slightly open. Its eyes were squeezed tight shut.

"No sign of violence," Farley said. His translator beeped and booped.

Captain R'kansssass hissed and hooted back. The translator said, "Passengers do not just die. Not on my ship.

"And," she said, "there are these." She gestured with a tentacle.

Farley's eyebrow went up. The room was unfurnished, which seemed to be the passenger's preference, except for a sleeping platform upholstered with pale chartreuse straw. The center of it was hollowed out in a space that would just accommodate the passenger, asleep. In the middle of that lay three perfectly ordinary, but perfectly incongruous, objects.

The plastic wrapper was common enough. On a cruise of this duration, a passenger who was disinclined toward food, games, or ogling fellow passengers had few other choices but to read. Farley peered at the title on the wrapper. A gaudy romance in Galactic Standard, with its covergram half torn through, blurring the image of a spectacularly mammalian humanoid in apparent distress.

Interesting choice of reading matter, Farley thought, for a passenger recorded as Scholar-Philosopher First Class, en route to the Interspecies Philosophical Congress on Derrida. But Farley knew a little about scholar-philosophers. The book would hardly have made his eyebrow twitch. The other two objects, however . . .

"A quill pen," he said, noting absently the tortured squawking of his translator as it tried to convey the concept. "No ink or any sign of use. And a handkerchief. Clean. No monogram. No mark at all, not even a manufacturer's label." He had unfolded the handkerchief to be sure. He folded it again. "Fascinating."

Captain R'kansssass hissed like a kettle on the boil. "Fascinating! Is that all you can say? Fascinating? One of my passengers is dead, and all you can say is—"

"Fascinating," said Farley. "And no reader for the book. Which implies—"

"Highgrassians do not read," said the captain. "They absorb knowledge, they say, through the skin. The ears, you would say. The computer would provide vocal feed. Not—" her tentacles flicked disdainfully—"this."

"So one might assume that if in fact this was a murder,

the murderer left the bookwrapper at least," Farley said. "And possibly the other objects as well."

"*Human* objects," the captain said. She seemed to have recovered her equilibrium. Her gills looked a shade less blue.

"In which case," said Farley, "I could be a prime suspect, if this is murder and not simple heart-analogue failure."

The captain's hide flashed from pearly pink through bright purple and back again. *Negation,* said the translator in retinal code. "You are the famous detective Mycroft Nkruma Farley. You are incapable of causing any death so obvious, or so frankly melodramatic, as this."

Farley had his doubts. Melodrama would have been blood, and edged weapons. But different species had different ideas of the dramatic. "So," he said mildly. "You've found me out."

"It is the captain's duty to know the identities of her passengers. And their occupations." Her voice through the translator sounded prim. "You are also, of course, the passenger under whose name you travel, the even more famous, dare I say notorious—"

"I am," said Farley. He returned the handkerchief to its place on the bed. "Your security staff will want to perform its own investigations, according to its own methods. If you would call them in, we can begin."

The captain bubbled and gurgled. "We must have discretion. We must! If the passengers discover that there has been a death on board—the panic, the morbid curiosity, the outrage, the lawsuits—"

"Your security chief, then," Farley said firmly, cutting through her babble, "and one of her most trusted, and most discreet, assistants."

The security chief and her trusted assistant discovered just about what Farley had expected, which was nothing. The computer had no record of any visitor or communication for the last shipday, except a steward with a cartload of fodder. That, once its contents were consumed, had been left in the corridor and duly collected. To all appearances, Its Excellency the Scholar-Philosopher First Class Grazer-in-the-Deep-Grasses had spent a completely quiet, completely and characteristically isolated shipday dozing, accessing the computer for information on Early Late New Neoplatonism, and revising the lecture it would be delivering at the conference.

Medical delivered a verdict of Death by Natural Causes. "Except," said the ship's doctor, "with a Highgrassian in that phase, there *is* no such thing as death by natural causes."

Farley invited himer to continue. The doctor was himerself in a transitional phase for an Eridanian, with the sweet, almost cloying voice of a male, but the dun plumage of a precoital female. Heshe smoothed back a feather that showed just a glimmer of iridescence, and clacked hiser beak in irritation. "Tolerate if you will, gentlebeing, a brief disquisition. Natives of Highgrass, like natives of my own world, undergo certain alterations as they mature." Heshe stabbed a button on the medconsole. An image appeared in front of Farley. It looked rather like a small dog.

"This," said the doctor, "is a newborn first-stage Highgrassian. At puberty, after a series of complex metamorphoses, it enters a second stage." Farley started. This was thoroughly humanoid, and quite familiar.

"That's a Fomalhautian dockhand," he said.

"That is a sexually mature male Highgrassian. Females are similar, but larger and less . . . glabrous."

Hairier, heshe meant. But also considerably more mammalian. Like, Farley realized, the bookwrapper he had seen in cabin 393B.

"Fomalhautian dockhands are male Highgrassians?" Farley said. It was not really a question. "Highgrassians are known for their total isolationism. And dockhands—"

"Dockhands are absolute nonentities," the doctor said. "Hired muscle, more economical than mechtechs. Need anyone know or care where they come from? These happen to be the unmated, unchosen males, who find that life on their own planet palls quickly, and who travel the spacelanes acquiring substantial wages which they then, dutifully, return through complex channels to their families on their homeworld. Since sexual congress is the trigger for the next phase, these never attain the metamorphosis, but die abroad or return home to a mate and metamorphosis or to inevitable and fairly accelerated death. Those who do metamorphose become the public image of their race, such as that representative who has so unfortunately been murdered on our ship.''

''I gather,'' Farley said, eyeing the image of the upright, dignified, togaed rhinoceros in what was clearly a university classroom, ''that in this phase, Highgrassians are virtually invulnerable.''

''Virtually,'' the doctor said, ''yes. To all intents and purposes, Philosopher-phase Highgrassians are immortal. They are not, it is true, indestructible. They can be killed. It takes a considerable amount of effort and application, and no little time. There was, in fact, a sect which devoted itself to a form of ritual suicide; the rites were a planet-year long, and extremely elaborate. If the victims were insufficiently careful, they never died at all, but simply accelerated their final metamorphosis.''

Farley regarded this latest image. In the light of the rest, it was hardly surprising. ''A sacred cow.''

''A final-phase Highgrassian,'' the doctor said with a snap of hiser beak. ''Placid, barely sentient, and content to graze its way into oblivion. Under the dogma of the Long Death Cult, death in Philosopher phase was more blessed, but death in final phase was honorable enough, and inevitable.''

''What else triggers final phase,'' Farley inquired, ''besides prolonged torture?''

''The Long Death Cult has long been suppressed,'' the doctor said. ''Final phase now occurs naturally and only, after a sufficient number of local centuries, under the stimulus of excessive population pressure. Or so I deduce, since Highgrassians will never leave their homeworld, and keep their population down to carefully calculated levels, particularly in the vicinity of their universities.''

''So if a Highgrassian wanted to commit slow suicide,'' said Farley, ''it would only have to invite all its friends and relations to live with it, and make sure that they produced plentiful offspring.''

''That,'' said the doctor, ''is disgusting.''

''Thank you,'' said Farley. ''So this death of a Philosopher, suddenly, with no prior warning, can only be murder.''

''It is impossible,'' the doctor said.

''In the current state of medical knowledge,'' said Farley, ''it is.''

* * *

He had not endeared himself to the ship's doctor. It was
not his job to be endearing, even in his current, public per-
sona. As far as the ship was concerned, he carried on in his
established fashion. He appeared in the casino. He sneered
at the health cultists in the hologardens. He wandered
through the accessible levels, making use of his breathing
apparatus where necessary, but avoiding the more hostile
decks, since a human in an impermasuit would at this stage
be excessively conspicuous. He dined each shipnight at his
assigned table in the seating reserved for oxygen-breathing
omnivores who preferred their nourishment dead on arrival.
That had been interpreted with some latitude in the case of
the Zki-riiiit whose scream and thrashing leap assured that
its prey was deceased when it reached the table, but eti-
quette forbade comment.

Without seeming to be a man-about-the-ship, he managed
to address as many of the passengers as attracted his, or the
computer's, attention. Sometimes it was even a pleasure.
The lady from Barthes University . . .

"I should point out," said Captain R'kansssass, "that Its
Excellency has been dead for half an eight of shipdays. And
you appear to be no closer to a solution that when its death
was first discovered."

"I wouldn't say that," said Farley, sitting back in the
conformachair. The captain had paid him the unusual com-
pliment of calling on him in his cabin. Her bulk, and what
appeared to be a leak in her breathing apparatus, filled the
room with a faint marshy redolence. Subvocally, he instructed the cabin's atmosystem to counteract the imbal-
ance. The system obliged with a whiff of heaven that also
happened to be Madame Tsi-Nyu's favored perfume.

"So?" the captain bubbled, oblivious to his distraction.
"You have suspects?"

"I may," Farley said. He sipped at the bulb he had ordered before the captain arrived. She had declined to join
him. In her agitation she kept overflowing the chairsling and
pouring toward the walls.

Farley suppressed a sigh. When he'd assumed his second
identity to take this cruise, he had expected to work. He
had not expected that work to be detection of a murder. It
was karma, he supposed, or a curse. In the media, death
attached itself to detectives. Beings dropped dead around

them. He had thought himself free of the myth; barked in the happy expectation of a T-month free from and all suggestion of death, detection, or disaster.

He squeezed the last drop of Glenlivet onto his tongue, rolled it until it sublimed into the ether of his hard palate, and set down the bulb. The captain was almost completely amorphous, a faintly blue-tinged, rose-pink mass with upright and quivering eyestalks.

Farley addressed her in his driest tone. "In examining the ship's manifest which you so generously provided me, and in inspecting the passengers' files, I was interested to note the peculiarly homogeneous quality of their occupations and avocations."

The eyestalks stilled. "This is a multispecies, multienvironmental ship," the captain said. "Surely you would not accuse us of the crime of excessive homogeneity."

"Certainly not," said Farley. "But I note that a substantial percentage of passengers are members of a charter voyage to the Interspecies Conference, either participants or their guests or attachments. Our victim was one such, and a rarity at that: the first Highgrassian Scholar-Philosopher to leave its homeworld in several standard decades."

"We are the favored line, and the favored vessel, for the Conference," the captain said with some pride. She had recovered herself sufficiently to resume her usual octopoidal shape. "We have been ferrying guests since the first gathering. And never," she said, growing agitated again, "have we suffered a single mishap."

"Certainly not," Farley said. "Your record has been exemplary. I myself chose this ship, and this particular charter, for that reason."

"Then it is fortunate for us," said the captain, "that you are aboard for this of all possible disasters."

Farley could not help but admire her agility of mind, although he deplored her lack of paranoia. "I could perfectly well have staged the entire affair for my own amusement," he pointed out.

"No," she said flatly. "You are not amused. Your stress readings indicate that you are considerably annoyed, reluctantly diverted, and deplorably fascinated by certain of the passengers whom you have been, for lack of a better concept, investigating. Do you believe that the murderer is a human woman of somewhat unexceptional endowments?"

"Madame Tsi-Nyu," said Farley with dignity, "is a charming lady of considerable intelligence and wit."

"She was also the last known being to speak to Its Excellency before its death."

Farley closed his mouth with care. "I see that I've underestimated you, Captain."

The captain quivered its anterior set of tentacles: a shrug. "I have a strong and pressing interest in the solution of this crime."

"Then you also know," said Farley, "that Madame Tsi-Nyu is a scholar-philosopher in her own right, and a colleague of Its late and yet-to-be-lamented Excellency."

"A rival, one might say," the captain said.

"But then," said Farley, "so are two-thirds of the passengers on this ship. No scholar is an honest friend to any other, as long as the law of Publish-or-Perish holds true."

"So I understand," the captain said. "Clearly Its Excellency was given no opportunity to publish; rather, it perished."

Madame Tsi-Nyu was at her scintillating best that shipevening, holding court in the oxybreathers' lounge. She was not a beautiful woman, as humans went. She was shorter than the norm, she was plumper than fashion decreed, her features were agreeable but irregular, her hair allowed, with scholarly carelessness, to go gray. None of which mattered in the least, once one had basked in the warmth of her charm.

She greeted Farley with delight. "My dear Mycroft! See who has consented to emerge from his lair tonight, and all, he says, for the pleasure of our company." Her hand, ornamented with a large and rather splendid Denebian opal, swept in a graceful gesture toward the being beside her.

Farley bowed in a particular, bobbing fashion. The alien bowed in return, a little less deeply, with a flourish of glimmering crest. "Dweller in High Places," Farley said. "You honor us with your presence."

"Oddly symbolic, is it not," someone nearby observed, "how often rank is implied by elevation."

The voice was human. The face was young, smooth, and self-consciously intelligent. "Ser diJon," Farley said by way of greeting.

The young man ignored him. "Elder," he said to the

alien, "is that, too, an Archetype: the high place, and the ruler as the dweller in it?"

"All things are a sign," said Dweller in High Places, "and the Types are in all that is or is perceived." The flick of his crest and the quick double blink of his eye was a smile. "Or so I attempt to teach. Ser diJon, is it true that you reckon yourself an analyst of Archetypes?"

"Oh," said the young man in evident confusion. "I'm nothing as lofty as that. I'm a critic, no more."

"A reviewer," Madame Tsi-Nyu said, "of popular fiction. He's to be a speaker at our conference, did you know?"

Farley knew. He watched the flush travel up the young man's face.

"Fiction is a mirror," the Elder said in a tone that the translator rendered as gentle, "as clear as any that there may be. Clearer than most, for a truth. Have you read the work of Merris deVane?"

DiJon's flush deepened.

Farley allowed himself a moment's pity for youth and snobbery. "I've read it all," he said, "or as much as I can find. Marvelous stuff. Robust. Swashbuckling. Not too badly written. Did you know the author is a pseudonym?"

DiJon was lost in mortification. The Elder looked politely puzzled. Madame Tsi-Nyu said, "Oh, is she? I'd wondered. Is she anyone we know, do you think?"

"Who's to tell?" said Farley. "I've heard that she may not be human, in spite of the name."

"If such is the case," said Dweller in High Places, "she is a master of your human psychology."

"No doubt of that," Farley said. "It's a shame she's sold and packaged so thoroughly in genre. She loses the respect she deserves, and would have if she sold less well, or suffered less lurid a reputation."

"Unfortunate," Dweller in High Places observed, "that popularity is so often mistaken for vulgarity."

"And the shadow for the Type," diJon said, so suddenly that Madame Tsi-Nyu started. Farley, who had kept the corner of an eye on him, noted that his flush had died to a ruddy glow. "Her books are perfect trash. Perfect. Every word is calculated to manipulate the psyche just so. When I reviewed *Far Cries Across the Worlds*—"

"That was in the *Newer York Times*, no?" Madame Tsi-

Nyu inquired. "Interesting analysis. Very. What was it that its like used to be called?"

"A hatchet job," the Elder said in precise and pedantic tones, "I believe. It was a masterful example of its kind."

"It was a frank analysis of a cultural phenomenon," said DiJon with a degre of heat. "If I had taken out the quotable lines, turned the summary around and grayed down the prose, it would have been a perfectly acceptable paper for the Conference."

"Is that what you'll be doing?" Farley asked. "Recycling your reviews?"

"A review," said diJon, "is not a piece of literary criticism. Each requires a different cognitive orientation, and serves a different purpose."

"Shadows again," the Elder mused, "and Types. How fascinating! I had never thought of these things in quite such a fashion. Is the book the shadow or the Type? Is the critic the true philosopher or the dreamer in the cave?"

"The reviewer is the recorder," Farley said, "and the consumer's guide."

"Of course you would say so," said diJon.

Farley smiled. "I do the odd review myself," he said, "and the occasional bit of criticism. Aren't we on the reviewers' panel together, Ser diJon?"

"Not that I recall," the young man said coldly.

"Well," Farley said. "I did sign on late. I haven't seen the program."

Ser diJon looked thoroughly disgusted. Farley broadened his smile until the young pup muttered something that might have been an excuse, and made himself scarce.

"That was not kind of you," said Madame Tsi-Nyu. Her eyes were laughing, Farley noticed.

"He's young," Farley said. "With luck and good feeding, he'll outgrow it."

"One may hope so," said Dweller in High Places.

"Yes," said Madame Tsi-Nyu when they had attained an agreeable measure of privacy. "I was the last to speak to Grazer-in-the-Deep-Grasses. So it is dead, then?"

Farley raised his eyebrow. "Someone's been talking."

"Someone has been deducing," said Madame Tsi-Nyu. "No one has seen Its Excellency in some shipdays. And that, while not uncommon, is suspicious enough, with the whispers one hears. The captain is unusually agitated for so placid a voyage."

"How many people know?" Farley asked.

She shrugged. It was a pleasure to watch. "Not many, I think. It had friends, but those are not numerous, and they respect its desire for privacy. Privacy is a great virtue among its kind."

"The greatest, I've been told."

"Maybe," she said.

"What did you talk about, then? Anything unusual?"

She regarded him levelly. He resisted the urge to squirm. He was a bare T-decade her junior, if that, and a professional in his own right—in both of his personae. Even so, she could make him rarely uncomfortable.

"Solomon al-Rahib Mycroft," she said, "one would think that we were in a detective novel, and you were the detective."

"I do not," he said grimly, "write detective novels."

"You certainly do not," she said. "As far as anyone knows. Why are you so interested in our late passenger?"

"It was murdered," Farley said.

She did not seem startled. "It would have had to be, wouldn't it? Since it was a Philosopher." Suddenly her eyes were full of tears. "It was so gentle, Mycroft. So wise. We spoke of nothing in particular—shadows, Types, signs and significations, the wind in the high grass, the taste of cool water in the sun's heat." She buried her face in his robe-front. "Oh, Mycroft! How could anyone have been so cruel as to kill it?"

Farley patted her and soothed her and did his best not to think of the baser passions. Her grief was genuine. He was sure of that.

Much later, and rather more rumpled than he had been when he began, he made his way along a corridor. It was deep in shipnight, and the lights were dimmed accordingly. He opted not to engage his augments, but made his way by natural vision, thinking of nothing in particular, letting his mind run on without his assistance.

The observation deck was all but deserted. There was nothing to see in nullspace, but Farley had an odd predilection for that degree of nothingness: neither white nor gray nor black, but somewhere in between. Some species went mad in contemplation of it. Farley found it soothing.

The shadow by the curve of the hull resolved itself into a tall-crested, vaguely avian, vaguely reptilian shape. Its eyes blinked, glowing green. It bobbed a greeting.

"Elder," said Farley, bobbing in return.

"Ser Mycroft," said Dweller in High Places.

There was a silence. Farley absorbed himself in the view, or the lack thereof.

At length the Elder said, "Here, of all places that are, one best understands the truth."

"Is there one?" Farley asked.

"Oh, yes," said the Elder of the Church of the Universal Archetype. "Certainly. Whether it is the truth that one wishes to see . . . that, I cannot judge."

"Is it true," asked Farley, "that in your belief, all species must be one, and all faiths one faith, united in the One Truth?"

"There is no *must,*" the Elder said. "Only *is.*"

"On Highgrass, Philosophers would disagree with you profoundly."

The Elder's crest flattened. "So they would," he said. His tone was mild. "There, each species must be sufficient unto itself, and each world should hold itself apart, lest it be contaminated by the evil of the Union."

"Yet a Philosopher came to the conference that represents all its race must abhor," said Farley. "You spoke often with it. Were you friends, after all? Or amicable enemies?"

"Both," said Dweller in High Places. "If friendship is to share a meeting of minds, and to take pleasure in it— then we were friends. If enmity is to find no common ground of race or creed or philosophy, then we were enemies. I am sorry that it is dead. I have seldom known any being who so wonderfully challenged my assumptions."

"It's not officially dead," Farley said.

"I know," said the Elder. "I knew when it died. Friend-enemies have such a bond."

Farley leaned forward. "Do you mean to say that you sensed its death?"

"I am not psi-rated," the Elder said, "nor if I were, would I have been attuned to one so alien. But when it died, I felt its passing."

"And you said nothing to anyone?"

"To whom would I speak? Whom would I trust?"

"Madame Tsi-Nyu."

The Elder flicked his crest, amused perhaps, or slightly surprised. "She is, indeed, one in whom to confide."

"And another friend-enemy?"

"A colleague," said Dweller in High Places.

Farley paused. His next question came slowly, each word framed with care. "Is it true that the Philosopher had introduced a new form of isolationist dogma, one that would, once it had been promulgated, severely undercut your efforts on certain worlds of the Union?"

"If so," the Elder replied with no evident hesitation, "it had not spoken of it to me. Nor, surely, would it have so far transgressed its own doctrine as to attend the Conference."

"Unless the sin was necessary in order to serve the greater good."

"Such a sin would require its exile and, if possible, its death."

"Exactly," said Farley.

Dweller in High Places drew himself up. He towered above Farley's not inconsiderable height. "Suicide is not a choice that a Philosopher of that race can make."

"Unless it is necessary," Farley said again.

"I can be no judge of necessity in any being but myself," the Elder said, and his voice was cold.

Farley took that as a dismissal. He bowed. His bow was not returned. When, at the door, he looked back, the Elder's back was to him, its eyes fixed on the void between the stars.

"Pseudonyms?" Ser diJon said. "Of course they interest me. Why a person would choose to write under another name or another identity—whether it's a form of concealment, or an almost ritual invocation of a different spirit—"

"Or gender," said Madame Tsi-Nyu. "Or species."

Farley was eavesdropping. He did not blush at it, even if he had been, like poor Ser diJon, pale enough for it to show. The scholar and the critic were sitting on a bench in the ship's garden. A rather sad-looking pale-green tree drooped over them.

"I've made a study of pseudonymous authors," Ser diJon went on. "Eventually it will be a book. Did you know how many of them are actually of a different species than they claim to be? More than half. And if you think that only promulgators of popular trash choose to hide themselves behind another name—I've found three major literary authors, so far, whose official biographies are unverifiable.''

"They may simply be extremely private people," said Madame Tsi-Nyu.

"Maybe," Ser diJon said. He paused. "Do you know very much about the Church of the Universal Archetype?"

"I know a little," Madame Tsi-Nyu said. Her voice was serene. "Why?"

"It's odd," said Ser diJon. "Their Sacred Book is right out on the net for anyone to read. But talk to a practitioner, get her going, and she almost always hints at more."

"Such as?"

"Well," he said. "Suppose that everything is a shadow of a Type, and the universe strives toward a universal truth. What if a person consciously lives a lie?"

"Much of social interaction consists of discreet concealments and words left unsaid."

"And the public Book condemns that," he said. "But what if a person pretended be something, or someone, that she isn't? For example—a pseudonymous author with a spurious biography. How would the Church regard that?"

"With regret, I would presume," said Madame Tsi-Nyu.

"It could be more than regret," he said. "In a fanatic, or in someone who takes the secret teachings too seriously."

"I can't imagine," said Madame Tsi-Nyu, "that even a fanatical Archetypist would go about scourging and flaying pseudonymous authors of popular fiction."

Farley, concealed behind a hedge, suppressed an urge to laugh.

Ser diJon, however, was young, and being young, had no sense of humor in such matters. "Oh, I can imagine worse. I can imagine a fanatic committing murder. If the crime were great enough—if the imposture were sufficiently appalling."

"Are you saying," she asked with a ripple of mirth, "that some enthusiastic proponent of the Archetype has an irresistible urge to rid the worlds of Merris deVane? Is it you, perhaps? Are you a secret Archetypist?"

Farley could not see diJon's face, but could well imagine

the flush that suffused it. "I am nothing more or less than I pretend to be. If I want to commit mayhem, I'll do it in a review, where the worlds can see."

"And so you have," she said. "So you certainly have."

This time Farley went to the captain, albeit at her request. She saw him in her office, a peculiarly characterless place that tried to be all styles and none, to all species and none. Its atmosystem was set to a bland all-purpose oxygen mix with a suggestion of salt flat and tidal marsh. Farley made himself comfortable in a conformachair and waited.

"Well?" the captain said. "What have you been doing?"

"Reading," Farley answered.

Her tentacles writhed. "What—"

"Popular fiction," said Farley. "Specifically, the works of Merris deVane, Musharrog of Deneb, and the Unnamed Romanticist."

There was a pause. Farley fancied that the sea-reek intensified.

"I thought," the captain said, "that I had asked you to solve a crime."

"It is a crime," Farley said, "how excruciatingly badly some of these books are copyedited, packaged, and produced. I'm quite certain that Musharrog's *Savage Saurian Passion* was gutted by what I hesitate to call its editor: there are glimmers of genuine competence, repeatedly and obviously hacked at or suppressed." He shook his head, taking no notice of the captain's bright blue gills. "Really, I'm going to have some very cutting things to say when I speak at the Conference."

"Have you forgotten that there is a corpse on my ship?"

The translator could not render a true shriek, but it provided a more than adequate imitation. Farley winced and waited for his ears to stop ringing. "Of course I haven't forgotten. I've been conducting investigations in my own fashion."

"By reading popular effluent and pursing attractive and not so attractive females of your approximate species?"

"Madam," said Farley coldly, "I am, as you are fond of pointing out, the famous detective Mycroft Nkruma Farley. I am also the notorious producer of popular effluent, Solomon al-Rahib Mycroft. In order to pursue the activities of the former, I must of necessity continue those of the latter."

"You do not produce popular effluent," the captain said. "You produce popular mindcandy with an occasional pretension to literary quality."

"So does Merris deVane," said Farley. "She really is better than her reputation."

"If the Philosopher was even a fraction as infuriating as you, it's small wonder it was murdered. Though how, with no record left behind, no sign of foul play, no hint of malice or deception among any of our passengers—"

"I wouldn't say that," said Farley. "There's a great deal of backbiting, particularly among the human-literature scholars. ShuManGa cut the august Professor Phathoumthong dead in the casino last night. Figuratively speaking, of course."

"The corpse in cabin 393B is not figurative," the captain said. "It is in stasis, awaiting solution of its murder and notification of its kin."

"You haven't sent notice to its next of kin?" Farley was shocked. "Do it, then, by all means."

"It is significantly less troublesome to send a subspace feed from normal space, than to do so from subspace itself. When we emerge at our destination, I will send the notice. By which time I hope to include as well, the name and motive of the murderer, and some assurance that the criminal has been apprehended."

"Send the notice now," Farley said.

"You've solved the murder?"

Farley looked up at the captain. She had risen in her excitement, narrowed and elongated and stretched her eyestalks to their farthest extent. "Not quite," Farley answered her. "But I have a lead. If you'll help me with a few small matters. . . ?"

They had laid the body of Grazer-in-the-Deep-Grasses on the bed in cabin 393B, turned on the stasis field, and applied safeguards. The captain herself had to penetrate the doorseal and assure the security system that the intrusion was authorized.

Farley counted a double handful of guests including himself and the captain. The head of security and her trusted assistant gravitated toward the wall and a position of watchful patience. The Elder of the Church of the Universal Archetype took stance beside the corpse, crest flattened in respect for the dead. Madame Tsi-Nyu stood a little away from him. The ship's doctor ruffled and muttered to himself, and possibly to hiser companion, a humanoid of substantial dimensions and lowering aspect. A Denebian scholar stood as still as the stone it resembled, until it angled a lambent eye in the direction of the last comer: Ser diJon in a hurry, skidding to a halt in the center of a circle of stares.

"Now," said the captain, drawing the eyes to herself, "that all have arrived, we can begin."

"Begin what?" Ser diJon clamped his mouth shut. His cheeks were crimson.

"I suppose you could call it an inquest," said Madame Tsi-Nyu. "It is that, isn't it?"

"In a manner of speaking," the captain said. "I have summoned you in particular as representatives of the passengers and crew, and as beings involved to varying degrees in the life—and death—of the esteemed Scholar-Philosopher First Class, may it graze the deepest grasses until the stars sleep."

Madame Tsi-Nyu blinked rapidly, eyes brimming with tears. The others seemed calmer, except Ser diJon, whom Farley had never seen otherwise than flustered. "Are you accusing one of us of murder?" the young idiot demanded.

The captain's gills shaded from shell pink to indigo. Farley moved in smoothly, coming to stand by the corpse. "We make no accusations," he said. "We're searching for answers, no more."

Ser diJon's eyes narrowed. "You," he said. "You're a pseudonym."

"My name is Mycroft," said Farley. "I am the author of *Foucault at Rest.*"

"So who are you really?"

"A literary gentleman," said Farley, "and sometime solver of riddles. Of which this is a peculiarly fine example. A noted scholar dead, it seems, of natural causes; except that Philosophers of Highgrass know no natural death. A locked room, a set of clues as cryptic as any Holmesian could ask for, and no sign or indication of foul play."

"Minute, localized, but very precise and lethal cerebral trauma," the doctor said, "is foul enough."

"What weapon can do that?" the Elder asked. His voice was quiet, his interest apparently without urgency.

"None that we know of," replied the chief of security.

She sounded angry. ''No weapon in our technology can deal a wound of that precise nature, or that perfectly calculated.''

''A medscanner can,'' said Ser diJon.

''A medscanner requires careful calibration, meticulous programming, and highly specific aim and focus.'' The doctor's beak clacked. ''There would be records of the 'scanner's transport to this room, and the victim would have had to cooperate in its setup and application. We have no evidence of any such thing.''

''Computers can be subverted,'' said the Elder, ''and records erased.''

''We did consider that,'' Farley said. ''If the ship's computer has been tampered with, the tampering was extremely skillful and its traces so far have been undetectable. To all appearances, the victim was alone when it died, and it died from no visible cause.''

''Then what left these?'' The captain held up the objects that had been found with the body: the quill, the handkerchief, the bookwrapper.

''A guest,'' Farley said, ''who knew how to subvert the computer.''

''One of *those* is the murder weapon?'' Ser diJon laughed. ''Chloroform on the handkerchief? The quill in the heart?''

''In a manner of speaking,'' said Farley. ''You are aware, I trust, that both Merris deVane and Musharrog of Deneb are present on this voyage.''

The Denebian stirred slightly. Its translator was set to a particularly low register, like gravel shifting. ''I am aware that I am here. And you, Solomon al-Rahib Mycroft. Sera DeVane . . .''

''Really,'' said Madame Tsi-Nyu, ''I am *not* she.''

''You are not,'' Farley agreed. ''The Unnamed Romanticist, however—''

She raised her fine arched brows.

''I've known that for months,'' Ser diJon said. ''I must say, Madame, *Don Juan Descending* was almost worthy of serious consideration.''

''Are you all impostors, then?'' the Elder inquired. He seemed considerably bemused.

''Say rather that most of us are more than we seem,'' Farley said. ''Except you, of course, your reverence.''

''I am a shadow and a lie,'' the Elder said, ''as is all that walks in flesh. Yet this much is true: We are forbidden to conceal our names or our works, even for our lives' sake.''

''Or that of your livelihood.'' Farley nodded. ''Suppose, then, that you discovered a great imposture, one so startling, and so disturbing, that your very faith was shaken. How would you receive it?''

''This was,'' said the Elder, bowing toward the corpse, ''truly, the Scholar-Philosopher First Class Grazer-in-the-Deep-Grasses. I have no doubt of it, nor can have. A great soul cannot be feigned.''

''Yet it can be disguised.''

''For what folly?''

''Folly, maybe. Or pleasure. Or simple playfulness.''

''We understand play,'' the Elder said. ''Lies, we do not endure.''

''And the liar, you put to death?''

The Elder was unperturbed. Others had come to attention; someone, perhaps Madame Tsi-Nyu, made a sound of protest. The Elder said, ''For the great lie, death. For the lesser, repentance.''

''You admit it, then? You confess? How did you do it?''

The Elder regarded Ser diJon with a calm and unblinking eye. ''I did nothing. What this late Philosopher did, we have yet to discover.''

''It wrote,'' said Madame Tsi-Nyu. ''Spoke, actually, since writing is not a Highgrassian vice.''

''Every philosopher teaches,'' the Elder said.

''Does every philosopher also compose works of popular fiction?''

Ser diJon, to give him credit, was the first to understand. ''Fiction? Popular fiction? *That* was Merris deVane?'' His eyes were wide. His mouth was open. He seemed to have forgotten how to shut it.

''That was Merris deVane.'' Farley considered the dead face with its curving horn. ''It was a she before it metamorphosed; a mother of many. It understood much that is common to every sentient creature, and some that is unique to the humanoid—having been humanoid itself, and singularly gifted with imagination and wit.''

''It was insane,'' said the humanoid who stood beside the ship's doctor.

''So are all Philosophers,'' Farley said.

''This more than most,'' the humanoid said. He looked

more human than most Fomalhautian dockhands, being smaller and less hirsute than the run of his kind. Even so, Farley thought that he could see a suggestion of the Philosopher in the curve of the nose and the angling of the skull on the neck. "It was my herdkin. It was called the Sublime, but also the Mad. It should never have ventured this voyage, knowing what it knew, being what it was. So we all told it—I more than any, who joined this crew in order to watch over it; for all the use I proved to be. It would not listen."

"It is never a Philosopher's inclination to listen to the young and the cautious." Madame Tsi-Nyu wiped her eyes. "Even to me it said so, after it told me the best of its secrets."

"To think," said Ser diJon. "I panned her—its—latest. I said it was too parochially Terran. Below even her accustomed standards. Feeble, hackneyed, and uninspired. But," he said, "I did grant that she showed an occasional small flash of wit."

"You were considerably less tactful than that," Madame Tsi-Nyu said with rare heat. "You called the book a waste of time, netspace, and promotional budget. You recommended that the author consider a career in commercial broadcasting—where, you said, her lack of imagination would make her an enormous success."

"It would," said Ser diJon. "The mass media would have been perfect for her talents."

He might have said more, but that was difficult with the dockhand's fingers wrapped around his throat. The Highgrassian lifted him a solid half-meter above the floor and shook him, snarling. The translator rendered the snarl in words. "You . . . said . . . what? You . . . wrote . . . what?"

"There," the chief of security said. "There, now." She did something; Farley did not clearly see what. But it convinced the Highgrassian to drop the critic. Ser diJon fell in a heap, gagging and clutching his throat.

Farley helped him up. He was trembling violently. When he could manage a sensible word, it was a snarl to match the Highgrassian's. "It was just a book review!"

"Yes," said Farley. "A book review. If it's good, it's wonderful. If it's bad, it's nonsense. Never forget, never forgive, and never take it seriously. That's the Author's Code."

"Unless one is a Philosopher," said the Philosopher's kinsman. "Then all that is true, is true, and all that is false, is wind. But if it is both true and false—"

"—it kills." Madame Tsi-Nyu spoke quietly, with her accustomed calm, but her face was set and still. The face, Farley thought, of a woman who has gone beyond fear to bitter courage. "I was delighted to discover, through deduction and a midnight confession, that our revered Scholar-Philosopher was, like me, a purveyor of anodyne to the masses. I brought the review to laugh over. Not—" Her voice broke. "Not to die for."

The Highgrassian did not leap at her as he had at Ser diJon. Perhaps he had no anger left. She met his eyes. Her own were full of tears. "I truly didn't know."

"No one knows," the Highgrassian said, "that words can kill."

"If one is a Philosopher of Highgrass," said Farley. "Words in a particular order, aimed at a particular target, in a being already approaching final metamorphosis, and practicing an art hitherto unknown to its people: lying in order to convey a truth more fundamental than truth itself."

"Writing trash for the mob?" Ser diJon had most of his insouciance back, if not his vocal facility. His voice was a croak.

"Writing what the masses will read," said Madame Tsi-Nyu. "Teaching them, maybe. Making them happy. It may not be a noble calling, but I reckon it a worthy one. I told Its Excellency so. Just—before—"

"Just before you read it Ser diJon's review," Farley said. His voice had no inflection. It sounded cold, he knew, and merciless. He could not help it.

"I only meant to laugh with it," said Madame Tsi-Nyu; "to share my own collection of bad notices, and to wonder at the folly of the young, as writers love to do. It was laughing when it died, Mycroft. Truly, it was."

"I believe you," he said. Not gentle even yet, but less cold. "And the quill? The handkerchief?"

"Signs," she said. "Trophies. Gifts for a practitioner of my own art. The pen that is mightier than the reviewer's scalpel. The handkerchief—"

"Keeping one's nose clean," said diJon. "Writing under an assumed name, to spare one's reputation."

She nodded quickly. "And the wrapper, of course, was

mine—my latest book. It was—'' She swallowed. ''Its Excellency was a fan of mine. As I was, of . . . of Merris deVane.''

''You wanted her—it—dead,'' diJon said. ''Royalties—rivalries—''

''No.'' Farley spoke before she could begin. ''That was a mistake. Concealing it, however, was an error of a different order. Why, Madame?''

''Fear,'' she said, clutching the handkerchief that was the twin of the one in Farley's hand, the one she had left with the body. ''And the hope that no one would guess, that it—it had died—of a book review.''

'' 'Sticks and stones can break my bones, but words can never hurt me.' '' The Elder blinked gravely in the face of collective surprise. ''Words are as deadly as anything that is. Words that are lies are the quicker to bring destruction. And words that are truth, but truth twisted by malice and envy . . . those kill most quickly of all.'' He turned his calm, terrible gaze on Ser diJon. ''You as much as she are guilty of this murder. She brought the words to the Philosopher. You wrote them. You edged and sharpened them to do the most harm, in the swiftest fashion, without mercy or restraint.''

Ser diJon opened his mouth, but nothing came out.

''Do you wish justice?'' the Elder asked the Highgrassian.

The Philosopher's kinsman rubbed his lightly fuzzed chin. His anger seemed to have died, or to have turned cold. ''What justice can there be now, with our greatest weakness exposed, and our greatest sage destroyed?''

''One might,'' Farley said carefully, ''place this gathering and this discussion under seal, and the participants under mindlock.'' His glance forestalled protest, or even response. It neither lingered on nor favored one face above the rest. ''One might also request that the perpetrators themselves—reviewer and revealer both—perform some suitable service to your world and your herdkin.''

''Such as become Merris deVane, and continue her career.'' The Highgrassian's demeanor was dour, its face implacable, but its wit, and its sense of justice, spoke to Farley of its dead kin. ''Both of them. Together.''

Madame Tsi-Nyu said nothing. Her face was hidden in her hands.

Ser diJon was appalled. *"Be* Merris deVane? *Write* that drivel?"

Farley knew a moment of perfect content. "How often have you indicated that you could do better in your sleep?" he asked. "Now you can prove it."

"But to collaborate—to work with—with—"

"With a highly experienced and notably tactful senior associate who wishes above all to atone for the harm which she has done." Madame Tsi-Nyu raised her head, squared her shoulders. Her courage, Farley reflected, was as admirable as her charm. "It's a solution worthy of Its Excellency itself, and it is no more than just. If," she said, "the authorities agree."

"They will," said Farley. The Highgrassian grunted, the captain bubbled assent. The Elder bowed its head.

Ser diJon was far from convinced. But Madame Tsi-Nyu had him in hand. The last Farley heard of him, he was still protesting, but with diminishing force. "But they were only words!"

"Words," said Madame Tsi-Nyu, "are the deadliest weapon of all."

MURDER UNDER GLASS

by Bob Liddil

This story was originally assigned to Allen Steele, who called one afternoon to say that *he* couldn't come up with a solution but that his friend Bob Liddil could. So, with Allen's blessing, the assignment was turned over to Bob.

> *Four aliens of different races are on safari on a wild, uninhabited planet. Their guide is a human.*
> *One day they show up at the spaceport and claim that their guide was trampled by an enraged alien beast. The authorities know this guide to be a very careful man and a crack shot, but also to be less than tactful in his treatment of aliens, and they suspect foul play.*
> *The four aliens are detained while a detective (any race you choose) is sent to the scene of the tragedy to determine whether the guide's death was caused by the animal or the aliens. The body has been buried, and when disinterred is pulped almost beyond recognition, but the detective unearths proof that the man was killed first and then trampled, and from this proof he is able to deduce which of the aliens killed him and which (if any) are merely supporting the killer(s) story.*
> *Write it up, insert the proper clues, and solve it.*

I hate being dragged out of bed during sleep-time. So you can imagine how thrilled I was when the com-buzzer went off at the Kilgarian equivalent of three a.m. Fumbling around in the dark for the blasted obnoxious thing making all the noise, I made a mental note to send whoever was on the other end to the snow dome for six months of igloo patrol.

Finally I found the com. "This better be more important than your life," I growled.

"Inspector," began a female human voice on the other end, "I hate to have to wake you up . . ."

"Well, I'm up now, so get on with it." My mouth tasted like the air inside of a pressure suit and my head was beginning to hurt. I was feeling positively evil.

"There's been an incident, sir," she sounded a little unsure whether she should continue.

"And?" I prompted. There had to be more. Nobody from the night shift would call me unless one of the damn domes had exploded or something.

"There's been a death, Inspector. One of the dome guides, a human by the name of Cobb Christian."

Now that was news. It meant that within a few days, the place would be crawling with regulators, news beings, and insurance investigators. It also meant that I'd be in my least favorite position, the spotlight. I decided right then and there that I'd better get the jump on the rush. Some being dying in a dome was bad for business. And we'd had a pretty good safety record up until now.

I said, "Okay, relax, I'll be ready in ten minutes. Send a transport around for me."

"It's already on its way, sir."

I cut the com link and activated the coffee maker.

When I signed up with Pinkerton's ten years ago to run security on Kilgari, I hadn't known much about the place. If I had, I would've probably stayed in the Navy. Not that this little backwater rock doesn't jump once in a while. Just the opposite. Every time a yacht full of rich tourists docks, the first thing they do is throw a party. Alcohol is the second largest industry next to expeditions on Kilgari, and City Dome definitely knows how to rock and roll. Off-world weapons are banned; you couldn't get one aboard a shuttle if you tried. Only licensed safari outfitters have them, and they're bonded for five million platinum apiece. So the worst damage any being can do to anybody else is to scuff them a little. Even the wogs—Kilgarian slang for "Wealthy Off-world Gentlebeings"—can't do much harm beyond the abilities of whatever might be attached to their appendages. The owners of this planetoid, in order to keep their resort status, have to seriously keep the peace. That means no crime and, in particular, no unnatural death.

I had just enough time to grab a cup of coffee, and throw on a jump suit and a rank vest before the transport arrived. The ride downtown was quiet. City Dome, at night, had its own kind of darkness, a red and green and blue aura from the building lights that reflect off the high glass. I used to be spooky about the domes. You know the old Earth science fiction, where the glass cracks and the outside vacuum sucks away the air. I used to read stuff like that as a kid. But in real life, it would take a direct meteor strike to hole a dome, and what little atmosphere Kilgari has burns up any small debris that might come along. The long-range scanners on the docking platforms above us would give plenty of warning about anything larger than a basketball.

About five minutes into the ride, I noticed we weren't going toward the Pinkerton building. Rather, we were headed toward the inter-dome tube station. As we pulled up to the front door, I could see a Pinkerton corporal waiting for me.

"Inspector Kruger?" She spotted me and greeted me pleasantly. "I'm Corporal Ross, from the records pool. I'm your field secretary on this case." This was the same voice I'd heard on the com-link just minutes before. If I'd known she looked like this, I'd have tried to be a little less grumpy. As I exited the transport, she handed me a file folder. Somebody must've warned her that I don't like or trust the electronic notebooks that are Pinkerton standard issue.

I said, "Where am I going?"

"Dome 16." She was wearing just a hint of perfume. That distracted me for a second. Then I said, "So, what happened with this guy, anyway?"

"Dome patrol got a distress call at 2300 hours yesterday from one of Christian's trekkers, saying that there'd been an accident. According to the preliminary report, he was trampled by a Kujata. We don't have any other details. The four trekkers are under house detention at the 16 Hotel and they're waiting to be cleared by you."

"Dome patrol won't clear them?" I was genuinely surprised. I would have thought that they would want to get those guests off-world as quickly as possible. This was beginning to arouse my curiosity.

"Apparently, they buried Mr. Christian. Dome patrol says they don't have the authority to dig him up. They called us."

I shook my head in amazement. This case was less than an hour old and was already beginning to sound like a made-for-broadcast tri-video. I followed Ross through the main terminal area to the VIP bay, where a private tube car had been rigged and was standing by. Very elegant. The VIP cars had dimmers on the lights. Dome 16 was at least a five-hour trip. I could get some shut-eye.

"Do me a favor," I said. "Take a couple of metros over to Christian's quarters. I've got a feeling that this one's not going to be cut and dry. Call me if something turns up."

"I'm on it," she said with a quick smile. How can anybody be cheerful on night shift?

As I stepped aboard the tube car, a female computer voice requested, "Destination, please?"

I answered, "Dome 16," then found myself a comfortable seat. I had a little reading to do before killing the lights.

The first three pages of the file reprinted the deceased's standard resident-alien dossier. You don't have to be anything except wealthy to come to Kilgari as a tourist. But to live here you have to know the Pope, be a member of the Ruling Family, or be really, really good at whatever specialty you're being hired for. Take me, for example, I'd been a Navy intelligence officer and I met the Pope once. Two out of three's not bad.

Now Christian—the man had been a Fleet Marine. He'd fought in the Tobago VI campaign, winning a distinguished service medal with six gold stars. He was wounded twice during the retaking of Sympac Science Station during the rebellion on Sympia III and had been held hostage for six years by the Islamic Jihad, during the "War to Destroy All Infidels in the Seven Sectors of Mohammed" campaign. He mustered out honorably from galactic service and spent three years as an independent mercenary, a for-hire body-guard to several different wealthy clients, finally coming to Kilgari with a recommendation from the president of Digitron-Teledyne, who also happens to be the tenth most wealthy man in the federated galaxy. That was page one.

This guy was something else. Page two listed more than a hundred weapons and type A through GGG explosives that he'd been trained to handle. He was also commando-qualified in desert, jungle, tundra, mountain, and under-ground tracking, and he spoke seven languages besides galactic, independently of the universal translator.

Page three listed hobbies, special interests and next of kin. Each section remained blank except for the words *none, none,* and *none.*

Pages four through seven outlined his credit. Not much out of the ordinary, a couple of thousand in the bank, company condo, the usual. So it seemed, at first glance, that Cobb Christian was married to his work. Nothing unusual about that. Takes a certain kind of being to tramp around the domes and put up with the idle rich for a living.

The last page outlined his corporate and domestic discipline record. Eleven complaints from City Dome Metro cops for drunk and disorderly, three off-world complaints through company channels alleging maltreatment of guests on safari. I found the latter interesting. All three complaints were handled at the executive level, and no fines were levied on the guide. That's outside procedure, meaning that he probably had a couple of friends in high administration.

At this point, I had a pretty fair picture of the deceased. Competent, rowdy, a little prone to alcohol abuse, cocky, well-connected, and less than fond of wogs. He also was a crack shot and extremely self-sufficient. Not the sort to get himself stomped to death by a dome creature, particularly one he worked around frequently.

At about that time, fatigue caught up with me. Laying the folder aside, I dimmed the light, closed my eyes, and tried to catch some zs.

* * *

I woke up to the smell of coffee, hot and black, just the way I like it. On the message screen blinked a note from Ross, saying "Good morning, sir, and good luck." She was taking this secretary thing seriously.

The next fifteen minutes consisted of an arrival, a short ride to the Dome patrol gate station and a call to the Dome 16 accommodation house to arrange a meeting with the trekkers. As sunrise began to lighten the dome, I sat behind a one-way glass window, sipping on my third cup of coffee, watching as they all filed into the interview room. One, in particular, a Kyzillian, seemed particularly agitated and it didn't mind letting the escort know it.

"Have you notified my embassy yet?" The universal translator spoke in a flat robotic monotone, but the Kyzillian was very animated and its appendages were waving around in a manner that indicated displeasure. "What about my * legal representative * being who deals with authorities*? Where is (it)?"

I figured I'd better get on with this before we suffered another casualty. As soon as it saw my rank vest, the Kyzillian launched into another tirade. I'm not known to be particularly patient. I told it, "Sit down and shut up!" and to my surprise, it did so immediately.

What a crew! A Kyzillian, two Lupinians and a Wapatai. The Kyzillian resembled a heavily-scaled snake, the Lupes looked like oversized gophers, and the Wapatai was, for lack of a better term, a short unantlered moose. At least they were all bipedal, but damn! What was this odd lot doing in Dome 16?

Stupid question, actually, when you think about it. The domes of Kilgari have only one purpose: recreation catering to the obscenely wealthy. Under each of the 21 domes lies an individually-terraformed ecosystem where different scenarios are played out for anyone who can afford the 600,000 platinum credits base cost. The higher the dome number, the more difficult and expensive the scenario, ranging from Dome 2, orchid and tropical rain forest hiking, to 21, the Snow Dome, where the expedition and guides are equipped with a spear, a fishing line, and ten days dry rations, for a 21-day blizzard trek. Dome 16 expeditions specialized in live animal kills, safari hunting for trophies. The interior is a veldt, modeled after Africa, Earth, except with a homogeneous mixture of creatures and supporting vegetation from planets all over the galaxy, predators and prey in a balanced environment. These four wogs were trophy hunters.

I said to the Kyzillian, "Okay, explain it to me. What happened? How did the guide die?" It protested fully ten minutes at being the first to be interviewed before it finally settled down to answer my questions. The field translator was an older model that cobbled the context a little, but I got the gist of it.

"We *had been* three days traveling on safari and *ending sleep period/beginning new wake period*. Our guide led us into a *depression in the ground*, saying to us that we were going to 'bag a big one' today. We set up a *technical term loosely meaning cross-fire zone* with myself on the point of the triangle and the guide in the center. The beast came out of nowhere. It charged past my position. I fired one round at it but missed. *Regret/sadness concerning loss*. Our guide was frozen with fear. He made no attempt to move and was trampled by the creature. We would have all been killed if we had not immediately taken cover where the beast could not get to us.''

The others from the party were quick to confirm the Kyzillian's claim. The details of my interview coincided with the individual statements the Dome patrol had gotten from them when they first came off the inside. It was this very agreement between the four on minute details that made me wonder if what I was hearing wasn't a planned, rehearsed story.

I researched the Kujata, the "beast," as the Kyzillian called it on the Dome patrol master terminal. I found it listed in standard inventory reference as a non-sentient, and from its picture, ugly beyond belief, looking like a huge, blubbery cross between a Terran whale with legs and an armored Grantinain rhino-beast. Formidable, true, but only by virtue of size. It would be easily capable of accidentally squashing some being if one got underfoot, but overtly attacking an experienced guide? Its confidential profile suggested otherwise. Not even an import, it carried a code "CC" according to the inventory schedule for Dome 16. "CC" stands for Composite Clone. It was a genetically-engineered tourist boogeyman, a sucker hunt for first timers. Things just didn't add up. Though hideous-looking and big as an armored personnel carrier, it should have been harmless as a puppy.

Although I had the authority to release them to Dome City, I ordered the wogs held. I wanted them handy for more questioning when I got back from the field. They all protested—none more loudly than the Kyzillian. That one was really starting to get on my nerves. Still, nothing to do now, but go out into the dome and retrieve the deceased.

* * *

The veldt inside Dome 16 is like no other environ on Kilgari. The temperature fluctuates between 30 standard degrees at night and 115 standard during light hours. Only a breath of breeze stirred the grass as our jeep made its way along the dusty road that led into the interior.

It took most of the morning to complete the slow ride out to the site where Christian had been buried. Two Dome patrolmen had been posted to keep the scavengers away, and judging from the number of dead hyenas scattered around the site, I guessed the duty hadn't been boring.

I watched as they uncovered the body. It was a mess. What hadn't been stomped into jelly in the attack had started to decompose. The heat and humidity, the bugs and the worms had already started doing their job, which was to reduce Cobb Christian to trace elements.

I said, "Bag him." Then I turned and walked away while they were doing it. I've seen a few casualties in my time, laser burns, blast victims. Nowhere in my travels, though, had I ever seen anyone so completely demolished as Cobb Christian. He'd been stomped so many times, from the look of the corpse, that I had to believe that whatever did it was pissed beyond belief.

"Uh, watch it, Inspector." The voice startled me, because I'd been lost in thought.

"Watch what?"

One of the young patrolmen who'd been on guard duty when we arrived had left his post to come over to me. He had a look of concern on his face. He said, "You don't spend much time out here, do you?" His tone was casual, rather than impertinent.

"Not really," I answered. "Why?"

The kid said, "Because you're standing right next to one of the deadliest clumps of vegetation on the veldt."

I must've jumped a yard, and I let out a yelp of surprise that brought the other guard running. Then I let out a laugh. The thing I had bolted away from was a rose bush.

I said, "Okay, kid, you got me." Apparently I was getting the rookie's treatment.

"You think I'm kidding, don't you?" the kid said. "Look, Inspector, Dome patrol puts each new recruit through the same indoctrination courses that the guides get. The flowers on that bush are a delicacy for one of the specimens, a veg-eater called a Fastiacalon. But the thorns secrete a poison that zaps anything that gets too close. See that pod, underneath? Watch this."

He went over to his jeep and returned a moment later with a packet of meat. Anticipating my question, he laughed and said, "Cats. We've got thirty different kinds of cats out here. They're fast and they're always hungry. Sometimes it's easier just to toss them a snack.'' I nodded in understanding. Educational, this Dome.

He reached out with his walking stick and pushed the end of it against one of the branches. Instantly, the other branches began to move as well, as if they had been stirred by a breeze. He nudged the tip of the cane into the center of one of the bright orange rose blossoms and then jerked it quickly back out again. The kid's movement came just a hair faster than the sudden closing of a dozen or so of the limbs on where the stick had been. He had already removed the meat from its wrapping. He just tossed it on the ground, three feet or so from the outer branches. He said, ''Stand back a couple of more yards, Inspector, and watch this.''

The branches parted and two flaps on the inner pod fell away, revealing a pastel orange interior wall, coated with layers of white spines. Nothing happened for a second or two. Then, with more speed than I would have bet on, a red tendril snaked out and speared the meat on the ground. Within no more than a minute, the meat had been dragged back into the interior of the plant, the limbs had reset to their original configuration, and it had once more taken on the appearance of an innocent rose bush.

I said, ''Shit!'' out of sheer respect for the plant and for the kid who knew what it was. I made a mental note to go back to Dome inventory again and find out why something this dangerous would be placed in the proximity of the guests. I had a feeling that the insurance boys did not know about this.

''Hmm,'' the kid said. ''Got a pair of tweezers?'' A thorn from one of those animated limbs had lodged in the body of his walking stick. I got a pair of grips from my evidence kit. Stainless steel; some things Pinkerton makes are worth having. Very carefully, I dropped the thorn into a glass tube and sealed it with an aluminum cork.

By now they had Christian scooped, bagged, zipped, and loaded. I motioned to the kid who'd just saved my hide to switch with the driver who'd brought me out to the site. ''You're with me now,'' I said. ''We've got things to talk about.''

* * *

By the time we reached the hotel, I'd acquired a complete education concerning the wildlife in Dome 16, both animal and vegetable. The youngster doing the briefing had requested to work on the veldt to fulfill a pre-entrance requirement for his PhD in bioengineering at Mars University. Then, instead of going into practice, he had returned to Kilgari and Dome patrol. The kid wanted to be a guide. One thing in particular that he said stuck in my mind long after he'd gone off to resume his duties. "You know, it's funny. In three years on the veldt I've never seen a Kujata."

I hadn't taken more than ten steps into the hotel lobby when the desk clerk flagged me to tell me I had a com-call. She indicated one of the private booths near the lift. Actually, I was grateful to be able to sit down on something softer than a jeep seat. I plugged in my KT&T card and said, "Go ahead," as the screen blinked on. It was Ross.

"Good," she said, "I'm glad I caught you. It seems our deceased had a couple of variables in his life."

"Go on."

"Well," Ross continued, "among his personal effects, we found a tab book for the racetracks on Kyzillia. It seems that Mr. Christian was a gambler and a heavy loser. Also, we found three fully-charged beam pistols, all set to kill."

"Heavy breach of company policy," I commented. "Is that it?"

"No, there's one more thing. We also found a commercial carrier ticket dated for today, on White Star Lines. His destination was Earth Colony 1800 in the Tri-Gama sector. It looks like he had planned to quit his job and head out to the Rim. The ticket was one-way."

I said, "Thanks, Ross, excellent work. Follow up on the gambling angle for me, will you?"

"You got it."

I cut the com.

Gambling is not illegal on Kilgari, although there is only one casino in Dome City. The racetracks on Kyzillia are another matter. Those snake pits (no pun intended) are home to the last bastions of organized crime in this part of the galaxy. If Christian owed money to one of the mobs, then the odds that his death was no accident rose dramatically. It occurred to me that having a Kyzillian in the dead guide's last tourist party, then finding he had a gambling problem, was a mighty long coincidence. The loose ends were all starting to fall together.

It had been a long day. I'd ordered an autopsy on Christian's remains, but that wouldn't be available until morning. I'd also ordered a toxic analysis of the thorn I'd brought off the veldt. That bush had been spooky. I'd been very surprised that anything that deadly would be placed in the proximity of tourists. I added to my list of things to do: finding out whose bright idea that thorn bush was. Then I pulled my call card out of the vid-com and retired for the evening. Best to chew big questions on a fresh day.

* * *

The com-buzzer went off at exactly 3:30 a.m. I swore a blue streak as I fumbled around, trying to find it. Then, when I finally did, I shouted into it, "Dammit! Doesn't anybody ever *sleep* on this planet?"

The silence at the other end lasted five seconds or so, and then a male human voice said, "Sorry to have to wake you, Inspector . . ."

I said, somewhat more calmly, much more quietly, and with as much dignity as I could possibly muster, "Someone better have died."

Another silence, followed by, "Actually, Inspector, that's why I'm calling. Someone *has* died."

Fifteen minutes later, gripping my first coffee of the day, I strolled into the Watch Captain's office at Dome patrol headquarters. I cut right to the chase. "Who's dead and how?"

"The Wapatai." he said simply. "And as to how, I've got somebody working on that now."

Now, I don't know much about xenobiology, mostly just general information. But there was one thing I would've bet a month's pay on: that moose didn't die of natural causes. I said, "Autopsy?"

"Already ordered one."

"Good. Put a guard on each of the other suspects and don't leave any of them alone. And roust that Kyzillian. Run a mob-connection cross-check on it and bring that and it to the interview room." I gave him an interplanetary Pinkerton access code for his terminal.

This had become a public relations nightmare. One need

not be a drive scientist to figure out that two deaths out of one safari party spelled more than coincidence. I grabbed another cup of coffee and headed for the interview room. Half an hour later, an escort brought in the snake.

"I protest!" It was now even more agitated than the last time I'd seen it. "My *representative to government* shall hear of this and you will be *performing janitorial duties on a Rim colony* by this time period tomorrow."

"I'm scared to death," I said sarcastically, but apparently the translator didn't pick up the inflection, because the snake shot back, "You should be."

I changed the subject. "Let's discuss the Kyzillian gambling syndicates."

It instantly made a sound of disgust, the Kyzillian equivalent of spitting on the ground. "Those *not translatable obscenity* disreputable *beings who consume the young of their own species* are beneath contempt." The translator was getting better, in my opinion.

The snake was now glaring at me as though it might be about to take my head off or something. To see its reaction you would have thought I had insulted its entire planetary population. "I am the son of one of the leading galactic traders in our system," it continued, "and the brother of General *no equivalent pronunciation* of the Kyzillian System Navy. I hold the rank of *minister in charge of a continental mass* in our government. I have related to you the details of the guide's death, as you requested and now, *untranslatable obscenity / reference to a deity*, I am ready to leave this miserable planetoid so that I may undertake my new mission in life, which is the complete dismantling of the Kilgari Corporation and the closing of this resort."

None of this added up. If the snake was telling the truth, the facts it had just related would make it a very unlikely crime family hit-being. Still, I had a dead guide on my hands, as well as a deceased nonhuman and except for the Kyzillian gambling angle, not much more than a gut hunch or two to go on.

Too much coincidence here. It *felt* like foul play.

* * *

I sent the Kyzillian back to its quarters without further comment and initialized a Class 24 security search on it and its family. If there is one thing Pinkerton connections *are* good for, it is the Coordinated Galactic Criminal Data Base headquartered on Data Alpha 3. With agency contacts in law enforcement stretched across ninety percent of the sectors in the galaxy, it would be a cinch to verify the snake's claim to royal connections.

The xenopathologist called at eight, a somewhat more civilized hour. By then, I'd received the report I'd requested from Ross, and also the biological background research I'd requested from the young PhD patrolman, concerning the Kujata and other seemingly strange life forms not entirely consistent with the "safari" motif of the Dome 16 veldt.

Ross' report closed one angle and opened another. An amount transferred from First Kilgari Savings, 18,000 platinum credits, satisfied the amount owed to the Kyzillians. That currency move had been performed on the day before Christian's trek on the veldt. The record confirmed that the transaction and the ticket buy had originated from the headquarters building of TKC (The Kilgari Corporation) in downtown Dome City. This was odd because 18,000 is a month's pay for a senior guide and there was no corresponding credit union code attached to the work. The funds had come from a company account. That meant that Christian's corporate guardian angel had bailed him out of his gambling trouble. Now it would be pretty easy to identify him and find out the reason for the special treatment. I put Ross on that trail, with instructions to bring whoever it was out to 16 to be interviewed by me.

The patrolman's report held some curious revelations as well. The Kujata, it seemed, was not the manufactured animal that my general access data base had led me to believe. There seemed to be no records on the cloning laboratory monitoring systems to indicate in which laboratory the creature was grown. Another oddity noted: both brochures and other printed materials listed the Kujata as being one of the most dangerous and elusive animals in the Dome 16 inventory. Yet no video record existed of it, and descriptions of it varied dramatically. Also, although considered a prime target, kill records seemed to indicate that no one had ever bagged one. Except (according to published reports), 16's top guide, Cobb Christian. The whole thing with this creature vaguely reminded me of a legendary creature from old Earth, a *snipe*. This often ferocious, rarely observed beast was used to teach young scout candidates lessons in tracking and capturing dangerous quarry. If I remembered correctly, much tracking but very little capturing was the rule with that particular Terran monster.

At ten, a Dome patrol courier brought me a printout of the pathologist's preliminary report on Christian. It read like a textbook version of a man being run over by a twenty-ton land vehicle. Every bone in the guide's body had been broken. Vital organs had burst under high pressure. Spinal separation, fractured skull. Probable cause of death: subject appeared to have been crushed by trampling. Cobb Christian's *snipe* had run amok on his body. At the bottom of the printout was a hastily scribbled note that said, *blood-analysis cross-reference with object provided pending.*

Now seemed like a good time to reinterview the gophers. Since the Kyzillian connection seemed to be evaporating and the moose had been eliminated the hard way, the Lupinians were all I had left. When they arrived, I offered them a seat, using the friendliest body language I could muster.

"Gentlemen," I said, casually, the translator offering my words as a series of variable frequency clicks and whistles, "tell me about the guide, Mr. Christian."

They looked at each other, then back at me, and neither said anything. Then they both shrugged at the same time in a gesture of "I don't know."

"Very well," I said. "Let me tell *you.*" From the information I'd gathered so far, I had a fair profile of the guide. "He was arrogant," I began. "He showed little respect for your species in particular, or for any of the nonhumans in your party." I noted subtle changes in the Lupes' facial expressions as the translator caught up with what I was saying. I ran with it. "He consumed alcohol in quantity and his behavior became more erratic as the expedition progressed. He became more verbally, maybe even physically, abusive. I'll bet you were glad when the beast showed up and stomped him into the veldt. Am I right?"

I admit it. It was a long shot. It was an old trick I learned in Navy Intelligence, used for interviewing prisoners. A human would never have fallen for it, but the gophers . . . they took the bait.

One said, "It is true. The human guide was a *unpleasant beast that wallows in garbage* and had said on more than one occasion that he would like to feed us to the lions. We are civilized beings, but there were times before the human's demise when I or my sibling would have cheerfully destroyed him. It is always sad when a sentient expires, but the guide was different. He deserved what happened.''

A minute later, I was called to the com. It was the pathologist.

''I did the extra tests you asked for, Inspector.''

''And what did you find?''

''Virostrychnine, in a very potent form on the thorn and in blood samples taken from the deceased.''

Bingo!

''Anything else?'' I asked.

''The cause of death was not the virostrychnine. That's only a neuro-paralyzer. In the absence of other events, it would've worn off in an hour or so and left him with a bad headache, not much more. The official cause of death, as far as I'm concerned, is still massive internal injuries brought about by being trampled. The guide was simply stomped to death.''

''Lastly,'' he said, and his tone became more confidential, ''about the second victim . . .'' I could tell he was trying hard not to laugh.

Less than thirty minutes later, I was notified that Corporal Ross and a Mr. Oppenheimer were waiting for me in a conference suite at the hotel. Oppenheimer was a junior vice president in the overseer's office. So this was Christian's guardian angel. Time to bring all the players together in one place.

* * *

I gave the watch captain a list of who and what I wanted, grabbed a cup of coffee, and took the transport to the hotel. They were waiting for me when I arrived. I introduced myself to Oppenheimer, but did not offer any more than a handshake and some chitchat. Ross had told him that he was being brought in to supervise the closing of the investigation. No need to say any more than that just yet.

As we took our seats at the conference table, the rest of the group began to arrive. The Kyzillian, being unusually low-keyed, arrived only ten steps ahead of the Lupes. Then came the two young patrolmen who had been guarding

Christian's body and their captain, and the pathologist. Soon, everybody was present. The last one in moved to close the doors, but I motioned him to hold off, indicating one more coming. Sure enough, the Wapatai, miraculously back from the dead, rolled up in a wheelchair, flanked by two medical technicians. Reactions were immediate and vocal, with the Kyzillian offering more and angrier comments than anyone.

"Now everyone is here," I said. "This meeting is being recorded. Does anyone object?" No one did, so I said, "All right, let's get on with this. For the record, the following are present. When I identify you, will you please indicate with a hand or appendage?" Then I did an old-fashioned roll call.

When I said, "Welcome back to the living," to the Wapatai, the moose responded with a loud snort. "Sometimes playing dead works, sometimes it doesn't," it said, roughly translated.

"Our Wapatai friend has an unusual ability to slow his heart rate, lower his body temperature, and simulate death when he's in trouble," I commented. "Most places would just call in the Wapatai ambassador and haul his 'dead' carcass away. Our doctor electroshocked his heart and damn near killed him trying to save his life."

The humans all got a good laugh out of it, but the off-worlders didn't see the humor, or maybe just didn't know what a good joke was when it came by. Then I began in earnest.

"What happened to Cobb Christian?" My dramatic tone was not lost on the new translation box I'd asked Ross to bring with her from Dome City. This translator model was much better at human inflection than the old one. I gazed around the room, allowing my eyes to rest on each one of its occupants individually. The gophers were calm, the snake fidgeted nervously, the Wapatai coughed and tried to smooth a patch of ruffled fur. Oppenheimer was the picture of poise, but right at his scalp line little beads of sweat were beginning to form.

"Cobb Christian was a bigot," I continued. "He mistreated the guests in his safari parties on several reported occasions, without incurring any disciplinary action from the company, thanks to you, Mr. Oppenheimer."

Oppenheimer turned an immediate shade of red and protested, but I ignored him and pressed on.

"He was heavily involved with gambling at the Kyzillian racetracks, an activity that you claim to know nothing about." I gave the snake a penetrating stare and it responded with negative body language but nothing verbal. "Those debts were paid off by . . . ah, surprise . . . Mr. Oppenheimer."

The executive was growing angrier by the minute and I was loving every second of it.

"So our four intrepid hunters go onto the veldt with a man who hates nonhumans so badly that he is about to resign and take a one-way trip to the furthest human colony on the Rim, just to get away from them once and for all, and does the guide get a little rough? Oh, yeah. And does he partake of a little alcohol? Again, yes, indeed. Now, each member of the safari party told exactly the same story. Identically, as though rehearsed, and that got me to thinking. It isn't reasonable for four nonhumans of three different species to come up with identical viewpoints of an event that they witnessed from four different angles, unless they've been very well rehearsed, or, better still, programmed in some way."

I looked over at the young Dome patrolman who'd rescued me from the roses. "Mr. Evans, you're an expert in xenobiology. How could these four have been tricked into believing that they saw Cobb Christian stomped to death by the Kujata?"

"Ah . . . telepathic image projection," he fumbled just a little. "It would require an esper rating of at least 17 on the Bridges scale to plant such a detailed recollection in four minds at the same time."

"True," I said, "and well-extrapolated. So, if we accept, for the moment, that the trekkers' versions of the guide's death are false, then, how did he die?"

The pathologist offered, "He was alive at the point where he was being trampled . . ."

I shot back, "Exactly! He was paralyzed. Not by fear, as our Kyzillian friend suggested in his interview, but from a dose of virostrychnine introduced into his body by a thorn from a very exotic rose bush—a bush which, incidentally, Mr. Evans was kind enough to keep me from being entangled in just a little while ago."

"So, how did Cobb Christian die?" I paused for effect. "He was killed by Dome Patrolman Evans."

* * *

My audience erupted into a babble of grunts, squeaks, squawks, snorts, and error messages from suddenly overloaded translator boxes. Soon, though, they all trailed back into silence. Now all eyes were on Evans.

Evans' face never changed expression. "Where did *that* come from?" he demanded.

"From the way things didn't seem to add up, right from the beginning. Murphy's first law of detective work. Eliminate the obvious, the probable, the possible, and what do you have left? The impossible. Corporate records, checked from Kilgarian terminals, backed up everything you told me: the PhD, the internship, the whole story."

"But it just didn't feel right, so I ran a Pinkerton background check on you, Patrolman. Before you came to Kilgari, you simply did not exist, and then, *bingo!*, here you are. Next, your appearance on Kilgari as an intern matches perfectly the last in a series of acquisition trips to the Unexplored Sectors made by Christian and seven other guides. Shortly after that, the first sales brochure advertising Kujata hunts began to appear. What you said out on the veldt clinched it for me. How could a PhD in xenobiology not have ever seen the most sought-after and dangerous beast under the domes? You killed the guide, all right. My only questions are how and why?"

Evans' body began to flow and melt, as it changed from human form into one roughly reminiscent of a Grantain rhino-beast, while still retaining the human face. Metamorph! *Shape-changer!* One of the rarest and frequently the most dangerous life-forms in the galaxy! Now *that* I had not anticipated.

Everyone in the room dived for some kind of cover. The only two left standing were this incredible creature and me—not because I'm particularly brave, but because I was pretty sure I knew who I was facing.

Rhino/Evans said nothing for the first moment or so, then, quietly, almost resigned, said, "How did you know?"

"Very simple," I replied. "You handed me the clues, one right after the other. I think you wanted me to know *why* Christian was killed, not just *what* killed him. He was killed because he kidnapped your mate, isn't that correct? Oh, and could you change back to Evans? You're scaring these others to death.''

Indeed, the Wapatai had already reverted back to its simulated death mode before the creature completed its change to rhino. Now, it had stopped breathing and looked stiff as a board.

Evans said, ''Close. Not my *mate*. My daughter. The females of my species develop much later than do the males. The ability to alter one's outer form, along with fundamental sentience, comes to them only in the second tri-century of their life span, thereby making them very vulnerable to those who would come and just take one away.''

I nodded in understanding.

''Christian came twice to our world, each time taking a female of our species while that one was in her dormant or *nonflux* state, unable to defend herself against him and his group. When they came back the second time, they showed an interest in the rose bushes, a vegetation that commonly grows on our world. I disguised myself as one of these and accompanied my daughter on her journey. Once here, it was a simple task to blend in to the facility and discover what it would take to return her to our world when she matured.''

''So,'' I interjected, ''by placing an aura of suggestion around the humans in your proximity, you were able to influence local computer records concerning the human disguise of Evans.''

''Exactly. Computer operators are the most suggestible humans I've known.''

I certainly agreed with that. I've dated a few.

''I knew it would take time to complete my rescue. Because she was so valuable, all the guides had orders not to kill the Kujata, only to track her and provide low power beam weapons for the guests to fire at her. But Christian had killed the first one and wanted to go on record as the only one to have done so.''

The great human hunter. I made a mental note to run psycho-screens on the rest of the Dome 16 guides.

''On his last safari, he brought a projectile weapon. My daughter had already begun her metamorphosis and Christian knew her patterns better than any other guide. He would have found her and killed her.''

"What happened then?"

Evans, who had now changed back to Evans, answered, "As a Fastiacalon, which is immune to the nerve toxin, I had retrieved a thorn from one of the rose bushes. I placed it and a small slinging device in the custody of the Wapatai. He was the most esper-sensitive and could be controlled completely without his knowledge."

One of the Lupines, from a position under a table, said, "You were in camp . . . just before it happened?"

"That's true," said Evans. "I had joined the party the night before, in this form, hoping to influence Cobb to hunt another trophy animal the following day. But talk of killing a Kujata dominated the conversation. He was obsessed with taking her horn as a trophy, something he'd been denied on his previous kill."

"Why didn't you use your esper ability to influence the guide?" That was Ross. Good question.

Evans laughed sadly. "Humans can be very single-minded. I tried to place a suggestion of other game in his subconscious, but unsuccessfully. The nonsapients, they were easy, but Christian couldn't be persuaded, and he was becoming aware of the attempt. So, at first light, I slipped away from the group and *became* the Kujata. I gave the order to the Wapatai to sling the thorn. With the guide paralyzed, he would be humiliated. By the time anyone figured out what was going on, it would be too late. Cobb Christian's last hunt would end in failure. But *She* appeared out of nowhere, enraged by the sight of him. He'd wounded her so many times. She just wanted him to stop hurting her. The paralyzer only lasts a few minutes and I could sense Christian gaining control of his body even more rapidly than would be normal. He would have killed us both. So I did what I had to do, then purged and reformed the group's memories."

"Why didn't you just put in a complaint with the authorities?" I asked.

Evans cast a sideways glance at Oppenheimer, who was partially hidden by a table. "I knew who was in charge of acquisitions. I also knew how important the Kujata hunt was to the tourist trade on the veldt. TKC's first consideration would have been the credits."

Evans knew the human species well.

"I'll trust you to see her safely home?"

"Of course," Evans replied. "It has been arranged for some time now. Her transformation is complete. Only her education remains."

"Then good-bye and good luck." I shook his hand, walked him to the door of the conference room, then closed the door behind him. Sometimes, being in charge is absolutely *great*.

"You . . . you *just let it go?*" That was Oppenheimer.

"That's right, Mr. Oppenheimer," I answered. "No need to detain it. Not that I could anyway. From where I sit, the guide's death was self-defense. Besides, I have another criminal case to worry about now."

Ross said to him, "You, sir, are under arrest for violations of the Sentient Beings Protection Act," and motioned for two patrolmen to flank him as escorts.

"You'll never make the charges stick, Kruger! That animal was caught on open range on a surveyed planet. You'll never prove criminal intent."

"Get him out of here. Take him to Dome City metro headquarters. I'll be along to file the charges in a little while." Then I added, "Dome 16 is closed to the public until I say otherwise. Captain, see to it, please."

He did, too.

*　*　*

I sent the four wog trophy hunters home empty-handed. Not even a refund. I logged the Wapatai *non compos mentis* for his role in Christian's death. It turned out that the Kyzillian really did have some mob connections. Needless to say, it did not cause trouble after I showed it the printout.

I filed my report with the Chairman of the Board of The Kilgari Corporation ten days later. My recommendation that the Dome 16 veldt tour be modified into a camera safari-trek was met with only modest enthusiasm . . . until I reminded him that the public relations nightmare surrounding the death of the guide had been effectively neutralized by announcing the creation of the Cobb Christian Memorial Video Trek for charity to be held once a year about this time. The positive publicity would be worth millions. *That* he liked, so I got my way.

I got a raise for keeping the media in the dark. The murder of Cobb Christian is listed on public records as an accidental trampling by an animal subsequently removed from the veldt. Pinkerton security files tell the real story, but nobody has access to them. They confidentially list the death as self-defense, by being/beings unknown, cross-referenced to the video record of that last interview with Evans.

Oppenheimer was allowed to resign and quietly return to Earth. No undue fuss was made, because there is no statute of limitations on prosecuting his particular offense, especially after I laid out the details of his criminal intent. He lied about Evans' World, as it is now listed, being a surveyed planet. I arranged a job for him, though. He's a Pinkerton security guard at the Greater Cincinnati Metro Convention Center.

Ross is now assigned to my office full time. Good secretaries are very hard to find and you never let one slip away. Not if you know what's good for you. And there's one other perk I got out of the Christian affair: standing orders now exist, in writing, never to wake me up . . . not even if one of the damned Domes *do* explode.

Now, how much more could someone ask for than that?

IT'S THE THOUGHT THAT COUNTS
by Michael A. Stackpole

Michael A. Stackpole's latest book is *Evil Triumphant*. He has recently been more active in creating computer games than science fiction stories, but this one shows that he hasn't lost his touch.

In a future society, a man kills his wife in what seems to be the perfect crime: no clues, no witnesses, perfect alibi. A telepathic policeman knows that the man did it, but telepathy is not legal evidence in court.

Write a story in which the telepath must, through legal means, force the murderer into revealing himself.

She walked into my office on legs long enough to be stilts. Gams like that usually only come out of a vat, but she looked baby factory original to me. The black sweater-dress hugged her tight, but the wide black belt, pearls, and the veiled hat told me she wasn't stalking a swain. She wanted something else and she figured I could deliver.

She looked up at me, flashing green eyes from a fox face. I felt something jolt through me. I checked to see that the Datamaster 301 desk hadn't shorted again, then I gave her a smile. She returned it, with interest, then clasped her gloved hands over her purse and held it against her flat stomach.

"Mr. Martel? Your secretary said I could come right in." She glanced down at the wooden chair in front of my desk. "May I?"

I nodded. A woman like her looks totally out of place in an office like mine. I keep it dark so I can't see how dingy it really is. The microwave over on the file cabinet has the stains of a million cups of nuked coffee in it. Optical data disks spill over the shelves; even their rainbow surfaces can't reflect the weak light. The couch is covered with old printouts from old cases.

It struck me, all of a sudden, that all my cases were *old*, just like my suit. Bad run of luck, but maybe it was changing. I nodded to myself and she took it as a signal to start. I could have told her different, but I didn't.

"I am recently widowed. My husband, Ken Cogshill, took his own life."

I'd heard it all before. Actually, I'd read it all before, straight from her mind. About a second before she spoke, the words appeared in her head and I had them. She impressed me—deliberate and direct. Most women don't have a quarter of that lag-time.

She blinked her big eyes, but made no move to brush away the single tear painting mascara down her right cheek. "I loved my husband, Mr. Martel, but he became involved with Richard Hybern. I thought it was just this Neo-men's movement, but Kenny, he became part of Hybern's inner circle. Ken gave him everything, then went out and killed himself. I have nothing."

I wouldn't have said she had nothing, but what she had wouldn't pay the rent or power. I watched her without saying a word. Most of my clients take this as tough-guy silence or stupid-guy silence. Okay, it could be either, but it gives me a chance to see if they're holding anything back as they assume I assume they are. If they are, it comes out, then I wait a bit more to see if they will spill it or think about yet more stuff they think I'd want to know.

She was holding a hole card, but she didn't want to play it. "I talked to some friends and they said Hamilton Martel was the best private investigator around." I saw the face of Mortimer Phibbs flash through her mind. I still had scars from that divorce case. "Mr. Martel, you have to help me."

"Ham. You can call me Ham." Sure, it's a dumb nickname, but it saved my life in the Steinberg cannibal case, so I stick with it. "I'll help you if you answer me one question, Mrs. Cogshill."

"Louise. Please, what is it?" She took off her hat and let a cascade of fiery red hair spill over her shoulders. "I want to be very open with you."

"Did you ever tell your husband that you went to see Hybern and ended up doing the horizontal tango with him?"

"How did you know?" Her cheeks reddened just a shade darker than her hair. She tore her gaze away from mine. "I guess you are the man I need."

She didn't know the half of it, but I let that slide. "You think Hybern confronted your husband with that news, and that's what drove him over the edge, don't you?"

I knew the truth before she answered. "Yes, no, I . . ." Purse opened and a handkerchief came out in time to catch the tears tooling down the mascara motorway. "Ken and I had been through a lot and we loved each other. He had strayed once, with his secretary, and I forgave him. I never assumed that meant I could . . . I knew we could have worked through it, but I felt dirty and ashamed. I felt *used.*"

Everything registered true on my built-in horse-pucky meter. "Okay, Louise, I can help you. You want me to find out if Hybern told your husband about your tryst and you want me to see if I can get you the family assets back, right?" I phrased that question that way on purpose. It made me seem altruistic and that's the priority she'd put on things anyway.

"Yes, yes, you understand."

I gave her my "I have it under control" smile. "I get five K a day, plus expenses." I sensed her shock because she knew, in the Phibbs case, I'd gotten twice that *and* stuck Phibbs for my new kidney in the process. What she didn't know is that I scale my prices in accordance with client-based eyestrain.

She nodded and reached her hands up to her neck. They came back down with the pearls dangling between them. "This is all I have to pay you."

I shrugged. "Let's go see my secretary. She can make the arrangements." I trusted Louise Cogshill, and she *believed* the pearls were cultured not synthed. I'd made a living proving that guilty husbands will say anything to wives, but I didn't want to tell her that Kenny might have pulled another fast one on her.

I let her precede me out to the reception area of my office. It was polite. It was also a joy to watch her walk. "Dolores, this is Louise Cogshill. She's our new client. We're billing her four large a day, plus expenses." When both of them looked at me in surprise, I shrugged. "She's a widow." With a walk.

Dol would have raised a questioning eyebrow at me if she

had one. She's a platinum blonde—real platinum, too. I rescued her from a blind date with a big magnet and used the data on a Prom hidden away in her to bring her former boss' house of disks tumbling down. She's been with me since, the loyalty and infatuation programs built into her working overtime since I turned out to be her white knight.

The pearls clacked gently in Dol's open right palm. She pulled them close to her face and a little red beam shot out of her right pupil. The laser scanned two or three of the pearls then clicked off. She looked up at me with electric Big Blue eyes and blinked them once. The pearls were genuine.

I guided Louise to the door, letting my hand rest on the small of her back. "I will contact you when I have something."

"Do you want my number?"

I winked reassuringly at her as I memorized the number floating in her mind. "I'll find it."

"It's unlisted." She doubted me.

"I have my resources, Louise." I made a note of her private line as well. "That's why I'm the detective."

She gave me a smile that made me forget what she was thinking. "They said you were the best. Good luck."

Luck is what you need when playing cards. I don't. I cheat. Every gamble for me is a sure thing. It may be immoral to bet on a sure thing, but I figured what Hybern had done to her and her husband was immoral. Fighting fire with fire.

Live by the sword, Hybern, and you can die by it, too.

I shut the door after her and turned to look at Dol sitting all prim and proper at her desk. She held her hands poised as if over a keyboard, but there wasn't one there. Her fingers worked phantom keys. Some folks call it a virtual keyboard. I call it a way to burn out those expensive little servomotors in her hands.

"Ham, I've sent the scan on the pearls down to Bronco. I have him on the phone now. He says he'll go fourteen on them, but we're bargaining. He wants to know if they're loaners or his for resale."

Even though I couldn't read her, I knew what she was thinking. She wanted me to sell the things outright and that way I couldn't make a gallant gesture to the widow Cogshill by returning them. "Loaner for now. They may be the only thing of her husband's she has left."

Dol nodded her head the way she always does. She says she has my best interest in her power supply. Says I'm a stalled car on the railroad crossing of love, but she's always there to pick up the pieces after the crash. "Yes, Mr. Martel."

"Dol, not this time. I'm all for you, you know that."

Her fingers stopped working. "Yes, Mr. Martel," she repeated, letting her voxsynther raise the pitch of her words for ironic effect. "With the sixteen-five I just talked out of Bronco, we're nine to the good over all our triple-notice bills."

I grunted, thinking. "Good. Look, I need you to run down everything on Richard Hybern. Ditto a file on Cogshill, too." I reached for my hat and shrugged my trenchcoat on. "I'm heading out for lunch. Tell the weasel I'm at Mickey's."

"How come you never take me anyplace, Ham?"

I knew where this conversation was going as if I were reading a script. I glanced over in the corner behind her desk at the silver pretzel the landlord's reps had made of her legs the last time I went overdue. "How much?"

She's got that innocent blink down pat. "Five."

"Do it." I smiled at her and opened the door. "Do it and I'll take you dancing."

Us telepaths are about as rare as honest politicians. I'm not sure why, but I have my suspicions. The Feds making insider trading a capital offense dusted some of us while I figure the spooks and Bureau picked up most of the rest. The Mob's got some interesting tests for telepathy, but the prize for passing is small, lead, and moves fast, so I stay clear of them.

I slid into my booth at Mickey's and scanned Arnie's mind for what was good to order. That drew a blank, so I checked for least toxic. "Burger, fries and some joe."

"Sure, bud," he snapped around a well-gnawed cigar. "Burn a cow and oil-boil some roots," he shouted at the elvis working the cookstove.

Coffee flowed like 10-W-40 oil into my cup. It would be a race to see if I could drink it before it etched the porcelain, but I gave it a head start. Letting it cool would make it harder to chew, but poaching my tongue wasn't on my list of things to do today.

The Weasel slid into the booth across from me, the cracked naugahyde tearing at his polyester double-knits like newshounds at scandal. He flashed me a big smile, hoping to provoke a reaction, but I shut him down. "How it be, man?"

I shrugged. The Weasel is a low-grade psychic. If I'm the Major Leagues, he's strictly T-ball. Reads emotions like greed or lust and works cons off them. I don't even know if he's aware he has that ability. I know he does because I can feel him tickling around, trying to get a read.

"Got a new case. You've worked some of the Neo-men's stuff, right?"

"Bly Institute lectures? Yeah." He gave me another grin. "All these suits ready to shed their synthskin and get back to basics. I got some connections and sell them 'Navajo' castoffs so they can be proper for their pow-wows."

His brain wrapped smugness around a label reading "Made in Moldova." "Nice scam."

"I even get their Halstons in trade. Resale on those is pure profit."

"Ever run into Richard Hybern?"

Arnie set my plate down and the Weasel recoiled like it was a traffic accident. Might have been the food. Burger looked like it had been forged, then shellacked. The fries . . . well, smothering them with ketchup was a public service. Besides, I needed a vegetable with the meal.

"Never him, but I've seen some of his recruiters. Colder than Marxism's promise, those dudes. They hang at Bly-athons and pull the elite with them to meet Hybern." The Weasel frowned. "Never take any of my customers."

"You're working different tiers of the food chain, babe." I broke a piece off my burger, forced it back to my strong teeth, and tossed some java down to lube its passage. "You've never worked a Hybern meeting?"

"Compared to Hybern, the Masons are a public gathering. Tight group. Members direct other members to check out a Bly lecture, then the Hybern recruiters go to work." The Weasel visualized me wearing a bullet-riddled dunce cap. "You're not going after Hybern, are you?"

"You know something I don't?"

He thought so, but by that time it wasn't true. "Folks

join his group for *life*, my man." He didn't mean a long time, either.

When I got back in the office, I saw a repair-meck kneeling behind Dol's desk. I might have thought something kinky was going on, but repair-mecks don't have the right tools. Two of his arms held her left leg braced while another pair slowly straightened it out. The last two, the dinky ones meant for fine work, were soldering connections on her stumps.

Her head swiveled all the way around to look at me. "I'll be an inch taller!"

Tossing my hat on the rack, I winked at her. "Files are on my desktop?"

"Yes, Mr. Martel."

I draped my trenchcoat over my couch and slid in behind the Datamaster 301. It wasn't the latest model, but it worked. The big, flat LCD display looked like a cartoon desktop and three folders sat stacked in living color on it. I touched the first one with my right hand and slid it down into place. Hitting the corner, it opened and I started reading.

Hybern started with the Bly Institute and looked, for a bit, to be the logical successor to the old man himself. Then the Wolf-Warrior schism hit the movement and the Blyers were reduced to running "Play nice" seminars at preschools. Hybern looked like he'd jump to head up the Wolf-Warriors, but he balked and disappeared for a while.

The Wolf-Warriors were a curious outgrowth of the men's movement. They rejected the logical fallacy of embracing the "warrior within" while abandoning the violence and hostility that came with that role. Like most misguided movements, they went overboard in the other direction, assailing Christianity and Buddhism as religions for "wussies." Embracing the Sadlerite Gospel of Casca the Eternal Warrior, they went to Guatemala to take over and form their own Militocracy.

The world quickly learned that NOW *did* have the bomb and the Wolf-Warriors did a fast atomic fade. The Bly Institute used their example as positive reinforcement about the folly of violence and jumpstarted the movement again. Hybern returned as a leader who helped men realize their full potential. When his list of successful clients became long enough, he split and set up his own group: Hybern Organization for Male Motivational Existentialism.

As I dug deeper into the clips, I saw the reason the Weasel had reacted so violently to my mentioning Hybern. HOMME had an unfortunate list of client suicides and accidents. The first couple of times HOMME was listed among the victim's affiliations, but after that all mention of HOMME was quashed. Touching the screen over the little checkmark icon on the scanned clips showed me how Dol had cross-correlated obits with other articles and pictures to make up the list of dead folks tied to HOMME.

Other articles Dol had found suggested a couple more people had found themselves in Louise's position. I saw two mentions of lawsuits to get money back from HOMME that the deceased had given before his death. One was settled out of court. Another obit told me the disposition of the second case.

The Cogshill file made for a quick read. Ken had been a fast-track executive with Mutual of Prudential-Tokugawa Insurance. He and Louise had been playing house for seven years, married for four of them. No kids. Ken's grandfather traded shrapnel for a Congressional Medal of Honor in Panama in '89. His father got a pass into West Point because of it. He resigned his commission in '32 to join the Ronald Reagan Brigade of the Tibet Tigers in the Sino-Tibet war. Ken was born six months before his father caught a fatal bullet in the fighting outside Lhasa in '33.

Kenny looked primed for Bly and Hybern. His father and grandfather were heroes but had paid for it in blood. Kenny opted away from military life. Not following them, he needed some sort of reassurance he was a real man. For me, waking up with Miss Bedroom-Eyes '49 every morning would have been plenty. Kenny wanted more and was willing to pay Hybern to get it.

And pay he did. According to the Cogshill account summary Dol had included in the file, Kenny transferred his entire savings to HOMME. HOMME was also listed as the beneficiary on an insurance policy he had. Hybern wouldn't get the insurance because Kenny had done himself—house edge for the company. The fund transfer, on the other hand, had been for over ten mondo, which was enough to buy anyone a dacha on the Black Sea and the government stability to keep it.

My mind revving high, I wandered out to the front. "Dol, how does this bank transfer thing work? How does the bank know Cogshill actually made the transfer to HOMME?"

She let out the closest thing to a sigh her chip could produce. It sounded like the wrong-answer buzzer on a vidgameshow. "I've explained this to you before, Ham."

"Humor me. I've still got bugs in my wetware."

"Widows, more like."

I winced. "Can the Eliza emulation, Dol, unless you don't want me to help you put those tin pins through the fox-trot."

She blinked once, giving me her full attention. "The bank supplies each customer with an account number and an access code. The first is supposed to be common knowledge and the second a deep, dark secret. Some banks even give good customers emergency codes so a transaction can be traced and stopped while appearing to go through. Prevents extortion."

"Huh. I never got one of those."

She stared at me to emphasize the adjective *good*. If my average balance were a thermometer reading, they'd have to recalibrate absolute zero. "Of course, folks are encouraged to change their codes often, but they seldom do or tie it to a number like their birthday."

I made a note to change mine. "So transfers are pretty easy to fake, right?"

Her head swung back and forth. "Banks use one more check. When you go to make a transfer, they feed back a word or phrase for you to type in. The computer checks the response time and typing patterns, then runs that by a file of examples they have from work you've done in the past. If things match, the transfer is authorized. Numbers you can steal. This you can't fake."

"Wouldn't that data base be limited for folks who don't type much?" Like me.

"Chances are people who don't type much don't have much money."

Like me.

"So Cogshill really did authorize the transfer to HOMME."

She nodded. "To the bank's satisfaction, he did. That's good enough for the Feds. If Mrs. Cogshill were to sue, she'd have to find a lawyer who wanted a loser."

"That much of a guarantee for a loss?"

"Not as good as the one you get with the Cybernags you bet on, but close." She extended both her legs and flexed her toes. "Now I'm faster than they are."

"What about the two suits against HOMME?"

"They involved real estate transfers. Different stuff. Brokers mess things up." She reached over on her desk and extended the glass bowl of batteries to the repair-meck. He took a 9-volt, then tipped the top of his head to her. She gave him a tinny giggle. He folded up his arms and stood.

The repair-meck headed for the door. I let him out, then reached for my hat. "I'm heading out."

Dol stood. "Let me come with you."

"I don't think so." Her head slumped forward, disappointed. I crossed to her desk and gave her a peck on the cheek. I ignored the fact that her flesh was colder than a proctologist's tools. "Head out for a trial run on those titanium trotters. Buy yourself a dress. Make it something nice. Real nice. For when we go dancing."

"You promise?"

"You're the apple of my eye, Dol." I winked at her. "Charge it to my account."

"Okay!" She looked at me with eyes like limpid pools of neon. "Where will you be?"

I gave her a patented "I'll be okay" smile. "I'm going to see Hybern. I want to find out what his thoughts are on this."

I'd had stale sandwiches tougher than the security man working the HOMME front office. A big guy in a maroon blazer, he flexed his pecs as he moved to bar my path. "Where do you think you're going, pipsqueak?"

I stopped, tipped my hat back, and looked up into his eyes. His mind had the typical bully feel to it. "I was thinking that spot back there, near the elevator, looked a bit softer for your landing, ace." A little question mark lurked beneath an ocean of laughter in his mind. "You got an ambulance service you prefer here?"

The question mark got a bit bigger. Like all bullies he expected me to be afraid of him, and when I wasn't, he began to wonder. I stepped closer, violating his personal space and bringing him into range for my secret weapon. Our gazes met and I let him have it.

If I work real hard and am in close, I can sometimes project a thought into someone's head. The trick doesn't work with women—reading more than surface thoughts off them might as well be torture and projecting is impossible. Women think differently than men. They're a lot like cats.

This explains why dogs are a man's best friend.

A long time ago I got the Weasel to dummy up a magazine cover for me. It shows me holding something that looks a lot like a World Championship Belt above my head. The magazine is titled "Killer Karate Today" and the headline reads "Minute Martel Hammers the Hulk." I studied that image harder than the IRS does a banker's 1040 form. I planted a comp copy in the bully's brain.

Worked better than planting a fist in his groin. He got all white and kinda sucked himself inward. 'Cept for his eyes—they bugged out.

"Mr. Martel to see Mr. Hybern."

A phone on the wall buzzed and the security man moved off to get it. I breathed a silent sigh of relief. Ever since folks had started using T1K Secmecks, that trick hasn't worked too well. Those machines think, or so I'm told, but their artificial intelligence is a marriage between that of Ted Bundy and the average Mako shark. Using a sociopathic Cuisinart to safeguard property might be some folks' idea of wisdom, but not mine. Mecks think in binary. Ones and zeroes. On and Off. If a T1K turns someone Off, even by accident, turning them back On requires microsurgeons with a taste for jigsaw puzzles.

The bully hung the phone up, then walked over to the elevator doors. He pushed the button and the doors opened. "Mr. Hybern will see you now. This elevator will take you to him."

I nodded and headed for the box. The guy touched me on the shoulder to stop me, then jerked his hand back like he'd been snakebit. "Excuse me, sir, Mr. Martel, but . . ."

"Yes?" I opened my coat so he could see that I wasn't heavy.

"No sir, not that." He smiled weakly. "Could I have your autograph?"

The Weasel doesn't work much, but when he does, what he does is good.

* * *

The elevator doors closed behind me. I braced for the ascent, then half-stumbled as it rocketed down. I started to regret not having Dol get me the plans for HOMME's building, but the elevator stopped short. I knew if I was being dropped into some trap the place wouldn't show on the plans anyway.

The doors opened onto a dark corridor. Walls looked like Lucite blacker than the coffee at Mickey's. The only light came from a dull red strip running along the top of the wall. I could see well enough to walk forward, but not too far. Behind me the doors slid shut silently.

The plush black carpeting smothered my footsteps like a pillow. Thin red stripes cut across the carpet every ten feet. They bled out from the thicker red strips bordering the walls like the sidelines in some corridor football game.

The corridor took a right-angle turn to the left after fifty feet. Another ten feet and it broadened out into a room. Same decor as the hall, but everything was wider, taller, and deeper. The room looked square, but the corridor bled into it at the corner. Funny how they'll pay architects to waste space like that.

Just over halfway into the room a stepped pyramidal facade of black Lucite backed Hybern's desk. Glowing red lines separated the slabs of the pyramid. Scarlet red light bled from around the edges of the design giving it a dim halo. A similar red strip, a bit brighter than the facade, ran around the edge of Hybern's ebony desktop.

The desk light and the facade combined to sink Hybern in bloody shadows. Red highlights glowed from his shaved head and his goatee looked woven from the same shadow they used to make his turtleneck and shirt. A big ruby sat in a gold setting on his left ring finger. He steepled his fingers when he saw me, then he nodded me forward.

"Welcome, Mr. Martel."

"Thanks." I walked forward and hid my surprise as a chair rolled out from behind the pyramid and stopped in front of his desk. "Who did your decorating? Dracula?"

White teeth showed in a grin I'd have figured threatening, but I got nothing from the guy. "Real men are not afraid of the dark."

"Real men don't live in it." I settled myself in the chair and hooked my hat over the corner. "I'd like to talk to you about someone who used to be in HOMME."

He leaned back in his chair, resting his chin in his right

hand with his index finger next to his temple. "Let me guess: Ken Cogshill?"

I nodded. "Very good. Care to show your work?"

"Elementary deduction, really. In the time it has taken for you to get here, I was able to check you out." He patted the polarized top of his Datamaster 9000 desk. "Among fourth rate detectives you have a following, Mr. Martel. Only Mrs. Cogshill is desperate enough to keep trying to find someone to investigate her husband's death."

"Okay, you're on target there—about her, not me." I narrowed my eyes in an expression that usually puts the subject of my investigation on edge. "She thinks you had something to do with his death. Cops ruled it a suicide, but if she's right, you've gotten away with the perfect crime, haven't you? Now why would she be after you?"

"She wants a scapegoat." The man remained a rock. I'd accused him of being a murderer and he gave me less reaction than the pizza delivery boy when I stiffed him on a tip. "She wants to assuage her guilt over Ken's suicide. She came to me first, accusing me of all sorts of heinous things. She claims we slept together and that my telling her husband about our fling caused him to kill himself. This is non-sense."

In the detective game you learn to see the signs of lying. Scratching the nose is one. Forced levity is another. Refusal to look someone in the eye is a big one. I go by all of those, and follow them up with a mental snapshot from the person talking.

I concentrated on Hybern as I asked, "Why would she say that?" Nothing.

He smiled effortlessly. "The woman is schizophrenic and delusional. She suffers from paranoia. Her inability to deal with the fact that her husband felt trapped in their life and killed himself has made her yet more unstable."

I should have seen it coming, but he misdirected me perfectly. I'd been in the mind of a schizo before. It's like looking at an X-ray movie. Everything is there, but reading Brett Easton Ellis' *The Bride Wore Black and Decker* is easier. Louise Cogshill might have been upset at her husband's death, but if she was crackers, then I was tuned-in to the same channel.

"You're lying!" I snarled and mentally pushed at him. I cracked through his defenses and caught his lie. I saw him showing Ken Cogshill pictures of his wife hugging her legs around someone who wasn't him. I heard Hybern muttering things about a man's honor and pride. Cogshill nodded, his head hanging in resignation, then I looked up at Hybern's face and saw him scratch his nose.

The trap closed on me faster than Broadway's *Tiananmen Square '89: A Musical Review*. I felt an alien presence in my mind. It was everywhere at once, but I couldn't pin it down. I felt like I was wrestling with a shadow. Worse, it was winning.

«You really want to know what happened to Ken Cogshill, Mr. Martel? I will show you.» I heard Hybern's laughter ringing in my ears, but it sounded very distant. *«Watch carefully.»*

Hybern rummaged through my brain until he found my bank account number and my personal identification code. Across the desk from me I saw him hit a series of icons on his desktop. He frowned. A vise pressed in on my head.

«Only $3000 in your bank account?» His anger pummeled me.

My fist clenched. *You think you're sore; that means Dol's spent $1000 on a dress!*

«Spare me.» Hybern did something that felt like he was taking steel wool to my brain, then my eyes focused. My interview with Louise played through my mind. Hybern lurked there like a pervert and watched it all. He caught my reaction to Louise's walk and froze my mental image there. *«She is fine, is she not? She was very good.»*

Every muscle in my body went rigid. *You bastard. If I get my hands on you!*

Suddenly I felt my hands around my own throat. *«You'll what? Do this?»* They tightened and I made a croaking sound. My thumbs pressed in on my windpipe. I felt the pulse in my neck thud against my fingers. I knew that Hybern could, in an instant, make me break my own neck.

Hybern came around and sat on the front edge of his desk, folding his arms across his chest. *«I could, but I'm more subtle than that. Both you and Mrs. Cogshill are a problem. I should have given Ken the order to kill her when he killed himself, but he wasn't strong enough for that. However, your interest in her suggests a solution to me.»* He touched an icon on his desk and I heard a phone dial tone. *«You're calling Louise and telling her to come here.»*

Never!

«*Never say never, Mr. Martel.*» He plucked her private number from my brain. He hit an icon on the desk that reversed the view so I could see everything, then punched the number into the dialing pad icon on the desk. The tones played out the first three bars of an old march, then it started ringing. I hoped it was busy, but she picked up and the Datamaster's hidden speakerphone filled the room with her voice.

"Hello?"

"Louise?" I heard myself say. "This is Ham. I'm at Hybern's place over on South King. I've been talking to him and he's interested in some sort of settlement." I tried to make my hands complete the job Hybern started, but he restrained me.

"Do you think it is safe?"

"I wouldn't be calling you if it wasn't. How fast can you get here?"

"Fifteen minutes?"

"Perfect," Hybern made me purr. "See you then."

He touched a button and cut the connection. «*Now you and I need to do some work to prepare for her arrival and your departure.*» He integrated our views so I could see things through his eyes. He punched up his bank account and arranged a transfer into my account. «*I think $500,000 looks like a sufficient amount for an operator like you to extort out of me. You manufactured evidence to link me with Ken's death after you and Louise, in the midst of a torrid affair, discovered HOMME had turned Ken into enough of a man to contest the divorce she asked him for.*»

Hybern gave me a devilish smile. «*I'll even use one of my "extortion" code numbers so the bank will return the money to me after you're gone.*»

All the pieces of the puzzle started to drop into place for me. "You have to be in the men's movement because the only folks you can read and control are men."

He didn't like that and punched a white-hot mental poker into my brain. «*No, I am not like you at all. You are a simpering fool who uses a minor talent to accomplish nothing. I detected your weakling effort up at ground level and decided to amuse myself with you. I am, you see, your mental superior. I use my gift to build empires. The corporate masters of this city, of this country, come to me for advice.*»

I pluck their desires from their minds, then present them back to them as goals. I synthesize bold strategies for them by pitting the strong against the weak.»

«Men like Ken Cogshill are only a small part of my empire. His position was more useful than he was. He cleared all the claims for survivor benefits that I got when my useless members had their accidents. He had decided to take his wife's advice and break it off with HOMME, but, like a man, felt he had to come and explain it to me himself. I was forced to make him kill himself.»

Not man enough to do it yourself, eh?

His face screwed up into a mask of disgust. *«My will, their hands. Watch, you will be the instrument of your own destruction!»*

Against my direct orders, my hands left my throat and settled themselves on his desktop. He slid the keyboard icon beneath my fingers and forced me to start typing. I vaguely remembered having hit the same series of commands before. The desk tied into an international data base. I picked out icons like a puppet with a twitcher on the strings. I ended up with a menu of airlines and flights in front of me.

«Any preference, Mr. Martel? Are you and Louise the sort of traditionalists who want a Costa Rican holiday? The winds won't blow wrong for another three months. Or, ah, I have it, a month at Club Med Antarctica. You'll pack plenty of sunscreen and keep each other very warm. Perfect.»

My hands selected Aero Hielo and Flight 4763, nonstop to Tierra del Fuego. I made reservations for me and Louise Cogshill. I got us confirmed seating. The video was even one I hadn't seen yet.

The machine asked me for preferred method of payment. I got my right hand halfway to my wallet to grab a card before Hybern reasserted control. *«Nice trick, Martel, but using your overdrawn Visa to set up a trace won't work.»*

My hands returned to the keyboard and dutifully typed in my account number and access code. The computer asked me to type in "Rosebud" as a check phrase and I resisted. *No!*

All the agony in the world crushed itself down to the size of a pinhead. It smashed down through the top of my skull, driving bone splinters into my gray matter. It got to the center of my brain and transformed itself into a sphere. It expanded and turned its surface into a razor-studded ball made of door screen material. It grew and grew, slicing and straining my mind.

I resisted until it started spinning. *I surrender, I surrender!*

«Resistance is useless.» Hybern reached over and lifted my chin up. *«Do it right or I destroy selected portions of your autonomic nervous system and you'll suffocate slowly.»*

I nodded. Folding all my fingers in except for the indexers on each hand, I carefully hunted and pecked out the keyword. I hoped the machine would reject it and send a warning flag out. It didn't. "Have a nice flight," it flashed beneath a smiley-face icon.

«How will I make you kill her?» He shrugged as if it were a minor matter. "We can decide that when she gets here. In the mean time, I see, during your sleazy little career, you've learned some nasty things about a lot of interesting people." He caught my thought about Louise. *«Don't expect her or anyone else to rescue you. When they leave the elevator, I'll pick them up, the same way I did with you.»*

He started drilling test holes for a muck-gusher in my brain. I saw bits and pieces of my life whirl past in dizzying confusion. Steinberg's mad face dissolved in blood. Bikermecks roared on through the puddle, drenching me. I tasted blood and smelled cordite. I felt the cold kiss of a knife and the hot fire of a gunshot. Faces popped up like targets and each one sank back into the obscurity from which Hybern dredged them.

A sidewinder smile twisted his lips. *«And just so you won't think I've forgotten you, I'll see to it that Dictameck in your office gets recycled into tin cans.»*

Not Dol! I pushed with my mind as hard as I could. He gave an inch. I tried to take a mile, but lost half an inch in the attempt. He shoved back harder. I felt my mind start to crumble.

Then I saw it. He saw it, too, through my eyes. The red laser-dot blossomed on his forehead like a zit on prom night. We both knew what it meant.

"Give it up, Hybern, we have you covered."

His control wavered for the second it took him to identify the voice through my memories, but that was all I needed. Coming up out of the chair I hooked a right fist at his gut. I missed and he tossed me clean across the desk. Twisting, I ended up in his chair, with my feet pointing at the ceiling.

I felt helpless and I fed that along to Hybern as he tried to defend himself.

Dol didn't need my assist. In the past I had cause to doubt whether or not the Sekmeht boards the Weasel had sold me for Dol were genuine. Rendered a copper Valkyrie by the lights, she drove at him like he was a Wolf-Warrior holding Girl Scouts hostage. Her left fist landed about where I'd meant my punch to. He doubled over and she dropped him with a right to the side of his head.

Dol vaulted the desk and pulled me upright. "Are you hurt?" Her laser scanned me for a second, then winked off.

I shook my head, but that hurt, so I stopped. "He dribbled my brain around inside my skull, but aside from that, I'm okay." I sat down in the chair the correct way and massaged my temples.

She cocked her head to the right, then blinked her eyes at me. "I just contacted the police. They say the feds are sending a couple of Hoovermatics to take him into custody. One of his disciples was a Senator."

"Wow!" I looked at Dol. She had a dark jacket over a red chemise and dark skirt. A black leatherette bag hung on a gold chain from her right shoulder. They matched the black shoes on her feet. I stared at her. "I'm stunned."

"I've called the cops for you hundreds of times before."

"No, the outfit." I swallowed hard. "Wow!"

"Oh, this?" She helped me up out of the chair and we walked toward the elevator. "You told me to get something so we could go dancing."

I nodded and smiled at her. "So how'd you know I was in trouble here?"

Her head waggled back and forth, which is her equivalent of a shrug. "I was buying the purse at the same time you charged the airline tickets."

"You thought I was taking off with Louise Campbell."

"At first." She fell mum as the elevator doors open and Bureaumecks rolled down the corridor. "Then you typed in the check code and I knew you were in trouble."

We got into the elevator and it started climbing upward. "How? The bank didn't kick it. I typed the word perfectly."

Her head swiveled toward me. "I know. I know you. You didn't miss a single key."

"Oh." I stepped back and looked at her again. "That outfit cost you a full K?"

"Of course not, silly." The elevator doors opened and I saw a suit bag draped like a shroud over the goon she'd coldcocked on her way in. "We have a date to go dancing. If I dress up, so do you. We are going, aren't we?"

I looked up and saw Louise enter the HOMME lobby. "Is it over?"

I nodded and felt her relief roll over me like a tidal wave.

"I don't know how I can ever thank you," her lips said, but I saw her mind had some fine ideas about gratitude. "Can we discuss things over dinner, tonight?"

I looked at her and thought about the plane tickets Hybern had made me book. Thought long. Thought hard. She could do a lot to make long, cold winter nights seem neither.

I shook my head. "Sorry, Louise, but I'm a stalled car on the railroad crossing of love." I shouldered the suit bag and slipped my arm around Dol's waist. "And tonight I'm dancing down the rails with a dame on steel wheels."

THE COLONEL AND THE ALIEN

by Ralph Roberts

Ralph Roberts, author of more than 30 books in other fields, here returns to his first love, science fiction.

The head of security is informed that there will be an attempt to assassinate the President of Earth within the next 48 hours. The only other things his informant related before being murdered himself is that the assassin was an alien, and that the weapon—which would not be a weapon in human hands—would almost certainly pass any kind of security inspection the killer was given.
Identify the weapon and the killer, and prevent the murder.

In the midnight hour, the Colonel finished reading the dead man's brain and the hologram faded away.

He sighed and stood up carefully in the manner favored by the elderly, moving from behind his desk to stand next to one of the tall windows overlooking Earth's never-sleeping capital city. It was night. A bright glow stretched in all directions, blending so distantly into the horizon that it was difficult to see where the lights of the city ended and the stars of the clear winter sky began. The navigation lights of aircars formed steady bright white and red streams in the allocated routes that passed far beneath his windows. Higher was the unmistakable pulsatingly purple grav field of a starship massively floating down to the port.

The Colonel was tall, trim, fit. His age was indeterminate but obviously of great years. His face was lined somewhat, and his hair silver. Yet, once he had risen and shaken off the stiffness that comes with sitting, he stood ramrod straight and moved with confidence. His eyes were what people noticed: blue-gray like a November ocean, they missed nothing and revealed nothing.

"This little is all we have?" the Colonel said to the window. "Just that the President of Earth is to be assassinated within the next forty-eight hours?"

"Yes, dear, it is," Agee, his personal computer, replied, her pleasant voice projected directly into his ear where none but he could hear. There was no need to speak aloud in replying to her, subvocalization worked just as well, but the Colonel was of the old school and often did so when alone.

He sighed. Van der Rant had been not only his Deputy of Security, but also a rare friend and confidant for over two hundred years. Now all that was left of a once-vibrant individual was a partial recording of the dead man's brain, relayed by an implanted personal computer similar to his own in the moment of dissolution for both.

"The president is to be killed by an alien, using a weapon that would not be a weapon in human hands," Agee continued, summarizing the fragment of brain recording. "Not only that, but it will almost certainly pass any security check. And none of our security devices witnessed Van der Rant's killing. Most unusual."

The Colonel turned from the window and looked across the spacious green and gold carpeted expanse of his office. Elegant antiques from around the galaxy rested here and there, peeking out of niches and giving the room a comfortable, cluttered patina of age. The office was perfect in every detail, and it had taken him over five hundred years to get it that way—the five hundred years that he had been Head of Security for the Republic of Earth and Confederation of Stars. He would never be a general because it would be a demotion from his present position. Many people had long since forgotten his name. To refer to "the Colonel," with a fearful glance over your shoulder, was enough. All knew instantly whom you meant. Especially those who would conspire against the Republic in these decadent times.

In the early days, there had been many thousands under his command—both humans and members of the other sentient races. Now, computers like Agee did most of the work, and intelligent devices maintained security. Van der Rant, his deputy, had been the only other live member of Security on Earth. On the hundreds of planets making up the Confederation, there was only one agent per world at most, and most agents handled entire systems, even sectors. Those other agents were too far away to help. It was all up to him, and he had little enough time.

Decisively, the Colonel left his office and approached the lift that would take him one floor up to the President's office. Old as he was, his earlier careful manner had turned into a quick-paced walk. Doors that would have issued flaming death to almost anyone else hurriedly dilated out of his way. They knew their master.

* * *

The newly-elected President of Earth for this decade was an alien—the first nonhuman ever to achieve the office. Her sex, if not always her actions, closely approximated that of female. She sat rigidly green, as was normal for her kind, playing some sort of incomprehensible board game with a crony who looked as much like her in dress and appearance as to be almost indistinguishable. To the Colonel, who had dealt in nuances for centuries, there was no doubt.

Both aliens suddenly became aware of his presence and momentarily displayed an emotion that was close enough to shocked surprise to be called that. It was, after all, long past the business day and there were legions of subtle but powerful security devices to spit annihilation on the uninvited and unauthorized, and that category covered everyone except her friend tonight. She had so ordered it.

"We have not yet met," the Colonel said coolly, "but you know who I am."

The President—her name was Navara, only that and nothing more—nodded, mimicking the human gesture with the ease of the consummate politician that she was.

"Few there are who do not know of the Colonel," she said, her accent perfect, yet underlaid with an exotic trill that was not unpleasing. Still, to the Colonel, it was obvious that she was less than enthused about his entry, and that annoyance was close to the surface. "We were briefed about you."

She wore a golden gown that hid most of her body, but her green head was smooth, hairless. Her eyes, mouth, and nose came close to human placement. She had two arms, each with slim hands having six fingers. Her overall effect was one of a beautiful but dignified matron. A mother-figure. A comfort-giver who was alien-yet-not-alien.

In short, she was electable although the election process had been controversial, and full of dirty tricks on all sides. Her party's tricks—the party which disputed the rule of the majority by the Earth-human minority—had had the best tricks of the four major parties. Two of those major parties were mostly comprised of humans, while Navara's party had both humans and humanoid aliens, the latter predominating. The fourth party was favored by alien races of nonhuman characteristics—methane breathers, intelligent crystals who took years to complete a thought, life based upon zinc and copper, which communicated only by coherent light, and others even more unusual.

This latter party had suffered the most at the hands of Navara's party, seeing victory snatched from its overconfident tentacles by an old and much-used political tradition called "an October surprise." In their case, distasteful cannibalistic practices attributed to their presidential candidate, which were only proved false *after* the election.

There had been much resentment evinced in all these political circles in thousands of star systems in the weeks since the election. Several investigations had been instigated. Many had not attended yesterday's inauguration, although attempts at reconciliation had also been launched.

Under the Colonel's seemingly dispassionate gaze, both President Navara and her companion grew uncomfortable. The Colonel had always been above politics, so much so that politicians often felt embarrassed and unclean in his presence. At least for a fleeting instant.

"Send the old dog back to its kennel," the other alien, whose name was Memnel, said in their native language. *"We can dispose of it later."*

Agee the computer did not bother to whisper a translation or voice a warning into the Colonel's ear. She knew full well that he understood the language the alien spoke.

"Old dogs may yet have sharp teeth," the Colonel said calmly and perfectly in the same tongue.

Navara raised a hand in a not-quite-human way that stopped her companion from making a retort. "I had hoped to do this at a more opportune time, but with a new administration comes changes. Your services as Head of Security will no longer be required. Memnel here, who happens to hold the rank of general, will take your position. You may depart after revealing to him all computer codes, overrides for the security devices, and the like.''

"Ask him how he got *in* here!" General Memnel demanded, obviously not realizing she had just shown that she already understood the Colonel's method of access.

The Colonel ignored the general, although Agee—with access to the unlimited data bases of his department—told him that the alien was head of Navara's people's secret police. Something a commonwealth within the Republic was not supposed to have. His agents kept track of all such, and adroitly uncovered and sabotaged plans not in the Republic's interest.

"It may be that I will resign in a few days," the Colonel said, unperturbed. "Until then, I will do my job. There is to be an assassination attempt. Within the next forty-eight hours.''

"I knew this would happen," General Memnel said, "The humans are not to be trusted. They do not easily accept their first alien president. We should move the capital off Earth without delay."

"The assassin is not human," the Colonel said.

President Navara was silent for a moment, thinking. She came to a quick decision. Self-preservation had won. "Your immediate resignation will not be necessary. After the assassination plot is foiled will be sufficient time.''

"But I can handle—" began General Memnel.

Navara interrupted him. "No, you will work with the Colonel. It is even possible he might teach you something. Now, both of you get out. I am tired.''

General Memnel looked as if he was going to argue, but a simple look from Navara caused him to desist. He stood, his manner denoting ill grace.

The Colonel smiled inwardly. Obviously he had knocked Memnel out of more than just the board game.

"Come with me," he said, turned, and left without glancing back to see if Memnel was following but, having orders from the President, the alien reluctantly did, cringing by uncontrollable reflex when passing through the doorway. No flames reached out for Memnel's life, however. The Colonel, through Agee, had instructed his devices to let the general pass unharmed.

* * *

Those of the general's kind did not show exhaustion after great exertion by a lack of breath, as would have an Earth-human—even one of much younger age—after trying to keep up with the Colonel. Instead, the general's limbs trembled and his skin glistened a lighter shade of green. He was all too glad to collapse without any attempt at gracefulness into a chair in the Colonel's office. Only the chair's rudimentary intelligence and quick catching movement prevented him from an embarrassing thump on the floor. It had been a harrowingly fast walk through the darkened maze of corridors, ever aware of the watching security devices, and afraid to lose sight of the old Security chief.

The Colonel was already seated behind his desk. Its surface was totally bare. This was to be expected in the paperless offices of the time, but there were no mementos, holographic photos, or anything else. Just bare polished wood. This was not true of the rest of the room. It seemed that every nook and cranny was full of an incomprehensible clutter of objects. To Memnel, it was just so much junk. Collectibles precious and valuable beyond price had no meaning to him.

He finally managed to speak, ignoring the Colonel's inscrutable, patient gaze. "Old human, you will of course tell all and reveal all. We have been ordered to work together by her Excellency, but the commands will be issued by me. You will do as I say. When this assassination plot is defeated, your services are terminated immediately. Is this understood?"

A brief smile crossed the Colonel's face, enigmatic even to those who understood Earth-human expressions. "In the centuries that I've served as Head of Security, has it not occurred to you that other Presidents would have wished to appoint their own person to such a powerful position? Perhaps you might have wondered why I am still here?"

They were speaking the general's own language, and there was a hint of warning in the Colonel's words. Memnel, unfortunately, did not catch the nuance—a failing the Colonel did not have in any of the many tongues, alien and human, that he spoke.

"It is a waste of time to play with him," Agee whispered

into the Colonel's ear. "His intellect is feeble. Let's get to work, dear."

"Do you understand," Memnel demanded, now recovered enough to lean forward on his chair and pound a fist on the Colonel's desk. "Navara may be soft, but for now she is the President and has given authority to me!"

"Yes, the meaning of your words is clear enough."

"As they should be, old one," the general said arrogantly. "Tomorrow I shall be Head of Security. After that, we shall see. The weak have no business ruling. Now, proceed! Explain every step to me."

The Colonel nodded, his face calm, blank. "The situation is thus: My deputy uncovered a plot against the President's life. The assassin is an alien—in this case, I take that to mean non-Earth-human. The weapon is something that the security devices will not see as a weapon, at least in the hands of its wielder. . . ."

He paused to let the import of this latter point sink in, but obviously the general did not comprehend.

"It could be anything, then?"

"No, it could not," the Colonel continued. "I designed those devices myself. They are very intelligent, as my deputy well knows. If it is something that they cannot recognize nor extrapolate to be a weapon, then we have a mystery indeed."

The general made what passed for a snort of derision. "And what other nebulous information do you have? Put your other agents on the job this instant. More solid data is needed for me to do my work!"

"There are no other agents on Earth. There were but the two of us."

Memnel stared at him blankly. "No other agents? But you should have thousands?"

"Thousands are not needed. In fact, it was only because of my age that I took on a deputy."

Memnel radiated contempt. "It is well that you are being replaced. We will need hundreds of agents for this city alone." He made a gesture with his head at the utter stupidity of the old human. "And just how reliable can the information of your dead lackey be?"

"Shall I crisp him, dear?" Agee asked. She, too, had thought highly of the deputy, Van der Rant. "Please?"

"Not yet, if you would be so kind," the Colonel subvocalized. Aloud, he said: "My deputy also provided precise and timely information. That is why he *was* my deputy for the last two centuries."

The alien was not impressed. "Why did he give you so little, then?"

"Due to most tragic and violent circumstances," the Colonel patiently explained. "He was off duty and not on a specific case. Whatever he found, it killed him before he could transmit full details. We have only a snippet of his thoughts to me before the great darkness took him. We know not where nor how he met his end. In the past there have been rare similar circumstances. Even so, this one was unique for its brevity and shortness of details transmitted. Something took him very quickly, indeed."

"You received a recording of his *brain?*"

"Yes, that is correct. It can be done, but it burns out both the brain and the implanted computer. Obviously it is only done in the extremity of dissolution of life."

Even Memnel had enough imagination to perform what passed for a shudder.

"Now," the Colonel said, "your President has not seen fit to provide me with her itinerary and office appointments as of yet. Obtain those and let us get started."

Memnel grunted and reached under his gown to cause his own personal computer to transfer the information to the Colonel's. The alien's personal computer was external and possessed a hefty power pack which the Colonel did not envy him having to carry around.

* * *

General Memnel's computer, unlike the general himself, was of substantial intelligence. In a time period of less than a second, it and Agee had correlated all pertinent data, and agreed upon their interpretation and presentation. A somewhat longer time elapsed while each computer explained those conclusions to the appropriate person. The general's computer took longer, since he kept asking it questions.

"*This* is who the President wants to replace you with?" Agee asked in amusement. "I wonder how he would have handled the affair that just occurred on Sirius VII," she added, then proceeded to give him the salient details.

The Colonel took in Agee's whispered reports, while

evincing outward patience and calm. His job was far more than merely protecting the President. Security was charged with handling anything that endangered the interests and well-being of the Republic of Earth and Confederation of Stars. Usually the devices on location dealt with the problems promptly. Agee monitored all of the encrypted links that networked all the agents, their personal computers, and the billions of intelligent devices belonging to Security all across the galaxy.

Agee constantly selected from the more entertaining events to regale the Colonel with from time to time. On rare occasions, there was a problem that needed his input. Perhaps once a century or so, he would have to travel off-world to attend to affairs in person. But no more than that. He had designed the system to work automatically, and generally, it did. In five hundred years, with the resources of the greatest government of sentient beings ever known, one can do a lot of adjusting and perfecting.

With a glazed look about him that the Colonel took to be information overload, the general finally spoke.

"Listen carefully, oldster, and I will explain."

"I would be most grateful," the Colonel said blandly.

"It is as so: The President has only one public meeting scheduled in the next two days. All private office business will be handled electronically, so her only personal exposure will occur during this dangerous, albeit necessary function."

"Indeed," said the Colonel, who already knew all the details, "she must urgently mend political fences."

Memnel ignored him, and continued his pedantic and condescending explanation. "A large delegation of elected officials and others from the three parties which suffered defeat will, in the interest of political unity now that the election is over, meet with President Navara. Some will present her with gifts of fealty, souvenirs, or advertising premiums, as is dictated by the traditions of their various cultures. Only these latter, during the next forty-eight hours, will have an opportunity to perform the assassination."

He paused triumphantly.

The Colonel sighed and bit to keep the alien general from taking all night—it would be morning soon enough and the meeting was scheduled for 0900 hours. "I see—and from this list you have deduced the assassin?"

The general performed an expression that was equivalent to a smirk. "I have narrowed it down to three: Senator Zarth of Zond, Representative Celu, and Executive Secretary Ulanto dar Freeg of the Purple Party."

"All aliens to Earth-humans, and all members of the Galactic Society for the Common Nesting of Sentient Kind," the Colonel said, giving the Purples their formal name. They were the party favored most by the nonhumanoid races.

"They are sore losers," the general said.

"And your reasons for suspecting these three respectable beings of long-standing service and impeccable reputation?"

The general ticked off his points: "Senator Zarth comes of a race that evolved on a hot, steamy world in which bacteria swim through the soupy air in uncountable numbers. For the primitive hunters of his race to get meat back to their females and cubs, they evolved the physical ability to turn their manipulative appendages into quite effective refrigeration coils, an ability retained to this day. Senator Zarth has only to freeze the plastic bladder of holy water he is presenting to the President and bludgeon her with it."

"Do not laugh aloud, dear," Agee cautioned unnecessarily, although it did take some effort on the Colonel's part not to do so.

"Secondly," Memnel said, "Representative Celu's race has the ability to emit noxious gases at great force."

"This I am aware of," the Colonel interjected. "They are seldom invited to parties since this is often an uncontrollable reflex."

The general paid him no heed. "Although normally merely offensive, what if Celu ingested poisons that would make his gas fatal to the President? Mercury vapor would be one such.

"Then there is the Executive Secretary of the accursed Purples. Her race had an ability similar to your Earth-sea puffer fish. She could either blow up rapidly and crush the President against the wall or, being as fanatical as I know her to be, over-inflate and explode in a suicidal snuffing out of our great President Navara.

"As to which of these three it is, I am not yet decided. Perhaps we should just eliminate them all."

"Yes, well thought out, indeed," the Colonel said.

"Don't be sarcastic, dear," Agee admonished.

The Colonel smiled fleetingly. "Unfortunately, the gifts are to be placed on a table well removed from the President and no one is allowed closer. Additionally, at the merest hint of any such actions as you have described, my security devices would vaporize the assassin. This is a long-established and well-understood policy. My devices are careful not to make mistakes, but act quickly and ruthlessly as need be."

"But . . ." Memnel began.

"Oh," the Colonel said expansively, "I do admit you've narrowed the list of suspects down dramatically, but to three hundred rather than three. We need not concern ourselves with the billions on this planet, but only those actually attending the meeting."

The Colonel suddenly became very still as he listened to new information from Agee. He pushed himself carefully up from the desk.

"Come with me. We have found where my deputy was killed. We will go to the port."

* * *

The port of Earth's capital city was the largest on the planet. Like the rest of the world, the Colonel's security devices had been scouring it all night looking for traces of Deputy Van der Rant. A flying eye, not much larger than a pinhead, had spotted something and alerted larger, more intelligent devices to investigate.

The Colonel and General Memnel now stood in a remote littered cargo hold of a huge starship that had grounded that very evening. One wall was starkly illuminated by the hot, white lights of several devices, but appeared as unchanged as all the other walls of the hold. The general was now displaying slight signs of being uncomfortable. The lights, perhaps?

"He was almost totally vaporized," the Colonel said sadly. "Only a few molecules of he-that-was yet exist on that wall which, being of almost eternal-lasting stuff, shows no worse for the wear. Enough matter for identification, far too little for decent burial."

The general did his shudder equivalent and looked around again. "Such energy, such unbelievable energy!"

"It also explains why there was no trace of him," the

Colonel added, more for himself and Agee than for the alien. "This ship came from off-planet with an empty hold, thus we had no devices in here. Somehow, Van der Rant was lured in here, still unsure enough of his suspicions to make no report other than letting his personal computer record events."

Agee whispered to him.

"Two groups of aliens arrived on this ship," the Colonel said aloud. "By chance, both are attending the meeting that will so soon occur. Each group breathes an atmosphere markedly different from our own and must be wheeled into the meeting in environment enclosures. Neither have anything that could remotely be considered a weapon and thus will easily pass my security devices.

"The Alinth are the more unusual. They exist in a soup of diluted acid, circulating through their bodies based most uniquely on both zinc and copper. They communicate by coherent light, generated naturally in their bodies and aimed through a lens in their chest at a fellow Alinth's receptor organ. The other group, called Y'll, swim constantly in brine, and resemble nothing so much as large Earth-sea shrimp. Like the Alinth, they are physically weak and would die instantly outside their environment enclosures."

The general listened to his own computer briefly. "Such also is my information. It cannot be them. Your agent met his death through some other means."

"Now that we know where the murder occurred," the Colonel continued, "we have correlated data from all devices in the port area—"

"Murder?" the general said, interrupting the Colonel—an act which many trillions of other beings would have thought twice about. "We are investigating an assassination conspiracy. What murder?"

"Some things take priority," the Colonel said coldly. "We in Security take the death of an agent very seriously. We will, of course, prevent the assassination, but bringing the murderer to justice is exceptionally important to us. I won't even ask why you did it, since I already know."

A moment passed until what the Colonel had said registered with General Memnel. "Don't be silly," he said. "I order you not to be silly."

The Colonel was unimpressed. "Several devices report how you met both groups of the non-oxygen breathers."

Memnel swayed, but regained control of himself. "Do they show me killing your agent, then?"

"No, your whereabouts are always accounted for."

"And what of *his?*" the alien said.

"There is no record of him since he went off duty, but he had the right to privacy and could order the devices to ignore him in a manner that even I cannot override. It was a right he had earned."

"Then you can prove nothing," Memnel said, his equivalent of a sneer very strong. His manner contemptuous, yet relieved.

"Of course we can," the Colonel said. "Other agents and devices in Security's network have long since penetrated your secret police. We know of your plot to overthrow your government and, by the happy circumstance of her election, you thought that by delaying the plot until now, you could take over the entire Republic of Earth and Confederation of Stars. It must have seemed like an incredible prize to you."

General Memnel sneered again. "It was and is. Besides, this prize is rightfully mine, since I engineered the election in Navara's favor."

The Colonel nodded. "This is truth. The October surprise that worked. With the eager assistance of the other three parties, we have the proof of that. We have also the evidence of your large payments of your government's money to the assassin."

Memnel was less confident now. "And who is this assassin? Which of the two?"

"Does it matter?" the Colonel asked. "I need merely order that neither be allowed within miles of the capital building at all."

"No! I have come too far to allow an old fool like you to stop me now!"

The alien slapped at his chest and his personal computer suddenly glowed through his robe. He removed it and the computer could be seen to be now surrounded by a dull red field of some sort. None of the Colonel's devices had reacted and the ones that had been illuminating the murder scene slowly let their lights fade to nothing. Only the dim ship's lights in the hold now existed.

Memnel carefully set his computer on the floor. "Now you will understand the reason for the large power pack," he said. "An imprisoning field is generated which also neutralizes your devices for a considerable radius. Do not try to move: you will only hurt yourself. You are both immobilized and incommunicado. I will come back and dispose of you later."

"I have already ordered that both alien groups be excluded from the capital," the Colonel said reasonably. "Give it up now and accept your fate. The penalty for killing an agent of Security is death."

Memnel's explosion of sound was certainly a laugh. "You are far too late, useless old dog. I have already arranged a special meeting for the President with the right alien group, purposely excluding it from the schedule you received. That meeting occurs in mere minutes. The aliens will easily pass your security devices. Their weapon will not be recognized as such until it is too late. Weak Navara will soon be vapor and President Memnel of the Republic of Earth and Confederation of Stars shall begin his long rule. All forces are in place and, with your death, your Security apparatus becomes mine. Now I must rush to oversee the delightful end of Navara and my ascension to total power."

Memnel laughed again, then turned ran from the hold. The Colonel waited patiently, listening to the retreating footsteps on the metallic floor of the corridor that gave access to the cargo hold. In a moment there was a brief, very intense burst of white light, then silence.

"Was he really that stupid, dear?" Agee asked. "He should have realized his vulnerability once he passed beyond the radius of his neutralizing field.

The Colonel shrugged. "The late general made many mistakes." He moved easily through the field, his devices, unaffected also, helpfully turning their lights back on and directing them so that he might not trip over the litter on the floor. One device easily deactivated the alien's red-glowing personal computer, neatly tagged it for evidence that was no longer needed, and brought it along in the Colonel's wake.

* * *

The Colonel and Agee were soon on their way to the President's office. The Alinth assassins, unaware of the fate of their employer, would be faithfully carrying out their murderous duty. There was no time to waste.

"It might be better," Agee said, "just to arrive, alas, moments too late. Let the killers solve the problem of Navara."

"This is not to be," the Colonel said. "Security protects its charges, whether they deserve that protection or not."

"She knew of the election rigging," protested Agee.

"And will pay for it," the Colonel said in agreement. "But not with her life."

"Copper and zinc, right, dear?" Agee said, just to let him know she had solved the mystery on her own.

Their vehicle took them crashing through a window on the President's floor, that being the quickest way, and the Colonel again walked unannounced into President Navara's office by a secret entrance.

* * *

Navara was watching as the delegation of Purples trundled through another door in their large environment enclosure. There were six or seven of them, dimly glimpsed through the transparent front and the acid bath that was their habitat. As the enclosure turned momentarily sideways to negotiate around a grouping of conference furniture, she saw that the rear of the enclosure was curved and of a shiny metal.

The enclosure began swinging back toward her. A glow seemed to be building in its interior. Navara suddenly felt fear. Yet Memnel had cleared these beings, had he not? And where was he? He had promised to be here for the meeting.

The Colonel suddenly stepped around her desk, having entered through an apparently blank wall behind her. He held up his hand and an immobilizing field sprang up. The environment enclosure ground to a stop, unable to bring its front to fully bear on her again. White-hot fury lanced out from the transparency in front and another grouping of furniture simply disappeared, as did a good part of the wall behind.

The doors behind the enclosure rapidly opened to admit a large device consisting mostly of a large tank on wheels. There was a burst of light as it breached the wall of the environment enclosure and inserted a hose.

"What . . . What is. . . ?" Navara began, but grew silent as she watched the Colonel calmly walk around in front of the enclosure and curiously look inside. Weak light washed out at him, but no harm occurred.

"How. . . ?" Navara asked.

The Colonel strolled back to her desk, hands clasped behind his back. Once again, a job was done and done well.

Navara slammed her desk. "How? What?" She was unable to think of any more words at the moment, and simply waited.

"An alien with a weapon that would pass security, *my* security, had to be unusual," the Colonel said. "The Alinth live in a sea of weak acid, which they circulate through their bodies. These bodies, being uniquely based on both zinc and copper, provide electrodes of opposing polarity for the generation of electric current. This, among other things, powers their communicative sources of coherent light which, because they live in a liquid medium, must be of considerable power to effectively work over any distance."

"They are *batteries!*" Navara said, understanding. "Living batteries! But surely even *they* cannot generate such destructive power with just their natural physical strength?"

"Indeed," the Colonel said in agreement. "However, six or seven individuals, when they have a parabolic reflector such as the back of their environment enclosure can direct and focus the power that each pours out. A quick infusion of a base to drastically weaken their acid bath has pulled their fangs for the moment."

Navara did her kind's equivalent of a comprehending nod, then became aware of more devices which had entered her office. Two of these now seized her gently but firmly.

"My best advice," the Colonel said, "is to never let someone as incompetent as the late General Memnel rig an election for you. A bit late, I admit, but valid nonetheless. All houses of the Congresses have voted for your impeachment. You are under arrest."

Navara sagged between the two devices, watched as other devices removed the Alinth environment enclosure, and knew her turn was next.

"You know," the Colonel said almost genially, as he comfortably took a seat behind her desk, "I should really not arrest the Alinth."

"Why not?" Navara asked. "They are assassins."

"Not from their viewpoint," he answered. "They communicate by coherent light." He waved at the devices to take her away. "They were simply making a rather forceful political statement," he said, as Navara was escorted out.

OBSCUROCIOUS

by Ray Aldridge

Ray Aldridge is a relatively new writer, but his name is no stranger to those who peruse the Nebula ballots, and his first novel has just come out to enthusiastic notices.

A chlorine-breathing ambassador from the Sirius system is found dead in his hotel room in an orbiting, multi-environmental hotel. He is alone in his room, the door is locked, and there are no marks on the body. The Sirius system is at peace, but they have a formidable military force, and since the hotel is owned and run by humans, they have given the human authorities twenty-four hours to solve the problem before declaring war.

1. Was he murdered or did he die from some other cause?

2. If he was murdered, how was he murdered, who did it, and what might the motive be?

The nameless messenger had come to Natty Looper an hour ago, terrified and carrying the chop of the Osiris Grand Hotel's security chief. The messenger had revealed nothing of the matter to be discussed, but he displayed the sort of barely-suppressed hysteria that Natty associated with major disasters. He had handed over a huge retainer, collected Natty's mark on a nondisclosure form, and left without a single informative word.

From the size of the retainer, Natty suspected that he was about to be asked to perform some impossible feat of detection. Find a way to save the universe or halt inflation. Find an honest person.

Natty Looper waited patiently, under the watchful gaze of a heavily-armed receptionist. He recrossed his legs, adjusted the straps of his ancient and authentic coveralls, scratched at one hairy shoulder. He did these things in a measured and unhurried manner, hoping to conceal a slight degree of nervous anticipation.

He sighed and got up, causing the receptionist to recoil fastidiously, as if she expected Natty to commit some unspeakably uncouth act. Spit tobaccy on the carpet. Ask for the outhouse. Comb a bird's nest out of his beard.

Natty sighed again, and wandered over to the great observation port that curved halfway around the reception area. He stood looking down at the old Earth below, at her deserts and still-blue seas, at her scattered fading patches of green. He looked up at the main hull of the hotel, which stretched forward of his vantage point for several kilometers, a mirror-smooth alloy surface dotted with thousands of glowing windows, nav lights, illuminated signs. In the middle distance, twenty kilometers past the Osiris, he could see the gleam of the small habitat where he kept an apartment—for those happy times when business brought him up to the Orbital Domains.

"Purty," Natty said to himself. Several of the nearest signs sensed his regard and rotated their image planes toward him; he found himself looking at a trailer for a performance of the Original Kachinadroid Dancers, an ad for a pheromonic hair tonic, and an ad for a new memory stimulant—"Now You Too *Can* Remember Those Important Things You Were Too Stupid to Notice When They Happened!"

Against the blackness of space, a huge free-floating holofield ran an advertisement detailing the delights of vacationing in the Caribee Enclave. A delicately beautiful woman balanced a huge hat on her head, and smiled at Natty. The hat was full of an implausible amount of tropical fruit; the woman reached up and plucked a banana. She peeled the banana in a languidly suggestive manner.

Natty turned away, just as the receptionist rose and said, "You may go in now, Mr. Looper."

He nodded pleasantly as he passed the receptionist, who looked as if she were holding her breath, just in case Natty smelled bad.

Natty walked along the fortified ingress, passing three sets of blast doors, which opened before him and closed behind him. The corridor doglegged twice before he reached the office.

The Osiris security chief rose behind her desk to greet him; her henchman was already standing. "Mr. Looper, welcome," she said in a pleasingly soft voice. She was slender, she wore her long black hair in a tied-back cluster of thick braids, and her green eyes had a Eurasian tilt. She wore an expression of professional nonchalance.

From an array of subtle signs—a tightness around the eyes, an artificial stillness, the way her bloodless hands gripped the edge of her desk—he could see that she was very frightened. "I'm Annadelle Rostov," she said.

He thought her dangerously attractive—but who wasn't beautiful, in the Orbital Domains? He reminded himself that the Osiris Grand was a small autonomous kingdom, and that this woman was its Lord High Executioner. He shook her hand gently and said "Howdy," as politeness demanded. As he held her hand, a moment longer than was entirely polite, her smile grew marginally warmer. "Call me Natty, Miz Rostov. Everybody else does."

"And I'm Annadelle," she said, sinking back into her chair.

The henchman was a huge man, whose hard face seemed set in a perpetual glower. He did not return Natty's nod.

"This is my assistant and personal guardian," Annadelle said. "He prefers not to use a name. Nor does he speak."

Natty shrugged. "Fine by me." He sank into a deep upholstered couch, which jackknifed his tall gangly body into an awkward position. He decided to ignore the discomfort.

She made a gesture and a thumping music filled the air, chopping away at "Okie From Muscogee."

Natty winced visibly. She waved her hand again and the music cut off.

"I thought you might be more comfortable with music from your own Enclave," she said, apologetically.

"Well, I appreciate the thought, Annadelle, but I ain't much of a fan of that cowkicker music. Heard too much of it as an impressionable youth, I guess." If she weren't eager to discuss the job, Natty Looper was willing to make small talk. "Buncha mean old drunks, singing through their nose hairs, all 'bout how their babies done left 'em—no damn wonder—and they feel like homemade shit, which is approximately what they look like, in most cases."

He was overstating the case, but not by much. Any talented new performers who did not hew to the narrow esthetic standards of the Appalachian Enclave had to choose between starvation and emigration to one of the few eclectic Enclaves. Or else they changed their music to conform. "Oh, it ain't all that bad," he admitted. "But you know what I mean."

"I suppose so," she said, and Natty thought that she might have been amused, were she less worried. "I should have known better. After all, you specialize in investigations across Enclave lines, so you're bound to have broader tastes than your fellow Appalachians."

There was just a hint of condescension in her manner, so Natty grinned and said, "Oh, only in some respects. Why, I can chug 'shine with the best of 'em. Ain't nothing I like better'n possum pie." He waggled his bare feet. "Cut my toenails ever six months, whether they needs it or not."

She laughed, and it was a far more pleasant sound than he had expected. "All right, Natty; I take your point. Now, let's get to business." She swiveled her chair and touched a dataslate built into her desktop. A screen on the far wall lit.

A Sirian bull's chitinous gray face filled the screen; his crimson scalp tattoos indicated a noble lineage and a high military rank. A brassy light gleamed on the alien features. The tiny silver eyes glowed with some intense emotion.

"He's a little pissed off, ain't he?" said Natty.

"Correct. This is Eternal General Lisefgethmeor. We received this transmission some five hours ago."

The image jolted into life and the bull showed his long incisors. "Earth cowards! Attention! Your doom is upon you. You have destroyed a great soul; now you will pay with your world's life!" The bull paused, seemed almost to be panting with rage.

"Dramatic feller," Natty observed, but Annadelle said nothing.

The bull continued. "When we arrive, our ships will burn your world to black glass." The monstrous face writhed; he turned his head as if someone had spoken off-camera. "Unless you can somehow prove to my complete satisfaction that you did not murder Ambassador Trafdechwanelter."

The screen went black.

Natty scratched at his beard. "Can he do it?"

"Probably. They've done it to other worlds. The Enclaves can't field much of a defense force. The Orbitals are even more vulnerable. If we had more time, if the Sirian fleet weren't so close . . . we could probably recall enough convoy cruisers to deal with them. But even if the Sirian fleet doesn't burn Earth black, a lot of people are going to die." She shrugged, a bizarre gesture, under the circumstances.

Natty felt a smothering fear, which he struggled to hold in check. The Sirians, he now remembered, were a militantly xenophobic race, with a reputation for "cleansing" the home worlds of races they found offensive. "How long afore they get here?"

"A little over sixteen hours."

"Holy batshit," said Natty.

"I couldn't agree more," said Annadelle Rostov.

"We need you," she said, after a while.

A silence ensued, a silence which Natty finally broke. "What the hell can *I* do?"

She sat back, and took a deep breath. She looked older than she had; her voice was small and weary. "Probably not much, Natty. But I have to try everything, and you have a reputation for being able to understand alien cultures. You've been successful in a lot of strange places, for a country boy. You've infiltrated Enclaves as diverse as HighRise City and the Yucatan Empire, you've collected bounties on body jumpers in Coastville and Baja Alabama. You were the lead investigator in the group that uncovered the Iberian Conspiracy."

"Yeah, but . . ."

"Some of the Enclaves are *very* strange, Natty. I want your perspective. I have a dead Ambassador in a locked, environmentally-sealed room. No one could have murdered him, but he's dead. The Sirians don't understand suicide as a concept . . . so I got nowhere with the General when I tried to tell him that the Ambassador must have killed himself. Will you take a look?"

Natty rubbed at his eyes. "What you need are xenobiologists. Xenoanthropologists. Xenocriminologists. Xenopsychometricians."

"I have them, Natty. They're crawling over the data like maggots, hundreds of them. Every government agency in the Enclaves and the Orbital Domains has at least one expert working on the problem. They're not coming up with any new ideas.''

"Well,'' he said, finally. "Can't hurt to take a look, I guess. But if the Earth gets burnt to a crisp, it ain't my fault. Hear?''

She cued a recording of the Ambassador's suite, taken through remote spycams. "We haven't unlocked the suite yet. If all else fails, we'll show the suite to the General and ask him to tell us how we murdered the Ambassador. It may delay him . . . though probably not. The Sirians don't have a high curiosity quotient, I understand.'' She touched her desk.

Natty watched as the spycam floated through the spartan interior of the Ambassador's rooms. The floors were bare metal, the walls a featureless white.

"Right homey,'' Natty commented.

"He was a warrior monk, before he joined their diplomatic corps. Very ascetic,'' said Annadelle.

The camera turned a corner and revealed a small comm room, equipped with an all-band holotank. On an uncomfortable-looking haircloth prayer rug, the Ambassador's corpse lay, already far gone into the peculiar decay typical of chlorine-breathing life forms, all puffed up like over-leavened bread and beginning to crumble into powder. The Ambassador was on his back, upper arms flung wide, lower hands clutching his crotch.

His spraddled tentacles were tangled around the base of the holotank.

"Cause of death?''

"Unknown. We have good scans of the body, but there's no sign of violence. The corpse was already somewhat broken down when we discovered it during a periodic spycam surveillance, so maybe we're missing something subtle. But as far as we can tell, he just stopped breathing.''

"So, who was he calling?'' Natty asked.

Annadelle shrugged. "That's the big question, I think. We're working on it, but as a Very Important Diplomatic Personage, the Ambassador had an extremely good privacy module on his datastream access, and it's going to take time to break his codes. Right now we're digging out the calls one at a time.''

" 'Calls'?''

''Yes. He made three calls in the waking period before his death. We've identified the first call. We expect to get the second within the next ten hours.''

''And the third?''

She shook her head sadly. ''Not before the General arrives, unless we get much luckier than we expect.''

Natty looked at her. ''You think the last call kilt him?''

''Yes.''

''But how? I reckon his tank was filtered against any deadly resonances. Right? And Sirians don't kill themselves, you say? So it wasn't like he got holt of Dial-a-Dread and got depressed.''

''No, his tank was completely filtered against destructive resonances. But I'm sure something bad showed up in his tank. I just don't know what.'' She glared at the screen, eyes like cold stones.

She turned those frozen eyes on him. ''The Ambassador's safety was my responsibility.''

''We ain't dead yet. Give me a nice room here, with a tank as good as the Ambassador's. Give me your security data—locks, surveillance systems, filter parameters, environmental lockins—and let me pick it over. I figger you're right—no way he coulda been murdered—but I'll feel better if I see the stuff with my own beady little eyes.''

''All right.''

''And . . . you got a record of that first call he made? Good. Gimme that, too.''

As he stood to go, clutching a handful of datawafers, he said, as if to himself, ''Obscurocious.''

''What?'' asked Annadelle Rostov.

''Oh. That's one of them hillbilly coinages. Sorta like 'ferocious obscure.' Or 'atrocious obscure.' Bodacious obscure. Or if we're talking 'bout lawyers it means 'loquacious obscure.' '' He winked, and her henchman bared his large teeth.

''No offense meant, iffen you're a lawyer,'' said Natty, and then he left.

The suite to which the henchman conveyed Natty Looper was a very comfortable one, with three pleasant rooms and a view of Earth. He stood and looked down at his world, wondering if it would see another day as a living planet.

It occurred to him that he was as safe as any human in

the system, for the moment. The Osiris catered to aliens of all sorts; the management specialized in providing comfortable accommodations for even the most eccentric life forms. There were probably more aliens currently in residence than humans, and so the Sirians would probably spare the Osiris during the first assault.

He felt no great relief; peeking into the future, he foresaw Sirian heavy troopers smashing in doors and dragging out the hotel's human guests.

He shuddered. He had to make an effort to stop thinking about the consequences of failure.

So he sat down and fed the datawafers into the holotank.

Two hours later he was certain that Annadelle Rostov was correct. There was no way the Ambassador could have been murdered. The locks were perfect, untouched. Untouchable, short of thermonuclear lances or other means of violent persuasion. The elaborate measures taken to safeguard the integrity of the Ambassador's environment precluded poisons, shock-filaments, hyperfibrillators, gas macros, neural resonators, feral microbodies, nanojects, suppressive radiants . . . all the tools of the modern assassin.

So it was suicide. Except that the Sirians, according to Annadelle, didn't understand the concept. Why was that? He sighed. Time to learn what he could about the Sirians.

The narrator was a woman from HighRise City; she spoke slowly and carefully. "The Sirians are that rarity among sapient races: a precisely determinate species. The length of their lives is fixed at birth; the scale pattern on the dorsal plates of a hatchling Sirian indicates its potential life span with an accuracy of plus or minus ten Standard days."

Natty Looper paused the recording and called up the Ambassador's biodata. Perhaps the Ambassador had simply reached the end of his span. After a moment, he shook his head. The Ambassador's age had been verified thoroughly— apparently the Sirians weren't above using the natural demise of a diplomat as an excuse to attack the host world.

No, the Ambassador still had a dozen unused years left on his longevity meter.

However, Natty was starting to understand why the Sirians didn't understand the concept of suicide.

He sat back, and tried to imagine what it would be like to know exactly when he would shuffle off the clay. How would he live his life? Natty usually enjoyed that sort of philosophical musing; his ability to put himself in strange shoes had been his greatest asset, had led him to a rewarding career, had allowed to live at least part of his life in the Orbital Domains, above the stultifying and regressive cultures of the Enclaves. But suddenly it occurred to him that he and all the other humans in the Solar System had suddenly become members of a precisely determinate species.

"Back to work," he told himself, and restarted the datawafer.

The narrator turned to a large flatscreen, on which an image of a male Sirian was projected. With a light pointer, she indicated the squat skull; the almost-human arrangement of eyes, flat nose, wide lipless mouth; the heavy upper arms; the delicate lower arms, with their long many-jointed fingers; the four tentacular psuedolegs. The image revolved slowly, then froze, again facing the camera.

"Note the armoring scales and lack of external genitalia. The Sirians evolved in a marshy, high energy environment, beset with numerous small, fast predators. On their world of origin, the narrow equatorial band of habitable lands was for the most part a featureless swamp. There were very few places of refuge available—only a few remnant basalt cores lifting above the ooze. They had no trees in which to take refuge, no caves, no hills. This perhaps accounts for their unusual reproductive strategy."

The screen image changed, to show a creature that only superficially resembled the male Sirian. It was low and broad, something like an animated green-brown rug, with numerous small psuedolegs showing at its margins. It had no discernible features, other than a scattering of large wet pores in its upper surface.

"The Sirian female," said the HighRise woman. "Researchers have not been allowed to closely examine any individuals of this gender, but it is suspected that they have no higher brain functions, and exist only as a bridge between generations. For every female hatched, slightly more than a thousand males are hatched. On the home world, the females spent their lives clinging to the rare stone outcroppings above the marsh. The males competed violently for the privilege of breeding the female; only a maximum of sixteen males succeeded. Immediately after breeding, these successful males expired. A fully gravid female produced approximately sixty-four thousand eggs. The hatchlings were initially nourished by the decay of their mother's body, after which the males dropped off the relative safety of the breeding crags into the swamp. The females remained.

"Most of the other males succumbed to the violence of the breeding competition. Those males that did not compete were the only sapient links between generations, and because of their determinate life span, this overlap was minimal. Xenoanthropologists generally agree that this biological impediment to communication between the generations is the major reason that the Sirians took such a long time to achieve a technological civilization."

Natty touched the *Pause* button. Had the Ambassador somehow met with a horny female of his species? It seemed unlikely. He twitched the holotank onto another informational track, and found out that at the time of his death, the Ambassador had been the only member of his species in the system.

He scratched his head. The datawafer still held vast quantities of information about the Sirians—their biology, social norms, hierarchies, technologies. Much of it would be gibberish to Natty Looper's unspecialized ears. Perhaps he should switch to another tack; he could always come back to the experts.

He called up the Ambassador's first call.

The recording contained both sides of the conversation, as was usual in calls made by Very Important Creatures such as the Sirian diplomat. Natty watched the Ambassador punch in the number; then the tank split into two image fields.

The connection was nearly instantaneous. The second image field filled with a pulsating mandala in scintillating silver and glorious gold; celestial music filled the room, high and pure. It swelled to a brief crescendo, fell sweetly away, and then an androgynous angel spoke.

"Greetings, seeker after wisdom. You have reached Gods Unlimited, where all sapient beings are welcome to drink deep from the healing waters of faith. How may we serve you?"

The Ambassador grunted, and Natty thought he could read the Sirian's alien expression. The Ambassador was disgusted.

"You may serve me by showing me your wares, thereby

demonstrating the vile weakness, the astounding credulity, the unforgivable sentimentality of your corrupt species.'' The Sirian spoke with a well-practiced air of cold implacability.

A floating personage appeared in the center of the mandala; a young woman with large breasts and a luminous halo. ''Skeptics are even more welcome than any other supplicants,'' she murmured.

''An end to these platitudes!'' the Sirian roared. ''Show me this madness humans call religion!''

''Patience, patience,'' she said. ''God is essentially unknowable, not to mention invisible. Before you can experience your personal epiphany, we must design a suitable mythic focus for your faith.''

''Patience!'' roared the Ambassador. ''Patience? I have no patience! Time slips away; the rate never slows for an instant, and we are all soon enough slime at the bottom of the World Muck. Show me your wares, or I will name you a fraud of the terminal sort, the sort that begs for instant expungement.''

A tiny frown creased the young woman's perfect brow. ''You must attempt tranquillity, seeker after wisdom. Our computers are working at their best speed; we've assigned your case our highest priority. But you are the first member of your species to visit the All-Shrine, so the process of development cannot be instantaneous. Soon . . . soon we will show you the perfect and highest expression of Sirian godliness—as determined by our deificatory system, which as you probably know has the most advanced software in the human worlds!''

The Ambassador opened his mouth to fulminate again, but a harmonious chime sounded, and the young woman said, ''Ah! We're ready. Watch, keep an open mind, and you will doubtless achieve transfiguration.''

She faded from the holotank, replaced by a murky darkness, broken only by drifting wisps of phosphorescent gas.

A voice began to speak in the harsh clicking Sirian language. Natty listened without comprehension, but then a slider bar opened at the bottom of the holotank, and a translation in small red letters appeared: *In the beginning was the Muck.*

Natty smiled, and fast-forwarded the image, to a sequence in which a golden light began to paint the tops of the birthing-crags. A cacophony of unpleasant sounds bubbled forth: untidy slurps, sucking noises, wet plops. Presumably this was inspirational Sirian music.

When the birthing crags began to grow beards and to develop large mournful eyes, the Ambassador roared with outrage. "Obscene!" he shrieked, spitting large greenish globules of phlegm against the camera lens. "Unendurable! When we sanitize the unfortunate world that evolved you, you miserable insignificant fraudulent pornographers, you'll be the first to burn."

He slapped the cutoff switch.

Natty sat before the dark holotank for a few minutes, musing. Already he sensed a pattern, or at least the glimmering of a purpose. The Ambassador seemed a volatile being, and he seemed to be very eager to find reasons to hate humans.

The holotank chimed. Annadelle's anxious face filled the interior, and for some reason Natty was reminded of an ancient pre-Emergence film, in which a wicked witch conjures the image of a young girl into a great glass globe. Annadelle was a grown woman, but there was a similar air of worried innocence about her.

"Natty," she said. "We have the second call. I'm sending a copy."

"Good," he answered.

She hesitated. "Do you have anything? Anything at all?"

"Well. Tell me this, iffen you can. Do you think the Sirians were jest looking for an excuse? To fry us?"

"Oh, of course. They're the most xenophobic space-faring race we've met with yet. But they have to have a good reason, or the civilized races would see to it that they got bombed back to the swamp."

"Religious insults ain't a good enough excuse, I take it?"

"Heavens no, Natty. If *that* were an acceptable reason to go to war, the universe would long ago have been blown to kingdom come. So to speak."

He liked it that she retained her wit, even in such grim circumstances. An interesting woman.

"I see. No, I ain't got nothing useful yet, jest some supposins and suspicions. Shoot me that second recording, and I'll get on with it."

"All right."

* * *

Natty watched as the Ambassador punched in the next number.

The destination field filled with a thousand hues, mingling and diverging in a whirling explosion of color. Atonal music, harsh and compelling, shuddered forth.

The image field flickered and coalesced, revealing a man with tangled spangle-braids and deep brooding eyes. "Interior Explorations Inc.," he said, in a resonant baritone. "How may we aid you in your psychic travels?"

The Ambassador leaned forward, his jaw jutting aggressively. "In that respect, I am sufficiently well-traveled. But show me your wares anyway, death merchant."

The spokesman scowled, and the transmitted image was enhanced so that his eyes glowed with dark red light. " 'Death merchant'? You got an attitude problem, scaly dude. We don't sell death; quite the contrary. We sell tickets to your interior landscape—psychoactive chemicals tailored to your particular needs, whatever they may be."

The Ambassador snorted dismissively. "I know you, monstrous creature. Your chemicals promise paradise, but deliver hell. This I know from the holodramas produced by your own regulatory agencies."

"You believe everything you see on the datastream, then?" Now the spokesman had an unpleasant edge to his voice, and a sneer curled his lip.

The Ambassador seemed to swell. "Intolerable! You will pay for this disrespect, worm of corruption. But first, show me what you can offer one of my exalted species. Then I will schedule your humiliation and destruction, as is proper."

The spokesman sighed. "Whatever, scaly dude. Let me run up a few parameters, and then I'll get back to you, okay."

He cut the connection.

Natty was puzzled. No deliveries had been made to the Ambassador's suite; so much was certain. Either the druggists had failed to come up with a suitable high for the Ambassador, or he had died before they had synthesized a suitable compound.

In any case, it seemed a dead end.

Natty sat back and stretched. There was a pattern here, if only he could see it.

He sighed. So far it seemed that the Ambassador was

exploring all the weaknesses of human beings, hoping to find something so disgusting that the other space-faring races couldn't object to a bit of racial prophylaxis.

He closed his eyes, and tried to make his mind empty. Something tickled at him, the ghost of an idea.

And then he had it.

Natty called Annadelle. "Iffen I can tell you who the Ambassador talked to last, can you get a recording of the call afore the General gets here?"

"Yes," she said. Natty could see that she wanted to believe there was hope.

He laughed, and a huge smile of relief stretched his face, almost painfully. "It's going to be okay, Annadelle. No kidding."

Annadelle's henchman hurried General Lisefgethmeor along the corridor, occasionally nudging the Sirian with a huge punch-gun. The General wore self-contained armor, a helmet in the semblance of some toothy predator, and spike-knee boots.

Natty and Annadelle followed a few paces behind.

The General snarled over his massive shoulder. "You can kill me if you like, but a thousand other bulls will step forward to take vengeance. And as a martyr to our great cause, my frozen zygotes will impregnate many females. A new permaglass breeding tower will be raised in my name. I have no fear of you puny creatures!"

Annadelle spoke soothingly. "No violence is intended toward your impressive person, General. As we said, we have determined the cause of the Ambassador's death to be accidental. We merely wish you to witness our proofs. We deeply appreciate your presence here; it will prevent a great deal of unnecessary bloodshed on both sides."

The General's only response was a skeptical rumble.

They sat the General down before a large holotank, in a small theater reserved for VIP screenings.

"I cannot imagine what you think you can show me."

"Probly not," said Natty Looper.

The General turned and glared at him. "Who is this offensive bumpkin?"

"This is the investigator who discovered the cause of

death," said Annadelle. "But now, give your attention to the tank, if you will."

The General grunted. But he returned his small eyes to the tank.

The Ambassador tapped at his terminal.

The tank responded with a display of squirming, naked human bodies, a complicated tangle of flesh, framing the words: *Hygienic Fantasies Unlimited.*

"Disgusting," said the Ambassador.

"Disgusting," echoed the watching General.

The logo was replaced by a man and woman locked in a complicated sexual posture. "How may we assist you?" said the woman breathlessly. She seemed marginally less involved in the act; the man was red-faced and his eyes were glazed.

They watched the Ambassador contemptuously explain his requirements, they watched the progression of images that evolved in the holotank's image field, as the Hygienic computers tailored the experience to the Sirian ideal. They watched the Ambassador grow pale and silent.

They watched the Sirian female undulate against the basalt.

At the bottom of the image field, a slider bar ran the translation of the slurps and warbles that now emanated from the tank: *GIVE IT TO ME BABY GIVE IT TO ME.*

Natty cut off the recording, before the General could succumb to the culminating heaves and hisses.

He was for a moment concerned that he had not acted quickly enough; the General was almost motionless, except for a palsied waggle of his head, which slowly ceased.

Eventually Annadelle broke the silence. "I hope you will agree that the Ambassador's death was an unfortunate accident. Of course, you may choose to sue Hygienic Fantasies in civil court. A case might be made for negligence, or even reckless endangerment."

The General darted a smoldering look at her. "You think this makes any difference? You have murdered a great soul; the weapon you used is irrelevant. We will burn the Earth clean with even greater enthusiasm than before."

Annadelle shook her head, smiling. "No one forced the Ambassador to employ Hygienic; if you sue, their lawyers will argue that he knew the danger and made no effort to avoid it. But this is irrelevant. You will not attack the Earth or any habitats of the Orbital Domains.''

''And why not?'' The General rose abruptly, shook himself. He seemed slightly less impressive to Natty Looper; judging from his painfully stooped posture, he now suffered from an unimaginably intense case of the blue balls.

Annadelle gestured and her henchman drew the curtains from a huge observation port, which looked out into space.

All the animated signs, whether attached to habitats or free-floating, displayed the images of wriggling female Sirians. Thousands of them.

The General gasped. The henchman pulled the curtains shut.

''If you attempt to attack us, not the slightest remnant of your fleet will survive.'' Annadelle's voice had gone metallic.

''We do not fear death,'' the General grated. ''We carry planet-bursters; if necessary we will blind ourselves and attack on autopilot. We are not the weaklings you take us for.''

''No? Then think about this. No matter how many of us you kill, a few human ships will survive. We know where your home world lies. The clouds that lie above the World Muck would make excellent projection substrates. Do you get my drift?''

When the last Sirian vessel had passed beyond the Oort Cloud, Natty Looper received another summons to Annadelle Rostov's office.

Her henchman seemed to be elsewhere.

She greeted him with an apparently genuine warmth and signed over his large performance bonus with cheerful gratitude.

She did not immediately usher him to the door, and he regarded her with a frankly speculative expression.

''What?'' she asked. A little color rose in her cheeks; she seemed very appealing. But also very dangerous.

''Oh, nothing,'' he said finally.

At that moment he felt a tiny pang of sympathy for the General.

AN INCIDENT AT THE CIRCUS
by Rick Katze

Rick Katze is a lawyer who has been active in Boston fandom for many years. This is his first professional story.

An alien carnival performer invites members of the audience to run it through with a sword, offering a prize if they can harm it. After a number of members try and fail—it is a hologram, and the real performer is backstage—a human takes the sword, hurls it through the curtains, and kills the alien. It turns out that the human used to work for the carnival, though not for this particular act.

This is more of a legal drama than a detective case. There is no question that the human killed the alien. Is it murder or not?

The spear hit Feilord in the chest and bounced off him.

"You are a weakling," he said in a most sarcastic voice. "I had thought you possessed some strength, but it is clear that I was wrong."

The audience burst into applause. The Great Feilord claimed to be immune to spears and now they had seen it with their own eyes. The show ended and they slowly left the circus in stunned amazement. He had been present in the flesh and the spears were real. No armor had come between the spears and his flesh. They did not know how he did it. Most left believing Feilord was really invulnerable.

The dry, hot summer season had just begun on Grundlor. Even night brought no relief from the heat. The circus, which had been traveling for three months, was scheduled to stay just one more month before leaving the planet. Samore, the manager, wished that it was sooner. The air cooling system in his office/residence strained to keep the area cool. He hated these warm planets, but he was a prisoner of the circus schedule.

Clayton sensed that Lina was tense. Not being sure what he had done, he asked her what was wrong.

Lina assured him that everything was fine between them. "It's the heat. Samore won't spend the extra credits to keep nonessential areas comfortable."

"He even worries more about the animals than he does us," agreed Clayton. "We're replaceable; they're not."

"I heard that Samore and Feilord had a fight earlier today about the heat in Feilord's tent. Feilord told him he would quit if it wasn't fixed immediately, and Samore threatened him if he made any attempt to leave the circus." Lina knew the time was fast approaching when she would have to decide between Clayton and Feilord, and, while Clayton would probably accept the decision to break their relationship with good grace, she suspected that Feilord would not, now that he was a big star.

At the mention of Feilord's name, Clayton immediately clamped down on his emotions. He didn't like Lina's involvement with Feilord, but he realized that only Lina could break it. There was still time before a final choice had to be made, but time was getting short. A Malakhi threesome may have been the most stable grouping in the Galaxy but, once bonding occurred, there was no escape short of death.

The discussion continued for some time before Clayton went back to his tent, where he found a note asking him to see Samore as soon as possible. As late as it was, he knew that Samore would cause a scene if he didn't make the attempt to see him immediately. Seeing the light on, he knocked at the door.

"Who is it! What do you want?" came the gruff voice from inside.

"It's Clayton."

"Yes! Come in." As Clayton entered the room, Samore said, "Don't bother sitting down. This won't take long. Shortages in your animal feed accounts have been discovered. You're fired. You have until morning to leave."

"You're lying! I haven't stolen a thing!"

After a lengthy shouting match, Samore finally admitted that Feilord wanted him fired. "He wants Lina and he doesn't want it to be a threesome. I don't have any choice.

Feilord's act is just too popular. You can be replaced; he can't. It's as simple as that.''

Clayton left, muttering about the terrible things he would do to Feilord.

Nighttime under the big top. The animals had been put into their air-conditioned cells for the evening, the dry winds greedily sucked the moisture from the air, and the last customer had long since left. The few remaining workers were drinking quint and smoking melam. Security had already activated the barrier which would cause the alarm to ring and automatic probes to be activated should anyone enter without authorization.

Shadows. Lurking in the dark. Two of the newly-cleaned costumes, neatly stacked in the tent, were selected. The slightly damp capes were carefully coated with a clear, odorless liquid that would dry within a few hours.

Old Rengreve was already hard at work that morning. The cats and the great chimps had to be watered; then, after their cages had been cleaned, they were given a light meal carefully calculated to assuage their hunger but not enough to affect their performance that afternoon. Two shows. No breaks.

Clayton had been fired last night. They claimed that he had been stealing, but Rengreve knew it was a lie. Management just didn't want to spend any extra credits even though the circus had always been profitable. Ever since the new owners had bought the circus nine months ago, changes had taken place. Admittedly, not all of them were bad from Rengreve's point of view. Should he pressure them for more money? Clayton's firing meant additional work for him. The thought slowly dissipated as he considered the risks.

Lina was just awakening. Eating a leisurely breakfast, she finally decided that with Clayton being fired, her relationship with Feilord would end immediately. Leaving the circus would avoid what otherwise would be an unpleasant situation with Feilord, who was becoming more demanding and self-centered. Before breaking the news to him, Lina decided that it would be prudent to make a few inquiries regarding openings for magic acts with other circuses.

Feilord had also gotten up early. Samore had not acceded to his demands for more money. As expected, Samore had blustered and threatened that his employer would hold him to the contract by hook or by crook. The man just didn't realize who he was dealing with this time; he had just laughed when Feilord threatened to go to court to break the agreement. Possibly the tent could be air-cooled, but more money was out of the question. Samore told him to think about it and give him his answer today.

So few of his kind had left their planet. They were simple folk, content to stay at home and mind the fields. Not him. It was unlikely they would find another of his kind who would want to leave home and join the circus. It had taken a while to perfect the act, but he now held the whip. If they didn't accept his terms, he would leave and find a circus that would give him an ownership interest.

And if he left, he would take Lina with him.

VP Arm attended the afternoon show. The kids had never been to a circus like this. An endless string of questions was patiently answered. Arm was bored, waiting for Feilord to appear in the center ring. He had heard stories about the invulnerable Feilord, but no specifics. People he knew just told him to watch the show and judge for himself.

The lights dimmed in the great tent. The other performers stopped. Even the ever-present clowns seemed to wind down.

There was a bright flash in the center stage which briefly blinded the audience, and then a man appeared.

"The Great Feilord has arrived! You have heard that spears cannot injure him. You probably suspect a trick. Watch and believe!" Samore made his announcement and left the platform. He would have preferred to stay, but Feilord would have none of that.

Collingwort brought three spears with him. "Will the people sitting in row 16, Seat 7, row 45, Seat 1, and row 4, seat 4, please come to the platform to demonstrate the invulnerability of the Great Feilord? To examine the spears and verify that they are truly deadly weapons, would VP Arm come to the platform?"

Arm had been surprised. He had been watching the performance very carefully, hoping to get closer since he still could not determine what the gimmick was. He approached the platform, examined the spears, and quickly concluded that they were just what they appeared to be. Rather than being requested to return to his chair, he was allowed to stay.

Collingwort handed a spear to the first audience member selected, who threw it at Feilord. It seemed to bounce off him.

Feilord looked at the athletic young man and, in a low but clearly sarcastic tone, said, "My grandmother can hurl a spear harder than that. Collingwort, please tell the next volunteer to fling it harder."

The next two men achieved similar results while Feilord taunted them about their inability to injure him.

The crowd was roaring when, suddenly, there was a slight flicker in the image where Feilord appeared to be standing. The silence was deafening, and Arm thought for a moment that there was going to be a riot. A sudden bright flash followed, and Feilord appeared, this time apparently in the flesh, saying, "Yes, that was a hologram. If it had not flickered, you would have been tricked. You see how easy it is to create an illusion to fool you. Before demonstrating that I am truly impervious to spears, I shall prove that I am really here. Will VP Arm come on the platform and physically examine me?"

Arm hopped onto the platform, cautiously moved toward Feilord while looking for another deception, and finally reached him.

"Please verify that I am not wearing body armor."

"He is not wearing body armor."

"Examine the cape which has been sanctified."

After thoroughly examining the cape, Arm announced that it was common cloth and contained no protective materials.

With a great flourish Feilord wrapped the cape around himself. "The Cape has been blessed by Krongh and will protect its owner from harm. You know that the spears are real. Collingwort will now have the three volunteers again cast the spears."

The first volunteer threw the spear. It hit and bounced off him. The audience was still looking for another trick. Feilord instructed Collingwort to give the next volunteer a spear. The second volunteer was about to toss it when suddenly Feilord froze.

Collingwort waited for Feilord to direct it be tossed. There was no response. Not like Feilord at all. "It is clear the Master has chosen to ignore you," he boomed in a loud, vibrant voice. Collingwort told him to throw the spear. Again it appeared to bounce off Feilord. When Feilord did not criticize the ability of the spear thrower, Collingwort, taking matters into his own hands, directed the final volunteer to hurl it and again, no apparent damage. The audience applauded but Feilord said nothing.

Arm's police instincts were alerted by Feilord's lack of movement. Something was wrong. Feilord had neither moved nor said anything after the first spear had been thrown. Even though the audience was impressed, he should have continued his banter to milk the last drop of appreciation from them. Even as he started off to join his family, Arm kept glancing back, convinced there was a problem.

Collingwort called for the end music. The show was over and the audience slowly filed out. After they had left, Collingwort went to Feilord. "You idiot! Why didn't you follow the script?"

Still no response.

Collingwort took the cape off.

Feilord was red-faced.

He was also dead.

Collingwort screamed.

Arm came running back, saw Feilord was dead, and smiled. The smile quickly disappeared. More people came. Arm directed that the police be called.

AVP Dane entered the tent with several investigators, saw Arm was already talking with one of the performers, and waited for him to finish. Arm summoned his subordinate over and explained briefly what he had seen.

The records quickly established Feilord's home planet. An immediate check showed the nature of his mutation. The soft outer skin was deceptive. The hardy rubbery hide underneath was virtually impregnable; the few scratches he had received were inconsequential. Arm suspected murder, but accidental death could not be automatically eliminated. He would have to interview the people.

The police had closed the circus grounds, bringing the employees into a common area where they could be interviewed and kept under control so that they could not talk to each other about what they had said to the investigators. With any luck the Compop would review the data being collected and list the most likely perpetrators of the crime, and the murderer would be found within a day.

Having heard that Clayton and Samore had argued the previous night, Arm sought out the former.

"Clayton, you have certain rights. After twenty-four hours, you may request a lawyer. Failure to answer truthfully will subject you to additional penalties. You do not have the right to remain silent. An officer's belief that you have lied is sufficient grounds to order a brain scan to determine the truth of your remarks. Do you understand your Ramanid Rights?"

Arm thought it was too bad that the brain scan could not be used indiscriminately, but almost twenty percent of the people suffered unfortunate side effects. Let the techs reduce it to five percent and he suspected it would be used routinely. Until then, using it on innocent people who suffered damage was frowned upon; more importantly, it caused black marks to appear on one's record.

"Yes, and I voluntarily renounce all rights to a lawyer since I am innocent and have no fear of the authorities. I will truthfully answer your questions."

"Tell me what happened since yesterday."

"Last night, Samore told me I was fired. There was a shortage in one of the animal food lockers. He claimed that I had sold the food. It was a lie, but Feilord had pressured him to release me. I spent the rest of the evening with Lina before leaving to sleep in my own tent. Lina seemed preoccupied and I did not wish to intrude any further, especially since she sympathized with my predicament. Today I talked with some of my co-workers, trying to find out what had happened. I felt that Feilord was jealous of the attention that Lina showed me. I intended to confront him, but he died before I could do anything. I swear what I have said is the truth."

VP Arm listened attentively. "How long have you known Feilord? Did he ever talk about his home planet?" With apparent aimlessness, questions were asked and answers given. Arm came to the conclusion that Clayton wasn't telling the whole truth.

Lina was next. After being warned of her rights, he asked her what had happened. She stated that Clayton had been with her most of the evening except for a short period. He eventually came back, and, after explaining about the situation, told her he was going back to his room. She had tried to get him to stay but he refused, saying that in his present mood it would be better if he left. Shortly after he left, she went to sleep. She finally admitted that her relationship with Feilord and Clayton had become too serious, and indicated that she intended to drop Feilord before bonding occurred. With Clayton's firing, she had decided to go with him, but had not yet told him about her decision. She had not said anything to Feilord.

Samore was then called into the makeshift office, warned about his rights, and interrogated; he was definitely not a pleasant person. Clayton had been fired because Feilord was jealous. Feilord had demanded more money because the act was generating huge profits for the owners, but understood that he had a contract with the circus and realized that he would have to honor it. He hoped that Lina would see the wisdom in having him replace Clayton. No, he didn't know the home planet of Feilord or anything else about him. The decision to hire Feilord had been made by the new owner of the circus.

Old Rengreve slowly entered the room and sat in the chair. He seemed bored and resigned to the interrogation. Arm ignored his initial impression when he made eye contact with Rengreve, whose own eyes were bright and penetrating.

Rengreve quickly admitted he knew about Feilord's racial characteristics. Seventy years on a tramp ship gave one a lot of information about the galactic Rim. He had considered selling the information to other circus owners, but in return for not saying anything, the owners of the circus provided him with a monthly bonus. He suspected that Feilord would soon demand a lot of money to stay. The contract would not hold him since the civil Court system suffered huge delays in processing cases, especially where only the rights of aliens were to be determined. In any case, he suspected that the owner would use other means to persuade Feilord to stay.

Arm interpreted this to mean that the owner, Fragmenti, had criminal connections; yet Rengreve was not afraid to demand money to remain quiet. Dane would have to check the records to find out about Rengreve. He was clearly more than he claimed to be.

Then Collingwort was brought into the room. He appeared nervous, and insisted that he knew nothing about the murder nor about anything else. He had been hired by the circus when they landed here and did not wish to leave his home planet when they went elsewhere. The money was acceptable, and with the secrets he was learning from Feilord he would be an important person when he returned to his village.

Collingwort's name told Arm a lot. There were a number of clannish areas on the planet that refused to have anything to do with the Galactic Empire. They remained in their enclaves, rarely admitting anyone without deriving a substantial benefit in return.

While the interviews were being conducted, other police were carefully searching the circus grounds. The small amounts of illegal drugs found in several workers' possessions were ignored; the weapons were confiscated. Except for one bottle, containing an unknown liquid that was concealed in a false bottom in Clayton's old room, nothing else was found.

By the time Arm returned to headquarters, the liquid had been analyzed. It was Zwart, an artificially produced compound that acted like a nerve poison when even a minute amount was absorbed through a scratch in Feilord's otherwise impervious hide. The report further indicated it was probably produced off-world. The cape had been literally coated with it. The spear would hit the cape, causing a small bit of the poison to adhere to the spear tip and enter through the scratch, resulting in Feilord's immediate death.

It was a simple case. Clayton and Feilord were Lina's lovers; Clayton was fired; Clayton blamed Feilord; Clayton knew about Feilord; Clayton killed Feilord. Simple.

Arm grimaced as he concluded the train of thought. If he knew about Feilord, why not threaten Samore with the information when Samore fired him—and even more importantly, when did he get the Zwart? He would have had to obtain it off-world long before there were any problems—which meant that Clayton was being framed. The murderer was still at large. Not so simple, after all.

Arm reviewed all the data and entered it into the Compop. The results were not encouraging. Clayton was the prime candidate; no one else even rated a mention. Arm concluded it was time to see the Captain.

The Captain was not in a happy mood. He had been reading Arm's report. Four complete background checks, with three of them extending off-world, would be expensive. The

City was in a financial crisis. All departments had been ordered to contain costs, and Arm wanted to spend all this money over a simple murder investigation of an alien. He called Arm into his smoky office.

"What's wrong with you? An open-and-shut case involving an alien no one is going to remember, whether or not we solve the murder, and you want to spend all these credits. Why?"

Arm had expected this. The problem was how to explain to the Captain what he felt. "I don't think this is a simple murder. Preliminary review indicates that the owner of the circus has criminal connections, one of the employees knew about the victim's weakness, and the evidence against Clayton is too contrived. While it *could* be just a lovers' quarrel that ended in death, I suspect a more complex situation which will require extensive research."

The Captain suggested that Arm investigate further before requesting the spending of more credits. If the situation warranted, he was reluctantly prepared to authorize additional funds.

The local reports concerning the people questioned and the Compop's conclusions were waiting on Arm's desk. Collingwort's was as expected: nine months away from home but no real legal problems. There seemed to be an increase in dug use in those areas where the circus had recently played. The Compop was invariably correct. The only problem was supplying enough information, and narrowly defining the parameters of the search to get the result. Its conclusions about Clayton were based on too many open-ended facts which invariably lessened its validity. One really needed to know almost all of the answers to get anything valuable from it. Samore had been involved in some violent altercation that was quashed before any official reports had been filed. That should be checked. Rengreve had a long but minor criminal record. The others were clean.

There were just too many clues; too many people who disliked Feilord. The evidence pointed to Clayton, but there was just too much evidence. Could Clayton, knowing he would be the prime suspect, have killed Feilord and then placed false evidence to cast doubt on his actions? There was still some piece missing.

The following day the report came in. The Compop was now making a drug connection. It was clearly inconclusive, considering the lack of facts, but it did fit with his own feelings about the case. He decided that Fragmenti was the most logical choice for the off-world search while Samore and Clayton would be the objects of the secondary search.

The Captain had expected something like this. "Tell you what I'll do," he offered. "Besides the local checks you can have two searches, including one off-world. If the information warrants it, I'll authorize the rest."

The reports turned up several days later. Compop was brilliant when it had a specific focus. It was useless if it had to compare all of its records to identify individual criminal acts. If they ever got it working right, he would be out of a job.

The circus had stopped at fourteen cities, nine of which had seen increased drug activity. Twenty years ago, Fragmenti had been caught distributing drugs. Since that time, there had been no record of criminal activity, but nine months earlier, he had bought the Invas Circus with a lot of money that he probably shouldn't have had. It seemed to make a reasonable profit traveling from planet to planet. He had previously owned other businesses which gave him the opportunity to travel and ship goods to countless planets with no fixed schedules.

The check on Samore produced little new information. While he seemed to be spending more than his salary would support, so did everyone else, and, except for that one incident, he kept a low profile when outside the circus.

Arm presented his observations to the Captain, who seemed both nervous and distracted by some other problem. When the Captain made no response, Arm said, "What's wrong?"

"There have been suggestions that you should arrest Clayton. Obviously there was a lovers' quarrel, not some drug-related killing. He had the motive, means, and opportunity to kill Feilord."

"Is that an order? If it isn't, give me two more off-planet searches. I need more information on Rengreve and Samore before recommending either of them for a brain scan."

The Captain had protected himself. The record, admittedly slightly edited, would show that he had attempted to dissuade Arm from taking further action should the situation blow up. If it didn't, Arm would remember that the Captain backed him at a time when he could have done nothing.

"You can have your extra searches," he said in a booming voice meant to imply that he wasn't subject to pressure.

The searches were instituted; the results were anticlimactic. The drug connection was obvious. Both Samore and Fragmenti had used other businesses for the past twenty years to cover their tracks, periodically buying and selling them so no suspicion would be raised.

Samore and Fragmenti were arrested. After denying all complicity in the murder, a brain scan was ordered.

Several hours passed. Arm was nervous. Evidence of the drug trafficking would not be enough; they had to be involved in the murder. Then the door to the examination room opened and the smile on the technician's face answered Arm's unspoken question.

Collingwort was brought to headquarters under arrest. As he sat in the specially-constructed chair, Arm towered over him.

"We know that Samore gave you the Zwart with instructions on how to use it. Tell me what you did and don't leave out anything."

Collingwort was frightened. He explained how he poured the liquid over the slightly damp capes, knowing that Feilord would randomly select one of them to use the next day. The liquid would reduce the magic in the capes, causing Feilord to lose prestige when injured. Feilord would not be in a position to continue opposing Samore—and Samore, in gratitude for this action, had promised to restore the magic to the capes and give them to Collingwort to use when he returned to his small village. He would be a mighty person to whom great respect would be shown. He never would have done it if he thought Feilord would be killed, and once it happened he feared that no one would believe him if he told the truth. Finally Collingwort admitted that he still hoped to get the capes to take back to his village.

Later that night Arm told Lina the details of the case.

"So why did you let Clayton and Rengreve escape punishment?" queried Lina. "There was no evidence in the brain scans that the Zwart had been planted in Clayton's old room and, more importantly, Collingwort stated that the capes were slightly damp when he doctored them. Freshly cleaned uniforms in this dry climate would never be damp."

Arm nodded in agreement.

"You are probably right in assuming Rengreve provided

the poison for Clayton to use. With Feilord dead and Fragmenti and Samore convicted of drug dealing, Rengreve should have no problem buying the circus and making a reasonable living. The circus was profitable before the advent of the Great Feilord, and I suspect it will be profitable with Rengreve operating it. If Samore or Fragmenti was going to plant evidence on Clayton, they would have used a method local to this planet.'' He paused and smiled ''As to why, if there is only one victim, you only need one murderer to complete the report. Think of the extra paperwork if I had to provide two separate chains each causing the death of the same victim!''

DEAD RINGER

by Esther M. Friesner
and Walter J. Stutzman

Esther Friesner has written a series of wildly comic sf novels with such wonderful titles as *Hooray for Hellywood* and *Gnome Man's Land*. Walter Stutzman is her sometime collaborator and full-time husband.

> *It is a crime punishable by death to kill a natural-born Man. It is a crime punishable by 10-25 years to kill a clone.*
>
> *A police detective comes upon the scene of a crime: there has been a murder at the home of a multimillionaire who has had himself cloned four times. There is a dead body, and four absolutely identical live bodies. Each of the survivors claims that he is the millionaire and that the other three and the corpse are his clones.*
>
> *Who is telling the truth, who killed the deceased, and why?*

Dead as a doornail. The phrase kept running through Gary's mind as they stood outside the library, waiting for the coroner to finish his on-site examination. Zack would've laughed. He'd have made Gary laugh too, in spite of the dead body slumped over that fancy-dancy inlaid table in there and its three panicky "siblings" milling around somewhere upstairs in this huge mansion and its very influential "patron" waiting for word.

When you heard that the cause of death was a finishing nail jammed into the brain stem through the base of the skull, a nail clean of prints, you knew it was serious business. Zack always said that when the business got that serious it was the best time to laugh. *Dead as a doornail.* Gary was maybe the only adult male who ever survived adolescence without learning how to laugh at really bad puns. That was what his partner Zack was there for.

Used to be there for. Zack was dead.

"So whaddaya think, Gee-man?" Zack's hand fell lightly on Gary's shoulder, too fast for him to object. Zack's eyes twinkled with brown mischief as they met Gary's cold, contempt-filled gray gaze. Zack's tongue clucked in Zack's mouth, but it wasn't Zack. None of it was Zack. It was a goddamned zombie, a parasite, a thief, a thousand other names Gary mentally threw at the creature who'd come to steal away everything, everything that had been the real Zack's territory, property, life. . . .

Goddamned clone, Gary thought.

Aloud he said, "Don't call me Gee-man."

Zack raised his hands in mock surrender. "Whoa! Sorry. No more, promise. But whaddaya think?"

"What's to think? It's the cause of death: a nail."

"One lousy nail. Crude. Common enough. Sonofabitch." Zack—the real Zack—always said it that way. You heard the mild curse come out as one word. And there was still the trace of Zack Molloy's long-smothered Brooklyn accent. You had to hand it to those biofeebs who swore a clone was as good as the real thing: they delivered.

Which was why a rich man like Clifford J. Pierce was now alive and well while one of his four exact duplicates lay dead as, yes, a doornail.

"Kinda narrows it down," Gary said.

Zack—the only Zack Molloy left alive to answer to the name—tore a sheet of paper from his pocket notebook and folded it into an origami crane. "How d'you figure?" he asked. "It's not like the government's controlling the sale of nails. Yet."

"I've got my reasons. You're the big brain. You guess." *The department paid enough to bring back that big brain, too,* Gary thought bitterly. *Earn the life you stole, you bastard.*

"Ooooo—kay." Zack tugged at the right side of his brown walrus mustache. The mannerism wasn't original with him; nothing was, Gary believed. Even the affectation of carrying a paper-filled notebook instead of a portapad computer linkup ("Can't do origami with one of those,

Gary-baldy!'' ''Don't call me that.'') was lifted from the dead.

It was all part of S.O.P., right along with the culturing of the tissue sample and the forced aging of the result. They'd told Gary all about how it worked when they were trying to get him used to the idea that his ''new'' partner wasn't going to be so new after all. Interviews with friends and family of the clone's ''source,'' v-tapes and photos of the ''source'' while still alive, intensive study sessions with the best psychologists and drama coaches money could lure to the government cloning center all combined to guarantee that the end product not only looked like but acted like the—what to call him? The original? The human template? When clones were commissioned by folk of independent means, the person placing the order was called the ''patron.'' How suave. How elegant. But when the original was dead, yet with a skill deemed worth saving, like Zack, he was called the ''source.''

What does it matter what they called you, Zack? Gary thought. *As soon as this clown surfaced, they all forgot you. You died; now you're worse than dead.*

''Oh, I can guess what you're thinking okay, Gary.'' Zack's clone tore off another sheet of notebook paper and started in on a fresh origami project while he spoke. ''Clifford Pierce is a man with lots of enemies; he said so himself. You can see what this estate looks like. He's got security devices in places I don't think they got at the White House. Retina print entry between one part of the *house* and another, man! DNA sampling just to get on the grounds.''

''A man like him doesn't have to take chances.''

''A man like him takes a chance every time he opens his mouth or takes a step outside. He's one very well-hated man, our friend Pierce. You don't control that much money and power without stuffing a little hate in the market basket, too. Especially when you've fixed it so most guys can't fill their own family's plates.''

Gary felt his skin start to itch. This roundabout style was Zack's—the real Zack's. It never used to bother him, waiting for his partner to get to the point, because after kicking up enough dust to bathe a baby elephant, Zack Molloy always managed to come up with one gorgeous, glittery, shining gem of a deduction.

Maybe this Zack would, too. It was what he'd been grown for, to keep a mind like Molloy's in service to the people. But Gary Jaggar didn't feel like waiting around anymore.

"Look, Zack, all we want is motive, means, and opportunity, okay? Means we got: the nail. Opportunity? Four craftsmen brought into the mansion to do some fancy carpentry in the—what'd she call it? That big room with the cloth ceiling and all that carved paneling?"

"Don't call me Zack." The words came soft, but steady; implacable. "It's Zachary." Then, as if they had never been said: "The Damask Room."

Gary shrugged off his partner's request. *Just be glad I don't call you what I'd really like to.* "So, good. And to get to the front door from the Damask Room at quitting time, they've gotta go past the library."

"You say that like Pierce lets his workmen use the front door." The clone's eyes got hard. "Pierce isn't noted for letting workmen have much of anything."

"I never said this crew came in here just like that." Gary shot Zack—*Zachary,* damn him—an irritated scowl. "I did some homework as soon as this call came in. The workers got hired by the foreman Pierce gave the job to. It was the foreman's lookout to run security checks on his men, then turn them in to Pierce's own guards. He did it by the book, except one of the original crew got sick at the last minute and he had to pull in a ringer: someone who could make sure the crew got the job done the way Pierce wanted it, and on time. Only now he's sweating bad because it looks like he was in such a hurry to show up with the four-man team of workmen he promised that he didn't check out this guy's credentials too good."

"Or perhaps he did," Zack murmured.

Gary snorted. "Who're you kidding? I talked to the foreman, remember? He's going nuts, doing everything he can to keep himself clean of this mess. Pierce is a real stickler for getting what he pays for and firing—hell, *blackballing* any worker who doesn't come through. I can see why that foreman grabbed a sub first and didn't double-check what the guy told him."

"Which was—?"

"Which was a phony name, for starters. He'd never've hired him if he'd known who he really was. No sane man's going to hire Willie MacCoun on purpose these days. Not if he wants to keep eating.''

"Willie MacCoun is a brilliant speaker," Zack opined. "Have you ever heard one of his public pleas in favor of reestablishing the right of the workers to unionize?''

"I don't got time for politics.'' Gary waved it away like a bad smell. "I've got my own troubles.''

"So do a lot of people like Willie MacCoun, only their kinds of work weren't considered 'vital' enough—like the firefighters, like us—to let them keep their unions during the Galvin Crisis.''

"Ah, what do you know about it? It was before your time. You weren't even outa the tube when—''

Zack's stolen eyes darkened, lost all trace of playfulness. For a moment, Gary felt as if he were staring at someone as far removed from Zack Molloy as he was from the Queen of China.

Stupid feeling. A clone was the exact double of its original, down to the last twist in the DNA. So exact, in fact, that when a man like Pierce opted to commission the maximum number of clones permitted him under the law, something had to be done to allow the authorities to tell one clone from another and all clones from their "patron.''

The creepiness in Gary's bones passed. Zack's eyes were their old, twinkly, copycat selves again. "I guess you musta read about it,'' Gay said a little hastily.

"Yeah, I guess I—'' The library door opened. The coroner's assistant stuck his head out and told them they could come back in.

The body was all neatly bagged for removal. Gary and Zack stood aside to let the stretcher pass. The coroner's assistant touched a key on his portapad and passed Zack the flimsy printout. "Just prelims,'' he said. "We'll let you know when we've done a full workup downtown.'' He and the other site-men cleared out.

Gary snatched the flimsy away before the clone could read it. There was still such a thing as seniority. Zack—the real Zack—had outranked him, but this *Zachary* didn't. Let him remember that.

Gary was still studying the flimsy when a timid rapping sounded behind him. He turned to see Clifford J. Pierce standing in the doorway. "Is it all right to come in?''

"Yeah, sure, Mr. Pierce.'' He felt awkward, telling one

of the most powerful men in the country that it was all right for him to come back into his own library.

Clifford Pierce smoothed back his iron-gray hair before speaking. "What a terrible thing to have happen."

"Sure was," Gary agreed. "That could've been you." He nodded the way the bodybag had gone. "Can you give us any idea who might've wanted it that way?"

Pierce paced around the big table, its highly polished inlaid surface casting back a perfect reflection of the billionaire industrialist's hawklike profile. He chose a leather-bottomed mahogany chair as far as possible from the place where the victim's body had been found and sat down.

"It's so hard to say . . ." There was a strange croaking quality to his voice. When Gary and Zachary had first arrived on the scene, Pierce's fiancée, Dr. Marcia Hoffman, told them that he'd picked up a chill en route to last night's benefit opera performance. He was also a heavy smoker, if the old society page photos were any guide—the billionaire never smiled for the camera unless he had a cigar in his hand. Add to those factors finding one of your duplicates dead in a house less vulnerable to infiltration than Fort Knox and no wonder he sounded rough.

"Haven't you any theories, gentlemen?" Dr. Hoffman herself now lounged against the doorjamb. She wasn't what Gary would call gorgeous—he'd be lying if he didn't say he liked them a whole lot younger—but she was still striking, for her age. Auburn hair so thick it kept escaping from the "sensible," pulled-back style suited to a professional, brown eyes touched with gold, a good figure, a tan that must've cost more than a few high season trips down to the Islands—not that Pierce couldn't afford it.

"Just one theory," Gary replied.

"If you can call it that," Zachary put in. Gary glared at him.

"Oh?" Dr. Hoffman raised one brow.

"Gentlemen, we understand if you're unable to discuss your findings with us at this time," Pierce said hastily. "Don't we, darling?" The adoring look he gave Marcia made Gary shudder. He could still recall the first time he'd noticed Robbie Molloy, Zack's widow, gazing at her dead husband's clone that same way.

No, not Robbie any more, either. *Roberta.* That was what *he* called her. He had a thing against nicknames, for some reason, but nothing against stepping into a dead man's shoes. And to judge by the way he looked at Robbie Molloy, nothing against parking those shoes under the widow's bed.

"Certainly. We're ready to cooperate with you in any way we can." Marcia moved gracefully across the room to stand beside her fiancé. "The sooner you can catch the murderer, the better we'll feel."

"It's, uh, not exactly murder."

"No?" The frown lines between Marcia's brows deepened.

"It's more—willful destruction of property; manslaughter at the most. It all depends on the judge. If the assassin had hit his intended target, he'd be looking at the maximum penalty, but since it's just a clone—"

"*Just* a clone?" The change in Marcia's voice was startling. The sweet, ingratiating tone was gone, shrilled away by indignation. "Property damage. Oh, that's rich. You're talking about a human life, not a—a high-class toy. But that's all a clone is to you, isn't it?" Gary didn't react. Why bother contradicting the truth? His impassivity riled her even more. "I don't think I care for your attitude, Detective Jaggar," she gritted.

Gary shrugged. "With all due respect, Doctor, as long as I get the job done, what's my attitude toward clones matter to you?"

The lady's voice frosted. "I'm a scientist, Detective Jaggar. Forgive me if stupidity happens to matter a great deal to me, especially when it takes the form of prejudice. For your information, I worked many years at Replicon, in their R&D division, before the government stepped in and took over. Even then, I was kept on."

"And that was where I met her." Pierce's hand stole up to clasp Marcia's. For a man with a rep for being all hard, honed edges, the man was showing a startlingly soft side.

All his adoration went ignored. "I know clones. They aren't just cookie-cutter duplicates of their originals," Marcia snapped. "Not past the genetic level. Identical twins have been born into this world for centuries, but no one ever dreams of—of *insulting* one by assuming he's the photocopy of the other!"

Zachary stepped in to deflect the lady's rage. "Look, Dr. Hoffman, we're not pretending to know as much about the care and feeding of clones as you—" (Was that quick wink he tipped Gary done because the real Zack would've gone for the "in" joke there, or was it Zachary's own?) "—but we do know the law, and the law says that there's a big difference between exing the source and exing the clone."

"Even a clone like him," Pierce murmured, shaking his head. A jagged sigh tore from his chest.

"Darling, don't upset yourself." Marcia was suddenly all attentiveness to her fiancé. "I know how much Caruso meant to you, but if it had to be his life or yours—"

"What? What'd you call him?" Gary checked the flimsy. "This says the cor—the deceased was named George."

"My little joke." Pierce didn't sound disposed to much hilarity. "I named them George, Tom, Ted, and Abe because—"

"Mount Rushmore." Zachary beat him to it. He looked at Gary and shrugged. "Hey, beats the hell out of Parsley, Sage, Rosemary and Thyme."

"But he was called Caruso." Pierce stared vacantly across the table at the chair where the body had been found.

"How come?" Gary asked. What he really wanted to ask was, *Who gives a fuck if you called him Noodles?*

Pierce blinked at Gary as if the detective had sprouted pink wings. "Why, for his voice! His incredible singing voice . . . gone, now. Gone forever." He blinked more rapidly, as if fighting tears.

"George really was quite gifted musically," Marcia said quickly, perhaps to cover her fiancé's uncommon show of emotion. "We were planning to have him receive operatic training."

"That's too bad," Gary mumbled. "But, uh, couldn't one of the others—?"

It was a mistake and he knew it the minute *after* he said it. *Oh, shit, get a load of the look in that woman's eye! Here comes the lousy not-a-cookie-cutter lecture again!*

But instead of the sermon Gary was dreading from Dr. Hoffman, all she said was, "That would be impossible." She looked down at Pierce. "Are you tired, dear?"

"A—a little." The man sounded badly affected by everything, and that chill he'd taken wasn't helping. He coughed violently as he rose from his chair. Gary could barely make out the words when he rasped, "If you don't require us any further, the hour is late—early, rather—and I would appreciate getting some rest."

"You go right ahead, Mr. Pierce," Gary said. "We'll call you if we need you."

Pierce nodded his thanks, leaving it to Marcia to say, "Olveira will show you out when you're done."

Zachary let them get almost to the foot of the sweeping spiral staircase before calling, "Oh, Mr. Pierce, there is one detail you could help us with. It concerns your own alibi—"

Marcia whirled, her face ablaze. "Are you *daring* to imply that Clifford—?"

The clone raised his hands. "I'm not questioning the fact that Mr. Pierce was attending the opera. A gala that big, half a dozen *papparazzi* probably caught him there. I was just wondering about something else: Were you aware that Willie MacCoun was in this house yesterday?"

Pierce tensed perceptibly. "Willie. . . ?"

"Top spokesman for restoring the right to unionize."

The billionaire's lips tightened. Now he looked more like the man his reputation had painted. "I'm familiar with MacCoun's position, sir. As you no doubt know, it is one I always have and always will oppose vehemently. As a matter of fact, I have been preparing a statement to a Senatorial investigative committee detailing the very real, very urgent reasons of national security which demand maintaining the unionization restrictions implemented by our government during the Galvin Crisis."

Grimly he added, "I was just going over the hardcopy in the library around three o'clock when George came in and told me I'd better get ready for the pre-opera cocktail party and banquet at five."

"It was a stunning performance," Marcia put in. "*Aida* with Honigsburg singing the title role, a reception afterward. We didn't get home until past midnight."

"Yes, that's right," Pierce agreed. "In any case, since I was rushed, I asked George to do me a favor and review the manuscript."

"You don't do all that on your PC?" Zachary raised one eyebrow.

Pierce's smile was a cold formality. "Call me eccentric, if you like, but I have found it easier to locate errors on the printed page than when my eyes are suffering CRT fatigue from watching pixels on a screen. Marcia and I were out of the house by four, as the gateman will confirm. When we came home, the door to the library was shut. I assumed George had finished work and closed the room before he went to bed. I went upstairs to prepare for bed, but after such an exhilarating evening I was unable to sleep. Finally, at around three, I thought it would be wise to review the speech, seeing as how I was wide awake anyway. When I didn't find it in my bedroom suite, I assumed George had left it in the library.'' He didn't have to tell them what he found behind that closed door.

''The coroner found the hardcopy on the table under the— under George's body,'' Gary put in. ''It went downtown with the rest.''

Cool blue eyes gave the detective a sardonic look that bit hard. ''I am less concerned with a disposable copy of my Senate speech than with the fact that a notorious rabble-rouser and probable traitor had the freedom of my home. The freedom, I suspect, to attempt my murder.''

''I don't get it,'' Gary said as they drove to MacCoun's last known address. It was a little past dawn, not much traffic on the freeway yet.

''What don't you get?'' There was just a hint of irony in Zachary's question, but like a good driver, he kept his eyes on the road.

''That big fuss about that dead clone, George, just because he could sing. What'd they call him—Elvis?''

''Caruso. You really ought to get out more, Gary.'' This time the hint was about as subtle as a thrown brick.

''Whatever. So if he was such a great singer, going to get opera training and all, why couldn't they just sub one of his siblings?''

''Like Dr. Hoffman said, it'd be impossible. Great singers depend on two things: proper breath control and the range and quality their vocal cords give them,'' Zachary explained. ''Breathing can be taught—it's part of a singer's training—but your vocal cords are an accident of birth.''

''How stupid do you think I am?'' Gary snarled. ''I know that much. So if it's something you're born with, and George and the others were all . . . *born* identical to Pierce, their cords oughta be identical, too. Why is George such a loss? Why isn't Abe or Tom or Ted the big singing sensation? Why not Pierce himself? Well, yeah, he smokes, but the others—''

"You can't tell the players without a scorecard."

"Say what?"

"Ever wonder about it, Gary?" Zachary steered the car off an exit ramp and into one of the less prestigious—to put it mildly—parts of town. "Ever wonder, when a man's rich and powerful enough to order more than one clone of himself, how he tells them apart?"

"Never thought about it," Gary admitted.

"No, you wouldn't. It's only clones."

Gary's eyes flashed. "Lay off me! How come it means so goddam much *what* I think about clones, *if* I think about them? As long as we get the job done, what does it matter?"

Zachary sighed. "What matters to us is what makes us human. It makes us individuals, in spite of what you'd like to believe. You, too. But never mind. My point is that, unlike the parents of twins, patrons of multiple clones don't claim to be able to tell their 'offspring' apart by love alone. For them, the cloning venture is generally dictated by business or political necessity. How else can the V.I.P. in high demand be two places at once? They can't waste time learning to distinguish between their . . . tools. They demand a discreet, reliable system of identification—something that will allow them to tell one clone from the rest without altering the outward appearance of any."

"What's the connec—?"

"Rings." Zachary drove down a bleak street where rundown apartment buildings slumped against one another for support. "Bioneutral plastic rings on the vocal cords. Insertion's easy, with the right tool. I never found out what the techs call it, but it works kind of like that gun for attaching tear-proof sales tags to merchandise. They let me watch 'em use it a few times while I was still going through socialization training at the government center. It's neat the way it slips a ring around one vocal cord per clone—the right, the left, it doesn't matter—and it's got a fiberoptic attachment so the tech can position the ring precisely before applying the surgical adhesive."

"That's important?"

"Not to you, I see, Gee-man"

"I told you not to call me Gee-man."

"As long as we get the job done, what difference does it make what I call you?" The barb stung. It was meant to.

"Look, I *know* about the rings. I read this." Gary rattled

the flimsy. "It was the first thing the coroner checked for, to see if the dead man was the real Pierce or just—or his double. See? Third line down." He read from the report. " 'Ring in place.' Then he says how his assistants checked out the other look-alikes in the house. Pierce didn't have any ring, but the rest had theirs okay." Gary rubbed his chin. "I don't get this jargon, though. "Abe, left, five?' What the—?"

"The positive identification position of Abe's ring," Zachary replied. "You can tell one clone from his sibs by a fast fiberop check. The rings are attached at distinct five millimeter intervals measuring down from the top of the vocal chord. Abe's is attached to his left vocal cord, five millimeters down."

"Oh." Gary looked out the window at the string of shabby storefronts, the hostile stares of the unemployed. "So I guess that's it, huh? It just worked out that where they attached the ring on poor old George's vocal cords gave him some kinda edge when it came to singing?"

"You got it." Zachary grinned. "And was that you I just heard saying 'poor old George'? Better watch it, Gary. I think that was human sympathy you just wasted on a clone."

"Oh, shut up."

They pulled up in front of the building that was Willie MacCoun's last known address. Not even the beauty of a May sunrise could wash all the ugliness out of a place like that. MacCoun's wife answered the door, rubbing her eyes and cursing the men who'd come to rouse her from sleep. When she heard who they were, she cursed louder.

But she cooperated. "Willie's not here. We're separated, okay?" Somewhere a baby yowled.

"Any idea where he is living now?"

Her skinny shoulders rose and fell. "He comes by here, sometimes. He brings us money, when he's got it. What he don't spend on whores."

"I see." Zachary regarded MacCoun's wife with the same speculative look the first Zack used when he was piecing together the real story behind the few scraps of fact some people were willing to give a cop. "Does he come by with the money regularly, or just after he gets paid for a job?"

Mrs. MacCoun's laugh was harsh. "What jobs, now? I told him to keep his dumb mouth shut, but he wouldn't listen. Unions again! That was all he cared about. I knew I came after the whores with him, but damned if I was gonna come after some stupid pipe dream. No one hires him when they find out who he is. Times he does get work, it's 'cause the foreman owes him a favor.''

"Lot of people owe your husband favors?"

She grinned with yellow teeth. "Usedta be, Willie was a pretty goodtime guy. Took his friends around with him to visit the bitches. Sometimes there was photos, y'know? Willie said it was just for laughs. Well, sometimes it keeps us from starving, so I guess we're laughing pretty good. And he's okay about coming by with the money right after he gets it, before he really goes to town. Maybe he'll go with one of them on his way over, but he makes sure we get took care of before he fucks away all his pay.''

They made a few more calls on their way back to the precinct. The foreman who'd hired MacCoun didn't have much more to tell. At five o'clock, they all reported to the service door to be searched and passed off the grounds. MacCoun—hell, no, he didn't *know* it was MacCoun, how many times did he have to swear to that?—was with them.

"Any time he wasn't?"

"I dunno. I don't remember."

"You were there all day," Zachary said. "What'd you do if you had to take a leak? Get one of Pierce's guards to hold it for you?" He winked.

The foreman was too stressed to get the joke. "Mr. Pierce's private secretary told us the rules while he was showing us how his boss wanted these replacement panels and this special fireplace mantel carved and installed.''

"What secretary?"

"Some guy, name was Taylor. He's the one hired me for the job. He said Mr. Pierce was pretty fussy about his house and he had a couple of specific master-class workmen he wanted engaged for this project; expert woodworkers. Tell you the truth, I was relieved to hear he'd picked his own boys, mostly. I mean, I knew them by rep, they were clean, Pierce couldn't squawk too much about the quality of their work after. Running the security check was easy, getting their passtags for the Pierce estate was easy.''

He grimaced. "Every time it gets too easy for me, I always wake up screwed. One of 'em called in sick that morning and I hadda grab a sub. Shit, I was desperate. Pierce wanted the job done in a day—Taylor made a big point about that—and no way we can do it shorthanded. I ask the jerk who let me down if he knows someone, and he puts me onto MacCoun, only he calls him Schowalter. Hey, Mac-Coun probably lied to him, too, who knows? So I take what I can get and we go in and we get the job done.''

The foreman shook his head ruefully. ''Done, all right. What's done is me.''

''You still didn't tell us whether MacCoun was ever out of your sight on the job,'' Gary put in, impatient.

''Yeah, once or twice. If we hadda go, Taylor told us to step on this button under the big table in that room and someone would show up to take us to the can.'' He managed a weak chuckle. ''Larson was the first guy hadda ring. You should've seen his face when his 'escort' showed up. Poor bastard almost peed in his pants.''

''Why?''

''Jesus, wouldn't you if it looked like you'd maybe pushed the wrong fucking button and brought old Pierce himself down on us? Yeah, there he stood, big as life; only it wasn't Pierce, of course, just one of his doubles, said to call him Tom. Brother, spooky? Weird. But we got used to it. Turned into kind of a kick, having Clifford J. Pierce himself there to take you potty.''

''MacCoun go?''

''A couple, three times, maybe four. Yeah, four at least. We were there all day, remember, lotta coffee, didn't get off until the evening. The Pierce place is so damn big, there's nowhere near it you can drain the snake—and I mean no-where! Shit, they got private guards all over that neighbor-hood ready to run you in if they catch you pissing against a tree. So I told the guys to take care of business once before we left.'' A feeble smile touched his lips. ''I'd'a been good nursery school teach, y'know?

''Anyhow, Tom marched us all down the hall, it got a little confusing, MacCoun and Larson came out first and wandered around some, staring at stuff—hell, you would, too, kinda things they got in a place like that—and Tom just about had a cow when he couldn't find them, but they turned up. He may look like Pierce, but he sounds different. Never get an iron-ass like Pierce in a panic like that dupe of his.'' The faint smile died. ''We got paid on the way out. Tom handled that, too. That's the last I saw of MacCoun and that's all I know.''

"When this guy you first hired told you to get MacCoun instead, did he tell you how to find him?"

The foreman nodded. "Had me call a number. It was a bar, but they knew him there and he got the message. I wish he hadn't."

They got the bar's address—a place deep in the blue collar slums, a dive surrounded by the cheapest of cheap hotels, arcades, and greaseburg eateries. The Dorado's big attraction was the promise of twenty-four-hour-a-day service, but the guy on dayshift didn't know MacCoun by any name and a photo clipped from the papers just got the usual, "Oh, yeah, that union guy, right?" response.

Outside the Dorado, Gary turned to Zachary. "Still think it looks like MacCoun's clean?"

The clone sighed. "I admit, it looks pretty bad."

"*Pretty* bad? Look, he was *there* and he hated Pierce. I'm not saying he planned it ahead of time. That last potty break was the perfect opportunity: Tom's busy trying to keep an eye on all the workmen, MacCoun and Larson wander away, probably split up, MacCoun happens to look in through the library door and sees Pierce—he *thinks* it's Pierce—bent over the table going over his speech. MacCoun's there doing carpentry work, he's got a toolbelt on, he takes out a finishing nail and—"

"Hammer," Zachary said.

"Huh?"

"Wouldn't he have a hammer in that toolbelt, too?"

"Sure, but—"

"How many people know that if you stick a nail in the base of someone's skull, it'll kill them?"

"Look, they know enough to be sure it's not gonna do their victim any favors."

"MacCoun's a simple man, Gary, the straightforward type. Oh, he's eloquent enough, but you heard what his wife said about how he's guaranteed himself the few remaining job contacts he's got: blackmail. Pretty primitive blackmail, too. He might've had the motive and the opportunity to kill Pierce, but when it comes to the means, he'd be the sort to whip out a hammer and smash a man's skull instead of tippy-toeing up behind him and jabbing in that nail. A nail with *no prints* on it, either, remember the report?"

"Workmen carry gloves."

"Give it up, Gary. Poor George's murder was Renaissance; MacCoun does things Neolithic style."

"Huh?" Gary repeated. Then, with a snort of disgust, he added, "Ah, forget it. Want to run down the Dorado nightshift, see if they know where we can find MacCoun?"

"There's someone else I'd rather talk to first."

"Who?"

"Mr. Pierce's private secretary, Taylor."

"Yeah, you're right. Funny, when we asked to speak to the house staff, no one mentioned anything about any private secretary."

"Precisely, Watson." Zachary winked. Almost in spite of himself, Gary winked back.

"Mr. Pierce and Dr. Hoffman are still asleep. This has been rather trying for them; for us all. May I help you?"

Now Gary knew what the foreman meant when he said how spooky it was, talking with one of Pierce's clones. Before, when he and Zachary interviewed the surviving three, it had been different. The uncanny effect was less when they were all together.

"Yeah, I guess so," Gary said. "Uh, which one are you?"

"Mr. Pierce named me Abe." The clone made a face which left no doubt that he despised his patron-given name.

"Okay, Abe, what can you tell us about Mr. Pierce's private secretary, Taylor?"

"Dennis Taylor? He's no longer employed here. He was dismissed the day of the murder, in fact." He relayed the information with no emotion whatsoever, but as he spoke, he began to crack his knuckles.

"Fired?" Zachary was immediately interested. "Why?"

Abe turned his impassive face to meet the cloned detective's eyes. "Sir, it is not my place to tell you your business, but I believe I can save you some trouble here: Mr. Taylor is not the eleventh-hour prime suspect you seem to believe you have uncovered."

"No?" Zachary tugged at his mustache. He sounded amused.

Abe's knuckle-cracking became more rapid and combined with Zachary's purloined mannerisms to irritate Gary so much that the detective snarled, "You're damned right it's none of your business! What are you doing, covering for Taylor?''

Abe's face flushed. ''I only wanted to help your investigation. If you'd rather waste time running down a red herring, it's nothing to me. I have no cause to cover for Mr. Taylor. Why should I?''

''Maybe because you clones are so hot to prove you're real individuals that you decided your way would be playing back-door man.''

Now every shade of color drained from Abe's cheeks. He turned from them both and left the room without another word. Almost as soon as he had gone, he was back.

Only it wasn't Abe. ''Hi, I'm Ted.'' Abe's sibling shook hands jovially. ''You've got to excuse my brother, he takes everything too seriously. I can fill you in on what he had to say, though. You know, about Taylor? No way did he kill George. He wasn't *fired,* his last day on the job was set a long time ago. Just bad luck it turned out to be the same day George was killed. See, with us around, Mr. Pierce realized that he didn't need Taylor's services any longer, so he worked out a really sweet severance deal for him and sent him on his way, no hard feelings.''

''Sure of that?'' Zachary inquired.

''Sure as I can be without reading minds. Listen, I wasn't around much yesterday until dinner time—Mr. Pierce had me taking his place at a reception at the Japanese Embassy—but Tom was, and he said that Taylor put him in charge of the workmen, then left around eleven o'clock, noon the latest. Mr. Pierce wasn't even *in* the library then.''

''We'd still like to talk to this Mr. Taylor.''

''Thought you might.'' Ted dipped into his shirt pocket and handed Zachary a slip of paper with an address and telephone number. As they were about to leave, Ted tapped Gary on the shoulder. ''Oh, one more thing. Abe says to tell you it takes a real asshole to tell a back-door man.'' He grinned. ''Nothing personal. Unless I'm Abe, of course. And wouldn't you just love to know?''

Too quick for evasion, Zachary's hand shot out and collared Ted, slamming him up against the doorjamb. ''You bet I'd love to know, Binky. So how about I give you a little something so I can tell you from the others? A couple of missing teeth sound good to you? A broken nose, maybe? Or how about—hey, I know they neuter you guys before they

let you out of the government center, but I can make the
job complete.'' His other hand jabbed in low. Ted gasped
and writhed. Zachary let him drop. ''Think about that the
next time you go calling my partner an asshole.''

Back in the car, Zachary yawned. ''Let's check out Taylor
and call it a day. No more we can do about finding Mac-
Coun until nighttime, anyhow, unless the APB on him
strikes gold. You with me?''

''I guess,'' Gary mumbled. Glancing over at the clone's
haggard but still-smiling face, he said, ''Here, move over.
I'll drive.''

Zachary got out and went around to the passenger side
while Gary slid over. As he strapped himself in he said,
''Thanks, Gee-ma—Gary.''

''Uh-huh. Um . . . look, Zachary, what you did to Ted:
you didn't have to. I been called worse.''

''Not while you were my partner.'' Zachary slumped
down in the seat and closed his eyes. ''Don't mention it.''

''Say . . . what you said about being neutered . . . you
didn't really mean—?''

''Yep.'' Zachary tried to make it sound like nothing.
''Come on, think about it and it makes sense. Can't have a
bunch of great genetic duplicates of this country's fat cats
roaming around loose. The paternity suit potential alone,
Mamma mia!''

''Oh. Hey, sorry.''

''Don't be.'' Zachary opened his eyes and gave him another of those old Zack winks. ''Neuter ain't impotent.''

Gary winced; Zachary couldn't help but notice. ''I bet I
know what you're thinking,'' he said.

''I doubt it,'' Gary replied.

''Oh, not exactly what you're thinking. F'rinstance, I can't
tell whether you're more disgusted by the idea of—me making
love to Roberta or Roberta doing it with—'' he hunched
forward in his seat and put on a burlesque Peter Lorre accent ''—a, a, a feelthy cloooone. Ahahahahaha.''

Gary felt himself go hot with embarrassment, but he kept
his eyes on the road and said nothing. He sensed rather than
saw Zachary slowly uncurl and lean back against the vinyl
upholstery.

''Look, man,'' Zachary said quietly, ''Cut me some
slack, okay? Some guys'd give their left nut to know the
answer to the big *why?*—you know, 'Why was I put on this

earth?'—but take it from me, it's no great deal. I *do* know why I'm here, and what good does it do me? The only reason I'm alive is because some upstairs creep decided your old partner's brain was worth saving on account of what he could do with it. You think it's fun, knowing you were put here so you'd turn out *just like* the man they grew you from? I mean, parents who look at their drooling newborns and picture 'em in the White House are easy to satisfy next to those biofeebs! Would you like it, always living with the feeling that if you happened to—if you *dared* to have a like or a dislike or a thought that wasn't *exactly* the same as your 'source,' you weren't just letting down Mom and Pop, you were betraying a whole fucking national trust?''

Gary kept driving in silence, but it didn't mean he wasn't listening. He could hear Zachary sigh and say, ''I love her. Not because he did, so I'm supposed to; I just happen to have fallen in love with my 'source's' widow. Predictable? But Zack Molloy wasn't a predictable man. You never knew, did you, that he'd follow you down to the docks when you got that 'come alone' call and jump out of nowhere when those three scumbags pulled heat on you and take out two of them before the third one waxed him.''

''He should've minded his own business,'' Gary said, jaw tight. ''He had a wife, kids, it was my tipoff, my bust. Stupid son of a bitch. Stupid goddam son of a bitch, get himself killed that way.'' He slammed the steering wheel with one fist and kept on driving.

He knew Zachary was gazing at him with Zack's eyes. Part of him felt sort of sorry for the poor clone. *No one asks to get born,* he thought, *but once you get born, at least you know you've got some choices. To have to come into this lousy world and find out you don't even get any say in who you're gonna be— Shit.*

''She love you?'' he asked so quietly that Zachary had to ask him to repeat. ''I said, does Robbie love you?''

''She says so.'' The clone's voice gave away nothing. ''I'd like to believe she does. You know, not that she's just latched onto me because I'm what she's used to, or because I'm her second chance to get it right with her first husband, or because she's scared of making a new life. And if she's just saying she loves me so the kids can have their old daddy back, I don't think I could stand that.''

''Yeah, that'd suck.'' They left the run-down streets behind, slicing through the heart of the city's commercial district and into the better class neighborhoods of the east side. Zachary closed his eyes and dozed; Gary drove. After a while, Gary remarked, "She means it."

"What?" The clone stirred and thumbed sleep from both eyes at once. Zack always used to do it one hand, one eye at a time.

"I said I know Robbie—Roberta—and if she says she loves you, then she loves *you*, okay? So don't sweat it."

"Okay." The big grin, the wink that belonged to a dead man. It wasn't so bad anymore. "No sweat."

"You gents looking for me?" Dennis Taylor leaned out the right side of his Reznik 280 and hailed them as they stood on his doorstep, ringing the bell.

Gary strolled over to the sleek red sportscar, noting with interest the old-fashioned English right-hand drive. "You Mr. Dennis Taylor?"

"In person." Taylor was a real California golden boy, tanned, blond, impossibly perfect. There were some dark smudges under his brilliant blue eyes, but that was to be expected: a man like that wouldn't keep a monk's hours. The only other thing that brought him down to human level was when he turned on phony charm so thick you could almost scoop it off him in gooey fingerfuls. "You must be from the police." He stepped out of his car with a dancer's grace. He wore navy slacks, a pink sports shirt open at the collar, and had a white cashmere sweater tossed over his shoulders.

"I'm Detective Jaggar and this is Detective Molloy. You get police calls on a regular basis, Mr. Taylor?" Gary had a feeling this guy was going to laugh. He was right.

When Taylor dropped the fake-sounding laughter, he answered, "I picked up a copy of the morning paper on my way home, and I figured it would be only a matter of time before you learned I'd left my employment with Mr. Pierce the very day of the murder." He leaned against the car, making no move toward his house, showing no indication he ever intended to invite them inside.

"It's not really murder, Mr. Taylor," Zachary said evenly. "Not when the victim was just a clone."

"Ah, you wouldn't say that if you knew old George!" Taylor asserted. "What a voice, what an incredible voice!

Even I could appreciate a talent like his, and I care for opera almost as little as Mr. Pierce.''

"Mr. Pierce doesn't like opera?'' Gary could swear he saw Zachary's ears prick forward, like a dog's. "Then why did he attend the opera the night of the crime?''

Taylor raised his hands, palms upward. *"Noblesse oblige,* Detective Jaggar. When I was still in Mr. Pierce's employ, I often wished I had a dollar for every time he and his cronies attended a symphony, a gallery opening, an opera benefit, or an art film screening when they'd all have been happier at home watching TV. I think the only one who ever honestly cared for music was Danielle. In Mr. Pierce's circle, cultural events are for being seen and networking.''

"Nice of him to take such an interest in George's talent, then,'' Zachary remarked. "Seeing as how he couldn't care less about music himself.''

Again that calculated laugh. "Very nice of him. Especially when so many of his associates are closing the status gap, getting clones of their own even as we speak.''

"What's that got to—''

"Oho, but how many of them will ever have a trained performing clone who can sing grand opera for his patron's dinner guests? Yes, very nice of Mr. Pierce.'' Taylor's eyes flashed as he caught sight of the look that passed between Gary and Zachary. "Don't mistake me, gents. I'm not condemning Mr. Pierce for his motives, I'm just trying to correct any misapprehensions you might have about the man. He always treated me well. Our parting was by mutual consent, and if you doubt the generous nature of my severance settlement, I'll be happy to show you my portfolio. Or refer you to my lawyer, if you persist in thinking I had any reason to want him dead.''

"No one's accusing you of anything, Mr. Taylor,'' Gary said, his voice level. He glanced at the car. "I can see how generous Mr. Pierce was.''

"Like it?'' Taylor beamed like a proud new father. "It's a little hard adjusting to the right-hand drive, but that's how they insist on making them in Nairobi. Fast, quiet, maneuverable . . . What can I say? It's love. Now, can I do anything else for you?''

"We wouldn't mind knowing where you were between the time you left Mr. Pierce's estate and six o'clock.''

"Gladly. I left the grounds a little before noon for a lunch

and racquetball date with Colin Yates at the Thistle Hill
Athletic Club, which kept us busy until five-ish. Then cocktails, of course, and a little informal celebratory dinner at
L'Obelix with Colin, Felicity Winter, Danielle Howe, Rose
and Kirk Delahunt. We finished at around nine thirty.
They're all in the book, if you need to check my story. Oh,
and you can check with the staff at Thistle Hill and *L'Obelix,* too. I assume that covers the time of death? The paper
didn't say when it was.''

''We'll let you know.''

''You're welcome,'' he returned too sweetly, and strode
up the brick wall to his front door. Halfway there he yanked
the sweater from his shoulders and swung it jauntily. Something small and bright flew from the soft fabric and landed
noiselessly in the grass.

Gary was already in the car, ready to roll, when he saw
Zachary pounce on Taylor's lawn like a cat after a mole.
His prize secured, the clone leaped into his seat, one fist
cupped tightly around whatever it was he'd found. Gary
waited until they were back on the freeway again before
asking what it was.

''Tacky,'' said Zachary, holding it up within range of his
partner's peripheral vision. ''Very, very tacky.''

Gary got a glimpse of bright colors and what looked like
a bird too ugly to live. ''It's an earring,'' the clone supplied.
''Shaped like a toucan. We should ask him about where he
went after that 'informal celebratory dinner,' once he
ditched Danielle and Felicity.'' Zack pronounced the ladies'
names with elaborate irony. ''You'd think a man with so
much high-class taste in cars would have better taste in
women. Or women with better taste.''

''Who knows?'' Gary shrugged. ''So, you gonna toss it?''

''Maybe.'' Zachary slipped it into his pants pocket.

Gary was too tired to argue or pry. He drove to the precinct, they filed their preliminary reports, and they both
went home.

The call came a good five hours before Gary was ready
to get up. ''They found MacCoun.'' It was Zachary. He
didn't sound happy. ''Dead.''

Less than an hour later they stood beside a slab in the
morgue and looked down at the livid face of the onetime
pro-union firebrand. ''Cause?'' Gary asked the attendant,

who handed him a short flimsy. "Heart attack?" Gary
looked at the hale, young body on the slab, then at Zachary
to see whether he was the only one who didn't buy it.

"It happens." The attendant was the stoic type. "He was
found in the Regal Hotel. Hourly rates, you know? We see
'em all the time: come and go." He thought it was funny
enough to keep on laughing until the coroner came up behind him and told him to put a sock in it.

"I'm glad you're here," the coroner told them. "There's
something I want you to see." He nodded them out the
morgue door and into a small lab. The folder on the counter
said "Pierce Clone: George." As they watched, the coroner
picked up the folder, took a marker from his coat pocket,
and drew a fat black line through the last two words. He
tossed it back down, scooped something out of a metal pan,
and pressed it into Gary's hand. The stunned detective
looked down at a small white plastic ring.

"It came loose during the full autopsy. The adhesive
doesn't hold as well when it's bonded onto dead tissue,"
the coroner said simply. "Congratulations: Now you're
looking at murder."

The Regal Hotel was only two blocks away from the Dorado bar, on a busy two-way street. The night clerk slept in
a crummy cubicle off the lobby—a "perk" that went with
the job—and he wasn't too happy when the day clerk woke
him to talk with the cops. He made it pretty obvious that
all he wanted was to tell them what he knew and crawl back
under the sheets.

"Yeah, he paid enough to keep the room until morning.
So what? Sometimes they do." His beady-eyed glower de-
fied them to ask *Here*?

"You ever seen MacCoun in here before?" Gary asked.

"Sometimes." The answer was given cautiously.

"And did he ever pay for the whole night?"

The clerk rubbed a stubbly chin. "Not often."

"Not at all, you mean."

"Hey, don't tell me what I'm saying! I just rent out the
rooms. Look, I'm not gonna give you guys the runaround,
say I don't know stuff I know. MacCoun turns up dead in a
room I gave him, him and that hooker, the sooner you get
the info you're after and get outa my life, the better."

Zachary grinned. "A man after my own heart. Okay,

mine host, tell us about this lady friend of the dear de-
parted.''

''What's to tell?'' The clerk screwed up his mouth.
''Shaggy blonde hair, big tits, nice ass, dressed in a coupla
skintights. She's carrying a big ol' shoulderbag, looks like
she's up for a day at the beach, right down to the iceshades—
shades at night, go figure! They all wear 'em, now and then.
Think it makes 'em look mysterious.''

''So she went up with him. When she came down, did
she look at all scared, upset?''

''Her? I dunno. Not sure when she came down. I hadda
leave the desk a couple times, and after he paid for the
whole night, I didn't hafta make Norm go up, knock, tell
'em time's up. Hey, you tell me the guy died on her, I bet
she got out fast and quiet.'' Again his square-tipped fingers
rasped over stubble. ''Although . . .''

''What?''

The clerk's bloodshot eyes sparkled momentarily. ''Probably nothing,'' he said, so that Gary was sure it was probably twenty bucks worth of something.

The bill in his pocket, the clerk said, ''They checked in
around eleven. Ten past I'm coming outa the back and I see
this woman go out in a real hurry.''

''The blonde?''

He shook his head. ''Much as I could see under that kerchief, she was a kinda dark redhead. She sure had the
blonde's shoes, though, and if she'd'a let that raincoat slip,
I bet I'd'a seen the blonde's clothes.''

Zachary leaned closer. ''Didn't you think it was weird,
after they paid for the whole night, she scoots out?''

''Hey, I didn't know it was her for sure and I'll think
when they pay me for it.''

''Well think about this: If you'd've gone up to check on
MacCoun then, you might've gotten him some medical help
in time to save his life. Hey, Gary, lend me your portapad!''

Gary slid it over. Zachary began entering a long string of
data. The more he typed in, the more nervous the night
clerk grew until the little man demanded, ''Whoa, hold it,
what're you doing? You mentioning me?''

''Right after the words 'criminal negligence,' uh-huh.''

''Hey, stop! Come on, cut it out! I didn't know for sure
it was the blonde. I told you she had different hair!''

"Wigs." Zachary continued to type. "Big deal. What about the shoes?"

"Shoes don't mean shit; they all wear them c.f.m. slings, y'know? It couldn't 'a been her. Look, I said she goes out ten past, right? So if your guy dies in the saddle, that's noways near enough time to get their clothes off, hardly; not for her to get outa *that* outfit. If they weren't doing it yet, how could he die doing it? And this girl goes right out the front door and picks up another john, so she hadda be a different one. Yeah, that makes sense." He looked pleased with the way he'd saved his hide.

"You saw her make the pickup?" Zachary asked, fingers still poised over the portapad.

"Sure. I hadda make sure she wasn't that blonde, didn't I? So I'd know nothing wasn't wrong upstairs." He lacked the experience to strike a convincing virtuous pose and soon let it drop. "She did nice on that one. Really fine car. He pulls up, sticks his head out right away, she musta give him a good deal, she goes around, gets in, they drive."

Zachary shoved the pad back to Gary. "If you did see the blonde, you'd be able to I.D. her?"

"Yeah, sure, no problem."

The clone reached into his pants pocket and dropped the stray earring onto the countertop. "Here's a little something to get you started."

Gary got off the car radio. The coroner had checked out Zachary's theory: potassium chloride. All the symptoms of a heart attack, hard to detect unless you looked close. Ten minutes was enough time for Willie MacCoun to get naked. Could be that while he was asking why his lady of the evening wasn't stripping too, she'd slipped him the needle.

A big bag can hold a discarded blonde wig, stow a kerchief and raincoat to cover up the cheap hooker's outfit when a lady's got to meet her ride. He went into the mansion to join Zachary.

Abe met him at the door, conducted him wordlessly through the house. "They are in the conservatory," Abe said at last, opening the French doors. A thin thread of music seeped out on the greenery-rich air.

"Thanks." Gary stepped in, but before the clone could shut the doors after him, he added, "Hey, I'm sorry. You know, what I said to you the other day." Abe only finished closing the doors, acting as if no one had spoken at all. Gary's first taste of unreality was bitter.

He shrugged off as much of it as he could and went toward the music. Pierce—the late Pierce—did nothing small. The conservatory housed a miniature rain forest. Crushed pink stone was underfoot, here and thre among the potted ferns and flowering trees stood a few white wrought iron chairs and tables, like you'd find in an old soda fountain. It was a good place for a private chat, or for a man to be alone with his thoughts.

A tenor's voice soared in an impassioned aria. Other voices jabbed back and forth across the music. Gary held himself back amid the fronds, eavesdropping. If he only listened, he could still pretend it was Zack doing the talking.

"—brought this clipping to prove it. You tell me if I'm reading the caption wrong: 'Clifford J. Pierce and his fiancée, Danielle Howe.' It's dated last Saturday. We spoke with her. She told us that she got a call early the morning of the murder from your former secretary, Dennis Taylor, canceling your date for the gala that night. She was very disappointed; she adores music. That wasn't half how bad she felt when you called her the morning after and broke your engagement. She said she never in a million years thought you'd drop her to go back to Dr. Hoffman. *Back* to her. You're a fickle man, aren't you?"

A harsh voice, roughened even more by recent tears, replied, "Stop toying with me. You know I'm not a man."

"I know you're not Pierce, because he's dead. And I know what you gave up so that you could step into his shoes. You loved music, George; you still love it the way he never did, the way that makes you special. I guess you love her more, if you were willing to let her do that to you, tear the music out of you when she removed your laryngeal ring so you could play Pierce and his body could be taken for yours."

"Marcia had nothing to do with it!" Gary, in hiding, could almost feel those words blast like a desert wind through the hothouse trees. "I killed him. I'll give you my confession right now."

"Why the hurry? So Dr. Hoffman will have time to escape? She can't. Dennis Taylor's turning state's evidence on her so we won't prosecute him as an accessory to the murder

of Willie MacCoun.'' Gary heard Zachary click his tongue.
''Never drive a car they'll remember.''

''Taylor. . . ?'' The clone sounded bewildered, pathetic.

He didn't cry until Zachary told him about the earrings—
how the night clerk at the Regal matched the one that had
dropped from Taylor's sweater to a pair MacCoun's elusive
companion had worn. ''When—about when did this happen?''

''No later than quarter past eleven. She said you didn't
get back from the reception until after midnight.'' Zachary's
voice dropped to a sympathetic murmur. ''She just meant
you, didn't she?''

''She left during the reception. No one pays attention to
who's where at those things. Afterward, I let her in by the
garden service gate.'' George's voice was a husky whisper.
''Minimal security, for here. We set it all up that afternoon.
As soon as she told me *he* was dead, I stepped into his
place, summoned the security chief, claimed the estate system was malfunctioning, ordered it all rebooted in a hurry,
before I had to leave for the banquet. The DNA was no
problem, but we needed my print on the retina scanners. It
was almost two in the morning when she came back. She
claimed it had taken her that long to locate MacCoun. She
was supposed to have done it alone.''

''Quarter past eleven until two.'' Zachary let it mean what
it must.

''She told me she loved me.'' George's once-glorious
voice cracked. ''God knows she had reason enough to hate
him after he led her on so long, then dumped her for Danielle Howe.''

''Not bad.'' Through the fronds, Gary saw Zachary tug
his mustache, Zack-style. ''Get top live-in medical exper-
tise for free. Clifford Pierce was one smooth businessman.''

''She told me the only reason she stayed on here after he
broke their engagement was to be near me. Me!'' Gary
watched the clone's frantic pacing back and forth, crunch-
ing the pink gravel. ''What about everything we planned?
Was she just going to leave me for Taylor?''

''Not with all you had on her.'' Zachary shook his head.
''No way she was just going to leave you.''

''You mean . . . she'd kill me? But she said—''

''When a big-time honcho like Clifford Pierce dies of a

heart attack, it's no surprise. Even if it's the same kind of heart attack she gave a little man like Willie MacCoun.''

"No! Marcia would never—! She loves me! She always knew *me,* who I really was, loved me for that, not just because I looked like *him!* You're lying, *lying!*''

Gary decided he'd played the spy long enough. George sounded like he was working himself up bad; he could turn dangerous. Gary figured right. Just as he stepped out of hiding, he saw Zachary try to lay a comforting hand on his fellow-clone's shoulder. With an animal groan, George pulled away, seized one of those iron chairs, and slammed him broadside. Zachary went down, George bolted.

"Halt! Police!'' Gary's command was an echo. The clone plunged into the greenery and was gone. Gary fired a warning shot that rebounded from the bulletproof glass, then flung himself down beside his fallen partner. "Zachary, buddy, you okay?'' No reply. Carefully Gary felt for a neck pulse. "Goddamnit! Don't you die on me, Zachary, don't you fucking dare die!'' he muttered fiercely. "I am not gonna lose another good partner like this. Ah, shit, why the hell didn't I just show myself?''

"Because we got laws against indecent exposure in this town,'' came the almost inaudible reply. Then: "Get it, Gee-man?'' and an I-dare-you smile that was no one's but his own.

Sealing off the estate was fast and easy; it was what the system had been designed for. The ambulance for Zachary almost couldn't get in, and it took more doing to locate George in one of the upstairs bedrooms—her room—then to have the guards override the retina-scan locks between floors, then between hall and room. It all took time.

She lay on her back with candles at her head and feet, the bloodstained silver letter opener that had found her heart tossed haphazardly nearby. There had even been time for George to find the other tacky wooden toucan earring and affix it to her right lobe.

Now he stood by the gilded antique writing desk, staring out the window. He turned and smiled weakly when Gary and the backups burst in. *"Tosca,''* he said, nodding at the tableau on the floor. "The scene where she stabs Scarpia to death and says—'' Abruptly he crossed the room to the bed-side table. Ignoring the orders to stop, he yanked a drawer open and thrust his hand in.

One of the backups was edgy; he fired. George spun back, hit the wall, and slid down, still grasping tightly whatever it was he'd lost his life to get. Gary was on him, jerking it from his hand: a mini-hypo and a vial marked *KCl*.

Still breathing, though the blood bubbled up and spilled over his lip, George gasped, ''—and she says—Tosca does—she says, 'This is Tosca's kiss.' This was going to be hers—Marcia's—her good-bye kiss for me.'' He laughed, and the blood was brighter. *''La commedia é finita.''*

DAW

Don't Miss These Exciting DAW Anthologies